SHANGHAI—1945

A HUMAN HELL LIT BY THE FLAMES OF WAR

Hata—the Japanese commander corrupted by pleasure and consumed by fear as his country's dream of empire turned into a nightmare . . .

Niki—the ravishing, sensual White Russian who was all things to men and women alike . . .

Dallin—the handsome, cynical adventurer playing a mysterious double game with icy nerve, iron will, and incredible daring . . .

Dominique—the image of innocence offering her body to those she hated to save the one she loved . . .

Becker—the ruthless Nazi "superman" making a savage bid for survival . . .

These were some of the men and women caught up in the rising inferno of greed, desire, treachery, and terror of Shanghai—as the noose around the city tightened and the last civilized restraints gave way. . . .

SHANGHAI

Big Bestsellers from SIGNET

SHANGHAI

Barth Jules Sussman

A SIGNET BOOK

NEW AMERICAN LIBRARY

TIMES MIRROR

SIGNET, SIGNET CLASSICS, MENTOR, PLUME, MERIDIAN AND NAL
BOOKS *are published by The New American Library, Inc.,
1633 Broadway, New York, New York 10019*

FIRST PRINTING, JANUARY, 1981

1 2 3 4 5 6 7 8 9

PRINTED IN THE UNITED STATES OF AMERICA

For Fritzi and Jen who
always had faith in me

SHANGHAI

Chapter One

At first glance, Felix Hacker seemed the most unlikely target in Shanghai for a Japanese firing squad. A timid little man with a plump, round face and a kind manner, he was often seen emerging from Madame Fouquet's Pastry Shop in the French Concession, clutching the familiar blue and white box that contained her famed chocolate layer cake with raspberry filling, and he could almost always be found at his tidy desk in the public library on the second floor of Town Hall at 22 Nanking Road near the Bund.

Felix was seldom idle or alone. The polyglot foreign colony of Shanghai saw to that, for they were always seeking his help. Six days a week the library was a meeting place for smartly dressed French matrons clamoring for the latest best seller on the Continent, pink-cheeked young English girls longing to lose themselves in a movie magazine, stiff-necked German engineers seeking highly technical journals, or gum-snapping Americans anxious for a peek at a stateside newspaper and the hometown baseball scores.

In spite of the constant demands for his attention, Felix always remained gentle and polite. Never irritated or abrupt, he would patiently fill requests, provide alternatives, and act as a living encyclopedia and unofficial guide to the Orient for a vast horde of bewildered travelers. Winter and summer, in

1

times of civil disorder and epidemic, Felix Hacker could always be found at his desk. His thirty years of dedicated service had earned him wide respect in the tradition-bound world of Shanghai.

But all this was in the past, for now Felix stood alone in the twilight, waiting to die in a brick courtyard behind Bridge House, the eight-story modern apartment building one block from Soochow Creek in the International Settlement, which had become the Shanghai headquarters of the Kempetai, the Japanese military secret police. Several strands of rusting barbed wire were looped around Felix's body, pinning him to the wall.

A sharp clanging noise rang across the courtyard, as Lieutenant Sumato, his shoulders bent, a curved sword dragging clumsily from his waist, shuffled wearily down the stone steps of Bridge House. Gray-haired at forty, with a narrow face heavily lined by sorrow, Sumato caused Felix a moment of anguish. It had never occurred to him that the one officer in the Kempetai he felt any regard for would be participating in his execution.

Sumato came to a halt at the bottom of the steps and gazed compassionately at Felix. Then, unable to delay any longer, he rounded the stairway to his right and flicked the switch embedded in the wall.

The beams of a dozen powerful floodlights illuminated the worn cobblestones, outlining Felix in their glare. Blinded, he shifted about, the barbed wire tearing tiny bits of flesh from his throat.

Sumato gave a loud, piercing command. A squat corporal, still fumbling with his trouser buttons, came racing past and dropped to his knees, hunched over the Nambu light machine gun, loaded and in place beside the stairway. Gripping the wooden handles, worn smooth from repeated use, he glanced sideways at Sumato, awaiting the signal to fire.

Across the courtyard, Felix was dazed by the speed of this final ritual. Perspiration dotted his forehead and he mumbled to himself in amazement, "*Gott . . . mein Gott.*"

The words filtered across to Sumato. Hearing them, he winced and was about to reply when a loud belch from the corporal brought him to his senses; he drew his sword, swinging the dull blade high into the air. For several seconds nothing happened, leaving Felix and Sumato gazing at one another in astonishment. Then the Nambu spat out its deadly fire, sending Felix reeling against the brick wall.

The ordeal of Felix Hacker was over but not his own, thought Sumato gloomily. Sadly, he dismissed his gunner and, troubled by questions he preferred not to confront, he mounted the stairs into Bridge House, grateful the tears forming in his eyes could not be seen from above by his superior officer.

Moments after he disappeared inside the building, a sturdily built Kempetai colonel, with hawkish features and the patrician manner of a Japanese aristocrat, leaned out the window of his office on the eighth floor. Annoyed because Sumato had failed to deliver the customary coup de grace to his victim, a guarantee against survival, Colonel Hata stood for a moment enjoying the first breeze of the evening, rising from Soochow Creek nearby. In the distance, the flag of the Rising Sun flew atop Garden Bridge, which marked the point where the Soochow, a minor tributary, merged with the much broader and heavily trafficked Whampoo River. Each time Hata saw that river with its array of large vessels surrounded by junks and sampans, it reminded him China was a mere twenty-four hours away from Tokyo by steamer. Nowhere else within the Japanese sphere of influence was there any place with such abundance of natural resources and such a vast marketplace for manufactured goods.

Hata turned his gaze to the south, to the celebrated Bund of Shanghai, an imposing row of concrete skyscrapers, once the world's tallest buildings (outside of Manhattan), that formerly housed the most prestigious trading companies, banks, clubs, and hotels in colonial China.

"Shanghai . . . the pearl of the Orient," murmured Hata; he was still in awe of this restless metropolis of nearly four million which overran the muddy banks of the Whampoo and was the gateway to the fertile Yangtze Valley.

Unlike many of its denizens, Colonel Hata, the commandant of the Kempetai, was well versed in the history of Shanghai. The Treaty of Nanking in 1842, which marked the end of the Opium Wars between China and Great Britain, resulted in the establishment of foreign settlements at Shanghai, Canton, Amoy, Ningpo, and Foochow. The treaty gave British citizens full extraterritorial privileges, including the right to enforce English law, conduct commercial enterprises, and organize a municipal government and police force within the boundaries of her settlements. By 1900, these privileges had been extended to the United States and sixteen other nations who had jurisdiction over the International Settlement of Shanghai, while France governed her own enclave, the French Concession. Together, the two areas under extraterritorial law covered thirteen square miles, an area in which a foreign populace of almost one hundred and twenty thousand lived, worked, and played, as shielded from the upheaval in China as if they were residing in London or on the Riviera.

Luxury hotels abounded in Shanghai, among them the Cathay and the Palace on the Bund, and the Park Hotel on Bubbling Well Road. There were a number of international banks—the Hongkong and Shanghai at Number 12, the Bund, the Russo-Asiatic Bank at Number 15, and the Yokohama Specie at Number 31. There were numerous shipping companies: the British P & O Line, the Blue Funnel Line, and the Royal Mail Steam Packet Company, all providing overseas passage, as well as the Canadian Pacific Line and the Dollar Line to the United States.

There were Protestant, Roman Catholic, and Russian Orthodox churches, two Jewish synagogues, and literally hundreds of Buddhist temples. There were four major department stores; two dozen western-style beauty parlors; dentists and doctors—even a hospital for dogs. Added to all this were automobile salesrooms and garages; American and British grocery stores; scores of dressmakers, custom tailors, wine and spirit shops, and six pharmacies.

Foreigners lived in stately homes and air-conditioned apartments on tree-lined avenues in exclusive areas. They attended gala parties given by extravagant millionaires and amused themselves with games of cricket at the British Country Club, gourmet luncheons at the Cercle Sportif Français, afternoon tea at Marcello's or the Scotch Bakery on Nanking Road, and, for men only, drinks at the famous Long Bar in the Shanghai Club located at Number 3, the Bund.

The other pleasures of the foreign colony included horse racing, greyhounds at the Canidrome, and jai-alai at the Avenue Joffre auditorium. There were a dozen first-class theaters that ran the latest motion pictures from Hollywood as well as the Municipal Council Orchestra, led by Maestro Paci, several English-speaking radio stations and three newspapers, plus over a hundred nightclubs whose taxi girls, whites and

Orientals of all ages were all too willing to provide a wide variety of sexual gratifications, assuming the price was right.

Until Pearl Harbor, and the complete takeover by the Japanese, Shanghai was the white man's paradise on earth. The signs in the public parks bore mute evidence to the reverse side of that coin: NO DOGS AND CHINESE PERMITTED.

It was a different world now, Hata gloated, and, hearing the creaking sound from below, he peered into the courtyard where two ragged privates, members of his overworked burial squad, had casually flung Felix Hacker's inert body into their wooden cart.

In Colonel Hata's mind, military justice had been served by the execution. Both sides, Japanese and Allies, knew the penalty for espionage was death. The risks were understood. It was also understood that if an agent willingly shifted allegiance and gave his captors enough genuine information, then bargains could be struck; accommodations might be made. It was with this in mind that Hata had originally offered to spare Felix Hacker's life in exchange for the precious black book he had compiled and for the names of the two men in charge of the spy ring that was plaguing the Japanese High Command along the East China coast.

But the roly-poly Swiss, a violator of his own nation's strict neutrality, refused to cooperate. Instead he endured twenty-four hours of incredible misery without revealing where the potentially damaging black book was hidden or the identity of the ring leader.

Hata sniffed at the night air, which was thick with humidity. It was impossible to keep from perspiring, and he noted bitterly that large patches of sweat were already forming on his freshly laundered shirt. The summer climate of Shanghai was an affront to Hata's fastidious nature, forcing him to bathe twice a day and change his uniform as often, in order not to go about smelling like an unwashed ricksha driver. Still, he reflected philosophically, being posted to Shanghai was far safer than an assignment in the South Pacific, the bloody scene of Japan's most tragic defeats in almost two thousand years of war, where battles at Guadalcanal, Iwo Jima, Saipan, and Okinawa had already taken a heavy toll. From the large group of men who had graduated in his officers training class in the Kempetai nine years earlier only he was still alive. The ashes of the others had been shipped back home for burial.

Turning from the window, Hata glanced at the cover of
the thick manila file in his right hand. There, in bold print
across the top beside the name Felix Hacker, were printed
the words: AUGUST 2, 1945, PRISONER DIED OF NATURAL
CAUSES.

Chapter Two

---◆---

Before the war the concrete skyscrapers of the Bund were lit twenty-four hours a day. From morning till night the broad avenue separating the imposing buildings from the wharves along the Whampoo River swarmed with activity. It was said the people of Shanghai never slept.

The Japanese occupation changed all this. Automobiles belonging to enemy nationals were confiscated, and gasoline, previously never expensive, was rigidly rationed and soared in price. Tourism virtually came to a halt, and imported goods were available only on the black market. Moreover, a strict curfew was imposed, allowing only those with special permits to be on the streets after nine o'clock in the evening, a deadline eventually extended to eleven o'clock.

Despite these wartime restrictions, the Cathay Hotel, at the corner of Nanking Road and the Bund, maintained its standing as the finest hotel in Shanghai and, by any standards, one of the most luxurious in the world. Twenty stories high, with a marble facade crowned by a pyramid-shaped tower, the Cathay had been built in 1937 by Sir Victor Sassoon, the Jewish millionaire whose vast empire stretched all the way to India and the Mideast. A few minutes after curfew on the same evening Felix Hacker was executed, the Cathay's elegant canopied entrance facing onto the Bund was practically

deserted except for a few massive prewar limousines, a
putty-colored army truck, and several exhausted ricksha
drivers squatting in an opium stupor beside their wooden
vehicles.

Fifteen floors above, Maximov Dallin stood at the window
of his suite in the northeast corner of the hotel. Below him
lay the legendary Hongkong-Shanghai Bank building with
its huge bronze lions guarding the entrance; the enormous
neoclassic Customs House with Big Ching, its clock tower
chiming on the hour; and beyond, the wide expanse of the
Bund now cloaked in darkness.

From the fading drone of the Superfortresses high overhead, Dallin could tell that the American bombers, returning
from raids on the Japanese Home Islands, had already swung
away from Shanghai and were heading toward their bases in
South China.

A few seconds later the air raid sirens sounded the all-clear
and Dallin heard the soulful plaint of Edith Piaf singing *"La
Vie en Rose"* on the phonograph mingled with the voices of
his guests who were attending the informal soiree he had held
nightly in his suite ever since he arrived in Shanghai nearly
three years before.

Maximov Dallin, a thirty-five-year-old White Russian, exuded an air of natural confidence that was enhanced by his
wide shoulders and powerful physique. He was fashionably
dressed in a tan linen suit, brown leather Wellington boots,
and an open-collared green silk shirt. His dark brown hair
was curly and thick, his brown eyes lustrous; a prominent
grecian nose robbed him of traditional handsomeness but lent
him a kind of dignity that was admired by the Chinese.

His suite in the Cathay Hotel was furnished with no
concern for cost. The rooms were decorated in the Bauhaus
style; the living room walls and ceiling painted in stark
white enamel, a rectangular rug of white wool woven with
bold multicolored stripes on the floor beneath a low glass
table. A rosewood chest topped with Italian marble and
several tubular chrome sofas and chairs in black leather completed the furnishings. On the walls were a few select abstract
paintings, among them a Josef Albers and a Kandinsky.

Like its tenant, the apartment was striking but impersonal.
To those who had had dealings with him, the White Russian,
while always accessible, was remote. He was quick to express

disapproval but slow to offer praise or betray his inner thoughts.

Among those remaining of the nearly fifty guests who had drifted through his apartment this evening, none thought she knew Maximov Dallin better than Niki Orlov, a fellow White Russian.

A willowy, seductive woman in her late twenties, her short black hair, delicate cameo-like face, and haunting dark eyes were accentuated by a long sea-green gown; an emerald choker encrusted with pear-shaped diamonds circled her throat. With every movement of her lithe body, she exuded an intoxicating sensuality.

When Niki noticed Dallin alone by the window, she broke away from the acid-tongued Parisian art dealer and gregarious Italian diamond merchant who had been boring her with gossip about the Duke of Windsor and his demanding American wife. Taking a glass of chilled vodka from a passing servant, Niki went over to Dallin.

"Another air raid alert but no bombing. Odd, isn't it?"

"Not really," Dallin replied, turning toward her. "Only means the Americans used up their bombs on the Home Islands."

"Fortunately for us! They bombed the hell out of the ghetto the other day."

"Since when do you care about the Jews?"

"I don't. But they do live here in Shanghai and one day a bomb may hit us too."

Dallin nodded. Then taking a pack of Camels from his jacket pocket he offered one to Niki and lit another for himself.

"Strange how these raids never bother you like they do everyone else." Niki smiled and slithered to rest on the edge of the leather couch, crossing her near-perfect legs so that they dangled invitingly before Dallin. "But then nothing ever does."

"What will be will be."

"Then it's true what Hata says—that you really believe in luck?"

"Without that a man is lost from the start." Niki nodded and made no reply. The phonograph switched records and began playing a love song by Billie Holiday just as mournful as the one Piaf had sung. Nearby, the art dealer from Berlin was arguing the merits of investing in paintings versus diamonds during inflationary periods.

"You *would* have a lot of records by Piaf and Billie Holiday," Niki said. "You really like to suffer."

"What makes you think I'm suffering?" Dallin was watching the gnomish Chilean Consul-General foxtrotting with a buxom Roumanian widow, the heiress to a vast fortune in Shanghai real estate.

"Because you never smile, and to make matters worse, tonight you're not even drinking."

"I can't. Business."

"You're not leaving Shanghai again?"

"Tomorrow night. Meantime I have problems over at the South Railway Station."

"Sounds serious."

"Only if the other side makes it serious."

"Is Hata going?"

"Depends on how reasonable the other side is."

"He promised to join me later upstairs at the Tower."

"Then he'll be there."

Niki laughed warmly. "He's not at all like you. He's predictable."

"What you mean is he's not like either of us."

"Now what have you heard about me?"

"Just that the redhead at the Pleasure Palace claims you paid her a visit the other night. And now she isn't sure who she likes more—you or me."

"Then perhaps we should all try it together sometime, so we can judge for ourselves. Or does that scare you?"

Dallin shook his head. Then he leaned closer and whispered, "Better we make it a foursome."

"I know." Niki smiled, wetting her crimson lips. "Only my Japanese friend doesn't believe in it. You know how conventional he is, even with our influence."

"You make him sound like a child."

"No," Niki answered, her voice taking on a note of sincerity. "But in the hands of the right woman, most men are like putty, no matter how strong they appear to others."

"And that's how Hata is with you?"

"Perhaps," Niki replied, sliding her foot suggestively against his ankle.

"Fascinating subject," Dallin said, edging away from her. "Let's discuss it someday. In the meantime, do me a favor and stay with this bunch while I go across town."

"Whatever you say, Mr. Dallin."

Bemused, Dallin brushed his lips lightly against her hand, then started to move away.

"Oh, wait!" Niki called out, drawing Dallin back. "There *is* one thing you can do for me."

"Name it. But hurry."

"Hata's birthday is coming up. I ordered a special gift from Switzerland months ago, and now they say it can't get through because of the American blockade."

"And this gift can't be found anywhere else but eleven thousand miles from here?" Dallin asked somberly.

"Be nice. Please."

"Okay. I'll have whatever it is delivered to the Nationalist Embassy in Berne, then flown over the Hump into Chungking. By this time next week it'll be on my desk. More I can not do!"

"Dallin?"

"What?"

"You're wonderful. Sometimes I think we're really just one big family—you, Hata, and me."

"You'd like that."

"Wouldn't you?" Niki replied teasingly.

"Niki," Dallin whispered into her ear. "if I so much as touched you anywhere, in ten minutes half the room would tell the Kempetai, and the rest would blackmail us directly."

With a laugh, Niki gazed at the Europeans and Orientals scattered around the living room, and decided she had to agree.

"Still, it's a pity."

"I never said it wasn't!"

Turning away, Dallin walked toward the bedroom. He paused for a moment to exchange a few pleasantries with a turbaned Indian money-lender, then was intercepted by Zabar, the balding Hungarian maître d' of the posh Tower Nightclub on the roof of the Cathay Hotel.

"Excuse the intrusion, Monsieur Dallin," Zabar said worriedly.

"If it's about your shipment, I already left word with Ferrara."

"You have? But I was never told."

"The freighter's arrived," Dallin explained patiently. "She's at Woosung. By tomorrow my people will have off-loaded her cargo of Argentinian beef and Persian caviar."

"A thousand thanks, Monsieur Dallin." Zabar beamed. "A thousand thanks."

A moment later Dallin was inside his bedroom with the door securely locked. He moved toward the right side of the huge bed and, reaching between the pillows, pressed a spot on the wall. He leaned back as the mirrored panel swung away from the wall above the bed revealing a compartment lined with firearms and ammunition.

Within easy reach of the bed hung a matched pair of Smith & Wesson snub-nosed thirty-eight caliber revolvers, alongside a row of boxes containing cartridges, a pile of various clips and magazines, and two German potato-masher grenades. On a higher shelf, resting on wooden pegs, were two gleaming submachine guns: a British Sten gun with a bolt handle and German Schmeisser with a box magazine. To their left hung two more lethal beauties: a pair of blue Bolo Mauser automatic pistols and a leather shoulder holster.

Dallin peeled off his jacket and slid the stiff leather holster over his left shoulder. Then he replaced his jacket and removed one of the Bolos from the wall. He shoved the gun with its steel-milled frame and six-inch barrel into his shoulder holster, dropped four clips with ten shots apiece into his jacket pocket, and nudged the mirror back into place, leaving the suite through a rear door that led directly to the service elevator.

The rear exit of the Cathay Hotel opened onto a wide alley. A maroon Bentley roadster, nearly fifteen feet long with flaring fenders, was parked there, Chinese chauffeur at the wheel. A squad of heavily armed Kempei motorcyclists surrounded the Bentley on all sides. As Dallin emerged from the hotel, all four Kempei kicked their motorcycles to life. Nodding to them, Dallin opened the rear door of the Bentley and settled himself comfortably on the padded leather seat.

A second later, sirens whining, the lead motorcyclists shot out of the alley and made a sharp right onto Nanking Road. They sped past a long row of darkened neon signs and storefronts, finally veering left. The convoy swept onto the Boulevard des Deux Républiques and past the crooked streets and ancient buildings of the "old city."

"This time I bring gun too, boss," the chauffeur shouted over his shoulder.

"If I need you we're both in big trouble," Dallin snapped back, lighting a Camel.

The Confucius Temple loomed against the sky on his left. Suddenly the motorcyclists switched off their sirens and headlights. The Chinese driver cut his lights and followed the escort across the tracks of the Shanghai-Hangchow-Ningpo Railway into the pitch-black yards of the South Station.

The Bentley glided to a halt beside a sprawling tool shed. The motorcyclists, their engines off, closed in around it, forming a silent phalanx.

Then the waiting began. As the seconds ticked by into minutes on the Bentley's dashboard clock, Dallin lit one cigarette after another, crushing them out impatiently. When the Chinese driver, growing restless, turned to speak, Dallin shushed him with an abrupt motion of his hand.

Finally, a low rumbling noise echoed across the railway yard. Dallin's gaze was riveted in the direction of the sound. Around the bend in the track, appeared a locomotive, a goliath from the turn of the century, hissing steam. In the darkness Dallin could barely make out the silhouette of the gondolas and boxcars behind it as the locomotive hissed and groaned to a stop.

At that very instant, a prewar Buick sedan rattled into the yard, followed by a ragtag gang of panting coolies. Its headlights flickered across the train, illuminating burlap sacks heaped across the gondolas and bulging from the splintered sides of the boxcars.

With the coolies bringing up the rear, the Buick jolted to a sudden stop beside the locomotive. All four doors swung open and shadowy figures hurried out to meet a small group that had descended from the train. Their loudly rejoicing voices carried over to the Bentley.

The celebration ended abruptly as Dallin, ordering his chauffeur to switch on his headlights, emerged from the Bentley.

His jacket deliberately unbuttoned, his arms swinging easily at his sides, Dallin quickly covered the stretch of open ground that lay between him and the group beside the train. For a moment the only noise was the sound of the gravel crunching beneath his boots. As he closed in, he got his first good look at the men gathered there: Peterson, the stocky, outgoing Swedish Red Cross representative; Father Joseph, the owl-faced minister of the Union Church; a pair of plump Chinese, whom Dallin did not know personally but recognized by sight as being affiliated with the Shanghai Christian

Brotherhood; and three bearded Jesuit priests from the Roman Catholic mission, whose soiled long brown robes indicated they must have spent the last few days aboard the train.

Silent and emaciated, the horde of coolies remained massed behind the aging Buick, waiting with empty sacks slung around their ragged, bent shoulders for the signal to unload the train. Dallin purposely avoided their suspicious gaze. Instead, he hailed the Red Cross official by name.

"Good evening to you, Dallin," Peterson replied politely, unable to conceal his alarm. "May I ask what you want here?"

"You don't sound too pleased to see me."

"What do you want from us?"

"If you don't mind, I'll come a bit closer," Dallin said, drawing nearer. "Shouting makes me uncomfortable."

With the exception of the husky Jesuit, who Dallin guessed was their leader, the others were perspiring heavily and looked extremely anxious. Whatever it was they had planned, it was clear that the last person in the world they wanted to encounter was Maximov Dallin.

"So!" Peterson said in a booming voice, "now you are comfortable, once again I ask you, Mr. Dallin, what is it you want here?"

"I came to talk about your train."

"This train has nothing whatsoever to do with you. We have permits. The written approval of the Japanese High Command and the Consular Corps."

"Precisely," Dallin agreed. "But you haven't got one from the Kempetai."

"What of it?" The husky Jesuit priest shot back. "I warn you, Dallin, we won't tolerate any more of your interference. You have wrecked our plans too many times in the past. Prevented us from carrying out our Christian mission of aiding the hungry and unemployed."

"Gentlemen, please," Father Joseph interrupted, "surely whatever our differences they can be settled without argument or harsh words."

"Don't count on it, Father," the Jesuit leader replied bitterly. "All this White Russian collaborator and black marketeer cares about is his own pocketbook. The fact that thousands—even hundreds of thousands—are starving in Shanghai because they can't afford the insane prices he wants for rice and grain doesn't bother him one bit. Does it, Dallin?"

"People are free to pay what they like." Dallin smiled. "You don't see me holding a gun to their heads and demanding that they buy from me."

"You don't need a gun. Not when you control the market and set the prices," Peterson complained, mopping the sweat from his flabby cheeks with a crumpled white handkerchief. "For the love of God, man, leave us in peace! Or doesn't the opinion of others mean anything at all to you?"

"Not when it interferes with business," Dallin said smoothly. "Now, I'll buy the whole trainload, every ton of grain and rice you've got, at three times what you paid for it. And I'll pay in gold, which is more than any good Christian ever did for me."

"Months of preparation have gone into this," the Jesuit leader objected. "What we have here is not for sale."

"Be reasonable," Dallin warned. "Everyone in Shanghai knows I've been accumulating rice, grain, and soybeans. My warehouses are crammed. If you unload what you've got here on the market I'll take a terrific beating."

"You can well afford it," Peterson said angrily.

"Maybe I can. But my investors can't. And remember, they don't take losing money lightly."

"When you say investors you mean Colonel Hata, don't you, Dallin?" the Jesuit leader said vehemently. "Go on, admit it. If we don't do as you want, you'll turn us over to the Kempetai."

"That isn't what I said."

"It isn't necessary," Peterson replied wearily, "Everyone in Shanghai is quite familiar with your methods of coercing hotels, bars—even Japanese generals—into doing whatever you wish."

"I didn't come to argue. If you don't want to sell, just say so. But keep in mind this is Shanghai, not Stockholm or London or the Vatican. What happens here is beyond the control of any of us."

"If I may say so, and may God forgive me if I am wrong," Father Joseph interjected, "never in all my years in the service of Our Lord have I ever met anyone as callous as you. We wish you no harm. Clearly what these gentlemen and I are doing is not for our own gain but to help those in need. We have thousands, many of them small children, going hungry in our hospitals, orphanages, and missions. At the prices your representatives charge we simply cannot afford to feed them. All we ask is that you let us carry out our plan. You have our word that not one gram of the rice or grain aboard this train will interfere with your monopoly."

"It's a pretty speech, Father," Dallin replied firmly, "and I don't doubt your sincerity, but there's no guarantee things will happen as you say they will. It so happens Du's people and some of the other factions in this city are watching us at this very moment. They'll be all over you the moment you try to take those sacks away from the yard. And I can't afford to let that happen. So take my advice. Sell while you can and with my gold buy what you need on the Shanghai market."

Disheartened, his voice quavering, Father Joseph replied, "This is something I can't answer myself. We'll need to decide among ourselves."

"You have everything figured out, don't you, Dallin?" the Jesuit leader said bitterly.

"Reality's plain as day and often not very pretty, but that's how I operate," Dallin replied, shrugging indifferently and fishing into his jacket pocket for a crumpled cigarette which he lit with a wooden match struck between his thumb and forefinger.

Their answer came thirty seconds later: a unanimous no. Disappointed but not really surprised, Dallin flung the newly lit cigarette onto the ground and walked toward the Bentley. Pausing to tell the Kempei motorcyclists they were leaving, he climbed into the car and ordered the chauffeur to move out.

"What about the supply train?"

"They want it, so let them have it!" Dallin replied grimly. As he sank back against the soft cushions, he let his mind stray to pleasanter thoughts.

While the Bentley sped smoothly away into the night, the Jesuits had already divided the coolies into groups and had started to unload the train. The emaciated Chinese threw themselves eagerly into the task; they swarmed aboard the gondolas and boxcars wrestling with burlap bags of rice and grain several times their weight. They edged the bags, one at a time, onto the ground so they could be emptied into the smaller sacks, which the coolies could handle with ease.

On the outskirts of the railway yard, a cordon of helmeted Kempei troops with fixed bayonets slithered quietly from their hiding places behind buildings and sheds, and in the cover of darkness, began closing in around the supply train. Unaware of the approaching danger; Peterson and the others helped the first wave of coolies, preparing to leave the yard, shoulder their heavy burdens.

Catching them all by surprise, the sharp note of a whistle blown by a Kempetai lieutenant signaled those soldiers assigned to carry torches to yank the three-foot-long kerosene-soaked straw sticks from their backpacks and ignite them. The flames illuminated the coarse faces of the Kempei encircling the train. At the sound of a second whistleblast, the soldiers carrying torches waved them vigorously overhead while the troops with rifles held them at the ready, steel bayonets glittering. Then the cordon moved forward at a trot.

Terrified by the sight of the advancing Japanese, the coolies dove from the gondolas and boxcars, and, carrying whatever they could, formed a seething, desperate mass beside the train. Racing over, the husky Jesuit priest tried to calm them, but instead, hearing the battle cry of the oncoming Kempei, the coolies panicked. Rushing by the beleagured priest, who stood with outstretched arms, they swept past the Buick, smashing Peterson to the ground, and bowled aside a stunned Father Joseph, before scattering in the general direction of the Whampoo wharves.

Ignoring the approaching Kempei, the Jesuit priest helped the Red Cross representative, who was reduced nearly to tears, into the Buick beside the dazed minister of the Union Church. Then snatching the official permit from Peterson, he charged wildly over to a squat Kempei lieutenant, protesting the illegal presence of his troops. The officer swung his long curved sword up against the throat of the Jesuit and, giggling, ground the document into the gravel with his heel.

Seconds later, the Kempei troops flung their blazing torches onto the densely packed gondolas and through the open doorways of the crammed boxcars. Instantly the flames ate into the dry burlap sacks, touching off the grain and rice. The fire spread from car to car with ravaging rapidity until the entire train was ablaze. Clouds of dark smoke swirled overhead, engulfing the Buick where Peterson and the others sat sick with grief.

When the blasts of hot air from the burning train began to sear their helmeted faces, the Kempei troops withdrew and, deploying into squads, marched off, their bayonets shining in the reddish glow cast by the fire.

A few miles away, in the International Settlement, the men and women involved in the Herculean effort of feeding the starving and needy stood on the rooftop of their headquarters and wept in dismay as they saw the flames streaking the sky. They had recognized the site of the blaze and knew what it meant.

Meanwhile, in the plush Tower nightclub high above the Bund, Dallin leaned casually against the marble bar, enjoying a neat Scotch, as he regaled his fellow black-market operators with yet another example of the foolishness of the good samaritans who had brought in the supply train.

Chapter Three

———————◆◆◆———————

At eight o'clock the next night, the uneasy slumber of a Kempei sentry dozing at his station by the stairwell was disturbed by the wail of the tortured Polish Jew echoing through the basement corridor of Bridge House. Eight floors above, where the screams of tormented prisoners could not be heard, Hata sat in his steamy office putting the final touches on the weekly report for his superiors in Tokyo. Even with the open windows, the overhead ceiling fan brought no relief from the oppressive August heat. Groaning, Hata crumpled the sheet of rice paper he had been writing on and reached for another. How he dreaded details. Summarizing the political situation or the persecution of the enemies of Japan was one thing, but describing the financial and economic mess gripping Shanghai was another. Against the American dollar and gold, the yen was sinking fast. The puppet dollar was already worthless, and even the value of the Nationalist one was badly eroded.

The decline in military production was another nagging problem. A substantial drop in the amount of raw material available had caused shutdowns at factories and mills, making a mockery of the goals set by Tokyo. The resulting massive unemployment had produced a social unrest never before witnessed in Shanghai's history.

19

He pushed the untouched sheet of rice paper away in disgust, resting his elbows on the eighteenth-century Chippendale partners' desk which, along with three matching chairs, had all been looted from the private apartment of an English millionaire, for Hata's office. On the edge of the desk, next to a solid gold lighter lay a family heirloom, a short samurai sword in a heavy iron sheath encrusted with precious stones.

On the wall behind Hata hung a portrait of Emperor Hirohito, a possession only the most privileged Japanese were allowed to display. On the other three walls of the office were tactical charts, a structural breakdown of the Kempetai chain of command in China, and a detailed map of Shanghai.

To the right of the doorway a sliding wood panel concealed Hata's official living quarters—a large room sparingly furnished with soft tatami mats on the floor, an ebony chest for kimonos and uniforms, and a shelf built into one wall displaying a photograph of Yasukuni, the famed Shinto shrine near the Imperial Palace in Tokyo, where the names of those Japanese soldiers who had fallen in battle were memorialized on tablets. It was believed by many, including Hata, that when a soldier was honored at Yasukuni, his spirit became immortal and he would be a warrior god protecting Nippon for eternity.

To Hata, the youngest son of an ancient samurai family, such shrines were sacred. Unfortunately for him, by the time he came of age there was little else a samurai background could offer but reverence for tradition. The great wealth of Japan was in the hands of a few Zaibatsu families, mercantile dynasties whose commercial interests had mushroomed into enormous industrial, financial, and trading companies that had a stranglehold on every facet of the Japanese economy and government.

The younger generation of the Zaibatsu families were educated at European universities or in the eastern part of the United States. Hata's parents could only afford to enroll him at a provincial college. While Zaibatsu offspring intermarried easily, thereby perpetuating the power and wealth of the great mercantile dynasties, Hata found himself spurned by a desirable wife in favor of a member of the new rich.

Embittered and disillusioned, Hata had joined the Imperial Army, the only means remaining to the impoverished samurai aristocracy of achieving power. Fortunately, through his prowess in athletics, always prized by the Japanese, Hata represented his nation at the World Olympics in 1936, which brought him to the attention of two of the country's most influential military leaders, General Hideki Tojo, Minister for War, and General Kenji Doihara, chief of the Imperial Army Intelligence Service. By aligning himself with the ambitious expansionist policies of these two ultranationalists, Hata was able to secure admittance to the Kempetai, the elite paramilitary organization with widespread police powers directly granted by the Emperor, who had given Kempei officers supreme jurisdiction over all their fellow Japanese as well as the citizens of occupied countries.

Hearing the chimes of the big clock on the nearby Customs House tower brought Hata's attention back to his report. It was then that he noticed the Felix Hacker file on his desk. Something would have to be done about all the dossiers in his possession, while there was still time, he realized. To continue the deception of declaring executed prisoners dead from natural causes was now not only absurd but could also be used against him in the future. Having made this decision, Hata rose from his desk and, moving past the large street maps of Shanghai on the wall, stepped into the long corridor that ran outside his office.

Immediately to his left, through an open door, was a high-ceilinged rectangular-shaped room that held the official records of the Kempetai. Here, in several rows of fireproof metal cabinets, arranged in alphabetical order and kept up to date by a squad of his most intelligent soldiers, were the dossiers of every person living in Shanghai who had ever been suspected of being an enemy of Japan.

The populace of Shanghai had been divided by nationality; the largest group was Chinese, but there were categories for Koreans, Indians, Hungarians, Poles, Czechs, and South Americans, as well as stateless Jews and refugees—in all, over two dozen nationalities. In addition, there were files for the opposing political factions that had chosen Shanghai as a battleground; Kuomintang and Chinese Communist; Nazi and anti-Nazi; Italian Fascist and anti-Fascist; Free French and Vichy French, White Russian and Soviet Russian. There were other categories for gamblers, kidnappers, smugglers, drug dealers, and gun merchants, as well as the local membership roll of China's two major secret fraternal societies—the all-powerful Green and Red Dragon still led by the notorious Shanghai gangster chieftain, Du Yueh-sen, who had retreated to Chungking with his good friend of many years, Chiang Kai-shek. Another file cabinet, long in disuse, held the dossiers of enemy nationals: citizens of nations at war with Japan since 1941—Americans, British, Canadians, and Dutch, who languished in prison camps throughout northeastern China.

But most important were the confidential dossiers locked inside a large steel safe. These contained the personal histories of every paid political assassin, informer, collaborator, information peddler, spy, and counter-spy that the Japanese Military Secret Police had discovered during their seven-year occupation.

Hearing a raspy cough from the other end of the corridor, Hata saw the bent frame of his adjutant, Lieutenant Sumato, emerging from the wireless room.

"Just in from Tokyo," Sumato announced, advancing slowly along the corridor with a handful of messages.

"What about the Norwegian?" Hata replied, taking the messages and handing over Felix Hacker's manila file.

"No news yet. We're searching the city now."

"You've taken the usual precautions, I suppose?" Hata asked sharply. "Port, rail station, airport, roads. And home searches?"

Hesitating, Sumato answered, "Not home searches."

Hata glared at his aide and snorted. He often wondered how his adjutant had managed to join the Kempetai. He sadly lacked the prime prerequisites of wealth, family, and influence. His formidable intellect and penchant for organization afforded the sole justification for his pallid presence which, even during exciting moments of glory, had remained spiritless.

Sumato, far from unaware of the critical nature of his superior officer's thoughts, lowered his eyes to the scarred stone floor. Even had he cared, which he no longer did, it would have been useless to attempt to alter Hata's low opinion of him this late in the game.

"You haven't forgotten Felix Hacker's black book, have you?" Hata was barraging him with questions again.

"No. But suppose there is none to find?"

"I assure you there is."

"But we have no proof," objected Sumato warily. "Only the word of a paid informant. A Caucasian at that."

"The man you're referring to has never been wrong before. Besides it's just like that fat overeducated librarian Hacker to keep a dossier on our role during the occupation," Hata insisted bitterly, raising his voice to add, "So you find it before I delegate other work for you to do."

With a shudder, Sumato recalled that split second when he and Felix Hacker had exchanged an astonished glance just before the gunner opened fire. Then ducking his face to hide his anguish, he murmured his assent and turned away from Hata.

Back in his office, Hata swept aside the incompleted weekly report to make room for the messages from Tokyo. Lighting a cigarette from a freshly opened pack of Chesterfield's, he began to read the first communiqué:

> JAPANESE HIGH COMMAND
> FIRST GENERAL ARMY HQ
> TOKYO
>
> PROCEDURE TO DEFEND HOME ISLANDS
>
> IT IS IMPERATIVE FOR ALL RANKS TO UNDERSTAND AN IMPORTANT TACTICAL ADVANTAGE HAS RECENTLY BEEN ACHIEVED OVER THE ENEMY.
>
> BY LURING THEIR FORCES TO INVADE OUR HOME ISLANDS WE ARE NOW IN A POSITION TO WIN THE FINAL BATTLE OF THE WAR AND OBTAIN AN HONORABLE PEACE FOR NIPPON.

Cursing in disbelief, Hata exhaled a swath of smoke and read on:

> ALL MEN FROM PRIVATE TO GENERAL MUST STRIVE HARDER FOR VICTORY. MUST ONCE MORE DEMONSTRATE SACRED LOYALTY AND A WILLINGNESS TO DIE FOR THEIR HONORABLE SON OF HEAVEN.

Hata slammed his fist against the desk, livid at the pompous stupidity of the High Command. At a time when steadfast officers like himself, men who had never flinched at carrying out official policy, were anxiously awaiting word on the course of the war, this sort of useless propaganda was the last thing they needed.

If only those fools had kept up the pace initiated back in 1941, Imperial Marines would by now be standing sentry duty at the White House. Instead, the once victorious military machine of Nippon lay shattered, her proud air force and mighty navy humbled. The High Command was adept at concealing the reasons for this situation, but Hata was not misled. His files bulged with communiqués that pointed directly to the causes. Japan had been unprepared for a long war. Her warships lacked radar; her fighter planes were too slow, poorly armed, and thinly plated. Her heavy industries were far behind American technology and productivity and, in any event, had now been all but bombed out of existence.

For almost six months American Superfortresses had been savaging the Home Islands. Waves of these four-engined monsters, flying at altitudes far beyond the range of Japanese fighters, had decimated cities, leaving hundreds of thousands homeless and countless others dead or wounded. Even Shanghai was a constant target for these long-range American bombers. Night after night they struck the shipyards, the warehouses lining the docks, and the railway centers. And all the while, the Japanese High Command in Tokyo kept issuing preposterous statements like the one he was now reading.

Angrily, Hata threw down the communiqué and went on to the next one:

> FROM CHIEF OF PRISONER OF WAR CAMPS
> ADMINISTRATIVE SECTION
> MILITARY AFFAIRS BUREAU
>
> SUBJECT: WAR CRIMINALS
>
> BECAUSE OF THE RECENTLY RECEIVED POTSDAM DECLARATION MADE BY THE ALLIES, ALL PERSONNEL WHO MISTREATED ALLIED POWS AND FOREIGN INTERNEES, OR ARE HELD IN EXTREME DISFAVOR BY THEM, ARE HEREBY PERMITTED TO REQUEST TRANSFER TO AN-OTHER COMMAND; OR IN CASE OF EXTREME JEOPARDY ARE TO BE PERMITTED AND HELPED TO FLEE WITHOUT A TRACE.

Shocked by the directive, Hata mulled over the words, "in case of extreme jeopardy"; he rose from his desk and moved slowly across the office. The Potsdam Declaration, only hours old, had already cast a deadly pall over Japan's surviving armed forces. Its terms were extremely clear: not only were the Allies demanding unconditional surrender, they were deliberately leaving the fate of Emperor Hirohito uncertain and vowing vengeance upon all enemy war criminals.

To Hata, the declaration was a blunt instrument of international policy, completely devoid of any logic or understanding of the Japanese mind. It was also certain to prolong hostilities until Japan's Home Islands were in ruins and her army and navy totally vanquished.

Coming to a halt before a tactical chart of China, Hata carefully studied the latest developments. In May of 1944, the Japanese Army had undertaken a major new offensive, advancing southwest across China, chopping up elements of the American Fourteenth Air Force, overrunning several garrison cities, and routing the Nationalist defenders. The latest campaign had culminated in a great victory for the Japanese. They had opened a corridor all the way from Manchuria in the north to Singapore in the south. They now controlled over half of China's vast population and were keeping a combined force of several million Nationalist and Communist soldiers at bay.

It was with a bitter sense of irony that Hata realized the Japanese were very close to finally achieving their military aims in China. After years of occupying the industrial east coast—years during which Chiang Kai-shek and the American ambassador had been forced to huddle inside Chungking's damp bomb shelters and Mao Tse-tung and Chou En-lai lived in Yenan's yellow sand caves while Japanese officers occupied the palatial mansions and grand hotels of Hong Kong, Peking, and Shanghai—the stalemate had finally been broken. No longer would there be any accommodation with Chiang Kai-shek. The Japanese High Command were carrying out their instructions to occupy the rest of China. But the battle order arrived too late, not only for Hata personally but for Japan as well. What good was conquering China when the Allies, sweeping across the Pacific, were on the verge of invading the Home Islands.

"Only a question of time before we're destroyed," Hata murmured.

China had exhausted Japan's energies, just as she undermined Hata's own will and loyalty. He had always been an ambitious man, true, but, until reaching China, he had never been corrupt. China had changed him, gradually weakening his will and corroding his spirit until at last here he was, using his influential position to further his black-market enterprises and spending most of his time with an erotic young Caucasian woman.

Lost in reverie, Hata thought of his partner, Maximov Dallin. As familiar with Shanghai's beautiful women as he was with the intricacies of the Asian black-market trade, it was Dallin who first introduced him to Niki Orlov, the only child of the infamous White Russian general, Count Aleksandr Orlov. Their relationship was the envy of every Japanese officer in Shanghai. And small wonder! Sometimes Hata himself marveled at his good fortune in having the love of such a headstrong, passionate woman. Of course, it had taken some adjustment on his part; indeed, Hata was still adjusting.

Thinking of the two White Russians, Dallin and Niki, lifted the dark gloom that had engulfed Hata. There is hope yet, he decided. Of course, it would require daring and great courage. Luck as well no doubt, as all worthwhile ventures did. But he could escape the trap closing in around him. He could flee China before the Allies arrested him as a war criminal.

"War criminal!" He spat out the phrase with vehemence, and a look of cold anger passed across his face. As commandant of the Kempetai—Shanghai Section, it was his duty to prosecute enemies of the Emperor. While others might shrink from torturing and executing saboteurs and spies, Hata could not. The express purpose of his being in China was to subjugate the civilian population so that the overall aims of the Greater East Asia Co-Prosperity Sphere could be accomplished.

His written orders came from the highest levels of government and they specified that he disregard the normal rules of warfare. The China campaign was considered to be merely "an incident," not a war, and those Chinese who defied Japanese rule were not lawful combatants but simply bandits.

It was the intent of Japan's ruling clique to force the Chinese into submission by any means necessary no matter how cruel or savage, should they fail to acknowledge Japan as China's natural superior. If all else failed, the Kempetai had been given orders to exterminate the Chinese if they stood in the way of Japan's New Order.

The idea that he might be persecuted for carrying out these duties incensed Hata. He was so preoccupied by the thought that he was not aware that Sumato had entered the room until the adjutant was at his desk.

"Miss Orlov phoned. She wishes to meet you at the Tower Nightclub within the hour."

"Very well. Order my car," Hata replied, gaining control of himself. "Any news on the Norwegian?"

"Only one report so far. He was seen leaving the Carleton Restaurant with his daughter."

"You mean he doesn't know we're after him?"

Nodding uneasily, Sumato shifted from one foot to the other.

"What about the black book?"

"Still nothing. Our people are still searching for it."

"Very well. That'll be all."

Sumato turned quickly for the door, his haggard face brightening for a moment.

"No, wait. There is one more thing." Hata smiled. "You knew Hacker personally, didn't you?"

For a moment Sumato could not move. When he finally turned around, his face seemed more anguished than ever.

"I borrowed books from the Municipal Library," he explained with a stammer. "Nothing more."

"You never spoke, never had any conversations with him?"

"About what?"

"Suppose you tell me?" Hata's grin was merciless.

Sumato was only too familiar with this form of questioning; he had witnessed his superior officer playing cat-and-mouse many times before. All Sumato could do now was hope and pray it was only a bluff, that whoever reported his acquaintance with Hacker knew nothing more.

"Perhaps we did have a few conversations about Western literature and classical music," he admitted prudently.

"Nothing about our affairs? What goes on here at Bridge House?"

"I have not betrayed my country," Sumato replied, his voice quivering with emotion.

"Yet someone leaked secrets about us to Felix Hacker so he could put them into his black book, didn't they?"

"I know nothing about that. I am not even sure there is a black book."

"Well, there is! And fortunately for me there weren't any copies made."

"But," Sumato insisted. "Everyone knows Felix Hacker was a highly respected scholar. And a dedicated librarian."

"Was he, now?" Hata lashed back. "That isn't what he admitted down in our basement."

"But he said nothing," Sumato protested, "only that——"

"Silence!" Hata interrupted. "You will never—never I repeat—contradict me. Do you understand that?"

"Yes, sir," Sumato murmured, his head bowed and torso twisted so that he almost resembled a hunchback.

"And as a Kempetai officer," Hata barked out at him, "your duty is to suspect everyone, isn't it? Especially scholars and theorists!"

"Yes," agreed Sumato, his face red with shame, although not for the reason Hata might have imagined. "But our Consular Corps insisted we observe the right of all neutral foreign nationals."

"Quite obviously they were wrong, weren't they?"

"Perhaps. But it's still their responsibility to uphold international law."

"After Pearl Harbor?" mocked Hata. "Don't be absurd."

The Tower Nightclub on the top of the Cathay Hotel offered a panoramic view of Shanghai and the mouth of the Yangtze to the west. The large circular room was furnished with chrome-trimmed tables and chairs, dark, frosted mirrors, and red velvet draperies. Once a haven for the Orient's American and European tycoons, the Tower was now crowded nightly with an assortment of high-ranking Japanese officers, war profiteers, sleek Chinese businessmen in double-breasted suits, and tantalizingly beautiful White Russian and Eurasian women.

Giacomo Ferrara, the managing director of the Cathay, surveyed the crowd from the marble bar that ran along one wall. He still found the nightly spectacle highly amusing. A gray-haired northern Italian with chiseled features and bushy eyebrows, he was impeccably dressed, as always, in a white dinner jacket, pleated shirt, black bow tie, and sharply pressed black trousers. As he waited for his chief barman, Igor, a mustached Bulgar, to mix his martini, Ferrara's experienced eyes scanned the nightclub, swiftly picking out those candlelit tables occupied by the most enterprising black marketeers and wealthiest refugees. These men were invariably accompanied by dazzling women, dripping costly gems and poured into revealing dresses. Much to his satisfaction, Ferrara noted with an ironic smile that these women favored imported French champagne and lavish amounts of Persian caviar, for which the hotel charged the equivalent of a dozen coolies' annual salaries.

On the podium, the Harlem Five, a black band from Haiti, switched from Shanghai jazz to the moody strains of a Cole Porter tune, causing Ferrara to shift his gaze to the couples foxtrotting on the dance floor beneath soft amber lights.

"To your good health," Igor interjected, placing the martini on the bar before Ferrara.

"*Grazie*," he said, lifting the glass to his lips; there was barely a trace of vermouth, he was pleased to note.

"So?"

"*Perfecto.*"

Igor beamed. "I am very grateful to you. My son-in-law was released from Bridge House this morning. Can you imagine—he's still in one piece. No fingers or toes missing, no teeth broken. Just some fleas and bad bruises."

"I'm glad for you." Ferrara smiled, still scanning the club's patrons. With a disapproving eye, he noticed a drunken Japanese admiral pawing a statuesque brunette with spectacular legs.

Igor went on in a whisper, "That White Russian Dallin charged a fortune to get my son-in-law out."

"He always does, but who else can get Hata to release a prisoner?"

"Nobody."

"Precisely. Nobody. And suppose Dallin had said no? Then what?"

"Believe me, I'm not complaining," Igor said hastily, stroking his mustache.

Even by the extraordinary standards of Shanghai, the White Russian was an unusually resourceful adventurer, no easy task in this international port which attracted so many wanderers in search of a fast profit. In his years as managing director of the Cathay, Ferrara had seen his share of these nomads, men and women of every nationality who traveled first class on the best ocean liners and frequented the finest hotels, and who shared one common aim—money. Most would resort to any deception or lie to achieve their goal.

Some, however, were true robber barons—men with vision, ingenious at manipulating people and building colossal fortunes from such mundane goods as hair tonics, aphrodisiacs, and Bibles; in Maximov Dallin's case, operating the most successful black-market and war profiteering syndicate on the East China Coast.

"Speak of the devil," Igor hissed, gesturing to Ferrara's right.

Colonel Hata stood in the doorway between Dallin and Niki Orlov. His entrance sent a ripple of fear across the crowded nightclub, for not one of the patrons, including high-ranking Japanese officers and officials, was immune from his power. Zabar, the normally aloof and imperious maître d', acknowledged the importance of the newly arrived trio as he hastily waived waiters and patrons aside and escorted them directly to their regular booth in the corner overlooking the dance floor.

The generals, diplomats, titled Europeans, and the stupendously rich paid their respects to Hata and Dallin as they swept past. Aware of the attention they were attracting, Dallin lowered his voice to a whisper as he continued his conversation with the Kempetai commandant. "I had no choice. It was either burn the train or lose control of the rice and grain market."

Hata paused momentarily to exchange greetings with an elderly Japanese admiral in a white uniform, then replied, "We would not have wanted our control broken, whatever the cost. So, while the incident surely hasn't done our reputations any good, it's nothing I cannot handle with the High Command or Consular Corps."

"Glad to hear that!" Dallin said, stepping aside while Hata and Niki moved into the booth, then sitting down opposite them. "Because for a while there I thought maybe I went too far."

"Don't concern yourself with it anymore." Hata smiled faintly. "Just tend to business and leave the rest to me. Which reminds me. When are you leaving for Nanking?"

"Midnight plane. Fat Ling's already reported in the Yangtze Gorges. But first I have to finish a deal over at the warehouse."

"You'll speak to Fat Ling about that matter I mentioned?"

"It's at the top of my list."

"Unfortunately that's where it must be," Hata turned his

attention to Niki, looking radiantly lovely in a delicate aquamarine gown and glittering diamond earrings.

"What's unfortunate?" she asked, leaning against Hata. "You two have been whispering to each other ever since we got to the hotel. Don't tell me there's more bad news."

Before Hata could reply, the wine steward brought over a bottle of Château Latour. Dallin gazed at its gold and white label marked 1929, then, approving the vintage, watched as the steward pulled the cork.

"Another batch of communiqués from Tokyo just arrived," Hata said. "The Allies have issued a declaration from their conference in Potsdam. It ends any hope of an easy peace."

The steward offered Dallin a partially filled glass. He sipped the wine appreciatively, then gave his consent for the steward to go on pouring.

"And what does the High Command say?" Dallin asked.

"Usual double-talk. Defend the Home Islands. Destroy the invaders on the beaches. Oh, yes. One thing more. They are allowing any officer or enlisted man who wishes to go into hiding to do so."

Perplexed, Niki left her glass untouched on the table. "Hiding from whom? I don't understand?"

"The Allies want revenge," Dallin explained. "Justice, they term it. Victors normally do. In any event, they've vowed to prosecute Nazi and Japanese war criminals."

"Oh, Christ!" Niki said, fiddling with her wineglass. "Why must things always change? Doesn't anything ever remain the same?"

Dallin and Hata knew better than to attempt an answer. Instead they sipped their wine in silence.

"It means you'd both be wanted, doesn't it?" Niki burst out.

"That's the general idea." Dallin frowned, stubbing out his cigarette.

"But what's going to happen to you? You can't stand on some beach throwing sticks and stones at the Americans like some crazy kamikaze, or go into hiding for the rest of your lives."

Once again Hata was struck by the fact that rebellion was yet another quality not often found in Oriental women; they would never permit themselves to become so impassioned, nor would they dare lecture a man. But Hata no longer resented this forcefulness in Niki. In fact, he had come to expect and look forward to it.

Seeing her dark eyes flaring and her soft round mouth tense with emotion, Hata reached down and gripped her slender hand. "Calm yourself, Niki. There is a way out. Dallin will arrange everything."

How typical of Hata, thought Niki, leaning against his shoulder. A Japanese man was taught from birth never to betray his inner feelings in public. At all times his face must remain composed and immobile; he must never reveal any signs of personal grief. This could only be done in private, when his emotions were permitted to run unchecked. Still, Niki was grateful that at least Hata no longer brooded for days before telling her what was on his mind, as had been his way when they first met.

Niki was fascinated by strong men. Hata, Dallin, and above all, her own father had filled her world with excitement. Now, however, in her father's case it was mixed with great sadness, for the doctors had found a malignant tumor in his stomach. They predicted he might linger for as long as another month but they could offer no hope. Ultimately the disease would spread and her father—Niki could not bear to go on thinking about it. As it was, she awakened at night fearing the thought of life without her father to protect and counsel her.

Still, she did have Hata. He understood her grief and had done everything he could to alleviate her father's suffering. Cancer specialists had been brought to Shanghai from Tokyo, Hong Kong, and even Chungking. No expense or effort had been spared, and for this she would be eternally grateful, Niki thought as she studied his lean, handsome face and felt his muscular thigh which pressed against her.

"In fact," Dallin announced, shattering her reverie, "one possible solution to our problem is coming our way right now." They watched as a portly, red-haired man with a heavily freckled complexion approached their booth. In his white linen suit, stiff old-fashioned collar, and narrow black tie, Obersturmbannführer Ernst Becker would have been noticeable anywhere.

He greeted them, bowing.

"Good evening, Fraulein Orlov. Gentlemen."

"Will you join us, Becker?" Dallin suggested politely.

"Thank you, I will. So nice to see you."

Smiling wanly, Niki found herself thinking again that there was a dark side to this German she would rather not know about.

"Wine?"

"Thank you, no."

Hata waved the approaching waiter away, then turned his attention back to Becker.

"May I speak freely?" the Nazi asked, glancing apologetically at Niki.

"We keep nothing from Mademoiselle Orlov," Hata replied.

"Of course." Becker smiled. "The fact is, Colonel, this Potsdam Declaration has me worried."

"That's understandable."

"*Ja,*" Becker acknowledged with a frown, "but you see, I have no intention of being sacrificed like a lamb. In fact, I've already arranged for a ship to take me to Argentina. To Buenos Aires, to be precise."

"Why tell us?" Dallin asked guardedly.

"Because, my dear gentlemen, I am in a position to offer you passage there as well. All of you if you so wish. We can all escape China before we are trapped and executed."

Up to this point, Niki had sat listening in dazed silence. Now, at the idea of fleeing China, of becoming an exile, she was filled with terror; she looked down and found her hands were trembling.

"It so happens we can depart very soon," Becker went on. "In about ten days, depending on when my ship arrives here in port."

"The fifteenth of August," Dallin calculated. "It doesn't give us much time—assuming we were even interested."

"*Ja,*" Becker replied forcefully, "but you know the political situation. If we're to survive this mess we must get out while we can. You saw what happened to us in Europe. The collapse. How quickly things change. I tell you there's not a moment to lose."

"Why not go to Europe?" Hata asked.

"Out of the question." Becker said vehemently. "Believe me, I know all about these things. In Argentina we will be safe. There are loyal Germans living there. Ones in high places who will protect people such as ourselves from the Allies, regardless of the pressures exerted on them."

"But why can't you—" Niki began to ask, when a sharp glance from Hata silenced her. Then he lapsed into thought. His intense concentration finally rattled even Becker's confidence.

"If you are still thinking we'd be better off in Europe," Becker blurted out, "let me quickly disillusion you. Those reports from Germany about the Allies carrying out witch hunts against Nazis are true. Believe me, with economic conditions as harsh as they are—people starving, no housing, women being raped, children selling themselves for a pack of cigarettes—plenty of us good loyal citizens of the Fatherland are being betrayed for the price of a loaf of bread. So listen to me, my friend, Argentina is the place for us. There the army and the police will protect, not hunt us."

"But for how much and how long?" Niki finally said with venom. "Or are your friends so generous they expect nothing in return?"

"Go ahead and make jokes, *fraulein*. But I tell you, the situation is serious," Becker replied, wiping the perspiration from his forehead with a crumpled white handkerchief. "So if my friends do wish something in return for their efforts, who can say they are not justified."

"Listen, Becker," Dallin explained tactfully, "it is not so much a question of money but safety that Mademoiselle Orlov has in mind." Grateful for his support, Niki gave him a fleeting smile.

Becker went on in the same loud, grating tone. "Safety? But I have already told you——"

"Enough of this," Hata interrupted sharply, making no attempt to hide his displeasure at the way Niki was being treated. "It's not necessary to raise your voice."

"Forgive me, Colonel," Becker said apologetically, wiping more perspiration from his freckled forehead. "But surely you realize I meant no disrespect. Why, time and again we Nazis have demonstrated our solidarity with you Japanese. Even the Führer on several occasions has said the Japanese are the Aryans of the yellow race."

"Most complimentary, I'm sure," Hata replied, exchanging a knowing glance with Dallin.

"Tell me, Becker," Dallin went on in a near whisper, "this ship of yours. What sort of vessel is she?"

"A freighter," Becker answered quickly, relieved to change the subject. "About eleven thousand tons. She is quite seaworthy and carries a highly experienced captain and crew. Now, as to passengers—frankly, I was hoping to keep the number down to, say, the three of us . . . or, if necessary, one more."

"And her cargo?" Dallin asked casually.

"Forgive me." Becker smiled. "I thought I had mentioned that her holds will be completely empty. You can fill them with what you will. Subject only to their capacity, of course."

"Interesting," Hata said, somewhat annoyed by the satisfied look on Becker's face.

"*Ja.* I thought you both would think so."

"How soon do you need our answer?" Dallin asked, lighting another Camel.

"How soon? Now would be best, but if necessary another day is all right too. Frankly, I am not prepared to wait more than that. You understand my head's on the block as well as yours. Our Nationalist friends may still have fascist links but they are too dependent on the Americans to shelter us for long. Don't you agree?"

"I haven't given it much thought," Hata lied, determined to avoid a conversation of this sort with Becker. "But as for your answer—one way or the other, you'll have it in two or three days. We can't do better than that."

"Very well," Becker said, sensing he was being dismissed. Rising quickly from the booth, he bowed stiffly to Niki, then made his way across the club toward the entrance. Being dismissed so abruptly angered him but he had no intention of permitting mere pride to interfere with profit, enormous profit if he was any judge of the fortune amassed by Hata and Dallin. As for Hata's offhand manner with him, it was to be expected. Ever since the fall of Germany, there had been a marked shift in the treatment bestowed on Nazis by their erstwhile Axis friends. Becker had become accustomed to it. These days many people, and not just the Japanese, seemed to take delight in belittling the dead Adolf Hitler. Even Jews actually had the nerve to come up to him and speak of the Third Reich in mocking tones. For certain, he thought, Buenos Aires must be better. Not that he too wouldn't have preferred going to Europe. That Hata, scoffed Becker, thinking he could survive the witch hunts, trials, and executions going on in Occupied Germany.

As Becker moved away from the corner booth, Hata felt Niki edge closer to him.

"You're not really planning to leave Shanghai with that overbearing Nazi?" As if to counter the seriousness of her question she casually removed a piece of lint from his uniform jacket.

"We'll talk about it later," Hata replied. "Why don't you have a dance with Dallin while I make a few phone calls. Then, looking at Dallin, he added, "Unless you mind?"

"Why should I mind?"

"I hate to rhumba in crowds." Niki pouted, as the Harlem Five launched into a feverish Latin tune, and Dallin rose from his seat.

"Then Dallin will change the music," Hata replied, rising from the booth to let Niki by.

"As you wish." Niki smiled, slipping by him and moving ahead of Dallin. They walked past several crowded tables to the podium, where Dallin motioned to the bandleader, a graceful Haitian in a purple tuxedo. He spoke with him briefly and seconds later, the bandleader waved his baton, and his musicians shifted from the rhumba to a slow foxtrot, surprising the other couples on the floor. Startled by the change in tempo, they stopped to watch the two striking White Russians dancing in their midst.

Curling her arm comfortably, her fingers touching Dallin's neck lightly, Niki murmured, "Doesn't the idea of becoming a fugitive again bother you? It reminds me of Russia. Of how we all fled from the Bolsheviks."

"History always repeats itself."

"Not if you listen to me. Give enough gold to the right Chinese and you needn't run anywhere. Others have, including my father. Let Becker become a fugitive. You and Hata stay here in Shanghai with me."

Dallin stopped dancing and looked closely into her lovely face. His expression was grim but his voice was gentle.

"Don't deceive yourself, Niki. Times have changed since men like your father fled here. The Chinese will bend rules for gold, that's true. But, with the Americans around, only so far."

"But if the Americans and Nationalists fear the Communists as much as people say, won't they need the Japanese Army, and especially the cooperation of the Kempetai?"

"The Americans view themselves as the moral leaders of the world. They'd have to change an awful lot to deal with us."

"Even at the risk of losing China to Mao?"

"Niki, believe me—if we remain, the day will come when they'll be after us like mad dogs."

"Us?" Niki laughed. "They wouldn't dare harm me. My father is a count. A general."

"From Czarist Russia. That dream was finished long ago."

"But you and Hata told my father . . . you talked so much about the future. About overthrowing Stalin."

"I know what we told him," Dallin interrupted impatiently. "But that was Hata's idea. Hata wanted it that way," Dallin said. "So now you see you have no choice but to come with us. Unless you're willing to risk what's happened to women in similar positions all over Europe."

Niki, an avid reader of newspapers, did not have to be reminded of the headlines. In France the Maquis shaved the heads of women accused of consorting with the enemy, then cast them out. In Russia and Eastern Europe such women were hung from telephone poles. Here in China there had been cases of mass rape and death by stoning.

Nonetheless, Niki had gone on seeing Hata. In the beginning she could easily have broken off the relationship. In the past she had always had the will to end an affair, even when the man was overwhelmingly attractive to her. With Hata, however, there were other considerations. He was handsome, to be sure, and a wonderful lover. But even more important, Hata was the commandant of the Kempetai. He was the most important man in Shanghai—more important than the governor-general.

From the outset, Niki had been thrilled by the power Hata wielded. Wealth, physical beauty, even intellect were always available to her, but Hata offered virtually unlimited power. And she found she enjoyed the feeling. It even gave sex, something Niki could never get enough of, a whole new dimension.

So, although on one level she could have broken off with Hata, but on another she could not. She had permitted her own desires to overwhelm all logic. At least until now, Niki thought. Because now the lark was over; the piper would have to be paid. She would have to flee China with him or remain to take her chances alone. Unless she could somehow get Hata and Dallin to use their combined influence and wealth to prevent anything from happening to her.

"I know Japan is out of the question for us," she said, "but there must be some hope of staying on in China. We have influence and friends. People like us never lose real power, regardless of who's in control—unless of course, the Communists take over."

"Perhaps," Dallin replied reflectively. "In any case, I've already put out feelers and I'm going up to Nanking to see Fat Ling, the Nationalist's go-between.

"I knew we could depend on you, Dallin," Niki murmured, tightening her grip on his shoulder as she followed him across the crowded dance floor.

Chapter Four

———◆————◆———

The August sky was a luminous blue, kindled with radiant stars. On the Bund, traffic trickled past the concrete machine gun bunkers guarding the Whampoo River. At ten o'clock a gleaming black Cadillac limousine whisked smoothly past the imposing Shanghai Club and stopped for a red light at the intersection of Nanking Road and the Bund.

At the same moment a pair of Kempei motorcyclists, their sirens whining, peeled away from the canopied entrance of the Cathay Hotel, closely followed by the maroon Bentley roadster and two more motorcyclists. Disregarding the red light, the Bentley pursued its escort south along the Bund past the halted Cadillac, affording the two passengers inside a clear look at Maximov Dallin. One of the two, the Norwegian Gustav Torg, still hardy at seventy with fine white hair framing a ruddy complexion and the palest of blue eyes, was able to view Dallin with almost Oriental detachment. But for his daughter, Dominique, a leggy golden-blond Nordic beauty with hazel eyes, high cheek bones, and a delicate profile, the sight of the treacherous White Russian collaborator was another matter entirely. Purely and simply, she detested everything about him.

"Well, if nothing else, at least we missed Dallin," Dominique said, flashing a wry smile at her father.

"Can't stand him, can you?"

"Nor the Tower Nightclub, which you never could before the war either."

"It's true," the Norwegian acknowledged with a shrug of his rugged shoulders, "but things change."

"They do indeed. Why ever did you sell the company to that vile man?"

"That hurt you a great deal, I'm afraid."

"No more than you. You just don't admit it. But really, I still don't understand why you did it. Was it Hata? Did he force you?"

"Let's speak of it another time," Torg said as the light turned green and the Cadillac got underway.

"You know we won't. We never do!" Dominique answered, grasping her father's large sinewy hand with her own softer one. "And you know how much I hate going into that nightclub. Seeing all those dreadful parasites feeding off one another and making up to the Japanese. Why must we go there at all?"

His blue eyes filled with sorrow, Torg studied the putty-colored army truck at the curb as his Chinese chauffeur wheeled the enormous limousine into the driveway beneath the canopied entrance of the Cathay Hotel.

"We go because one hears things at the Tower that can be heard nowhere else in Shanghai."

"But why?" Dominique asked in frustration. "What good does hearing what goes on do you? You're no longer a China trader."

"But I will be again when this war is finally over," the Norwegian insisted firmly, gazing solemnly at his daughter.

A bulky Ukrainian doorman in a braided shirt and peaked cap swung open the rear door of the limousine and stood aside as Gustav Torg and Dominique climbed out. Walking arm in arm, they had almost reached the hotel doorway when the back panel of the parked army truck dropped down with a clang. Three Kempei soldiers, bayonets fixed on their rifles, charged across the wide stretch of sidewalk, their burly sergeant in the lead.

"Gustav Torg?" the sergeant demanded.

"Yes."

"You're under arrest."

"On whose orders?"

"Kempetai," the sergeant barked, his eyes on Dominique. "Her too. Both of you come now to Bridge House."

"Not my daughter," the Norwegian replied firmly.

"Her too. Bridge House," the sergeant repeated, reaching for Dominique's shoulder.

In a flash, Torg stepped between them and rammed his massive fist into the Kempei sergeant's nose. Then, taking Dominique in tow, he bulled his way past the other three soldiers who stood dazed at the sight of their leader bent over on the pavement, thick spurts of blood coming from his nose.

As she was propelled ahead by her father, Dominique caught sight of Plitov, the night manager of the Cathay. Plitov, a short, bearded Russian in a black cutaway, was poised anxiously inside the elegant marble lobby, a formation of a dozen or more Chinese bellboys in black caps and white jackets behind him.

As her hand touched the revolving door, Dominique heard her father shout, and before she could make out the words, she was pushed through the revolving door. Losing her balance, she went sprawling into the lobby at the feet of the shocked night manager.

"My God, what is happening?" Plitov cried as he rushed to her assistance.

"I'm not sure . . ." Dominique started to reply, only to see all three Kempei soldiers pounce on her father and drag him away. Screaming, she broke away from Plitov and rushed back to help. Hard as she pushed and shoved at the revolving door she could not budge it. On the other side the burly sergeant, his broad face streaked with blood, was leaning with his shoulder against the glass divider.

Sneering at her pathetic efforts to move the door, he slid his hands to his groin, slowly undid his trousers, and began urinating on the glass.

With a groan, Dominique shut her eyes, and by the time she reopened them, the glass divider was covered with urine and the sergeant was hurrying toward the curb, shouting to his men to load Gustav Torg aboard the truck.

Dominique threw herself against the glass divider of the revolving door with a cry. Plitov gripped her firmly by the elbow. "Can't you see. It's too late. No one can help him now."

The doors of the putty-colored truck swung shut with a loud bang. The engine revved up; smoke poured from its exhaust as the driver shifted noisily, and the truck pulled away from the curb with a jolt.

"What's happening?" Dominique wept, confused and overcome by the sudden loss of her father. "Why didn't you do anything?"

"What could we do? What could anyone do?" Plitov replied, guilt-stricken. "It would cost us our lives to interfere."

"Where is Signore Ferrara? I must find him."

"Upstairs in the Tower," Plitov replied. "I will telephone at once." He moved toward the reception desk on the other side of a row of potted plants backed by a large gilt-framed mirror.

"No!" Dominique called out. "It'll be faster if I go up there myself." She wiped the tears from her cheeks and dashed off. Dodging a party of Japanese naval officers and their European girlfriends as they emerged from an elevator, she ordered the startled operator to take her immediately to the Tower Nightclub.

The Harlem Five were just breaking into a Louie Armstrong melody when Dominique entered the room and was greeted by the maître d'.

"Good evening, Mademoiselle Torg."

"Good evening, Zabar," Dominique replied anxiously, "I was told Signore Ferrara was . . ."

Her words trailed to a stop as she saw Colonel Hata making his way across the dance floor toward the corner booth with Niki at his side.

"Pardon me," she said, slipping past Zabar, who looked at her strangely. She moved hurriedly between a double row of crowded tables, reaching the booth just as Hata sat down.

"Dominique!" Niki called out before she had a chance to say anything. "I've been trying to reach you for months, but they always tell me you're not at home."

"I'm sorry, Niki," Dominique replied, avoiding her former classmate's eager greeting. "I must speak with Colonel Hata."

"Who's stopping you?" Niki replied, badly stung.

"What is it, Mademoiselle Torg?" Hata asked, reaching for his wineglass.

"You know me?" Dominique said, unable to hide her surprise.

"Of course. Niki often speaks of you. After all, you are old friends, I believe."

Dominique blushed. They had been friends until Niki began seeing Hata. "Forgive me for barging in like this, but your soldiers have just made a horrible mistake."

"It wouldn't be the first time," Hata joked. "Which mistake is it now?"

"It's not funny. They've arrested my father. Dragged him away in a truck right in front of the hotel. So I would be very grateful if you could have him released at once."

"Then you think his arrest was an error?"

"Of course. Wasn't it?"

"Curious," Hata said, taking another sip of wine.

"I'm afraid you're confusing me. What is so curious?"

"No questions, if you please. A Kempetai officer must not be spoken to with disrespect."

"I was not being disrespectful. I was only——"

"Stop this!" Hata ordered. "You will leave us now."

There was a chilling tone to his voice which made Dominique hesitate. She looked over at Niki, hoping her old friend would intercede, but Niki was enjoying her discomfort. Taking in the situation, she gazed up from the table, her eyes fixed on Dominique's lush bosom, and a faint smile crossed her lips.

Dominique shivered. It was not the first time she had been aware of Niki's ardor where she was concerned. Trying to put it from her mind, she addressed Hata firmly. "It's my duty to inform you that my father and I are citizens of Norway, a neutral nation. And I have no intention of leaving here until you at least explain why he has been arrested."

"You go too far," Hata snapped.

"Stop bullying me!"

Leaping up from his chair, Hata drew himself to his full height. "For the last time, I warn you—do not test my patience any further."

An uneasy silence spread over the club as its patrons turned away from their own conversations to listen to the exchange between Hata and Dominique. More frightened than she had ever been in her entire life, Dominique was tempted to leave. Hata had earned his reputation at the expense of many innocent people and she hardly imagined public opinion would affect his actions now. Every instinct told her to get away while she could, before his wrath was unleashed against her. But she knew that by going now, she would seal her father's fate.

"Perhaps I may be of some assistance, Colonel?" Giacomo Ferrara inquired, approaching the corner booth.

His face taut with anger, the Kempetai commandant

started to reply when Niki placed her heavily-jeweled hand over his and whispered something. Unable to hear their exchange, Dominique was suddenly aware of a hand at her elbow.

"You'll be safer in my office downstairs," Ferrara murmured, inching nearer. "Leave me to speak with Hata."

Dominique shook her head slightly and waited until Hata finally turned back to her, his face now calm and composed. His first impulse had been to punish this Caucasian bitch, have one of his Korean bullyboys make her suffer terribly for her audacity in speaking to him in such an arrogant manner, but Niki felt it would be going too far. She had convinced him to treat her differently.

"You wish to know why your father has been arrested. Am I correct?"

"Yes. Please," Dominique replied politely, trying to hide her relief at the abrupt change in his attitude.

"Very well." Hata nodded. "Our investigation shows your father has been spying for the Allies against the Japanese Empire."

"Spying? My father?" Dominique gasped. "But that's impossible. My father isn't a spy."

"I assure you there has been no mistake. His execution will take place in due course," Hata announced coolly, rising from the booth with his arm extended toward Niki. "Now you must excuse us. I wish to dance."

Dominique was numb; then, all at once, the full impact of Hata's words struck her. She started after him, when the whole room seemed to tilt and the floor came rushing up to her. Dizzy, she staggered another step, then sagged to one side. Seeing her falling, Ferrara sprang forward, managing to catch her before she hit the floor. He lowered her gently into a nearby chair.

On the dance floor, Niki draped one arm lazily over Hata's shoulder. "You've never wanted her?" she whispered into his ear.

"Dominique Torg? Never."

"Pity," Niki said as she watched Dominique being carried away by Ferrara and Zabar. "I bet you'd enjoy her."

"So would you," Hata said spitefully, suddenly reminded of times he preferred to forget.

"You're jealous." Niki laughed, kissing Hata warmly on the mouth and holding him tighter. From the rigidness of his body she could tell he was angry. The idea that she was attracted to other women infuriated him. He had found out accidentally during a late-night party at the Pleasure Palace, a luxurious brothel owned by Dallin and Hata that catered to rich Japanese and Chinese businessmen. Hata had been called away on an emergency and when he returned, he had found Niki in bed with a voluptuous redhead. Her wide-ranging inclinations had caused a bitter fight between them. Although Niki was finally able to calm Hata down, she had never before seen him so upset. For a moment she had been certain that she would be the next victim of the Kempetai commandant.

"You could have her if you wished," Niki murmured, not content to let the matter drop.

"I'm not so sure."

"What woman wouldn't offer herself to save her own father?"

"You didn't," Hata said resentfully, brushing his lips against her glossy black hair. Aware of her hardened nipples pressing against his chest, Hata felt his desire for Niki rising. He could never get enough of this woman. At times his submission to her plagued him. How easily she was able to bend his will, even in her desire for other women, a taste that repelled Hata. Logic told him to rid himself of such a self-destructive relationship before it was too late, but deep within he knew it was impossible. There were too many other things going wrong in his life for him to deliberately take an action that could only result in suffering for him. He often wondered if others saw how Niki dominated him. It was a glaring reversal of Japanese tradition, in which the female was expected to follow and obey every wish of the male, whether it be her father, husband, brother, or eldest son.

"I'm starved," Niki whispered. "Let's go to that Viennese cabaret in the Jewish ghetto."

"If you like," Hata replied, confirming, at least to himself if no one else, that the commandant of the Kempetai was at times a pawn in the hands of this willful Caucasian woman.

After he brought Dominique into the tiny alcove off the steamy kitchen and placed a wet towel across her forehead, Ferrara sent Zabar away and stood quietly beside her.

"How do you feel?" he asked gently.

"Terrible. How could my father be a spy?"

"Gustav Torg is one of my dearest friends," the managing director replied.

"But is he a spy?"

"I doubt that. But what finally counts is what the Kempetai believe, and Colonel Hata is the Kempetai. Now I'd better see you home."

"Not yet. I can't just leave and let that sadist murder my father," Dominique protested, bolting from the chair. Overcome again by dizziness, she sank into Ferrara's outstretched arms.

"Listen to me carefully," the managing director said quietly, an eye on the sweating faces of some of the kitchen staff who were watching the two closely. "You're not the only one in Shanghai who has good reason to hate our Kempetai commandant. But if you wish to help your father you must not cause another scene. Hata will not tolerate it. I know his limits."

Realizing that what Ferrara was saying made sense, Dominique straightened up and smoothed back a strand of hair that had fallen over her forehead.

"I'm sorry. I'll be all right."

"You're sure?" Ferrara asked with concern. "If you wish, we can stay here another few minutes, or however long it takes."

"No. That's all right. I'll really be fine now. You've been very kind. I appreciate it."

His face flushed with embarrassment, Ferrara led Dominique across the kitchen, passing along a narrow aisle that separated a row of refrigerators from the restaurant stoves where a team of Chinese dressed in white swarmed about the flaming burners.

"They'll torture him, won't they?" Dominique asked, as Ferrara guided her past two wiry Chinese cooks in food-stained aprons.

"I manage a hotel, not the secret police," Ferrara said evasively, knowing only too well that at Bridge House the Japanese were trained in the use of torture and, given time, could make anyone confess to what they wished, even someone with as much character as Gustav Torg.

"You haven't answered my question."

"The essential thing is to act quickly," Ferrara said, stepping aside for a gaunt kitchen worker who was wheeling a vegetable cart. "All that can be done to save your father will be done. You know how dear he is to me. I shall contact Dallin at once and insist he convince Hata to free your father, even if it means my going deeply into his debt. Now will you please calm yourself?"

Nodding, Dominique felt a chill run through her at the thought of having to ask anything of that arch collaborator Dallin. Ever since he had come to Shanghai she had known only misery. First, it was the personal shock of discovering that the White Russian had purchased her father's business, Gustav Torg & Company, then her increasing shame as his true purpose for taking over the company became apparent to everyone in East China, including Gustav Torg.

"Problem is, I just heard Dallin is going to Nanking and may not be back for days. But I shall inquire at once."

"Dallin wouldn't have helped us anyhow," she said flatly. "I'll see our consul or ask General Mishima to intercede."

"Under normal conditions that might work," Ferrara said, "but I fear, when it comes to spies, not even the governor-general of Shanghai or the Consular Corps can control the Kempetai."

After Dominique drove off in her chauffeured Cadillac, Ferrara paused at the mail desk in the lobby tended by a very old Chinese in a navy blue jacket with brass buttons.

"Tell me, Lu, has any mail arrived for a friend of mine, a Monsieur Munk?"

"Is he registered, Signore Ferrara?"

"Quite right. It'll most likely be under 'hold for arrival.' "

"Ah, like your Mexican friend—Pacheco," Lu replied, reaching into a corner cubbyhole of the walnut mailboxes lining the wall behind the desk.

"Exactly," agreed Ferrara. "Only Senor Pacheco won't be receiving any more mail. He decided to bypass Shanghai and return directly home."

Lu shuffled expertly through the thick pile of letters marked HOLD FOR ARRIVAL, eventually coming to the last one with still no sign of the name Munk.

"I'm afraid we have none," Lu said, glancing up. "But if one does arrive, shall I have it sent directly up to your suite?"

"Please do," Ferrara murmured as he started across to the reception desk where Plitov, the night manager, waited.

Chapter Five

———◆◆◆———

Due south of the Bund, in the French Concession, the road running parallel to the Whampoo River is called the Quai de France. At its most southerly tip, the Quai abuts on the native quarter of Nantao, where the waterfront offices and godowns of three of Shanghai's greatest prewar trading companies—Butterfield & Swire, the China Merchants, and Gustav Torg & Company—were to be found. Until 1941, this area teemed with overworked coolies lugging huge burdens of cargo between warehouses and the steamers lining the wharves. By 1945, the only vessels left were the rusting hulks of two half-sunk freighters, while the Quai de France, once the center of bustling commerce, now served as a gathering place for the unemployed coolies and warehouse workers of the district.

At the massive iron gates of the smallest godown, with the faded sign GUSTAV TORG & COMPANY overhead, several Kempei motorcyclists straddled their machines and nervously eyed the mass of unwashed, starving Chinese loitering on the Quai. Beyond the gates, within the courtyard of the brick warehouse, the maroon Bentley roadster stood parked, the Chinese chauffeur asleep at the wheel. Behind her was a putty-colored truck carrying a full squad of Kempei troops armed with automatic weapons.

On the other side of the courtyard, facing the warehouse entrance, four pimply-faced Chinese youths in badly cut suits leaned lazily up against a garish yellow Packard with white sidewalls. Strung out next to them were a dozen late-model American trucks repainted a dull gray. Inside the warehouse, just off the entrance, three Chinese sat facing Maximov Dallin around a table covered with shiny gold bars.

Two of the Chinese, the Lee brothers, dressed in double-breasted black mohair suits, watched with Dallin as Tung, a rotund Mandarin in a navy blue robe, patiently weighed each bar on a small metal scale, then tested it by taking rubbings with a rough stone and comparing the scrapings to a color chart resting at his elbow.

The White Russian was accustomed to being the lone Caucasian in a veritable sea of Chinese. Chain-smoking cigarettes, his light brown suit jacket badly rumpled from the intense heat, Dallin paid close attention to the weighing of the gold. The process was tedious at best. Tung, the finest gold assayer in Shanghai and a long-time employee of his, was known for his thoroughness and a tendency never to hurry. This, coupled with the Lee brothers sudden attempts at cordiality, did not make things any easier for Dallin; something about their eagerness to please had aroused his easily ignited suspicions.

Restless, he rose from the chair and moved to the open doorway of the office. From there the White Russian scanned the sacks, crates, and boxes piled in long rows from one end of his warehouse to the other. In one corner a gang of sweating coolies was at work among stacks of wooden crates under the watchful eyes of several youthful gangsters in cheap European-style suits. One by one, the crates were pried open, the contents examined and counted, then the lids sealed shut. Each stack of crates was marked. The ones labeled penicillin, quinine, morphine, and insulin were separated from the others containing American cigarettes and whiskey. Off to one side of the crates loomed a large bulky object covered by a tarpaulin.

Crushing the butt of his cigarette beneath his hand-tooled English boot, Dallin lit another with a wooden match and suddenly remembered a Kempetai report Colonel Hata had shown him some time ago. The report, filed by a reliable informant, concerned a gunman working for the Lee brothers, who, in his zeal to make good, kidnapped the only son of a family related to the gangster lord of Shanghai, Du Yueh-sen, himself now in Chungking and a highly trusted adviser to Generalissimo Chiang Kai-shek. After the Lee brothers discovered the blunder, they had swiftly released their victim and made profuse apologies, but it was too late. Fiercely proud and just as greedy, Du Yueh-sen sent word that he was levying a huge fine on the hapless Lee brothers, not unlike one he extorted from Chiang Kai-shek in 1927 for insults heaped on him with the arrival of the Nationalist Army in Shanghai. History showed that Chiang had paid and now, thought Dallin, it was the Lee brothers' turn to repeat the gesture, which to his calculating way of thinking probably accounted for their sudden offer of friendship. But friendship to what end, Dallin wondered gloomily.

As his mind was weighing just what they were planning, the younger Lee brushed against Dallin and shouted to his henchmen to have the tarpaulin removed from the bulky object alongside the crates.

Then, turning to Dallin, he asked in a high-pitched voice, "Brand-new, you say?"

"Let me show you," Dallin replied, leading the way across the warehouse to where two workmen in baggy black cotton pajamas were rolling the cover off a cream-colored Cadillac with gleaming chrome bumpers and white-wall tires.

"1945, is it?"

"That's right," Dallin said, pointing to the original General Motors factory sticker glued to the rear window on the passenger side. "One of the few they made this year. She came by ship to Bombay, then overland by rail and truck to the Gorges, and by freighter on down to Shanghai. Courtesy of a Nationalist general."

"Crazy Americans," the younger Lee giggled. "If they're not careful they'll give away the whole country to Chiang."

"You know what they say," agreed Dallin. "Uncle Chump from over the Hump."

Nodding, the younger Lee ran his slender finger along one glistening front fender.

"You're a very smart man, Dallin. You always deliver. Very rare quality in a Caucasian."

"If I didn't, why do business with me?"

"So true. But ours has been a very beneficial association."

Over the past years they had often had dealings. Dallin would bring in contraband from Free China and turn some of it over to the Lee brothers at an enormous profit. By using a syndicate of agents, the Lee brothers would resell the goods in Shanghai.

Up until now, the arrangement had been marred only by the petty complaints made by the Lee brothers regarding the quantity and quality of the merchandise. Dallin had grown used to their chiseling and their attempts to get cheaper prices. In general, he went along with them, mostly because they were a power in the city, and from the start he had charged extra to compensate for their haggling, which was another reason why this current transaction seemed different. For the first time the Lee brothers made no attempt to haggle, complain about the quality of the merchandise. In fact, they had not caused any problems at all, which was precisely what worried Dallin.

Hearing his name being called out, Dallin noticed the chubby gold assayer waving to him from the office doorway, "Must be finished," Dallin said. "How about your men, Lee?"

Scratching at a hairy mole on his face, the younger Lee spoke briefly to a slender Chinese whose baggy suit looked as though it had not been cleaned or pressed in months.

"Our count is okay," the younger Lee confirmed, turning back to Dallin.

"That's it then." The two men started away from the shiny Cadillac.

"How soon until the next shipment?" the younger Lee questioned, hard-pressed to keep pace with Dallin.

"I told you before. A week. Ten days."

"For us the sooner the better. In Shanghai plenty of people want luxury goods. The more they cost the better they are. Plenty of people say that cash money is no damn good. Much better to invest in expensive things."

"I'll try to help you keep them happy."

"You're a very smart man."

Inside the glass-enclosed office, Tung slipped the last gold bar into a leather valise and snapped the edges closed. "Okay, we go now." He grinned.

"Let's do it!" Dallin replied, turning to the elder Lee brother and shaking his hand, then doing the same with the younger one,

Less than a minute later, Dallin and Tung were settling into the rear seat of the maroon Bentley. The Chinese driver, no longer asleep, gunned his idling engine, then, tailed by the putty-colored truck, he followed the Kempei motorcyclists out of the courtyard.

Heading south on the Quai de France, past trenches of gun emplacements, they swung west into the native quarter of Nantao, cutting through narrow winding streets with only inches to spare, then on across crowded intersections, past noisy Chinese jostling around food stalls selling fried noodles, steamed dumplings, and assorted spicy pork and chicken dishes sizzled over open fires. Sirens whining, the Kempei motorcyclists opened a path through the densely packed streets, emerging finally on Avenue Edward VII, which divided the International Settlement to the north from the quieter residential French Concession.

Here the broad avenue resembled a great Parisian boulevard. Buildings blacked out in conformance to the strictly enforced Japanese ordnance rose ominously, casting shadows over the lonely Japanese sentries who guarded gun emplacements hastily constructed to ward off the expected Allied invasion. As he watched the shadowy figures in their saucer helmets rush by, Dallin was swept by a feeling of alienation.

A mile past the racetrack, the motorcyclists turned onto Yates Road and sped past a long row of silk and embroidery shops. Slowing, so the Bentley and putty-colored truck could overtake them, they swept by the Roulette Club and led the way into the walled-in driveway of the McTyeire Girls School, where a green Packard was parked with its motor running.

Not waiting for the Bentley to come to a stop, Dallin swung his door open and turned to Tung.

"See Hata gets that gold and no one else."

"You'll be all right?" Tung asked, squeezing his large frame past Dallin as he got out.

"Once I'm on that plane for Nanking, I will be."

"Suppose the Lee brothers think you're still carrying the gold?"

"That's what I want them to think, my friend. Just tell Hata the Lee brothers are up to something. He'll know what to do."

Concern etched on his face, Tung pressed the heavy leather valise against his ample belly and turned to Dallin.

"Maybe you better forget Nanking and come with me. Maybe less profit but maybe longer life."

"And throw away a quarter of a million? Not a chance!"

Dallin shut the door and waved as the Bentley took off after the Kempei motorcyclists.

"The Nanking plane is always late," the Chinese driver shouted over his shoulder, as the needle on the speedometer shot past sixty.

"It's not the plane I'm worried about."

"You think maybe the Lee brothers set us up?"

"Maybe," Dallin answered, glancing out the rear window at the truckful of Kempei struggling to keep pace.

Except for the harsh drone of the powerful military motorcycles an eerie silence engulfed the Bentley as they sped through the dark, deserted streets.

"Once Shanghai was all neon lights and noise. Plenty of noise. You remember, boss?" the driver shouted, jamming the gas pedal to the floor.

"I remember," Dallin said, lighting another Camel with a wooden match.

"Think Shanghai will ever be the same again?"

"Maybe."

"Maybe, yes? Or maybe, no?" The driver chuckled as the Bentley turned onto tree-lined Hungjao Road and raced past Rubicon Creek and the Municipal Council Nursery. In the distance a line of blinking red and green lights signaled the final approach to Shanghai Airport.

The Kempei motorcyclists cut back their speed, coasting past batteries of anti-aircraft guns strung out along the road. The convoy arrived at a heavy wooden barrier. Twin machine-gun bunkers flanked the barrier, sealing off traffic in both directions. A full squad of infantrymen, bayonets fixed to their Nambu rifles, stood guard in the road, led by a stocky corporal in a visored cap. At the sight of the Kempei motorcycle escort, the corporal shouted for the barrier to be lifted, then waved the other two vehicles behind them on through.

The Bentley glided quietly past, following a winding two-lane road dotted by bomb craters. It rolled by a row of blasted hangars and repair sheds. Parked on the runway and silhouetted by the flickering red and green lights were the shattered fuselages of stripped Zero fighter planes and twin-engined Mitsubishi bombers—all that remained of the once-proud Imperial Army Air Force in China.

"The Yanks have really given this place a fancy plastering," the driver griped, spinning the wheel sharply to the right to avoid a crater.

"Good bomb sights," Dallin replied, studying the ruins of a large hanger off to his left. "Something the Japs don't have."

"No sign of the Lee brothers, huh, boss?" the driver brought the Bentley to a gradual stop at the entrance to the main terminal building.

"So far," Dallin answered grimly, reaching for the leather valise stowed on the floor of the rear seat, identical to the one used to carry the gold. Leaving the car, Dallin paused for a moment alongside the four goggled Kempei motorcyclists. He slipped each of them a handful of American dollars, then strode briskly into the terminal.

The place had seen happier days. A near miss by a five-hundred-pound bomb had left both floor and ceiling badly cracked. Water seeped up through wide seams in the floor from broken pipes, leaving murky puddles filled with debris. One interior wall of the terminal was minus large chunks of plaster and scarred by fire. Flames had spread to the roof, exposing the crossbeams. Sandbags had been piled against the damaged wall to prevent it from toppling.

Nearby, just off the entrance, was a makeshift bar, where a sloppy Cantonese woman in a badly stained apron served tepid green tea and Shanghai bottled beer. The cups were of chipped porcelain and the beer not even a local German brand but a cheap Chinese imitation, a sad reminder of the splendid circular teakwood bar, looted by the Japanese, where prewar passengers had gathered before boarding international flights to San Francisco, London, and Paris.

Now only a few tired civilians in shabby clothes and a party of melancholy Japanese officers huddled together at the makeshift bar perspiring from the sweltering heat. Dallin detoured around a watery mess on the floor. He gripped the leather valise tightly in his left hand and approached the ticket counter in the center which was manned by a pair of Japanese consular officials in blue uniforms.

Beyond, in the rear of the terminal, separated by a rope cordon, were two lines of waiting passengers standing before closed, heavy steel doors. One line was nearly twice the length of the other, and the passengers, mostly civilians with families, were loaded down with luggage.

"Hello, Mr. Dallin," the senior consular official, a bushy-haired Japanese with thick eyeglasses, greeted him. "Going to Nanking again so soon?"

"Afraid so," Dallin said politely, presenting his Nansen passport, Shanghai identity card with photograph and green stripe indicating he was a foreign national. He held back for last a letter signed by Colonel Hata personally authorizing Maximov Dallin to travel anywhere he wished in Occupied China.

"Papers in order." The senior consular official grinned, passing the documents back with a prepaid ticket. "Everyone knows Mr. Dallin is special good friend of Kempetai."

Slipping the Japanese a neatly folded American twenty-dollar bill in return, Dallin asked, "What's going on? Never saw this place so crowded."

"Very bad weather in the Home Islands the last few nights. Tokyo flights cancelled."

"Still bad weather, huh," Dallin murmured. "What about Nanking?"

"Nanking? Good weather. No worry. Wait over there, please." The Japanese pointed sideways at a wooden bench that stood against one wall beside a heavy steel door. Dallin saw about a dozen passengers seated there, a dismal bunch compared to the eager passengers on the Tokyo line whose excited voices filtered back across the terminal. Pocketing his documents and ticket, he thanked the official and started over to the Nanking gate. Halfway there, he noticed a couple of hard-faced Chinese in baggy dark suits had joined the group at the bar. Ignoring them, Dallin sat down on the wooden bench beside the other passengers headed for Nanking.

As he did so, a burst of static reverberated from the overhead loudspeakers, followed by a high-pitched voice announcing that the Tokyo flight was cancelled due to bad weather. At first the Tokyo-bound crowd seemed oblivious. Then, as the words sank in, they gathered their belongings and, loaded down with luggage and parcels, moved slowly past the senior consular official in silent resignation. For several months now flights had often been cancelled because of bad weather, a euphemism for yet another massive American air raid on the Japanese Home Islands.

Dallin had more immediate concerns—the two newcomers at the bar, who seemed excessively interested in him. Dallin was positive they had something on their minds, and if so, his fellow passengers would be no help. Some were listless junior officers toting briefcases full of black market cigarettes and whiskey. The remainder were worried Chinese puppet officers in tan uniforms, who were far from happy about leaving Shanghai. As a whole, the puppet troops and the officials of the Nationalist government of Nanking were a sorry lot. Led by Wang Chei-wei, the one-time heir of Sun Yat-sen, they were recognized by Japan as the sovereign ruler of China; in reality, however, they were used to enforce unpopular economic and political programs and had swiftly earned the distrust and scorn of both the Japanese and Chinese.

As Dallin was considering using the telephone at the ticket counter to contact Bridge House, the door to the ladies room burst open and a blowsy peroxide blonde emerged. She gave the Nanking group a cursory glance, then started over to Dallin, who knew her. She was a Hungarian refugee named Marta Fodor, and as Dallin well knew, she looked a lot better from a distance than close up. Although she was no more than thirty, whiskey and drugs had aged her by ten years. Nonetheless she had managed to snare a Chinese puppet general and had sat out the war years safely in a mansion in Nanking with a fleet of expensive automobiles and plenty to eat, which was more than most other European refugees could say.

"Nice to see a familiar face," she said, sitting down beside Dallin. Nodding, Dallin offered her a cigarette, then took one for himself and lit both.

Slowly exhaling a dense cloud of smoke, she scanned the terminal and finally focused on the two young Chinese at the bar.

"Worried?" Dallin asked, leaning his elbow on the leather briefcase resting on the bench between Marta and himself.

"Only since the day I was born. How about you?"

"Oh, I've had a few good days in between. How's the General?"

"Not very well," Marta replied, adjusting her skirt to reveal a well-rounded leg encased in nylon. "You'd be the same in his position. But then you've always been lucky."

"How so?"

"You've never had to choose. You've just serviced both sides in this damn war."

"Like a whore, you mean?"

"I don't mean to sound bitter . . ." Marta hesitated. "Only I don't want to go back to Nanking to die."

"Then don't go."

"It's not that easy," she said, biting her lower lip. "Those two by the bar. The ones in their grandfathers' suits. The General sent them to make sure I do go back."

"I was wondering who they belonged to."

"Now you know."

Marta fidgeted nervously, the spike heel of one shoe tapping out an uneven rhythm against the stone floor. The sound was beginning to annoy Dallin.

"Shanghai's a big place," he said, trying to distract her. "You have friends."

"Friends?" Marta laughed cynically. "Sure I do. But they all want to go on living. Becomes a nasty habit, I guess."

"The General can't be all bad."

"He's a traitor, but just because he betrayed China doesn't mean I have to hang with him, does it?"

"You lived with him in the good times."

"Sure. And he got all he paid for. Or don't you believe me?"

"Oh, I believe you all right," Dallin murmured, sorry he had gotten into this conversation. He tried to ignore the way her silk dress clung to her body, outlining her heavy, sagging breasts.

"Dallin?"

"What?"

"Help me?"

"Don't see how I can," Dallin said, crushing his cigarette beneath his boot.

"You could talk to those two. Make them see things my way. Then later I could get away. Fly to Hong Kong or make my way overland to Chungking."

"What makes you think they'll listen to me? If what you say is true, the General must be paying them plenty."

"You're rich. Pay them more. You won't be sorry. I swear." Marta caressed his hand, and parted her legs just enough so that her inner thighs were bared and inviting. "What do you say?"

Dallin was about to say no, but he never got the chance. Instead the pair pushed off from the bar and started directly for him just as the heavy steel doors at the rear of the terminal burst open and two more Chinese in black pajamas charged inside waving old-fashioned Colt revolvers and firing as they ran.

At the first sound of gunfire the Nanking-bound passengers scattered, leaving Dallin and Marta by themselves on the bench. Letting out a howl, Marta grabbed the leather valise from Dallin and dashed for the terminal entrance. Dallin swiftly covered the gap, keeping Marta between himself and the pair of Chinese, who were now waving ugly-looking switchblades.

"Get away from me!" Marta screamed.

Two quick glances showed Dallin he was trapped. The Chinese at his rear had cleared the terminal of all opposition and in another moment would be upon him. Ahead his escape was blocked by the knife-wielding pair, who had drawn far apart and were coming at him from different angles.

Dropping to one knee, Dallin seized Marta by the ankle and, twisting hard, sent her plunging belly down on the floor. In the same motion he pulled the Bolo Mauser automatic from his shoulder-holster and planted two slugs apiece into the pair ahead, tearing bloody holes in their chests. Not bothering to see how fast they were dying, Dallin swung around to cover his rear. He need not have troubled.

A long, savage burst of rapid fire from an 8-mm. Nambu submachine gun caught the pajama-clad Chinese by surprise, pitching them into the air like paperdolls. Riddled from groin to chin, they skidded to a dead stop against the ticket counter. Glancing over his shoulder, Dallin recognized the benign face of the bowlegged gunner Ganghi, the most highly rated executioner in the Kempetai, scrambling in his direction from the terminal entrance.

"Can do, Dallin," the Japanese offered, waving the hot barrel of his weapon at Marta, who was crawling away from the valise.

"No! Don't! Please!" she begged.

"Colonel Hata say lady real bad number. Work both sides of street."

"It's not so. I never did anything wrong. I never did," Marta wept, pleading for her life.

"You sold me to the Lee brothers," Dallin whispered hoarsely. "For how much? Tell me."

"A steamer ticket," Marta admitted with a sob, her heavy breasts quivering. "But, you see, I had no other choice. Dallin . . . they threatened to . . ." The short bark of the Nambu drowned out her words as she sank to the floor.

Chapter Six

━━━━━━◆━◆━◆━━━━━━

Gustav Torg lay on his back, strapped tightly to the narrow wooden table. His nose was broken in two places, his eyes were badly swollen, and ugly green welts covered most of his face. From the cellar corridor outside, the anguished cries of tortured prisoners penetrated even the thick stone walls of his cell. Not once since he was dragged into the basement of Bridge House had that haunting chorus of appeals for mercy ceased for more than a few minutes at a time.

Lying there, helpless, Gustav Torg watched as Yoshijiro, his barrel-chested torturer, approached. He had a huge shaven head and beady, bloodshot eyes and he wore only a filthy loincloth. To the Norwegian his appearance was not that of a fellow human but of some pitiless underworld creature who had seen hell and stayed on to enjoy its pleasures.

Swallowing a mouthful of cold noodles, Yoshijiro let out a loud belch, then lifted a rubber hose from the tiled floor and clamped its wet nozzle over the Norwegian's bruised face.

Trapped, Torg was aware of his own muffled screams as the nozzle dug painfully into his shattered nose. Pleased, the Kempei torturer gave orders for Koki, his pop-eyed assistant, to begin.

The assistant bent over a large metal sink and spun the

59

faucet. A jet of water shot through the hose, rapidly filling
Gustav Torg's nostrils, then backed up in his throat and
mouth, choking him. Struggling wildly but in vain, Torg
fought the leather straps that pinned his battered body to the
wooden table.

For hours now, this same pair of Kempei soldiers had been
systematically torturing him, first stripping away the flesh
from his feet with steel rods, then using bamboo slivers to pry
loose his fingernails and toenails in an attempt to force him
to confess his role in the spy ring.

From the moment of his arrest at the Cathay Hotel the
Norwegian had been prepared for this ordeal. His only solace
in the midst of this dreadful pain was the thought that his
daughter was still free, that somehow she had managed to
find refuge inside the Cathay, safely out of the hands of the
Kempetai.

"Enough! Get him up!" Hata ordered as he sauntered
through the doorway, the picture of military precision in his
sharply pressed breeches and carefully shined knee-high
leather cavalry boots.

Racing to obey, Yoshijiro quickly unfastened the metal
clasps securing Gustav Torg's straps and yanked him by the
shoulders into an upright position on the table.

The Norwegian's head fell to one side and water came
spurting from between his cracked lips. A little bit more and
he would have drowned for sure this time, Torg thought, as
he battled to catch his breath.

Hata paced the cell, waiting for the Norwegian to regain
control. The sight of mutilated flesh repelled him and he
resented having to deal with Torg personally. Finally the con-
vulsions came to an end, and the Norwegian sat hunched
over the edge of the table. His white hair, sodden with blood
and sweat, fell in thick strands over his bruised forehead.

"Be reasonable," Hata said softly. "The deception is over.
It's futile to go on this way. Felix Hacker told me all about
you and the other man in charge of the ring."

Almost a full minute passed before the Norwegian lifted
his head; his pale blue eyes raked the Kempetai commandant's handsome face. He knew the Japanese was a con-
summate liar.

Recognizing the skeptical expression in Torg's eyes, Hata
smiled. "Unfortunately Hacker's dead, otherwise I'd have him

tell you all this himself. The fact is, whether you believe me or not, I even know all about his precious black book."

At last the Norwegian finally understood. He had wondered why Hata was so determined to break him. In view of what was happening to Japan it had made very little sense, but the mention of the black book made everything much clearer. The leadership of the Shanghai Ring did not interest Hata half as much as the black book. By destroying those damning pages Hata could delay, and possibly evade, Allied retribution for his role during the occupation of Shanghai.

But what puzzled Torg was how the Kempetai commandant had learned that there was a black book. Hacker had never told him—of this much Torg was sure. He knew the gentle librarian would sooner have died than let his precious document be destroyed.

One other thing puzzled Torg: Hata had mentioned that the Norwegian shared the leadership of the ring with another man, but Felix could not have told him because as far as he knew, Gustav Torg was the only leader of the Shanghai Ring.

That meant someone else must have talked to Hata. But who? Who could have infiltrated and learned so much about the Ring's operation without being detected?

"Well?" Hata demanded, his patience nearly at an end, "do I get the book?"

"You get nothing," the Norwegian replied hoarsely. "Not one word from me now or ever."

"Stupid old man!" Hata raged. "You think this is the same Asia you and your imperialistic Caucasian friends came to forty years ago. You think we will go on tolerating your preposterous sham that Occidentals are superior to Japanese. Why, our POW camps are filled with officers, graduates of Sandhurst and West Point, begging on their knees for an extra bowl of rice."

"That may be true," the Norwegian answered, as the throbbing pain in his head intensified, "but soon those same camps will be filled with Japanese war criminals like yourself."

"If that day ever does come, it'll be too late to save you."

"Just the same, it's coming," the Norwegian said, lifting his swollen face to stare unafraid at Hata.

Raging at the man's defiance, Hata gestured with his right hand, and the barrel-chested torturer lashed out, delivering a brutal kidney punch that toppled Gustav Torg on his back, writhing in pain.

"For over two years I have lost face because of your activities here in Shanghai. Now I have you, and I want that book. Do you understand? I want that book!"

"Nothing! Ever!" Torg gasped, clutching his side.

Frustration marring his good looks, Hata motioned again and the burly torturer struck out, this time shattering what was left of the Norwegian's already twice-broken nose.

"Then it's too late for you, Mr. Torg," raved Hata. "Or must I cite the number of planes lost, ships sunk, trains and tanks and bridges blown up because of your spy ring? Or tell you what we've learned about that traitor Busch at the Shanghai Airport. The so-called good German. Good for whom? Or would you prefer I begin by telling you about your fellow Scandinavian, Peter Hansen, our esteemed former port captain whose knowledge of Japanese shipping schedules enabled subs from the American fleet to block the East China Seas . . ."

It was several moments before Hata, carried away by his own rhetoric, realized that the Norwegian had lost consciousness. Infuriated by this final insult, Hata signaled the two torturers to continue their efforts, then he strode from the cell, unmoved at the anguished cries echoing through the corridor.

Two minutes later, after reprimanding a loose-tongued sergeant for peace-mongering, Hata stood alone, seething with anger, on the roof of Bridge House, peering across Shanghai at the ruins of Chapei to the south. Although it was still early in the morning, it was already hot. He heard the drone of an airplane and, looking west at the horizon, saw a twin-engined American B-17 approaching. More propaganda leaflets, Hata raged, watching the lone American pilot bring his craft around for a pass over the city. Just a year and a half ago, a daylight mission like this would have been unthinkable. Within a matter of minutes silver Japanese Zeros, their pilots' fingers on the trigger, would have torn across the sky to meet him. But now, Hata reflected bitterly, very few Japanese fighters were left in China, much less in Shanghai.

Shifting his gaze to the Garden Bridge and the Whampoo River, Hata saw a small freighter fleeing the port to escape the bomber. His flight was unnecessary, since the Americans only bombed in squadrons, yet Hata envied the freedom of the freighter's captain as he sailed toward Woosung where the

Whampoo River merges with the Yangtze, then empties into the sea.

Catching a final glimpse of her stern disappearing in the distance, Hata was reminded of Ernst Becker's proposition. It rankled Hata to leave Asia, a continent he helped free of the white man's oppressive presence, and to flee, moreover, with a Caucasian he could not afford to trust.

Hata needed no one to tell him that Argentina was a nation where Orientals were low on the social and economic scale, as was the case the world over, except in the sphere dominated by Japan. Once Hata set foot on South American soil, he would be at the mercy of Caucasians, men who, by nature and upbringing, would band together to rob him of his fortune and perhaps even his life. Although he had not confided this to Niki, the notion of being thrust into a situation where the Oriental was an inferior plunged Hata into the blackest of depressions.

Chapter Seven

———————◦═══◦═══◦———————

A gilded cupola crowned the red brick mansion of Count Aleksandr Orlov in that part of the French Concession known as Little Russia. The building contained twenty-five rooms including a full-scale ballroom and indoor swimming pool. The landscaped grounds with a formal rose garden stretched over three acres and were surrounded by a fifteen-foot-high wall covered with shards of broken glass.

Precisely at noon, Niki climbed out of a hot bath, dried her smooth, rounded buttocks and small upright breasts with a thick green towel, then wrapped herself in a peach-colored silk robe. After morning coffee and fresh croissants, she went directly to her lavish dressing room, decorated in fashionable ocean liner Art Deco, and, settling herself before the chrome mirror, began applying makeup.

Half an hour later, satisfied with her work, she left the bedroom and made her way past the upstairs servants who were vacuuming the oblong Peking blue rug that ran the entire length of the hallway. As she turned the corner at the far end, she paused before the full-sized baroque mirror and studied her reflection. She noticed the faint hollows beneath her eyes. Ever since her encounter with Obersturmbannführer Becker she had not been able to sleep. Even scalding hot baths, the normal remedy to calm her volatile nerves, failed to ease her fears and help her sleep. And when she had been able to shut her eyes and doze off, there were always those horrible dreams—frightening ones of ugly men in uniforms pursuing her relentlessly from place to place around the world. Niki did not need that Austrian Jew, whatever his name was, to explain their meaning; nor could she expect Hata, or anyone else who had not shared her experience, to understand their effect upon her.

The earliest memories she could recall, dating back to the Bolshevik Revolution, were the backdrops for haunting nightmares. Never would she be able to forget how she and her mother were driven from St. Petersburg, then forced from town to town; abandoning relatives, friends, and one possession after another, until finally, in Vladivostok, the Countess died of pneumonia and Niki sailed alone on a rusting steamer for Shanghai. It was a wretched experience, one which she would resent until her dying day. Never, she swore, would she ever permit that to happen to her again. Not Nationalists, Communists, Americans, not even Hata would make her a vagabond. What counted above all was security. Not necessarily marriage at this stage, she realized, unable to rid the thought of Dominique from her mind, but certainly the stability of her own home and a city, if not a country, where she was known.

This much decided, Niki turned away from the mirror and, knocking gently on the door opposite, entered her father's bedroom. Dimly lit even at this hour of the morning, the room reeked of whiskey and medicines. From where she stood, Niki could see the icon of the Archangel Michael that hung over the bed. At least four hundred years old, it had belonged to her great-grandfather and had been in the family mansion in St. Petersburg for more than a century. This, together with the large copper samovar that was used for making tea in the library downstairs and a priceless collection of Fabergé miniatures, gifts from the Czar, were all that remained of the costly furnishings of two town houses and a half dozen estates which had once belonged to the Orlov family in Russia.

Seeing her father stir, Niki moved nearer to the bed. Count Orlov had grown even thinner during the past week. His sleeping cap, a custom she had always found absurd, considering the heat of Shanghai, was tilted back at a sharp angle, exposing his almost bald head. His cheeks, even his nose, were a sickly gray, and his usually imposing mustache was drooping.

It was an unsettling sight for Niki, who had always been proud of her father's distinctive aristocratic looks. From the yellowed photographs in the family albums, which she spent hours flipping through, Count Orlov, who preferred to be referred to as General, had once cut an extremely dashing figure.

"Niki, my dear, come here," the General called out, suddenly sitting upright in bed with both hands resting on his lap.

"How are you feeling, Papa?" Niki asked, moving closer to the bed and noticing, as she did, her father's slender fingers which had loved to fondle women, cards, and gold—and always in that order.

"I feel . . . I feel," said the General hesitatingly. "Better I don't tell you how I feel. All it would do is upset you even more. But bring me a whiskey, a tall one, and tell me of you. Of your good friend Colonel Hata and how the fortunes of war are affecting him."

Earlier in her father's illness she never would have brought him the whiskey he adored, but now that the doctors gave up all hope for him, Niki would no longer deny her father anything that pleased him.

Smiling despite his pain, the General shifted around in the bed to watch as Niki reached for the decanter of his favorite Scotch whiskey. His daughter's fragile beauty never failed to remind him of his dead wife, whose looks combined with wit and spirit had broken more than one heart—and damaged more than several friendships. But back then, before the Great War, life was lived on a grander scale, the General thought sadly. Not like the present where airplanes, radio, and telephone cut short man's satisfaction in every area of human endeavor. In life itself, Orlov concluded, remembering how he fought with the Cossacks, sacked Turkish villages, lost estates in the Ukraine over dice, and spent nights with sultry gypsy enchantresses and sunny afternoons playing croquet with perfumed princesses. An accomplished bon vivant, he had risen with the sun and gone to sleep with the dawn many times. But in the end, the enchanted world he knew had vanished. Lenin, Trotsky, and the worst bastard of them all, Joseph Stalin, had wiped away a golden era, sending its principal players off into exile where they cropped up as doormen, pimps, and warlords' bodyguards in Shanghai. But not Orlov, not Count Aleksandr Orlov, for he had acted in his own behalf. What he had done was dishonorable. Plainly it was theft, but nevertheless he had done it. He had sacked the paymaster's office that last day in the field against the Bolsheviks, taking millions in gold bullion just hours before boarding the last steamer from Russia.

For over twenty-four years now, Orlov had lived with the infamy of that deed, lived with the condemnation of his former fellow officers, who blamed their poverty on his greed. How many threats and ultimatums they had delivered, Orlov recalled. So many he had forgotten them all, except for the demand itself: the gold bullion contained in the paymaster's trunks, gold which had purchased the luxury and security of this mansion. For the General too yearned desperately for security. What good, he reasoned, would his giving up the gold do? It would only be shared by hundreds—thousands if entire families were included—and ultimately it would be dissipated. Instead, it was devoted to maintaining his style of life and battling his perennial enemies, the Russian Communists.

"Your whiskey, Papa," Niki repeated, holding out the glass for her father. Lately these reveries of his went on for several minutes at a time, she realized, noticing with anxiety the rapid change in his health.

"Tell me about the war," Orlov said, breaking away from his memories and reaching for the glass.

"It's getting very bad for the Japanese. Soon they expect the Americans to invade the Home Islands."

"All fools, that's what they are. Americans joining forces with Stalin. Giving the Communists all that aid. And now forcing Japan to her knees, when she's the only force in Asia capable of battling Mao . . . stopping Communism from spreading."

"Papa," Niki said, hesitating, "Hata's leaving. He's making plans to escape from Shanghai before the Nationalists and Americans arrive."

"A wise man. Where's he going to?"

"South America. Argentina."

"He goes far, but then he has good reason."

"He wants me to go with him. Says if I don't, the Nationalists here in Shanghai will treat me like a collaborator."

Nearly a full minute passed as her father absorbed this information. Finally he asked, "You trust him, this Hata?"

"I love him."

"Trust I asked, I'm not interested whether or not you love the yellow dwarf."

"Yes, I trust him," Niki answered, smiling at her father's terminology. Yellow dwarf was an expression many Russians, especially those who fought during the Russo-Japanese War of 1905, used to refer to the Japanese. If the Axis powers had not been the White Russians' greatest hope in freeing Russia from Communist control, her father's hatred for the so-called yellow dwarfs would never have altered, and she would never have been permitted to consort with Hata.

"You say Hata wants you to accompany him?"

"Yes."

"Good. Then do so. Go with him."

"But, Papa," Niki said, the tears filling her eyes.

It was not easy for Orlov to say what he did. He could well understand her tears. If there were any left inside him he too would cry. But the years had taught him the necessity of letting go. Hadn't he let go of Mother Russia, his estates, his wife, his mistresses, his comrades-in-arms; all that was left was the icon above his head, the samovar and the Fabergé collection, and Niki, his precious daughter. And now all this, including Niki, must go. There was no other choice. How could he permit his daughter to remain here in Shanghai, a city eventually doomed to the Communists and a place where his own enemies were just waiting for an opportunity to strike.

"I agree with Hata," he said stubbornly. "Go at once. The longer you stay here the more dangerous it will be for both of you."

Stunned by her father's reaction, Niki sat down on the bed. She never expected her father to feel this way, never imagined he would willingly send her away. How could he be so callous, she wondered, seeing him more clearly now: an old old man, his face shrunken, his body wasted by the cancer that was eating him alive. It was like being confronted by a total stranger. He was so quick to let her go, so quick to pull away the underpinnings of a relationship which had offered her so much security all these years that they had been together in Shanghai. It must be the result of this disgusting disease, she decided.

"Don't you want me here with you?" Niki asked softly, stroking his hands tenderly.

"Tears if I say no. Tears if I say yes. Of course I want you to stay. But for what? My funeral. We both know there isn't much longer for me. And as for Shanghai, her fate is decided as well. The world we knew is gone. The easy life for Europeans in Asia is over. The Bolshies . . . the Communists . . . don't you see . . . they're coming!"

"But what about me," Niki sobbed, unable to keep back the tears which streamed down her cheek. "What about me? I don't want to wander the world . . . go from country to country like I did with Mama."

"And you won't, you won't," Orlov consoled her reassuringly. "Not if you follow my advice and do exactly as I say. Will you do that?"

Nodding, Niki reached past her father for a handkerchief from the night table. She dabbed carefully at her eyes, wiping away the tears.

"Good. Now listen carefully," Orlov went on in a whisper, looking toward the door to make certain no one was there to overhear him. "Everything I have . . . all the gold will be yours. You will never have to worry, never have to work, never have to do anyone else's bidding. Not if you act wisely and follow my advice. Hata's a strong man. He will protect you. He will help you reach Argentina safely. But once you are there . . . once you are there . . . you will leave him. Understand me. Leave him. You will not tell Hata what I tell you. Not tell him anything about my gold and where it has been hidden all these years, for not only your Japanese friend but our enemies will be after that . . . be assured, they will be after that. No! Instead you will find another man, not an Oriental because an Oriental will be of no use. No! Pick someone like your friend Dallin. A shrewd businessman. A survivor. Win his heart and make him take you to Europe. To Europe! There you will be safest of all and he can protect you . . . and you can make him even richer than he already is. But never never trust him or anyone else . . . and never believe the Bolshies. They will always lie, always try to get you to go back . . . to . . . to . . . to . . ."

Still clutching Niki's hands, Orlov fell back against the pillows. His face was grayer than it had ever been, his eyes sunk deeply into his already sagging cheeks.

"Father, I . . ." Niki started to say, then suddenly leaped up from the bed and crossed to the window. Standing there numbly, peering down at the rose garden, she found all her illusions had been destroyed by her father's words. She realized there was truth in what the other White Russians had said about him for years. Only she had been spared her father's cynicism, his twisted hatred for the Communists and anyone else who was after the gold he had stolen. And now, even at the point of death, he was still at it, manipulating his daughter's best interests to preserve the gold he hoarded, God only knows where, Niki thought.

"Tomorrow you will feel better," General Orlov's voice echoed more strongly across the room. "Tomorrow we will begin making arrangements to outwit my enemies again . . . and again . . . and again!"

Chapter Eight

———————————

That night, the fourth of August, two hundred and forty miles northwest of Shanghai, just beyond Nanking, Maximov Dallin stood quietly on a windswept ledge of rock overhanging the Yangtze River. Worry lines beaded his sun-bronzed face, and his mood was grim as usual. Ahead, shrouded by impenetrable darkness, the Yangtze thundered, her swift current sending masses of white water swirling up against the battered granite cliff where Dallin was standing.

Off to his left, downriver in a small cove, a Japanese steamer lay at anchor surrounded by a flotilla of heavily laden junks from Ichang, a treaty port at the entrance to the famed Yangtze Gorges. Here the river narrowed sharply and, marked by what seemed to be a never-ending series of rapids, worked its way through mountainous terrain so forbidding it made the passage to Chungking, almost four hundred miles away, one of the most dangerous water routes in the world.

At six thousand tons the steamer was one of the largest on the Yangtze. She had been built in an Antwerp shipyard in 1899, for a Dutch company—the Java-China-Japan Line—and she was equipped with three good-sized holds capable of storing anything but railroad cars and oil. By 1941, no longer considered seaworthy, the *China Star*, as she was then known, had been confiscated by the Japanese Navy and rechristened the *Ikado Maru*. She had been pressed into service on the Yangtze until a bomb from an American B-25 had blown apart her cargo mast, rendering her booms useless.

Aboard the junks, lit by the flickering deck lamps of the *Ikado Maru*, dozens of Chinese Nationalist soldiers in tan cotton uniforms moved about listlessly, lugging heavy crates. On the Japanese steamer, half-naked coolies, watched over by dozing Japanese soldiers in brown khaki, stood in a single line receiving the crates from the junk and transferring them, man to man, until they were lowered to rest in the cargo holds.

Except for the tingling sensation in his gut, Dallin had very little to criticize in this latest black-market operation. The Chinese Nationalist junks bringing the U.S. Army PX merchandise were already anchored in the cove when he arrived aboard the *Ikado Maru* in this no-man's-land deliberately maintained by both armies. Happily, both the Nationalist and the Japanese troops assigned to guard the buyer and seller during these immensely profitable transactions seemed content enough with their share and the half-dozen cases of Scotch brought along by Dallin to help them pass their idle time.

Yet something was troubling Dallin. From long experience he knew it was always the unexpected in China that proved lethal. His first trip upriver, two and a half years before, had been a perfect example. Then a gun-happy company of Chinese Nationalist troops, angered by the cut paid them by the Chungking trader Dallin was dealing with, opened up with their machine guns, slaughtering a dozen coolies on the deck of his steamer. The whole transaction would have ended in disaster if the Nationalist commander, a distant relative of the all-powerful Soong family, had not appeared in time and straightened out the misunderstanding. There were other incidents as well, ugly tales not directly involving Dallin. One Nazi businessman, double crossed by his own men, was thrown alive into the angry waters of the Yangtze and never seen again. Another merchant, a European with important connections in both camps, literally lost his head to a Chinese puppet general infuriated at not getting his cut of a sale. The general had mounted the merchant's head on the prow of his convoy's lead vessel as a warning to other smugglers.

Despite the growing number of violent incidents along the Yangtze, too many fortunes were being made to stop the war profiteers and black marketeers from continuing to move goods. From Nationalist-held territory came vast quantities of beef, grain, and salt, as well as valuable minerals and stocks of U.S. Army equipment, including ammunition, jeeps, and trucks. In the opposite direction, from Occupied China, flowed sugar, gasoline, cigarettes, medicines, industrial products, and luxury goods. So much trade went on between the two avowed enemies that it gradually became clear to all, even to those American advisors pledged to support Chiang Kai-shek, that there was collusion between the highest Nationalist and Japanese levels of command. This connection was eventually confirmed.

By the spring of 1945, the flow of trade became abruptly one-sided; the Burma Road was finally open, and supplies began pouring into Free China from American bases in India. The Nationalists no longer had to rely on the Japanese and Shanghailanders for basic necessities or luxury goods. In fact, the reverse was now true; Occupied China and, to a growing extent, Japan herself were now dependent upon the Nationalists.

Whatever the circumstances, the black marketeer's life was a tight-rope walker's balancing act at best. It called for an almost feral sense of danger and nerves of iron.

Hearing muffled footsteps on the ledge behind him, Dallin jerked the Bolo Mauser from his shoulder holster and spun around.

At the sight of the gun, the gaunt Korean in black cotton pajamas halted a half-dozen paces away. "They are waiting," he informed Dallin.

Nodding, Dallin peered over the Korean's sloping shoulder. Behind him, in a cave cut into the side of the mountain not twenty feet away, a group of Nationalist and Japanese officers and a potbellied Chinese merchant were seated at a long wooden table.

"Get the cargo manifest," Dallin ordered. "Double-check it for anything our fat friend may have forgotten. He enjoys little tricks like that."

The Korean swung about on his straw sandals and padded silently off down the dark trail. Dallin shoved the Mauser into his holster and made quickly for the cave. Inside, a hanging oil lamp shed just enough light for him to make out the faces of the men seated there. He slipped past the three Japanese officers and took a place at the far end of the table with his back to the rear wall. Seated to his right, across from the Japanese, were three Nationalist officers. The table was strewn with bottles of Scotch and jars of domestic pickles. Dallin poured himself a shot from an open bottle, then sat back listening as pint-sized Captain Osho described how wonderful their lives would be as soon as the war was finally over.

Dallin recalled with wry amusement that only two years before, this same Japanese officer had been singing a far different tune. Back then, swelled with pride over the Japanese victories in the Pacific and Southeast Asia and giddy from their stunning success over the arrogant Caucasians, Osho had proudly described how the New Order would bring prosperity to all Orientals, and especially to the Chinese.

Near the entrance to the cave, Ling, the potbellied Chinese merchant, was stubbornly explaining several items missing on his cargo manifest to the equally stubborn Korean.

Witnessing the deadlock, Dallin reflected how little the war had affected the businessmen on either side. Only the armies had been changed. At the outbreak of the war in 1937, the Japanese were bursting with confidence; equipped with the latest weapons, they were ready to fight and die for their Emperor. With shiny spurs on their leather boots and high-visored caps they stormed across Marco Polo Bridge, sending the unprepared Chinese into flight. Time after time, the Chinese, hampered by corrupt Kuomintang generals, shoddy armaments, and scarcely any training, reeled before the mechanized Japanese onslaughts. Shanghai was one of the few places where the Chinese made a valiant and courageous stand; given orders by Chiang Kai-shek to hold their ground, the 19th Chinese Army hung on until it was nearly decimated by enemy planes and artillery firing at point-blank range. In so doing, Free China won a victory in world opinion but suffered the loss of some of her finest troops. Meanwhile those very troops, mistreated, poorly fed, underpaid, and left to die on battlefields, soon understood that the unofficial policy of Chiang Kai-shek was not to wage war against the Japanese at all, but instead to wait for America to do it for him while he prepared to destroy the Communists. Eight years had passed since those dark days, and in recent months the tide had changed completely. The Americans had done precisely what the Generalissimo had hoped they would. They had swept the

Japanese aside in the Pacific and were now closing in on the Home Islands.

Dallin turned to the stocky Nationalist major on his right, a middle-aged Cantonese with two gold-capped front teeth. "How's Chungking these days?" he asked.

"Too hot," the major chuckled, "and filled with too many smelly Americans."

"All crawling with gonorrhea," added the young Chinese lieutenant with a severe crewcut, who was in the middle beside Captain Chen, a morose-looking northerner with a terribly scarred face.

"Too many Americans everywhere these days," snapped Captain Osho cynically. "In France, Germany, Italy, and on their way here."

Neither the Chinese officers nor Dallin made any attempt to reply. In the awkward silence that ensued Dallin topped his glass with more Scotch, then offered the open bottle to the badly-scarred Nationalist captain.

"Thanks," he said in a cultured tone, holding out his empty glass. "You know Chungking well?"

"Can't say I do," Dallin replied, filling it nearly to the brim.

"Lucky for you. The corruption there is enough to make anyone puke. Thanks to scum like us."

"Speak for yourself!" the stocky major said sharply. Then, turning to Dallin, he explained, "When Chen drinks, he gets serious, and when he gets serious, all he thinks of is how China should be but never will be. At least not in our lifetime."

"It could be if we tried," Chen shot back stubbornly.

"It'll never be," the stocky major insisted. "Too many problems. You solve one, and ten more crop up."

"Not even we could solve them all," Osho laughed, belching aloud.

"They could never be solved by you Japanese!" Chen shouted, slamming his glass down onto the table. "And they never will be with the Generalissimo. But they might be with someone else."

"Who else is there?" blurted the young Nationalist lieutenant, without thinking. "Unless you mean Mao?"

In just seconds a hush fell over the cave; Nationalist and Japanese alike stared hostilely at Chen.

He remained hunched over the table, looking unafraid, indeed, relieved, that his secret was finally out.

"Hate me if you wish," he said calmly, "but you all know what I say is true. Only the Communists fight the Japs. Only Mao helps the peasants. And it's only the Kuomintang and the Japanese who steal from our people."

"That's enough!" screamed the Nationalist major, shaking his fist. "What you say is treason."

Dallin was tense, anticipating trouble. He knew from experience it was a short step from liquidating Communist sympathizers to murdering rich White Russian collaborators.

Without warning the Korean squatted down beside him and announced matter of factly, "Ling's short ten thousand in goods."

"Some theft can't be helped," the fat Chinese merchant said anxiously, as he approached Dallin. "You know how Chungking is! They stole from the cargo before I left."

"Let's get on with it," Dallin said brusquely, Ling's lies a welcome interruption to the confrontation brewing between the Nationalist captain and the others.

Rising slightly in his chair, Dallin unfastened the lower buttons of his shirt and pulled off the money belt strapped around his waist. Catching everyone's attention but Captain Chen's, Dallin slid the zipper back along the entire length of the canvas belt and neatly bundled packets of crisp American one-hundred-dollar bills poured onto the table.

His small eyes narrowed, Ling ran his tongue excitedly over his fat lips in anticipation and moved closer to the pile of currency.

"Hundred thousand U.S., less ten," Dallin said casually, slipping one bundle back into his coat pocket.

Captain Chen remained sunk in thought. While the others greedily eyed the money heaped on the table, Ling eagerly traded places with the stocky Nationalist major and whispered, "I check the bills first, okay?"

"Suits me," replied Dallin. "Only blame any bad ones on your Shanghai brothers, not me.

Ling scooped a crisp packet of bills from the table and withdrew a powerful Zeiss magnifying glass and a brand-new hundred-dollar bill from his bulging briefcase.

"The best counterfeiters in the world are in Shanghai," the stocky Nationalist major observed as Ling painstakingly compared Dallin's currency with his own.

"Not only for American and British currency but for German as well—that is, if anyone is stupid enough to still want some of Germany's," Captain Osho snickered and everyone but Dallin and Captain Chen burst out laughing.

Hours later, Dallin was still seated at the table with his back to the wall, watching a dense cloud of cigarette smoke drift slowly out of the cave into the star-filled night. The others had already left, supposedly to return to the junks and the *Ikado Maru* to wait out the dawn. Only Captain Chen, snoring loudly over at the far end of the table, remained in the cave. Reaching out, Dallin gently shook his left shoulder. The Chinese woke with a start, stared about bleary-eyed, then, rubbing one badly scarred cheek, lifted a bottle of whiskey and began to pour himself another drink.

"They're outside, waiting for me to leave," Dallin explained softly.

Not surprised, Chen leaned back against the chair and replied, "What does it matter? Now or later, the end will come just the same."

"Where did you get those scars?"

"Burma," Chen said, a spark of pride in his voice.

"With Vinegar Joe?"

For the first time all night a genuine smile creased Chen's mutilated face. "General Stilwell taught us how to fight and how to be proud of our country, but Chiang grew afraid. He had Stilwell recalled to the U.S."

"I heard the Chinese troops took a liking to him."

"Why not? He came here to fight the Japs, not play games like our leaders and let the U.S. do it for them."

Shrugging, Dallin said, "Big country. Big problems. What can you really do about it? Long as you get yours, right?"

"Wrong."

Shrugging again, Dallin dug his fingers into a crumpled pack of Lucky Strikes lying on the table and lit one. As he inhaled, he kept one eye on the entrance to the cave. "When I leave here, they'll come for you. What they have in mind won't be pretty."

"Why should you care about me?"

"Trouble's bad for business even when it happens to idealists."

"How can they fear people who only want social justice,"

Chen said bitterly, flinging an empty pack of cigarettes into the dirt. "Nothing makes much sense anymore."

"Maybe people don't want change. Say what you like, but China's had nearly a decade of war. We've all gotten used to living like this. Chinese Nationalist, puppet, liberal, Japanese, White Russian, all of us."

"You mean people would rather go on with this rape, theft, and useless killing?"

"And take squeeze and make beneficial arrangements to sweeten their own pockets. Way I see things, ideology like yours or the Communists' is pretty heady stuff to people who've grown lazy and corrupt."

"If you mean war is easier than peace," Chen said, eyeing Dallin a bit strangely, "then I don't understand them or you."

"Don't blame me. It's not my country."

"No. But you live in it, so you cannot escape responsibility. My father was a follower of Sun Yat-sen. When Chiang betrayed the revolution in '27 and sold out to the bankers and the gangster Du at Shanghai, my father left the Kuomintang and searched for another way, a democratic way to unite China and get rid of the six despotic families."

"What happened to him?" Dallin asked, rising from the table and starting slowly out of the cave.

"He was tortured, then murdered in Happy Valley by Chiang's secret police, the Blue Shirts."

"That's what I figured," Dallin concluded sourly. "Take my advice, leave before they come for you. And stay away from the river. They'll expect you to head that way."

"Dallin?"

"What?"

"Who are you?"

At the entrance to the cave, Dallin reluctantly came to a halt and turned around. Seeing a ray of hope on Chen's face, Dallin started to say something, then had second thoughts, and replied, "You already know. A White Russian emigré. A businessman. A man without a country. Why?"

"Is that all you are? A China trader?"

"Isn't that enough? It's made me rich."

Disappointment registered on the mutilated face, "I had hoped you would answer me differently," Chen said. "In that, as in so much else, I guess I was wrong."

"I guess so," Dallin murmured.

Dallin left the cave and plunged into the night. He moved quickly down the mountain, following the trail that wound between massive boulders to the river below.

He was halfway there when gunshots rang out from the direction of the cave. Then he heard the sound of men running and cursing in Chinese and Japanese. Dallin quickened his pace, making his way down the mountain, into the cove, and back onto the *Ikado Maru*. Having made certain the Korean was seeing to the placement of cargo in the holds, Dallin went onto the bridge and leaned against the railing.

Back on the mountain, flashlight beams were criss-crossing in the darkness. Dallin followed their rapid movements for a while, then, frowning, turned away as Ling came bustling up to him.

"Soldiers are so stupid!" the potbellied Chinese merchant said, spitting into the water and narrowly missing a Nationalist private on the junk below.

There was another burst of gunfire as more screaming echoed down from the mountain, sending Ling into peals of laughter. "Idiots chasing each other around in the dark. Sometimes I wonder why we allow them so much control over our lives."

"So we have time to make money," Dallin said quietly. Then, deliberately changing the subject, he asked, "What's Chungking like now?"

"The end's so close I'm glad I'm not in your shoes, my friend. The official word is that the Allies will hang people like you by the balls."

"I'll worry about that when it happens. What about America. . . ."

"My son's the one who reads the magazines. *Life, Look, Colliers, Saturday Evening Post.* He can't get his fill. He wants to finish school in the States. He says the factories there are busy day and night turning out ships, tanks, guns, whatever you want. There's no stopping American production, he says. It's more than the rest of the world's put together."

"Must be so," Dallin agreed. "I even heard Comrade Stalin praises the Americans."

"For now. Which reminds me!" Ling brightened. "I've got nylons, Coca-Cola, Bulova watches, RCA radios. Take your pick. Much as you want. The Chungking warehouses are loaded."

"How about penicillin?"

"Fifty thousand doses in original U.S. Army wrappers. You need more, I get more."

"How soon can I take delivery?"

"Can't be too soon for me." Ling smiled happily. "What about the fifteenth?"

"That should be all right."

More gunshots resounded from the mountain, followed by a terrible scream. Almost at once the flashlights converged on a point in the distance. Dallin and Ling fell silent, the slamming of the hatches behind them the only noise.

The Korean appeared without warning at the railing. "Ship ready."

"Good," Dallin replied. "Get below and check on the men."

Dallin waited for the Korean to start across the deck, then turned to Ling. "What about antiques? Any more of those large stone Buddhas from the Yun Kang caves?"

"You want more antiques? What are you doing with all the ones you and Hata already bought from me?"

"That's our business. Yes or no?"

"Suit yourself," Ling chortled, the rolls of fat around his belly swaying as he laughed, "but if I were you and Hata, I'd be looking for a safe place to hide rather than buying more rare treasures."

"You have any ideas?" Dallin asked, making no attempt to conceal his interest.

"For you I might."

"And Hata?"

"The Jap is too hot. He can't be helped."

"How much?"

"Why talk money now? When you're ready we'll discuss the terms."

"Include Hata?"

"I already told you it can't be done."

"Think it over."

"It's a waste of time," Ling said, his usually genial face turning grave.

"In China accommodations can always be found—for enough money."

"Not this time. Not for war criminals like the commandant

of the Shanghai Kempetai. Besides, why should you worry about him as long as I save your neck?"

For once Dallin had no answer. He stared in silence at Ling's cherublike face, wondering what, if anything, could touch this mercenary Chinaman's soul.

Chapter Nine

In Shanghai a light drizzle was falling as Gustav Torg's black Cadillac limousine turned off Bubbling Well Road into the well-lit circular driveway of the Roulette Club. The Chinese chauffeur brought the limousine to a stop beside the doorway, and Dominique stepped out almost at once, wearing a sleeveless white satin gown cut low enough to reveal the fullness of her pale breasts. She acknowledged the doorman's respectful greeting, then started up the broad marble steps into the white Victorian building.

The last seventy-two hours had been agony. When she returned from the Tower Nightclub she had discovered her home ransacked, the servants, especially her old amah, totally cowed by the Kempei intruders. Every room of the three-story mansion had been searched, all the closets and drawers turned out, books, papers, and personal objects thrown carelessly about. Nothing was left untouched. Whatever appeared to be suspicious had been carted away to Bridge House for further examination.

From the butler Dominique learned that the Kempetai were desperately searching for a diary or book of some sort which they had apparently not yet found. When Dominique questioned the butler further, however, she got nowhere, meeting the same taciturn manner he had displayed to the Japanese.

To compound her confusion, the elderly custodian of a small office building near the Holy Trinity Cathedral, used by Gustav Torg to conduct his private business, had telephoned to report that the place had also been raided by Kempei soldiers and that all her father's correspondence and files had been transferred to Bridge House. He too had overheard the Kempetai officer in charge instructing his men to look for a diary or book.

If all this were not enough to make Dominique unsettled, what followed surely was. First, she had made a frantic visit to the Norwegian Consulate on Szechuan Road where there had been a maddening wait until the first secretary could be located, to learn that nothing official could be undertaken until the consul returned from Chungking. The next day Dominique wasted several more hours at the governor-general's mansion trying to obtain a personal interview with General Mishima. She was finally told by an obnoxious aide that such meetings required a written application and a minimum of forty-eight hours' notice. Fortunately, not all her hopes rested on getting their help. It so happened that she was justified in asking a favor from one of the most influential men in Shanghai, perhaps someone who was not as powerful as Hata in an open contest of strength but surely a man as adept and wily as anyone else at compelling the Kempetai to spare Gustav Torg's life.

With this thought in mind, she hurried across the plush lobby, past two watchful Corsicans in dark suits, and entered the main casino.

It was a vast, high-ceilinged room with a plush dark brown carpet and glittering crystal chandeliers. Shanghai's wealthiest and most prominent residents were gathered at the various gaming tables, which were manned by other sharp-eyed Corsicans in sleek tuxedos. In their midst a row of bland-faced Chinese cashiers seated inside chrome cages nonchalantly doled out stacks of different-colored chips in exchange for carefully weighed gold bars and closely scrutinized American and British currency.

At the long mahogany bar, on the far side of the room, more than twenty-five feet from the nearest gaming table, were some of the city's highest-paid informers, pimps, opium dealers, and gangsters, men and women of widely divergent nationalities, most of whom had been cast adrift by the war and were determined to profit at anyone's expense.

Nationalist agents, Soviet spies, Kempetai thugs, and Green Dragon Society fingermen mingled freely among this bizarre collection of human flotsam, tolerated by the tightly knit Corsican management that controlled the Roulette Club, just as long as whatever trouble these people caused took place off the club's premises.

On a wide balcony overlooking the bar, near a small circle of tables reserved for the biggest plungers, was the private booth of Robert Salat, the director of the Shanghai Roulette Club. From his vantage point high above the main room, the lean, stylishly dressed Corsican could keep an eye on the play going on below and around him.

He was seated alone, as was his custom. A bottle of vintage Dom Perignon rested snugly inside a sterling silver bucket close by the table.

"*Ciao*, Robert," Dominique said warmly, as she approached his table.

Whatever unpleasant thoughts had been clouding the Corsican's handsome face vanished at once. In seconds nothing seemed to exist beyond Dominique's golden presence.

"*Ciao, cara.*"

"You look pleased but not surprised," she said, slipping into the booth opposite Salat.

"In Shanghai bad news travels fast."

"I should have known," Dominique said with a slight smile. "Ferrara is right. Our consulate can't help, and getting to see General Mishima may take days."

"What else did Ferrara say?"

"That Dallin is my only hope."

"Yet you come to me?" Salat said, as he motioned a waiter to pour the champagne.

"I trust you."

Pleased by this remark, Salat watched as Dominique's glass was filled. Then, lifting his glass, Salat touched it gently to hers and murmured. "*Salud.*"

"Is Ferrara right?" Dominique asked, sinking back against the seat, her hazel eyes intent on Salat.

"Dallin and Hata are partners, that much is clear. But how much weight that carries when the spy is someone Hata has been after for so long, who can tell?"

"Then you think . . . you believe my father's guilty too?"

"Think about it. What does Hata gain by punishing the wrong person this late in the game? He doesn't need a scapegoat to please his superiors. Not anymore. But he does need to destroy evidence of his war crimes. Evidence collected and written down in a book."

"So that's what his men were searching for? Still, I don't see what this has to do with my father."

Salat hesitated. It pained him to hurt Dominique. He would have given anything to avoid it.

Seeing his anguish, Dominique averted her eyes, but it was too late; the tears cascaded down her cheeks.

"Don't, Dominique," Salat whispered, offering his handkerchief. "Everything will be all right. You have my promise."

"It's unfair of me, I know," she sobbed. "I shouldn't involve you in my problems. But I don't know where else to turn."

"You've turned to someone who cares . . . will always care . . . I hoped you would come."

"Truly?" Dominique asked, her eyes glistening.

"Truly."

Stroking her hair, Salat put his arm around her and drew her close. As she nestled against him, Dominique could not help sensing the irony in finding so much comfort in the arms of the one man, outside of Hata, with the most menacing reputation in East China. How little people really knew about Robert Salat, she thought as she looked up at him. His lips gently brushed against her forehead and finally moved to her unprotesting mouth.

"It's been so long," he whispered. "So very long."

"I've missed you too," Dominique murmured, stroking his smooth cheek acutely aware, not for the first time, just how attractive he was.

"One of Du's men should be here tonight."

"The Chinese gangster?"

"Yes. They've swapped money for hostages with the Kempetai before."

"Is Du my only hope?"

"For the moment."

"Oh, God."

None of it made sense to her. Gustav Torg had always insisted they abide by the rules the Japanese had set down for neutrals. He even made Dominique promise never to criticize the occupational authorities, although both he and his daughter were sickened by the atrocities the Japanese committed in China.

Out of love and respect for her father, Dominique had adhered to his wishes, although much of the time it was not easy. She detested the barbarism and arrogant ways of the Japanese in Shanghai. Now, to her complete amazement her father was charged with espionage against them, which could only mean one thing: either her father or Colonel Hata was lying to her. And since she had never had any reason to doubt her father before, it seemed clear that Hata was the liar.

"In the last few weeks four men have died," Salat said, as though reading her thoughts. "Busch over at the airport, a Danish sea captain at the port, and one of the senior Chinese railroad officials at the main station."

"Allied spies?"

"Hata thought so."

"You mentioned four?"

"Felix Hacker too," Salat added reluctantly, turning away for a moment to sign a chit for a gambling credit brought by a turbaned Sikh attendant.

"Felix Hacker dead?"

"Executed."

"I can't believe it. That shy little man. Why, he used to visit our home three or four times a week with those chocolate cakes from Madame Fouquet's that I . . . oh, my God! Then it is so, and Felix could have given my father over to the Kempetai before he died?"

"It looks that way," Salat said cautiously, "only don't be too harsh on him because, if he did inform on your father, he didn't do it willingly. Otherwise he'd still be alive. Like the one who sold Hacker out."

"But who would betray such a wonderful man?" She paused. "Dallin?"

"Maybe," Salat said grimly. "All I know is rumor has it was someone from the Cathay Hotel."

Dominique sank back against the seat. So it was true after all. It seemed unbelievable. A ring of spies operating in Shanghai under the nose of Colonel Hata, with her father and Felix Hacker two of its members. She had known that there had been acts of sabotage against the Japanese, that there were innumerable agents in the market for information. But Gustav Torg! Her father! One of China's leading traders and businessmen, conspiring with the librarian from the Municipal Council Public Library? Not to mention a German, a Dane, and a Chinaman at the railway. It was too fantastic for words. Coming from anyone else, Dominique would never have accepted it for one moment, but Salat was not just anyone.

The two had met by accident a year before Pearl Harbor. She was returning from a shopping expedition in the French Concession and had ordered her driver to stop at the Royal Tea Room on Nanking Road near the Cathay Hotel. Discovering all the tables but one occupied, and that one marked Reserved, she had waited at the pastry counter, marveling at the assortment of desserts, when in walked Salat, looking extremely dashing in an ivory linen suit.

Before Dominique realized what was happening, he had persuaded her to join him at the table marked Reserved. She soon found herself telling him about her student days in Paris, from which she had just returned. It was a city Salat knew well, although from a different vantage point.

When she had first gone to Paris, in 1937, it was a mecca for political refugees fleeing Hitler's Germany. The sad-eyed men and women, many of them already world-famous artists and writers, had made an impression on Dominique. At the mercy of the pro-fascist French police, unable to find work, and without proper visas, most of them spent long days and nights huddled together in cafés on the Left Bank. Homeless, their money and hopes for a better world vanishing, they nevertheless managed to go on debating art, music, literature, and above all politics.

When the war they talked about finally became a reality, Dominique realized she had to go back to China, if she ever hoped to see her father again.

On her return, the great port of Shanghai had seemed unchanged. For most foreign residents Shanghai offered vast privilege and great comfort. Undisturbed by the First World War, when business had soared to record heights, Shanghai's foreign residents saw no reason that this next war would not be just as profitable for them.

Despite their optimism, however, a few cracks were beginning to appear in the colonial facade. True, the Occidentals continued attending the usual run of parties and other social functions, but they could not ignore the Japanese Army and Navy units that had been stationed in the Chinese sections of

Shanghai after the bloody conflicts of 1937. Nor could they block out the daily skirmishes on the streets of the International Settlement and the French Concession as Kempetai henchmen hunted Nationalist and Communist agents, intent on liquidating Chinese collaborators.

It was in this tense atmosphere that Dominique and Salat met. From the start of their affair they purposely avoided old friends and acquaintances, preferring long drives alone into the lush rice country in Salat's sleek twelve-cylinder Bugatti, the only one of its kind in China. There, far from the city, they talked for hours at small, out-of-the-way restaurants and spent dreamy afternoons on crystal-clear lakes sailing past enchanting pagodas.

It was during this period that Dominique learned about the Paris that Salat had known in his underworld days. He had been born in Corsica, where his family long had ties with the island's most powerful criminal syndicate. At eighteen, Salat was shipped off to Marseilles to get experience in the syndicate's operations. He worked with a gang of Corsicans who specialized in robbing provincial banks in France and Italy. Salat's job was to serve as the gang's gunman, a job he excelled at. The gang attacked the Bank of Paris in broad daylight; getting away with several million francs, they managed to reach their hiding place near Lyon, but Salat was betrayed to the Sureté by an informer, and a French court sentenced him to ten years for bank robbery. He escaped after serving one year, and made his way first to North Africa, then out to the Far East where the Corsican syndicate operating in Macao had need of a man with his talents. He changed his name to Salat and established a completely new identity.

When Dominique first heard Salat's incredible tale, she hadn't known whether or not to believe him. She quickly decided that all that really mattered was their desire to touch and kiss and be alone with one another, particularly since the whole world around them seemed to be coming apart.

Salat was thirty-two and quite a ladies' man. Dominique was ten years younger and, despite her years in Paris, still a virgin. Oddly, Salat never made demands on her. It was she who was responsible for their sleeping together, a decision she never regretted.

When Gustav Torg returned from the interior, he already knew about his daughter's romance with Salat. Every taipan employed informers, and the Norwegian was no exception;

no businessman could operate in Shanghai and expect to be successful without them. The Norwegian was no ordinary tai-pan. He had come ashore penniless from a burning cargo steamer and, with only his fists and determination, he made a fortune in China. In less than a decade, he built a trading empire with offices throughout the interior of China and in every principal capital of Europe.

Curiously, the fact that Salat was a Corsican gambler and a gunman had not upset Gustav Torg as much as his daughter had imagined it would. The Norwegian's main concern was that she might marry impulsively before giving herself a chance to know other men. Torg had asked that they stop seeing each other for a year, at the end of which time, if Dominique still felt the same way, he would give her the most lavish wedding in the port city's history. She had little choice but to accept.

The lovers spent their last day together in Soochow, a quaint old city of narrow canals and arched stone bridges of-ten called the Venice of China. At first Dominique hadn't had the courage to tell Salat, until he questioned her, having sensed trouble from the moment he had arrived at her home. Fighting back her tears, Dominique explained her father's position and his firm insistence they not see each other for a year until she was positive about her feelings.

Salat's eyes had taken on such a deadly look that she was sure he would lash out and strike her. When Salat saw the look of fear on Dominique's face, he drew her tightly to him and told her not to worry.

Dominique was grateful that Salat had not made her break a promise to her father, although she knew that if he had asked her to run away to Hong Kong she would have gone.

As the war finally spread to Shanghai, their one-year trial separation was soon swept away in the bloodbath that rapidly engulfed China. Salat was gone for long periods; the Japanese occupation had an enormous effect on the Corsican syn-dicate which operated most of the finer gambling houses of Southeast Asia. Several groups viewed the war as a chance to wrest control of the casinos away from their Corsican owners. It fell to Salat to stop these usurpers. The China coast was soon filled with rumors of the dashing Corsicans' ruthless treatment of the syndicate's enemies.

Only after Bastia, the director of the Roulette Club and Salat's closest friend, was murdered by the Kempetai did he return permanently to Shanghai. By then both he and Dominique sensed their moment was gone, that too much blood had been spilled. Salat had gone too far this time. For even if Dominique still wanted to marry him, Salat would no longer agree. In a country like China, human life was the cheapest commodity, and Salat was marked for death by many powerful enemies. He would never place her life in the same jeopardy.

But now that her father's life hung in the balance, it was Salat that Dominique had turned to.

Pockmark Shen, the merciless gangster lieutenant of Du Yueh-sen, was by far the most grotesque Chinese that Dominique could ever recall meeting. He was obscenely fat with tiny black eyes buried in bulging cheeks pitted by smallpox scars. Their meeting took place inside Salat's teak-paneled office at the rear of the balcony. Pockmark Shen, his swollen body draped in a loose black silk gown, was seated in a heavy chair flanked by two granite-faced Chinese bodyguards whose revolvers were outlined against their tightly fitted jackets. A fourth Chinese, a spindly-fingered accountant, was hunched over a small table across the room, busily wrapping rubber bands around thick piles of currency, which he then dropped, one by one, into a battered leather satchel at his feet.

Throughout the introduction by Salat, Pockmark Shen never smiled. If the grotesque Chinese took any interest at all in their meeting his tiny black eyes never revealed it.

"Colonel Hata is no friend of the Green Dragon Society," he finally replied in a surprisingly high-pitched voice. "Sometimes he does business with us, but always on very unfair terms."

"But you can buy my father's freedom?" Dominique asked coolly.

Brushing aside her question with a wave of his hand, Pockmark dug his thick fingers into his eyes, massaging them for a long time before saying, "A very difficult man, Colonel Hata. Very difficult people, the Kempetai. Very bad for spies they catch."

Dominique glanced over her shoulder at Salat. From his grim expression she could tell the meeting was going badly. Mustering her flagging spirits, she swung back to the Chinaman.

"Mr. Shen," she said firmly, "there's no proof my father is a spy, and since he is a neutral foreign national, I'm sure someone of your importance can persuade Colonel Hata to release him."

"You say Kempetai has no proof. Maybe Kempetai says different."

Discouraged, Dominique fumbled for a reply. Salat broke in: "All Mademoiselle Torg needs to know is can you buy her father's freedom. If so, for how much?"

Nodding, Pockmark Shen said, "Okay, I speak with Chungking. But spies cause much trouble for Japanese and Chinese."

"Thank you very much," Dominique said as warmly as she could; the Chinaman, moving incredibly fast for a man his size, flung himself out of the chair and toward the door, still flanked by his two bodyguards, the accountant trailing with the leather satchel.

Seconds later, Dominique and Salat were alone in the office.

"Not very successful, was I?" Dominique said, folding her hands nervously in her lap.

Salat didn't reply at once. Instead he drew a slender gold case from his inside jacket pocket; he offered her a cigarette and, taking one for himself, lit both.

"Spies cause much trouble for Japanese and Chinese," he murmured, repeating Pockmark Shen's exact words as he exhaled a thick swath of smoke.

"You mean he won't help even for money?"

"I mean Boss Du in Chungking may have his own reasons for not wanting your father alive."

"Then why didn't he just say so," Dominique said heatedly.

"Because it's un-Chinese to say no. Now calm down. Give Pockmark a day or two."

"And then what? Suppose the answer is no."

"Then I'll handle things."

"How, Salat? You can't invade Bridge House."

The telephone rang on Salat's walnut desk and he moved across the office to answer it. A minute later, after telling his chief croupier to grant a steady customer a new line of credit, he started back for the sofa.

"Your father hasn't much time. Four, maybe five days. I've seen what the Kempetai can do to people."

Dominique couldn't keep from trembling. She remembered

hearing about Bastia, a legendary figure in the Corsican underworld and Salat's closest friend. In tears she had listened as Salat described the cruel punishment inflicted on Bastia for defying Colonel Hata's demands to share the profits of the Roulette Club. She was also aware how much suffering the syndicate's orders, forbidding any revenge against the Kempetai commandant, had caused Salat.

"If Hata won't deal with us," Salat said, starting back across the office, "there's another way to save your father than raiding Bridge House."

"What way? Tell me."

"It's better I don't. You must take my word for it. There's something here in Shanghai that Hata and his partner Dallin cherish much more than some book or executing Allied spies." Salat sat beside her.

He tilted her face up to his and kissed her for a long time.

"That last night together. What was it you said about me?"

"That you lived too near the edge," Dominique said reluctantly. "But I never stopped loving you. I don't think I ever could."

Chapter Ten

————◆————

The Yangtze is the third-longest river on earth. It flows for nearly four thousand miles in an easterly direction from Tibet to the East China Sea, a world unto itself. Generations of Chinese fishermen and sailors, dating back centuries before Christ, have lived and died, never leaving its mile-wide banks.

Dallin was reminded of this as he stood at the porthole of his cabin, watching a heavy downpour lash against the *Ikado Maru*'s wet decks. A few minutes more and the storm would pass. The sky, now a dark gray, would turn a brilliant blue again and the hot sun would burn down upon the river. But until then, for at least an hour, the oppressive humidity that plagued eastern China during the summer would be tolerable.

Outside in the corridor Dallin could hear the Japanese officers laughing. Murdering the Nationalist Captain Chen had left them in a good humor, and they had come back to the *Ikado Maru* itching for more fun. Fortunately for Dallin, there was another case of Scotch in the galley, and he was comforted by the knowledge that Nanking would be coming up on the steamer's port side by nightfall.

Ignoring the raucous laughter, Dallin unfastened the shoulder holster, strapped low against his rib cage, and slid the Bolo Mauser beneath the pillow on the bunk. Then, swinging both legs onto the thin mattress, he stretched out with his head resting against the damp pillow, his eyes fixed on the ceiling overhead. His thoughts strayed to the dead Nationalist officer. The tragedy was so typical of China. Where else could a man die so easily for one careless remark?

Rolling over on the bunk, with his face buried in the pillow, Dallin recalled other men and women he had seen slain during the war years. Good people, intelligent people, usually the best of the lot, who paid a high price for their ideology. Dallin cursed their naiveté, their vulnerability. To survive in China took guile, shrewd planning, and luck. Only fanatics—and even they knew better—went about speaking their minds to others.

"Luck." Dallin sighed. No one knew better than he the role luck played in human affairs, not just in achieving success but in simply remaining alive in this war-torn country where the balance of power changed overnight and danger was never far away.

The Chinese called it *joss* and had many symbols for it. To them the color red symbolized good luck. Male children meant luck. So did chubby hands, thick earlobes, and small feet. According to native logic, big feet were suited for labor. Since people who labored were usually poor, a person born with big feet was usually unlucky. To Dallin's way of thinking it all pointed to a man's destiny being largely beyond his control—left to his *ming*, the Chinese word for fate.

Joss, ming, luck, fate; he was turning the words over in his mind when a hard knock on the door brought him up short.

"What is it?"

"Trouble," the Korean replied through the closed cabin door.

It was an understatement. There was more trouble than Dallin had bargained for or could do anything about. By the time he and the Korean got out of his cabin and onto the bridge deck, an entire platoon of heavily armed Imperial Marines, their brown camouflage uniforms and white leggings soaked from the rain, had stormed aboard the *Ikado Maru*. The Marines quickly overwhelmed the detachment of Japanese soldiers guarding the hatches on the main deck and began herding them toward the forecastle.

Dallin recognized their leader at once: Colonel Takamori Juzo, the notorious butcher of Leyte. Untamed and fierce, Juzo had bushy hair, gold-capped teeth, and a scraggly beard.

He wore a torn campaign jacket and carried a curved sa-murai sword and huge revolver strapped at his chunky waist.

"Hello, Dallin," Juzo shouted, booting a slow-moving Chinese seaman out of his way.

"I heard you were stationed in Manchuria."

"You mean with the Kwantung Army?" Juzo grinned slyly. "We pulled out of that deathtrap weeks ago."

"Afraid of the Russians?" Dallin asked, eyeing the squad of husky Imperial Marines armed with submachine guns fanning out on the deck around the Korean and him.

"Right!" Juzo grinned. "You would be too if you saw what we have. Some crack army! No artillery, tanks, or planes. The Soviets will roll over us like we did the Americans back in '42."

"Doesn't sound good."

"It stinks," Juzo said, his well-aimed spittle spotting the Korean's sandals.

Dallin glanced quickly at the Korean, then looked toward the wheelhouse, where two Marines with bayonets on their rifles were guarding the elderly, pipe-smoking captain of the *Ikado Maru* and the vigilant seaman at the helm. On the main deck below, two rows of Marines were shepherding their prisoners over to the forward hatch, forcing them at gunpoint down the metal ladder into the suffocating hold.

Captain Osho and another officer backed stubbornly away from the ladder, objecting loudly to this treatment. The Ma-rine platoon leader, a sturdy six-footer, shoved his way through the column of prisoners and, getting a grip on their collars, dragged them screaming over to the edge of the hold and flung them inside. Seconds later the pint-sized Osho's shrill scream ended in a dull thud.

"How's my aristocratic friend Hata these days?" Juzo asked, pleased with the efficiency of the platoon leader.

"Alive and in power," Dallin replied warily, familiar with the long-time feud between the two men. More than once, the sophisticated Kempetai commandant had expelled the crude Juzo from Shanghai for his free-wheeling tactics and abuse of the occupation laws. Each time Juzo had made a meek apol-ogy and appealed to the High Command to be allowed to re-turn.

"And the Tower Nightclub?" Juzo asked, wetting his thick lips. "Still jammed with beautiful women?"

"The finest in Shanghai. All trying to get away with some rich Nazi or facist."

"Smart. I'm getting out too," Juzo said, his grin replaced by a somber expression. "Soon as I've finished a little business. I'd already be gone if I hadn't lost all my money at Salat's roulette tables the last time I was in Shanghai."

"You shouldn't gamble."

"Sometimes I win. Besides, what I have in mind isn't a gamble. It's a sure thing."

"I wouldn't count on it," Dallin replied, his voice taking on a hard edge.

"We're wasting time." Juzo shrugged. "You have a permit for the cargo in your holds?"

"You know I haven't."

"That's too bad. For you."

"I've got something better than a permit. And you know it," Dallin warned, feeling the presence of the Nambu sub-machine gun at his back.

"If you mean Colonel Hata," Juzo spat again, this time not bothering to miss the Korean's brown feet, "he's important all right, but in Shanghai, not north of Nanking."

"Hata won't like my being robbed."

"He won't even know about it," Juzo replied, shouting orders.

Two Marines swept forward. A hulking brute, cradling his submachine gun in one elbow, tore the Bolo Mauser from Dallin's shoulder-holster. The second Marine, missing one ear, ran his calloused hands over the Korean, removing a dagger taped low against his back.

"Dirty Korean assassin!" Juzo hissed. "Only people I know worse than Caucasians."

Unruffled by these insults, the Korean ducked his head stupidly about, then dove across the deck, his lunge for Juzo's throat falling short as the two Marines sent him crashing back up against the bulwark wall. Letting his muscular arms drop to his sides, Juzo swaggered over to the Korean, halting just inches away.

"Cowards, all of you!" he hissed. "Back-stabbing, grenade-throwing Korean dogs! You shot Baron Saito, blew off the leg of Foreign Minister Shigemitsu, and nearly blinded Admiral Nomura in Shanghai. All because you want to be independent. You can all go to hell!"

Juzo kneed him savagely in the groin. Moaning, the Korean doubled over with the pain. Juzo lifted the Korean's sagging chin, then smiling, brought his fist crashing down on his skull.

"Easier in the old days," Juzo grunted, turning to Dallin. "Now you fight harder for less because the clever ones like your friend Hata have stolen everything not nailed down while fools like me in the field ended up with nothing. Well, that's all over, I tell you."

"It's not too late," Dallin said cautiously. "We can still come to some beneficial arrangement."

"Does this arrangement of yours offer me more than I can get by taking your cargo?"

"Steal and you'll be hunted. My way you get something, which is a lot better than nothing, and nobody will be after you."

"It wouldn't be enough," Juzo insisted angrily. "I need money. Big money. Before China goes down in ruin."

"Don't be a fool. You'll never reach Japan alive. Hata won't let you. The Kempetai won't let you."

"Are you threatening me? A goddamn White Russian collaborator telling me, a full colonel in the Imperial Marines, what I can do?" Clearing his holster in one fluid motion, Juzo swung the narrow barrel of an 8-mm. semiautomatic pistol, closely ressembling a German Luger, against Dallin's jaw.

"Still think you can tell me what I can do?"

"I'm trying not to think about you at all," Dallin replied evenly, his lustrous brown eyes staring off into space.

Chortling, Juzo slid his right thumb slowly back over the steel-gray semiautomatic until the hammer was fully cocked.

"Beg me, Dallin?"

"Drop dead."

Juzo smirked and squeezed the trigger. The hammer struck an empty chamber with a resounding click.

Not surprised, Dallin struggled to keep his eyes averted from the pistol still inches from his jaw.

"I ought to kill you, Dallin. I really want to, you know."

"You still might. You haven't left China yet."

"Trouble is, I need you to get out."

"That's life, my friend."

"You're goddamn right, you arrogant White Russian bastard," Juzo snapped, lowering his weapon.

Not long after, Dallin and the Korean found themselves between decks locked inside an unused machine parts locker just above the boiler. They squatted facing one another, with their backs against the wall. Coarse hemp linked their ankles together and bound their wrists separately behind their backs. There was no ventilation; the air was stale and hot from the boilers below.

"Offer Juzo gold," the Korean said vehemently.

"Won't work. He needs something no one will know he has. Like our cargo. You heard him. Manchuria's rotten. The Kwantung Army's been stripped clean to defend Japan and the Pacific."

"We're done then."

"Maybe."

Falling silent, both men were deep in their own thoughts when they heard the *Ikado Maru*'s engines crank to a halt. They were thrown across the cabin and slammed up against each other. Suddenly the engines hummed again and the *Ikado Maru* went ahead at half speed with her rudder put over and her stern swinging wide as the steamer picked up speed, turning in a full circle and moving off in the opposite direction.

"Back north," the Korean said, feeling the bow of the steamer plowing against the swift-running current.

"Must be taking her to the Gorges," Dallin reckoned, listening to the throbbing of the *Ikado Maru*'s engines. "Easier to sink her there and move inland with the cargo."

"He'll get away with it."

"Maybe, we may get lucky yet."

Scowling, the Korean leaned his gaunt frame up against the cabin wall and shut his eyes. In seconds he was snoring. Dallin would have preferred joining him, but if he were to survive there was a lot to be done. Even so, the idea that in another twenty-four hours the *Ikado Maru* should have docked in Shanghai and been under the protection of his partner Hata didn't make the situation any easier.

Returning to Shanghai was always the best part of any run. There was the unloading of the cargo, a short visit to Bridge House to pay his respects to Hata, then time to rest in his luxurious suite at the Cathay Hotel, the sweetest moment of all. A hot bath, a shave, a change of clothes followed by a good meal and several hours of sex at the Pleasure Palace, and Dallin would be ready for all comers. And come they would! Every war profiteer and black-market operator, Chinese and European alike, all with a hot offer and an attractive proposition to get rich off the new cargo.

Instead, Juzo had appeared and now things were turned around. Worse, the cargo was up for grabs and his own fate could go either way. Dallin mulled over all this. Some hours after, when he judged it was dark, he kicked the snoring Korean awake.

"Reach down with your teeth and pull the blade out of the heel of my boot."

They took turns. First the Korean held the finely honed Swedish blade between his teeth and sawed through the ropes binding their ankles. Then Dallin turned around and, holding the blade with two fingers, slit the rope securing the Korean's wrists. A moment later, the Korean performed the same service for him.

His hands and feet freed, Dallin used the blade to pick the locker door. Then, pressing his ear up against it, he remained still for a while until he was satisfied there was no one guarding the passageway. Still taking no chances, Dallin slid the door open a crack and peered out. Directly ahead, the narrow passageway was deserted. Off to his right, there was also no sign of life, not even from the companion ladder that led down to the boiler room. But off to the left, six feet away, at the bottom of the companionway leading up to the main deck, a burly Imperial Marine was sleeping with a rifle across his heavy thighs.

Motioning for the Korean to stay put, Dallin gripped the Swedish blade tightly between the thumb and forefinger of his right hand and stepped out of the locker. In a fair fight, Dallin knew that the Marine, who was trained in the arts of self-defense, would have the edge, but Dallin had no intention of being fair. He intended to kill quickly and survive. That much decided, he made his way through the passageway, his left shoulder brushing the wall; a foot from the companionway the Marine began coughing. Awakened by the vibration of his own body, the Japanese shifted position on the stairs, then rubbed his broad nostrils with both hands.

In the same moment, Dallin tore the rifle away and plunged his blade deep into the startled Marine's chest. In shock from the blow, the Marine fell back against the companionway and groped wildly at the two inches of Swedish steel penetrating his chest just above the heart. Anxious to

end it, Dallin rammed the Marine in the face with the
wooden stock of the rifle. There was a sickening sound of
splattering cartilage, then a faint moan as the Marine sank
down against the steps. Dallin was forced to turn away, repelled by what he had just done.

Then there was a grunt, followed by a blur of motion, and
the Marine was upon him, spinning Dallin sideways and
loosening his grip on the rifle, which went skidding across the
deck. His bloodied face contorted by rage and determination,
the Marine pushed Dallin aside and went for the rifle.

Dallin caught him and clubbed him hard on the side of the
jaw with his fist. The blow sent the Marine into the wall and
down on the deck. This time he stayed there. Dallin used his
boot to make certain. Then he bent over and yanked his
blade out of the dead Japanese. Wiping it clean on the dead
man's trousers, Dallin looked up to find the Korean beside
him.

"Check the fore hatch," Dallin ordered, tossing him the
rifle. "Then meet me on the bridge."

Nodding, the Korean balanced the long-barreled rifle
lightly in his hands and started up the companionway, leaving
Dallin alone to drag the burly dead Marine into the locker.

Moments later, grasping the Marine's dagger in his right
hand, Dallin climbed out of the companionway onto the
main deck of the *Ikado Maru*. The steamer was moving at
full speed without her running lights. Over the bow it was
pitch-black, no visibility at all. Off the starboard and port, oil
lamps flickered on the distant banks.

A gust of wind swept up from the Yangtze, bringing with
it a thick spray of water that soaked his face and clothes.
Dallin was grateful for the change after being locked below
deck since early afternoon. The sound of a human voice filtered out of the night. Then another voice rose in reply.
Judging by the direction the voices were coming from, Dallin
guessed they were sentries or lookouts posted at the bow.

Turning toward the stern, Dallin groped about for the ladder attached to the deck housing. Finally his fingers wrapped
around a clammy iron rung, and springing upward, he began
to climb toward the bridge. Once topside, Dallin crouched
low and made his way across the slippery deck. He halted
a few feet from the rectangular-shaped wheelhouse. One of
Juzo's men was at the helm, silhouetted against the wrap-
around window.

Finding the helmsman alone was a good break. Now the question was whether to deal with him or wait for the Korean to arrive. Dallin preferred waiting. There was more chance of success, less chance of an alarm being sounded. On the other hand, Dallin reasoned, if he waited too long someone else might come along.

The sharp clang of metal made Dallin forget his decision. Someone was scaling the deck ladder portside. It was too loud for the Korean. Besides he wore sandals, Dallin remembered, ducking just in time to avoid a hulking figure that moved past into the wheelhouse.

Dallin clung tightly to the railing, the swift-running Yangtze at his back. Inside the wheelhouse he could hear the two men talking. Then one of them struck a match. A brief glimmer of light illuminated Juzo's face. The renegade Marine wore an olive-green sweater and a battered campaign cap, its narrow visor pulled low over his roguish face.

Dallin cursed his fate. The odds had changed considerably now, his chances of retaking the *Ikado Maru* fading appreciably. Angered, Dallin heard the clamor of static, then a torrent of unintelligible words coming from the wireless shack ahead. He saw the Korean crawl past.

"Over here," he whispered, grabbing his bony shoulder.

"I almost ran into Juzo," the Korean hissed back frantically.

"He's in the wheelhouse. What's it like below?"

"No good. Full squad of Marines at the hatch. More on deck. Get slaughtered trying to get our men out. Besides you've seen what they're like."

"I know," Dallin said. "No damn good against Imperial Marines." The situation confronting Dallin was getting more lopsided by the moment. He mulled over the few options left him.

"We'll deal with Juzo, then swim for it."

"Leave now, I say. I want Juzo more than you, but why risk it?"

His question was a logical one, except for the fact that Dallin, not the Korean, was partners with Hata.

"Just do what I tell you," Dallin said firmly. "Go around to the port side. When I make my move, take out the helmsman."

The Korean hesitated. Then, muttering something that went unheard by Dallin, he moved off into the night. Dallin waited another thirty seconds, then edged his way carefully along the railing until he was opposite the open doorway of the wheelhouse, where Juzo stood with a cigarette dangling from his mouth. The helmsman was beside him, holding the tiller and staring ahead at the dark Yangtze.

Dallin gave them time. He would have preferred not doing this, but as long as Juzo lived, he would be a problem to Hata, which hardly served Dallin's own interests.

"Juzo?" Dallin called out softly, padding silently through the doorway of the wheelhouse.

Bewildered, Juzo turned as Dallin swung his dagger upward, then over, slashing the corded throat of the renegade Marine colonel. His bandy legs buckling, Juzo fell against the chart shelf. Blood poured from his severed jugular vein in thick spurts. Shrieking, he fought to stay on his feet, clinging desperately to the oak shelf made slippery by his blood.

Nearby, the wiry Japanese helmsman, cowed at first by the suddenness of the attack, reached for the general alarm button overhead. Overtaking him, the Korean swung the rifle up at the ceiling, mashing the helmsman's fingers just inches from the button. Cracking him in the head with the rifle barrel, the Korean herded the whimpering helmsman out of the wheelhouse.

Meanwhile Dallin was busily engaged in keeping the *Ikado Maru* on course. At the helm, he could hear Juzo, behind him, slowly choking to death.

Juzo stared glassy-eyed at Dallin. "White Russian bastard," he grunted, blood dripping from his thick lips. Then his hands slid slowly off the edge of the oak board and he sank down onto his haunches, dead.

The Korean reappeared in the doorway. "Nice work." He grinned.

"He's dead; that's what counts," Dallin said stony-faced. "Now, leave the rifle and get going. We'll meet in Shanghai."

"What about you?"

"I have things to do. Get moving!"

The Korean propped the rifle up against the wall, and a moment later, there was a faint splash off the starboard and Dallin was alone again.

Inching the tiller gradually toward starboard, Dallin put the *Ikado Maru* on a diagonal course for the north bank of the Yangtze. Her bow pitched heavily as she cut across the powerful cross-current. The deck rolled beneath Dallin's feet.

Gripping the tiller tightly, he held her steady. The *Ikado Maru* stayed on course, bearing in for shore.

The seconds ticked by slowly. Dallin's forehead was beaded with sweat. Every instinct told him to abandon the tiller and take to the river, but he held his ground until the flickering oil lamps that dotted the north bank, faint only a short time before, were brighter. Breathing easier, Dallin shifted the lever on the engine telegraph dial to STOP, and a moment later the *Ikado Maru* creaked to a halt.

Jabbing the general alarm button overhead, Dallin ducked out of the wheelhouse, ignored the clanging bell, and, hoisting himself onto the starboard railing, sucked in as much of the night air as he could and dove clear of the drifting *Ikado Maru* into the muddy waters of the Yangtze.

Chapter Eleven

————◆◆◆————

At the far end of a busy shop-lined street in the heart of Nantao lies the popular Willow Pattern Tea House. Flanked by several ancient temples and guildhouses, the Willow Pattern, with its ornate wooden facade and painted curved roofs, stands on massive stone pillars amid an immense pool of water and is reached by four zigzag footbridges.

It was nearing noon when Dominique left the black Cadillac limousine at the north gate of the native quarter and, braving the searing sun, made her way on foot along Rue Montauban. She wore a loose red Egyptian cotton dress with an open collar, and her long blond hair was pulled neatly back into a tight bun. Turning off Rue Montauban, Dominique walked through a maze of narrow crowded streets past tiny shops offering silks, pewter, ivory, and brass. She skirted the hordes of jugglers, bird vendors, magicians, and other tradesmen hawking services and wares at the edge of the pool and crossed one of the wooden bridges that led into the tea house.

Since Salat's call late the night before, telling her of Pockmark Shen's refusal to help her father, Dominique had felt alone and vulnerable. Not even the Corsican's assurances that Gustav Torg would be freed could alleviate her anxiety. She was shocked that the Nationalists in Chungking had refused to trade with the Kempetai for her father's freedom. Their

104

firm rejection dashed all her hopes and had thrown her into total confusion.

Did it mean Gustav Torg was not an Allied spy? Or was this the Nationalists' way of keeping her father from exposing their own illicit ties with the Japanese? Most frightening of all was her suspicion that her father was merely an innocent victim of the Japanese Secret Military Police, someone with no connection whatsoever to the Nationalists but nonetheless destined for death simply because of a whim on the part of Colonel Hata.

From a table on the second floor of the tea house, Dominique watched as two emaciated jugglers beside the pool below deftly flipped porcelain plates high into the air, then caught them on the tip of their noses. At the finish of their performance the patrons of the café broke into polite applause and threw coins to show their approval.

Dominique lifted the glazed pot decorated with figures of Mandarin functionaries and poured herself another cup of oolong tea. Inhaling the perfumed fragrance, she surveyed the people seated around her. It was a typical Shanghai tea house patronized by Chinese; there were students, merchants, minor government officials, and several clusters of very old men with wispy white beards and black skullcaps, who seemed to delight in eating watermelon seeds and making sucking sounds over their teacups.

Growing restless, Dominique glanced at her watch. She had found herself doing this often lately, desperately aware of each minute of every hour that her father's situation remained unaltered.

Finally the sound of a powerful engine echoed down the street and Dominique peered out. A pair of Kempei motorcyclists were followed by a white Chrysler limousine with an open driver's compartment; the car swerved to a halt a few feet short of the zigzag bridge. Her heart pounding, Dominique watched as the chauffeur, a Kempei soldier in uniform, leaped from the Chrysler and, shoving aside a few pitiful beggars, opened the rear door. Niki Orlov stepped out. Her black hair shone brilliantly in the strong sunlight. Unlike Dominique she wore the latest Parisian fashions—a tailored silk skirt with pleats and long-sleeved blouse from the House of Chanel.

As she followed her chauffeur into the Willow Pattern, Niki marveled at how quickly her mood changed from bleak despair to passionate anticipation. No one, she realized, not Hata, not even her father, could have prevented this rendezvous. Her desire for Dominique Torg, which had lain dormant for years, had surfaced at last. Niki mounted the broad staircase to the upper floor of the tea house and joined Dominique at the small round table in the corner.

"Sorry I'm late." She smiled, moving her manicured fingers seductively along the edge of the table. "But with all of these fortifications the Japanese are building, traffic is just awful."

"I'm sorry too," Dominique replied softly. "I didn't mean to hurt your feelings the other night."

The apology pleased Niki. She could not take her eyes off Dominique. Her blond hair shimmered like fine-spun gold, a halo around her high cheekbones, straight nose, and hazel eyes. With no makeup other than a faint touch of tawny red lipstick, Dominique's face had the pristine beauty of a Grecian statue. All that she needed was a robe, Niki thought, one she could lift slowly over her naked thighs and drape loosely around her slim hips.

"Can we talk about my father?" Dominique asked, upset by Niki's intense scrutiny.

"I expected we would. Only I'm not sure I can be of any help."

"Speak to Hata for me. He'll listen to you."

"He isn't so easy to talk with."

"But you've always known how to handle men. Even at school we used to rely on you for advice."

It was true. Niki had always been ahead of the other girls in her class. She had reached sexual maturity early and it had fallen to her to explain the peculiarities of the male body to all her friends at the McTyeire Girls School, a task she had performed with relish.

"My father's life depends on it, Niki," Dominique pleaded. "I know we haven't seen much of each other since the war . . ."

"Whose fault is that?"

"Mine, I know."

"I phoned your house every week for months. Not once did you call back. Not once. And now you want me to help you. You should ask the very man you condemn me for loving."

"It's true I'm a hypocrite," Dominique admitted lamely.

"What you're saying is right. But I can't take it now, Niki. Not now. Please."

Dominique leaned across the table, her eyes imploring Niki. She buried her face in her hands, struggling to keep back the tears. This was not going at all the way she had hoped it would. She had vowed to somehow undo all the years when Niki was the group leader and Dominique one of her followers, but old habits die hard.

"Let's go back to my place. It'll be a lot more comfortable for us to talk there," Niki said, stroking the soft skin of Dominique's slender wrist.

"Niki . . . I . . ."

"Do you want my help or not?" Niki interposed sharply. "You saw how Hata feels. And you certainly didn't help matters the other night at the Tower by acting so superior."

"I wasn't being superior. I lost my temper. You know how I am when I get angry."

"Yes. But this isn't high school anymore. The Kempetai kill people! Now, are you coming or not?"

Nodding half-heartedly, Dominique watched as Niki dropped a few Shanghai dollars on the table. Then, rising together, they made their way out of the tea house and across the wooden bridge to the white Chrysler and its motorcycle escort.

Now she really had made a mess of it, Dominique decided, nearing the limousine. Once inside there would be no turning back; no escaping Niki's insatiable sexual appetite. Those manicured hands would fondle her naked breasts and explore her silky thighs. Dominique might prevail on Niki to stop for old times sake. She might even make her angry enough to temporarily lose her desire. But in the end Niki would have her way. Over and over again, Dominique repeated to herself that this was not really happening to her; that it was just a fantasy.

A few feet from the Chrysler, Dominique slowed her pace, letting Niki get ahead of her. "I'm not going, Niki. I've changed my mind." And before her words could register on Niki, Dominique hurried down one of the side streets.

Hearing the sharp click of Niki's high heels on the cobblestones behind her, Dominique darted around the corner into Jade Street. There were a dozen streets of this kind in the Chinese quarter, resembling narrow alleyways more than actual streets. Most had enclosed passages overhead and were lined by tiny shops, dealing in jade, ivory, brass, or silk.

It was lunchtime. Except for an elderly woman in a long black gown seated outside her shop, the alleyway was deserted. Dominique looked around frantically for another way to escape, then, giving up, hurried toward her. The woman, in her seventies, with gray hairs sprouting from her chin, was cooling herself with a paper fan. Her feet, peeping from the hem of her gown, were misshapen mounds of flesh, not more than four inches long and wrapped in black gauze.

Dominique greeted her politely, then glancing sideways to make sure Niki wasn't in sight, she slipped into the shop. It was tiny and lined with shelves of jade objects, ranging in color from translucent white to dark grass-green.

On the lowest shelf, nearest to Dominique, were earrings, bracelets, pendants, and hairpins. The next featured figurines of Buddhas, elephants, tigers, and Chinese horses. On the two uppermost shelves rested the most expensive pieces—graceful Ming Dynasty vases of the highly sought-after greenish-white jade.

Pretending an interest in the display, Dominique kept away from the doorway, until she finally saw Niki go past, followed by the Kempei chauffeur. By then the elderly shopkeeper had come inside and was standing behind her. Doing her best to control her nerves, Dominique decided it was safer to remain a bit longer. She pointed at the pink Buddha of happiness in the corner of the second shelf and said she wished to buy it. A few moments later, certain Niki was gone, Dominique left the shop holding the pink figurine of a seated Buddha and started hurriedly along the sun-splashed street.

"Something you need badly?" Niki asked, stepping from a doorway just ahead, taking Dominique by surprise.

"Actually I did always want one," Dominique mumbled, unable to look Niki in the eye.

"The Buddha of happiness," murmured Niki, stroking the jade figurine's smooth rounded belly with her long fingernails. "I wonder is anyone really happy for very long?"

"You sound depressed."

"If I am, it's your fault."

"I'm sorry," Dominique blurted, "I really am. But imagine how I feel with my father in Bridge House."

"We could still go to my place. Talk things over. You

know I want to help," Niki insisted, letting her hand slide gently against Dominique's breast.

"Not today, okay? I just don't feel like being cooped up. Too nervous I guess." Clearly it was not okay. That much Dominique could gather from the look of disappointment on Niki's face, as she turned toward the Kempei chauffeur who was a few yards away.

"Well, there isn't much to do around here." Niki frowned as she gazed at the deserted street.

"How about a walk?" Dominique suggested hopefully. "We can share your parasol."

Shrugging, Niki opened the parasol and held it so it shielded both of them from the sun; arm in arm, they strolled down Jade Street.

"It's so terribly humid. How do we stand it?" Dominique said, aware of the heat of the cobblestones beneath her feet.

"Shanghai summers are always dreadful."

"Remember how before the war no one would be caught dead in the city during July and August."

"My father always took me to the mountains."

"I remember your house. It was lovely, with the swimming dock in the center of the lake."

"You were the lucky one," Niki said, staring directly at Dominique. "Every year going on those grand tours of Europe. Visiting Rome, Florence, Paris. You never knew how much I envied you. God, how I wanted to get away from China in those days."

"You always said how much you hated to travel. Hated to leave your home."

"I hated to leave it for good. But a grand tour . . . Those fabulous hotels. Marvelous restaurants. Sidewalk cafés. It seemed so glamorous, like it must have been heaven."

"I never knew that's how you felt," Dominique said, suddenly worried by the ubiquitous Kempei chauffeur at their heels. "Does he always follow you?"

"Always." Niki frowned. "Colonel Hata's afraid someone may try to kidnap or assassinate me."

"Has anyone tried?"

"No. Thank God!"

"He's been very good to you. Hata, I mean."

"Very. Especially since my father took ill——"

"I hadn't heard," Dominique interrupted. "Is it serious?"

"He's dying," Niki whispered, coming to a halt. "Another month, maybe a few weeks. He can't last much longer."

"It doesn't seem possible."

"I know. Just a few years ago we were little kids. Care-free rich little kids. Then the war came. And now my father's dying of cancer."

"And mine's in Bridge House," Dominique added, her eyes taking on a haunted look.

"Do you remember the Old Dragon Wall?" Niki asked suddenly.

"Sure. The one in Mandarin Gardens where we played after school. Why?"

"Come on! I'll show you!"

Taking Dominique by the wrist, Niki dragged her around the corner into a lane that connected Jade Street with the next trade street.

"What's so important about the Old Dragon Wall?" Dominique gasped, taken by surprise.

"Only this!" Niki replied, leading her into a narrow opening between a parked truck and the oval gate wall of an ancient guildhouse. "All I've thought of is doing this . . . of being alone with you."

Before Dominique could say or do anything, Niki was kissing her lips; caressing her hair, and pressing her breasts against Dominique's, moving closer until their thighs were touching.

"I've dreamt of this a thousand times," Niki whispered, pinning Dominique to the wall, the heat of her thighs burning through her skirt.

"Don't, Niki. Please." They could hear the footsteps of the Kempei chauffeur as he ran past, looking for them.

"Stay with me, Dominique. I'll do anything you want. Anything. But please don't leave me." Niki's eyes were glazed, her mouth moist and hungry.

"I must go, Niki."

"Stay just another minute."

Dominique was eager to leave, but she needed Niki's help.

"If I do, you'll speak to Hata?"

"I swear."

"Today?"

"Yes. Only don't go. Not yet. Promise you'll stay at least until I—"

Niki broke off in mid-sentence, unable to go on. Instead,

her lips curled in a strange smile, and she reached over, touching Dominique's face. Then she ran her slender fingers slowly down to Dominique's breasts, cupping them gently in the palms of her hands. "I want you," she murmured. "I want you so very much."

"Niki?" Dominique shuddered.

"What?"

"No more. Okay?"

"But I want more. Much more," Niki insisted, shutting her eyes and forcing Dominique's hands down between her legs.

"Niki?"

"I need you . . . please."

"First speak to Hata about my father," Dominique heard herself whisper. "Then talk to me about your needs."

Not bothering to wait for a reply, Dominique pulled free and headed back to the street, arriving just as the Kempei chauffeur came running in her direction.

Chapter Twelve

<hr/>

The taste of raw tuna still in his mouth, Lieutenant Sumato moved wearily along the eighth-floor corridor of Bridge House, past a series of glossy black-and-white photographs of American battleships and heavy cruisers sunk at Pearl Harbor, defeated enemy troops being paraded through the streets of Manila, General Percival surrendering to Yamashita at Singapore, and half-naked British troops laboring under the torrid sun in Malaysia.

But Sumato was unware of them as he concentrated on the double column of names on the sheet of rice paper he was holding, names of the Chinese and Occidentals slated for execution in the next few hours.

As he glanced over the list, Sumato rued the day he was drafted into the Kempetai. Not that he did not wish to serve his Emperor. If anything, his problem came from wanting to serve him too well, but the crimes committed by the Kempetai against the native and foreign populace of Shanghai had upset him badly. Sumato had sailed from Tokyo with the sacred mission of bringing the New Order to China. He had been willing to cast aside the past, forget his years as a student in the intellectually enlightened community of Nagasaki and the subsequent period, during which he had taught history. He had dedicated himself to the Emperor

Hirohito. But in so doing, he found himself involved in harassment, torture, even murder. Was this his noble purpose in coming to China? Sumato was appalled by his fellow Japanese. How could they act as they did? How could they so easily put aside the values of social interaction, imbued in them from birth and practiced in Japan, to rape and plunder and kill? In the end, Sumato thought, they would leave behind a trail of blood so thick that, given centuries, the memory would not be erased. His conscience was plagued by his own role in this war.

The words of the Potsdam Declaration rang in his ears: "stern justice shall be meted out to all war criminals, including those who have visited cruelties upon our prisoners," calling up vivid images of Americans, Englishmen, Dutchmen, and Australians, reduced to walking corpses, being herded into the courtyard, then shoved against a wall before a firing squad or forced to their knees to meet the swordsman's razor-sharp blade.

Nearing the end of the long corridor, Sumato grunted in response to a greeting from two of his subordinates, then rapped on the door to Hata's office and, without waiting for a reply, entered. The sound of an American swing band on the radio across the room greeted him. Glancing to his left, Sumato saw Hata was not at his desk but was seated on a tatami mat in the small chamber beyond the open sliding panel. Wearing a black kimono with a silver dragon painted on the back, Hata knelt before the photograph of Yasukuni Shrine, sniffing cocaine from a small spoon. The irony did not escape Sumato.

"Yes? What is it?" Hata finally asked, his lean face unusually animated.

"The execution list is ready for your signature. And the radio room reports losing contact with the *Ikado Maru*. She hasn't answered signals for the past few hours."

"Have you tried the emergency code?" Hata asked, placing the tiny spoon carefully into the silver box holding cocaine and initialing the paper nonchalantly with Sumato's pen.

"None of our signals draw a reply," Sumato said. "According to the Yangtze River patrol, the *Ikado Maru* hasn't been heard from or sighted since she steamed north of Nanking three days ago."

On hearing this, Hata rose from the tatami mat and

walked quickly to his desk. He lifted the telephone receiver and ordered the Bridge House operator to connect him with the Kempetai commandant in Nanking. Replacing the instrument, he turned to Sumato.

"Any change with the Norwegian?"

"Nothing yet. He refuses to discuss the ring."

"Not the ring. It's the black book, Felix Hacker's report, that I want. How many times must I tell you that!"

"According to our men he's said nothing about that so far either. In fact, he won't say anything, and if he's abused any further I doubt if he'll even be able to."

"Put him back in his cell for a day. But no more than that." Hata scowled, reminded of other prisoners in the past as stubborn as Gustav Torg. Most of them had talked eventually, but it had taken time and by then what they had to say was not worth listening to.

"I received a report about Herr Becker," Sumato's voice interrupted his thoughts.

"What about Herr Becker?"

"According to one of our Ronin, he was seen last night entering the offices of the Iberian Navigation Company on the Bund. He stayed half an hour, then left in the company of Senor Rossio."

"The Portuguese?" Hata said, surprised, thinking how clever the Nazi was to charter a neutral ship for the run to South America. "Very good. See our man's rewarded. And add Senor Rossio to our surveillance list. I want them both watched around the clock. Anything else?"

"Yes." Sumato hesitated. "I'm afraid there's also a report about Mademoiselle Orlov."

"What about her?"

"She was observed meeting Dominique Torg at the Willow Pattern Tea House."

"When was this?"

"Earlier today. They met at the tea house, then strolled through the Chinese quarter together."

"Nothing more? They didn't go off anywhere?"

"No. Not according to the chauffeur's report . . . but . . ."

"Well, what is it?"

"He lost sight of them for a few minutes. When he finally located Mademoiselle Orlov, she was in an alley alone. In a rather delicate state."

Angered, Hata wondered what made Niki do these things.

She knew how upset it made him. Hata studied Sumato's haggard face, hoping for an explanation, which he knew would not be forthcoming, then turned away. He was brooding about his involvement with the White Russian woman.

Suddenly it occurred to him that there was a way to solve two nagging problems with one action. "Arrest her," he ordered sharply.

"Who?" Sumato asked in confusion.

"Dominique Torg."

"But . . . she's done nothing wrong."

"Arrest her anyway," Hata insisted, dismissing his adjutant with a slight wave of his hand. Pleased with his decision, Hata returned to the tatami mat. He reached for the tiny spoon and, bringing the cocaine up to his nostrils, gradually forgot Niki and the disappearance of the *Ikado Maru* and his partner, Maximov Dallin.

Five floors below, the Norwegian inched away from the door of the chain metal cage and tenderly propped his mangled back up against the wall. The position was not ideal for his lacerated body but at least he was alone.

There was a sadistic logic to the methods the Kempetai used to destroy a prisoner's morale and self-confidence. Upon his arrival at Bridge House, the Norwegian's clothes had been taken away and he had been issued a ragged pair of cotton pajamas, the same pair, torn and bloody, that he was now wearing. Then he was thrown into a dark, foul-smelling cage not much larger than the one he now occupied; it held twenty other prisoners—men and women of all ages whose neglected bodies were covered with lice and bruises. They were forced to squat on their haunches for hours on end and were forbidden to talk to one another.

His first moments in that cage had made Gustav Torg violently ill. The powerful stench of unwashed bodies, of festering sores and human excrement, took away his breath and turned his stomach. At first he thought he had been thrown in a cage of madmen.

Now, at least, he was alone. He was uncertain just how much more punishment his aged body could take. It seemed clear that his stubborn resistance had only provoked his captors to embroider on their brutal craft.

During his first session, the Norwegian swore he would not scream or cry out, but after biting through his tongue several times, he realized he could not hold out much longer. It shamed him to whimper like an abused animal, but in the end he decided all that counted was his denying Hata the information he so desperately sought.

So far he had not revealed anything of importance, but the abuse to his body was considerable. Both feet were three times their normal size and too raw to walk on or even touch. His toenails as well as his fingernails had been torn off, exposing the nail beds. Huge purplish bumps covered both knee caps, and several of his ribs were cracked—all the work of the same instrument, a heavy wooden board. His face, permanently windburned from his years at sea, was a swollen lump; simply opening his mouth caused him intense pain. He was glad he could not see himself, he decided; the sight would undoubtedly make him lose courage.

There had already been several suicides during the Norwegian's stay at Bridge House. Given the frailty of the human spirit, it was not surprising. It was the only way a prisoner had of saving himself from his torturers.

But Gustav Torg would not permit himself such an escape. His religious convictions would not permit him to take his own life. There would be no avoiding what lay in store for him. All Torg could hope for was a quick end and that the information Hata wanted never passed his lips.

As a trickle of blood seeped down from an open wound on the top of his head, Gustav Torg recalled how it had all begun.

During Christmas of 1942, a coded message had arrived at his office from the Norwegian government in exile in London, ordering him to organize a spy network against the Japanese. Despite an initial reluctance, the enterprising Norwegian set about the task with the same diligence that marked everything he did.

His first contact was Felix Hacker, not that he had expected the gentle librarian to become an Allied spy, but Torg wanted to utilize Hacker's easy access to a large group of people so that he could move about Occupied Shanghai without attracting the suspicions of the Kempetai.

Torg and Hacker had innumerable discussions, trying to locate men they felt were capable and willing to spy against the Japanese. Their first recruit was a diehard German socialist, a master airplane mechanic. His real name was Anton Knoll, but he had assumed the identity of one Karl Busch upon his arrival in Canton in 1939, swapping everything he owned for the dead man's papers. It was that or be detected by local Gestapo officials and sent back to the Third Reich where he was a wanted man.

Anton Knoll had fought against Franco during the Spanish Civil War, serving under André Malraux in the International Squadron. Following the defeat of the Republic, he chose to live in the Orient rather than seek refuge across the border in France. It had proved a wise decision, since most of Anton Knoll's fellow volunteers, fugitives like himself from fascist regimes, were imprisoned by the French, then starved in concentration camps, and finally turned over to their native governments on France's surrender.

Anton Knoll had purchased the identity papers of Karl Busch the day he arrived in Canton, and before another twenty-four hours had passed, Knoll, now known as Karl Busch, was en route to Shanghai for a new career as a technical advisor to the Japanese, hired to service two dozen tri-engine Junker 52's recently purchased from the Nazis.

The second agent Torg and Hacker recruited was Chung Lee, a sixty-year-old Chinese railway official at Shanghai's North Station. An incorruptible Mandarin from a prominent family, Chung had seemed a likely candidate to the Norwegian, for his wife and three sons were among the tens of thousands murdered by the Japanese in the sacking of Nanking. Chung Lee would never forget nor forgive. At the time Chung Lee agreed to work for the Allies, Japanese troops were disembarking in great numbers at Shanghai harbor and then being sent by rail to bases throughout northern China. Information provided by the diligent Chung Lee ultimately enabled the American Fourteenth Air Force to carry out bombing missions which had a disastrous effect upon the Japanese land forces.

The third person approached was a retired Danish sea captain, Peter Hansen. An old friend of Gustav Torg's, he leaped at the chance to sabotage Japanese shipping. To the crusty old Dane, battling one Axis partner eased some of the frustration he felt at the Nazi occupation of his beloved Denmark. Perched high in an abandoned warehouse on the edge of Woosung, at the mouth of the Yangtze, Hansen kept a close watch on the vessels steaming in and out of the port of Shanghai. His accurate reports were used by the American

Sixth Fleet to sink enemy troopships and sorely needed outgoing supply convoys.

The procedure Felix Hacker established to receive information from these agents was deceptively simple. For that reason, it met with Gustav Torg's speedy approval. Once a week,
during regular business hours, each agent would visit the Municipal Council Library, ostensibly to borrow or return books.
In actuality the books they returned contained data destined
for Felix Hacker. Whenever one of them had something urgent to pass on he would telephone ahead, requesting a certain title. The Swiss librarian would reply by saying the book
in question was not listed in the card catalogue; he would
then meet the caller by "accident" that same evening at a
prearranged spot. For Busch it was a German beer garden
near the Kaiser Wilhem Institute, the Nazi propaganda center
in Shanghai. Chung Lee was assigned a popular Nantao
restaurant, well known for its northern Chinese cuisine and
mixed clientele. The place selected for Peter Hansen was a
busy waterfront café owned by a Swedish sea captain's
widow, a gigantic woman with a booming voice and risqué
sense of humor who regarded the Japanese as beastly little
gnats, though never to their face.

Not one of these three agents had any inkling of the other
two, of the role Gustav Torg played, or how their information was transmitted to Chungking. From the outset, the
genial Swiss, humming Mozart and eating chocolates at every
meeting, would cheerfully insist on absolute security. Unnecessary knowledge, he stressed, especially as to one other's
identity, only increased the danger for all of them.

Remembering this, and how determined Felix Hacker had
been to avoid detection by the Kempetai, the Norwegian
grieved at the despair he must have felt at being forced to
disclose their names.

Somehow, despite the gravity of his own situation, Torg
could not find it in his heart to condemn his old friend.

The Dome Café resembled its famous Left Bank namesake
in more than just decor. Situated at the intersection of Thibet
and Bubbling Well roads, it attracted a colorful mixture of
Europeans, many of them in their early twenties, who regarded themselves as budding intellectuals, poets, writers, and
painters. They gathered there daily; seated on cane chairs at
brass-rimmed tables amid film posters of Renoir's *La Grande*

Illusion and *La Règle du Jeu,* of Chaplin's *Gold Rush* and *Modern Times,* they would argue away the hours till curfew, frequently clashing over the merits of the upcoming trials of Laval and Pétain in France, the shocking defeat of Winston Churchill and the unexpected triumph of the Labour Party in Britain's general elections, and the sudden hard-line policy of the Soviets and their lingering presence in eastern Europe.

Yet the moment Dominique arrived at the Dome for a late afternoon coffee all conversation ceased and an uneasy silence swept over the café. None of those seated, her long-time acquaintances and former classmates, invited her to join them, or did more than coolly acknowledge her presence. They sat stony-faced, hoping she would change her mind and leave. Dominique had witnessed this sort of behavior before; while their moral cowardice upset her, she was in no mood to tolerate it. Refusing to be cowed, she slipped into a nearby booth and ordered a café au lait. Then, as she waited, she clasped both hands firmly in her lap, considering her next move.

"You must not let them bother you," Salat murmured, sitting down opposite her. "They're afraid of the Kempetai." He looked very debonair in a light gray suit with wide lapels, a blue shirt, and navy blue tie. His black hair was combed straight back from his forehead, and it was only as he waved the waiter away that Dominique noticed the somber concern in his dark eyes.

"You aren't afraid," she said, leaning closer with both elbows resting on the table.

"That's only because I've had . . . how shall I put it . . . a peculiar personal history."

"At least you've never pretended to be something you're not. Not like these phony intellectuals and artists with all their pompous talk of liberty and political justice."

"Dominique!" Salat interrupted, touching her cheek with his hand. "How long have you been here?"

"Not very long. A few minutes."

"Good," Salat murmured, watching a middle-aged Eurasian, who was leaving the telephone booth by the service bar. "Where is the ladies room?"

"Do you need to use it?" Dominique laughed until she saw there was no gaiety in his face. "Behind us," she said, suddenly sober. "In the hallway."

"Is there a rear door out of here?"

"At the end of the hallway. Why?"

"Never mind why. Just do as I tell you. Act as if you're going to the ladies room, then slip out the rear. We'll meet on the corner. Now go."

"Salat? What's wrong? Has anything happened to my father?"

"Do as I say, Dominique," Salat insisted, keeping his eyes on the Eurasian two booths away. "We've already wasted too much time." Nodding her head, Dominique got up and made her way across the café and into the hallway.

Suddenly aware that Dominique was no longer in sight, the Eurasian put down his newspaper and hurried after her. As he moved past, Salat stretched out his leg and tripped him. Then, voicing apologies, he helped the Eurasian to his feet, and clipped him just above the right ear with the heavy handle of his 9mm Browning automatic.

Seconds later the Corsican was out the front door and rushing toward the corner where Dominique waited. At that moment, a green Buick sedan screeched to a halt and four Japanese in western dress charged across the pavement into the Dome Café.

"What's happened?" Dominique asked, alarmed.

"Hata's ordered your arrest," Salat replied, leading her quickly toward his silver Bugatti touring coupe, parked at the curb.

"Niki! She must have betrayed me."

"Hata doesn't need a reason. Now get in and let's get out of here!"

Before they could move, the Japanese came rushing out of the alleyway at their rear and opened fire with revolvers. Salat pulled Dominique down on the pavement, using the long narrow hood of the Bugatti for cover. The bullets fell wide, tearing into the concrete and blowing out the rear tires.

Suddenly a truck rattled past. Salat gave it time to block them from view, then, with Dominique in tow, bolted across the street into an alley. Boxed in by tall buildings and overflowing with garbage, some cans piled three deep, the alley ended at the rear door of a modern apartment building.

"Let's run for it!" Salat urged, starting into the maze of garbage cans.

They were just beyond the first pile when another flurry of gunshots rang out and bullets crashed into the metal cans, then went ricocheting about wildly. Diving down, Salat and

Dominique hid behind a barricade of cans. Pressed close together, her face was just inches from his; her long blond hair grazing his shoulder.

"Kempetai! You come out now!" a raspy voice cried arrogantly from the street.

"I can't involve you like this, Robert," Dominique whispered. "I'll do what they want."

"No, you will not!" Salat snapped, sliding the heavy Browning from his jacket.

"Kempetai! If you don't come out, we come in!" the raspy voice screamed again.

"Robert?" Dominique implored.

"Listen carefully. At the end of the alley behind those cans is an apartment building. Use the stairs and get onto the roof. From there go across to another one. The farther away the better. Then find someplace to hide. An apartment, a hotel room, whatever. Stay there until dark, then phone the club and ask for Caro. Someone will come to take you to safety."

"What about you? I can't just leave you here. Not like this."

"You can and you will. I'll buy us some time, then make my way out. And you better take this along."

He made a slight movement and a tiny nickel-plated Kolibri slid from his sleeve into the palm of his left hand.

"Up close it's good six times. Just point it and keep squeezing the trigger until whoever's bothering you stops. Now get going, and don't look back."

"I don't know what to—" Dominique stopped in midsentence and flung her arms tightly around Salat, hugging and kissing him. As more gunshots rang out, he pushed her on her way.

Watching the street, Salat inched back behind a double row of shoulder-high garbage cans, then made a small opening between them for the barrel of his automatic. He settled down to wait, knowing it would not be very long.

Sixty seconds later a wiry Japanese with eyeglasses dove into the alley and rolled to cover against the wall. Salat still waited, his finger wrapped loosely around the trigger of the Browning, as more gunshots ripped into his abandoned position. Then a second Japanese, this one with the strapping build of a wrestler, sprang into the alley beside the first and, exchanging a few words, started to advance with him.

Salat opened up, pumping two slugs apiece into each

Japanese and sending them screaming back against the garbage-strewn pavement. It was good work, but it gave Salat little comfort. A Kempei soldier wearing a brown saucer-shaped helmet ran past the mouth of the alley, and a minute later, a Nambu light machine gun raked the brick wall above Salat, showering his gray suit with thick red dust.

The odor of rancid cooking oil inside the apartment building, filled her nostrils as Dominique fumbled around in the dark until she finally located the stairway. She hesitated, wondering if she should wait for Salat, when a long burst of machine-gun fire followed by the booming sound of the Browning automatic sent her rushing upstairs.

Salat jammed a fresh magazine into the butt of the automatic. He had two more in his pockets. That made thirty-nine cartridges in all. Ordinarily that was enough for any hard action, but now, hearing the Kempei noncoms deploying their men around the opening of the alley, Salat wished he had brought two or three dozen and a grenade as well. Pointless to dwell on that, he decided, and swung the barrel of the Browning into the small opening between the cans. Sighting quickly, he fired. The shot brought down a Kempei private, who spun around and flopped over in a dead heap. It was a cheap victory as far as the Corsican was concerned. He longed for a head-on confrontation with the man responsible for all this—Colonel Hata.

A rumbling noise, growing steadily louder, shook the pavement. With a grinding crash of steel, an armored car smashed past two parked automobiles, climbed the curb, and slammed against the corners of the adjoining buildings. Its advance into the alleyway blocked by the width of its fenders, the turret of the armored car swiveled and a 40mm cannon poked its ugly snout at Salat.

The blast shook the walls, demolishing garbage cans and sending down a shower of deadly metal shards. Salat lay flat on the ground with both arms shielding his head. Even so, the explosion hurled him across the alley, burying him under a mountain of debris.

Inside the apartment building, windows rattled and the stairway quaked. Amid cries of terror, Dominique lost her footing and slid downward, finally grasping onto the railing to break her fall.

She was positive Salat had been killed in the shelling. Quivering, she lowered herself onto the step, wrapping both arms around her body to still her trembling. As she heard someone mounting the stairs on the run, she lifted the nickel-plated Kolibri in her shaking right hand.

"Thank God!" Dominique gasped as Salat, his swarthy face smeared with red dust, rounded the landing. She let the weapon drop.

"There's a Jap armored car downstairs. Come on!"

Encircling her waist with his arm, Salat led Dominique up the last flight of stairs and across the roof to the corner of the building overlooking Bubbling Well Road. Below, a cordon of Kempei stood guard, diverting the light flow of traffic.

Northward, the next building over was separated from them by a gap of three feet. It's roof, considerably larger than the one they were on, was lined by long rows of concrete chimneys. Barely visible beyond the last row was the lush green landscape of the Shanghai Racetrack.

"Keep down!" Salat warned, pulling Dominique away from the low wall bordering the roof just as a bullet from a high-powered rifle tore off a chunk of plaster nearby. "Sniper," he explained grimly. "Must be a whole company of Kempetai down there."

Shivering, Dominique heard whistles, then guttural commands, as Kempei troopers swarmed through the streets, deploying around the building.

"We're trapped, aren't we?"

"Not if we get across that roof and take cover between the chimneys till dark," Salat said, watching the sun setting behind the clouds off to the west.

"Then what?"

"First things first!" The Corsican smiled and led her by the hand to a section of roof where they could safely cross over to the next building.

The Kaiser Wilhem Institute, a solid gray stone building, built before the First World War, was situated on Bubbling Well Road, not far from the Shanghai Roulette Club. Once the headquarters for the Gestapo and local Nazi party, the Institute had been abandoned three months earlier at the time of the Third Reich's surrender. On the first floor, a pasty-face Obersturmbannführer Becker, his eyes ringed with fatigue, sat alone in his large office, both feet up on his messy desk and only a flickering oil lamp for light. On the walls around him, portraits of Hitler, Goebbels, Goering, and his own personal mentor, Gestapo chieftain Heinrich Himmler, were tilted at odd angles, gathering dust. On the second floor, directly above where Becker sat, was the most powerful radio transmitter in China, a German-made wireless capable of reaching around the world to Berlin.

"Disgusting!" Becker muttered, looking at the flickering oil lamp and thinking bitterly that things had come to an insane pass when the Shanghai Power Company could cut off the electricity of the highest-ranking Gestapo official in China simply for failing to pay his bill.

His heavily freckled face twisted with frustration as Becker deliberately shifted his legs, toppling a thick pile of official reports onto the floor. Who was interested in the glory of the master race and the Axis partnership now, he thought miserably. Small wonder! An entire nation, the invincible Deutschland, with the most energetic and efficient people on earth, lay in ruin, while he sat eleven thousand miles away in the dark.

"Gott in himmel!" Becker moaned aloud, wondering how those dumb bastards in Berlin had screwed things up so badly. How could anyone in his right mind make the tactical blunder of invading Russia? An army of five million and over seven thousand airplanes and tanks destroyed in one year!

And as the not incidental offshoot, Ernst Becker, the man entrusted with bringing the Final Solution to China was left without enough money to pay the electricity or telephone bills, much less buy his own way to safety!

Glumly, he recalled how, during the Nazi heyday, the Kaiser Wilhelm Institute had been the scene of nightly political and social gatherings. The theater downstairs drew capacity audiences of Japanese officials and influential European and Chinese civilians, all cheering the Nazi march across Europe. Austria, Poland, France, Holland, Norway. Sounds of the blitzkreig and tramping jackboots rang in his ears. To be a Nazi really meant something then. A Thousand Years, Hitler had proclaimed. A Thousand Years!

"I'd have settled for just my lifetime!" Becker thought dolefully as he contemplated the exorbitant price the Iberian Navigation Company demanded for chartering a freighter. Neutral bastards. All through the war, the citizens of Portugal, Spain, and Switzerland had gotten rich by playing the Axis off against the Allies. And now they were out to soak him personally. The only way out now, Becker decided, was to convince that procrastinating yellow dwarf, Hata, that Argentina offered the best refuge.

He lifted the telephone receiver to his ear and waited impatiently for a dial tone. Hearing none, he began pounding the cradle with his free hand until the realization that the line was disconnected struck him.

Incredulous, Becker hurled the receiver to the floor. It landed on the pile of official reports already there. Fuming at the black fate which had beached him on this distant shore, he anxiously paced the gloomy office. He caught sight of Adolf Hitler's portrait hanging crooked on the wall, and in a sudden burst of impotent anger, he sent it crashing to the floor.

The great bay windows of the Cathay Hotel's dining room faced east toward the China Sea. Two stories high, the enormous room was filled with excellent reproductions of French Regency furniture; elegant cut-crystal chandeliers shed their soft light on the delicate golden-hued fabric that covered the walls.

Two hours before the towering French doors were opened for the evening meal trade, Giacomo Ferrara patiently inspected the personal appearance of every member of the dining room staff, as was his weekly custom. It was tedious work, but necessary, as Ferrara had learned years before. Only by exercising constant diligence could the superior standards of the Cathay Hotel be maintained.

As it was, the Pacific War had made sizable inroads in the Cathay's ability to serve her select clientele. Such imported delicacies as white truffles from Italy, hams from Parma, cheeses from France and Holland, to name only a few, were no longer available. Fortunately liquors and wines were never a problem. The cellars of the Cathay had been amply stocked with enough bottles of vintage French and Italian wines to last out the century, if necessary—even at the rate the Japanese were indulging themselves.

Which served to remind the managing director once again how drastically his clientele had changed. There were so few world travelers anymore. Even the number of affluent refugees reaching Shanghai was down to a trickle. The Cathay had to rely largely on her regular long-term guests—high-ranking Japanese officers and government officials, an Indian rajah and his entourage, a dozen exiled Chinese warlords, an array of European nobility, including one Italian duke, and a colorful assortment of other foreign nationals, including Maximov Dallin, who were rich enough to afford the hotel's steep rates.

Finally, his eagerness evident, the last in a long line of waiters approached Ferrara. The managing director knew that this lanky Chinese, with round shoulders stooped from age and many years of service, took enormous pride in his work. Ferrara gave him special attention, noting that his black jacket and trousers were scrupulously clean and freshly pressed, that his gray hair was cut short, well above the ears, and his fingernails carefully trimmed and spotless.

"Excellent," murmured the managing director in approval. Beaming, the Chinese bowed slightly, then quickly rejoined his colleagues waiting in rows four deep beside the kitchen doors. Ferrara signaled to the staff captain standing beside him, a portly Austrian refugee, that the session was over, and strode out of the dining room.

A few minutes later, the elevator deposited him on the tenth floor, where his private suite was located. He unlocked the double doors, switched on the hall lights, and went into the living room which overlooked the Bund to the south and the Whampoo River to the east. Pouring himself a half glass of dry English sherry from a crystal decanter resting on a credenza, Ferrara skirted the Italian Renaissance pieces in which the living room was furnished and halted before a small oil painting of Piazza San Marco by Canaletto. A family possession, it had come from their ancient palazzo on the Grand Canal in Venice.

"Ah, Venezia!" sighed Ferrara. Just the thought of that island city, unique in all the world, made him long for home. He felt he had been born in the wrong era. If he could have chosen, he would have lived in the Renaissance, surrounded by the genius of Raphael, da Vinci, Verrocchio, Michelangelo, Titian, and Tiepolo. Ferrara regarded his own civilization with bitter derision.

"They were giants!" he murmured. "All we have now are buffoons like Mussolini and barbarians like Adolf Hitler."

It was sad. What was a man of culture like himself to do? Where was he to go?

Plagued by his unresolved thoughts, Ferrara gazed out at the purple sunset over the badly mauled Japanese warships anchored in the Whampoo River, graphic evidence of the sorry state of Japan's ambitions. Even now the Communists were said to be moving toward the coast, hoping to occupy Shanghai when the Japanese surrendered.

If it were true, which Ferrara did not seriously doubt, the fanatical disciples of Mao would have little patience with his kind. Capitalistic lackeys! Imperialist dogs! Colonial overseers! In his time, Ferrara had heard all the catchphrases.

Sipping the last of his sherry, he made his way back for a refill. A few feet short of the credenza, Ferrara stiffened as he noticed for the first time a square manila envelope resting upright against the sterling silver ice bucket. In the center of the envelope in bold lettering were the words: MONSIEUR MUNK—HOLD FOR ARRIVAL.

Swiftly breaking the seal, the managing director extracted a single sheet of paper and read the three words in bold print that lay before him: DALLIN IS MISSING

Stunned, it was some time before Ferrara had the presence of mind to crumple the paper into a little ball, place it in a marble ashtray, and set fire to it. Moments later it was black ash.

Bridge House seemed strangely silent, devoid of the usual screams, the cries for mercy as prisoners were hauled from their cages and dragged through the long corridors to the torture chambers in the basement. For the first time since his incarceration, Gustav Torg had been spared this ordeal. Instead, he squatted on the floor of his lice-infested cage. He knew if he tried to lie down or walk, which, considering his condition was impossible, the guard outside would take delight in punishing him.

He was still wondering what the silence meant when a guttural command from the guard alerted him that someone was coming. Normally, apart from torture sessions, this only occurred at mealtimes, when the panel at the bottom of the cage door would slide open and a chipped bowl would appear. But he already had a bowl on the floor beside him; the stench of the putrid fish soup lingered in his smashed nostrils.

The Norwegian glanced at the door as a haggard-faced Japanese officer, whom he had never seen before, shot back the bolt and entered.

Even though he was certain the sentry spoke no English, Sumato whispered. "Felix Hacker was my friend."

"Yes?" Torg replied, his pale blue eyes brightening with interest.

"Out of respect for his memory, I wish you to know Felix Hacker revealed nothing. Not your name, or any of the others. If he had done so, especially if he had given up the black book, he would be alive today."

"I don't understand. Then how did . . ."

"Colonel Hata lied. The man who betrayed you is European. I don't know his name or nationality. Only that he lives at the Cathay Hotel."

His heart beating rapidly, the Norwegian was unable to control the excitement that raced through his body. "Thank you," he finally replied. "But why do you come now? Surely it's dangerous for you."

"Because . . ." Sumato hesitated, his face reddening with shame. "I wish you to remember that not all Japanese are like Colonel Hata." Before the Norwegian could respond, Sumato had turned and stumbled out of the cage.

Hours later, long after the chipped bowl was reclaimed and the guard had gone off duty, to be replaced by another half-drunken one, Gustav Torg remained squatting in the same position, contemplating Sumato's words.

The possibility that Hata had sent him simply as another ploy to extract a confession occurred to Torg. Ultimately, however, he discounted this thought. Gustav Torg had dealt with many men in his life, and he felt positive that Sumato was telling the truth. It did not make his situation any easier, however. Quite the reverse. It meant that only the Norwegian knew the black book's hiding place, which meant Hata would now *have* to get the information from him.

For the first time since his arrest, Gustav Torg wanted to die. He briefly considered suicide, despite his beliefs. How else could he guarantee that under torture he would not reveal his secret? There was little doubt in his mind that he was marked for more sessions with his sadistic captors. Torg was familiar enough with Oriental behavior to comprehend the reason for Sumato's embarrassment. He was ashamed because he knew his superior, Colonel Hata, was planning infamy far worse than all his previous ones.

Chapter Thirteen

———◆———

"Must be the sixth of August," Dallin mumbled. He lay bone-weary on a steep, thickly wooded hillside, his entire body and most of his face covered by dead branches and leaves. In the distance beyond the morning mist he could barely make out the fog-shrouded mountains bordering the Yangtze.

A rustling sound caught his attention. He peered at a cluster of pine trees nearby and saw a doe nudging her shiny black nose warily through the branches. Sniffing danger, she whirled and went crashing back into the woods.

Relieved, Dallin shoved aside the pile of dead branches and sat upright. His cheeks were rough with two days' growth of beard, and fatigue lines creased the corners of his eyes. His clothing was torn and stained by earth and sweat.

At first glance, his situation seemed grave, but Dallin had faced other problems in the past that were worse. Still, the letter from Hata authorizing him to travel was gone, as was his identity card and prized Bolo Mauser.

From experience, Dallin knew that an unarmed Caucasian without papers on the Yangtze was a dead Caucasian, and away from the river, there were other dangers just as lethal. Deserters turned bandits were only too willing to slit a throat, Oriental or Occidental, for a Mexican silver dollar, and Nationalist and Communist guerrillas were ever on the lookout for Japanese collaborators—especially one as notorious as Maximov Dallin.

With hunger gnawing at his belly, Dallin shrugged off these unpleasant images and started down the hillside toward a trickling stream hidden in the tall grass. It was not much more than a couple of feet wide and pebbly at the bottom. He dropped to his knees and dipped his face into the slow-moving water. Drinking his fill, he leaned back with his elbows resting on the grass. A frog, its hooded eyes curious, vaulted over his legs and disappeared into the stream, followed by a whirling butterfly with velvety black and rust-colored wings.

Frogs, butterflies, tall grass smelling of fresh dew; it was all so tranquil, so different from life in Shanghai. Slowly, inevitably, bits and pieces of Dallin's past began to rise up, battling their way through the protective shield that he had deliberately thrown around himself in order to live.

In late September, 1942, an urgent message was received in code at the Kremlin in Moscow from OSS headquarters in Washington. It requested an authentic set of White Russian identification papers for an American intelligence officer who was being sent into Occupied China.

Shortly thereafter, Soviet agents operating in the Chinese city of Tientsin, near Peking, located a thirty-five-year-old Russian emigré, Maximov Dallin, a businessman with a Nansen passport and valid Japanese identification papers. According to the report forwarded by them, via Moscow to Washington, the subject, Maximov Dallin, was suffering from a trauma commonly found in many Russian exiles—a relentless yearning for his homeland and a terrible malaise which made it impossible for him to adjust to his present circumstances.

On the basis of this report, Major General Lavrenti Pavlovich Beria, chief of Russian state security, and the official responsible for filling the OSS request, decided that Maximov Dallin should be given the strongest assurances of favorable treatment and repatriated immediately to the Soviet Union.

Later, in compiling his review of the case, Major General Beria noted ironically that the happily repatriated Maximov Dallin had barely completed a detailed summation of his experience in China, before he was taken screaming from the Kremlin and put into an unheated railroad car which carried him off to the gold mining camps in the frozen wastes of Siberia.

By mid-December, 1942, less than ninety days after dispatching their request, a recently recruited major at OSS headquarters in Washington opened a thick envelope that had been carried into the United States inside a diplomatic pouch; it contained a detailed dossier on Maximov Dallin along with a complete set of identity papers.

Two weeks later, an American OSS agent tumbled out of a U.S. Air Force Dakota southwest of Shanghai. By dusk he was standing in the sparsely furnished offices of Gustav Torg & Company, gazing at the famed Bund skyline. Fully briefed on his mission, the OSS agent, known now as Maximov Dallin, had been informed of the austere nature of the Norwegian. Yet nothing had prepared him for the uncarpeted room with its battered rolltop desk, straight-backed hardwood chair. and lone portrait of Norway's King Haakon VII.

Light on his feet even at seventy, the lean Norwegian rose to greet his visitor from Chungking. Pleased that his people had managed to get Dallin safely past the Japanese guardposts ringing Shanghai, Gustav Torg was anxious to meet the man the OSS had chosen to carry out their mission.

Yet after a brief introduction neither man spoke for a few minutes. Instead each stared unabashedly, trying to take the other's measure. Finally, impressed by Dallin's sober manner and sturdy physical presence, Gustav Torg said: "Inside this room you may say whatever is on your mind. Outside I insist you maintain your cover. While I can count on the loyalty of some of my people, there are others, some whose names I have not yet learned, who have accepted money and favors from the Kempetai."

"Lovely," Dallin said, unable to disguise his concern.

"You are worried?"

"I'd be a fool not to!" Dallin frowned, glancing out the window at a Japanese gunboat roaring across the Whampoo in pursuit of a fishing junk with an enormous eye painted on its paddle box.

"At least we agree on the danger," Torg replied. "As you can see, the Japanese are everywhere and in great numbers. The Kempetai alone employ several thousand informers, in addition to their own staff, and they don't hesitate to use their special powers to arrest and execute without formal charges or evidence. There's no law in Shanghai anymore but their law; no reprieve from their cruelty. Make no mistake, Mr. Dallin, the Japanese mean to show the world they are superior to the Caucasians by humiliating them in every way possible."

"Sounds like you're having second thoughts," Dallin said, studying the Norwegian.

"I've had second thoughts from the start. Didn't they tell you?"

"It would have made no difference."

"Still they should have told you. When the OSS first sent someone to see me, I told him that Japan and Norway are at peace. I would do nothing to jeopardize my country's neutral status, whatever my personal objections to the Japanese might be."

"What changed your mind?"

"I received a coded message from the Norwegian government in exile, signed by the Prime Minister himself on behalf of King Haakon VII, directing me to comply with any request made by the OSS."

"Hardly the best way to make friends. Trusted ones."

"I will do my duty, I assure you." The Norwegian gestured toward the portrait of the king. "Whatever my personal feelings, I am still a loyal subject of my king."

"But you don't like it much."

"Does that bother you?"

"What bothers me is you don't seem to understand we're fighting a war. You live in the Orient. You know as well as I the Japs don't give up. They go on fighting until they're dead. And even then they sometimes beat you."

"I assure you I recognize the need for defeating the Axis, Mr. Dallin. But for me it's a question of ethics. The Japanese permit me certain freedoms because I am neutral. In return, I feel obliged to keep my word."

"Your word?"

"Yes," the Norwegian said forcefully. "I know in some quarters a man's word is not important. But to me it's always been everything. As you should know, here in Asia it's a fact of life for a China trader. We don't have contracts. We don't resort to courts to settle disputes. We rely on a simple handshake, understanding from experience and reputation that the other man will fulfill his part of the bargain. Should someone break this bond he'll never be trusted again, he might as well be dead. Nothing will ever restore him to his former good standing."

"For a businessman you're one hell of an idealist," Dallin said, impressed despite himself by the Norwegian's integrity.

"And for an American you're remarkably ruthless. You see, the choice presented to me is far from simple. Either I am disloyal to my king and country or I must violate my word with the Japanese. In either case I stand to lose."

"A no-win situation."

"Precisely. But that is something I have grown familiar with ever since this war began. Now we'd best be going."

"Where to?"

"My home. It's nearly dinner time. I prefer we do our talking there."

A few minutes later, Dallin and Gustav Torg were seated in the rear of a black Cadillac limousine heading north along the Bund.

"Quiet, isn't it?" Dallin observed, noticing few cars and hardly many more pedestrians on the wide avenue skirting the Whampoo River.

"The Bund is completely changed. Since the Japanese confiscated all enemy business interests there aren't many of us still using these office buildings. Unless you count Japanese military officers and officials."

The Cadillac slowed to let a bulldozer pass into a machine gun bunker under construction, then rolled by a row of 105 mm. anti-aircraft batteries to Nanking Road where the Palace and Cathay hotels occupied adjoining corners.

"I was given your home address," Dallin said casually. "Is it still the same?"

"Yes. On Avenue du Roi Albert in the French Concession."

"Then why are we going to Hongkew?"

Before Gustav Torg could reply, the Cadillac gained speed, shooting past a group of Japanese sailors negotiating with a European prostitute in the public gardens of the shuttered British Consulate. The car mounted the steel trestle spanning Soochow Creek. On the far side of Garden Bridge loomed the huge gray mansion of the Russian Consulate. Off to the right, below the bridge, a shiny black Shanghai junk, its deck piled high with dull green tea leaves, was making the sharp turn from the Whampoo River into the creek.

"You're familiar with Shanghai then?" the Norwegian asked warily.

"Enough to know that your place is in the opposite direction."

"Correct. But you see Bridge House lies just across the bridge."

"You're taking me to Kempetai headquarters?" Dallin asked, a look of anger on his sunburned face as he stared at Gustav Torg in disbelief.

"Not for the reason you think."

"How do you know what I'm thinking?"

"Permit me to explain," Torg continued with obvious reluctance. "Japanese law requires all foreign nationals living in Shanghai to register at Bridge House. It's merely a formality. Something every visitor to the city is obliged to do."

"Negative," Dallin shot back. "I have all the papers I need, including a curfew pass, which I would have shown you if you had bothered to ask."

The Norwegian swiftly drew a small Beretta automatic from his jacket pocket. Moving half a second faster, Dallin shoved the gleaming barrel aside and pressed the snub-nosed barrel of his 38 caliber Smith & Wesson revolver against the Norwegian's chest.

"Now give me the real reason."

Shrugging, Gustav Torg replied, "I suppose I owe you that much. The cruel fact is, if you don't pass the Kempetai interrogation now, you surely will never pass it later if you are caught, which could mean the lives of the people I have recruited for your mission, as well as my own."

"Jesus!"

"Forgive me, Mr. Dallin, but China teaches us to be devious in order to survive. Under the present circumstances, this seemed the only logical move to make."

"To sacrifice me?" Dallin said, pressing his revolver against Torg's heart.

"Only if you are not as capable as Chungking claims. You know how the Japanese treat their enemies. I had to be sure."

"It's not your profits you're worried about?"

His blue eyes reflecting pain, Gustav Torg replied, "I'm afraid my past reputation for success dies hard. Another year of war and Torg and Company will share the fate of every other legitimate trading company in China, neutral or not."

"Which is?"

"Bankruptcy," Gustav Torg said, with the weariness of someone who has done everything possible to alter his fate. "Now if you put your gun away, I will inform my driver we're changing destinations."

"Forget it," Dallin said roughly, regretting his previous question.

"Pardon?"

"It won't be necessary."

"I'm afraid I don't understand," the Norwegian said, genuinely puzzled by Dallin's insistence.

Fifteen minutes later, after being ushered into Colonel Hata's office on the eighth floor of Bridge House by two surly Kempetai guards with fixed bayonets, Dallin wasn't sure he understood either.

"You live in Tientsin?" Hata asked, leaning back in his chair and gazing with deep interest at the tall curly-haired Caucasian standing calmly before him.

"Until three months ago I did," Dallin replied, plunging easily into his cover story.

"Three months?" Hata repeated, glancing down at the Japanese identification card and Nansen passport lying on his desk. Then, toying with the green passport, he added, "This is issued by the League of Nations and quite useless, you realize. Diplomatically or otherwise."

"It's all I could get. Being a Russian in exile."

"Three months, you say?"

"Give or take a day."

"Why are you not afraid of the Kempetai, Mr. Dallin?" Hata asked sharply.

"Why should I be? The Japanese are a great and wise people. Everyone living in East Asia should be grateful they have come to free us from the oppression of the Americans and British. I know I am—grateful, that is."

"You like the Japanese people?"

"I believe in your plan for Asiatics," Dallin went on forcefully, "with basic rights for Russian emigrés as well; we hate the Soviets and have suffered just as the Japanese have from callous Europeans and Americans."

"I see," Hata replied, weighing his words carefully. "But why have you been away from Tientsin so long?"

"I was on my way here when I came down with malaria. I nearly died, but a peasant family in a village up north took me in and cared for me. They saved my life."

"What was the name of this village?"

"It's got no name."

Hata looked up suddenly, his flaring nostrils betraying his suspicion.

"But it's easy enough to find on a map," Dallin continued. "About thirty-five miles west of Chefoo. The family's name was Laou. I never can forget them. Saved my life, they did."

Giving Dallin a sour look, Hata began jotting down the information in large blocklike characters on a sheet of rice paper; then, without pausing, he asked sharply, "What is your reason for coming to Shanghai?"

"Money," Dallin answered bluntly, fishing in his side pocket for a crumpled black Turkish cigarette and lighting it with a wooden match struck with his thumbnail. "It's simple. Everyone knows the real China fortunes are made here in Shanghai."

"Before the war?"

"During it, too!"

"So you think you'll make a fortune here in Shanghai?" Hata asked, appraising Dallin differently.

"I've met a lot of Chinese and Japanese who have. Don't know why a White Russian can't do the same." Dallin smiled, drawing on his cigarette.

Colonel Hata rose swiftly from his chair and, ignoring Dallin, began pacing about his office. Finally, he halted to gaze out the window at the Bund skyline; then he turned toward Dallin and said, "You will show more respect for a Kempetai officer."

"Colonel?"

"Bow I say!" Hata screamed.

The two guards swung their rifles around. Dallin snatched the burning cigarette from his lips and, ducking his head, bowed toward Hata.

"Lower."

Fingers nearing the floor. Dallin bent over as far as he possibly could and stayed there, catching a fleeting glimpse of Hata as he returned to the desk and sat down in his chair.

"Now suppose you tell me the truth?"

Dallin didn't really wish to change anything, but the tone of Hata's voice told him to shuffle cover stories quickly.

"Actually I've been near Wuhan."

"Go on," Hata said, tapping the end of his pen against the palm of his left hand.

"It was only business. Nothing special. Really, it wouldn't interest you."

"Suppose you let me decide that. The merchandise involved, please?"

"Tires. Some spare auto parts left by the General Motors Company in their Tientsin warehouse, from before the war."

"War material?" Hata smiled.

"No. That's not what I said."

"And these tires and auto parts. Who purchased them?"

"A Japanese company."

"Name of the company, please," Hata asked, tilting his pen toward the rice paper.

"Funny! I don't seem to remember."

"I see." Hata smiled again. "Tell me this. Your venture, was it profitable?"

"Profitable enough."

"Come now, Mr. Dallin," Hata questioned with sincere interest. "I didn't ask how much. Only if you were satisfied?"

"The fact is, I would have made double, or even triple, if I had had a Japanese officer in with me."

A glow of contentment came to Hata's face as he went on. "I understand you are acquainted with Gustav Torg?"

"I've done business with him. He was kind enough to drop me off here."

"You know him well?"

"As I said, we've done business in the past. We're not what you might call friends or even close acquaintances."

"Interesting!" Hata concluded, leaning back in the chair and crossing his legs casually. "You will wait in the next room, please. I'll call for you when I'm ready."

After Dallin had left the office, flanked by two guards, Hata pored over his identification card and Nansen passport with a powerful magnifying glass. Still perturbed and lost in thought, he placed a long distance call to the Tientsin section Kempetai headquarters. A few minutes later, as he examined the way the photograph was glued to the passport, his call came through. Hata held a lengthy conversation with the Tientsin commandant, prolonged by a delay as he referred to his files. When Hata finally replaced the receiver, he was unable to hide his agitation.

Meanwhile, in the corridor outside the office, Dallin sat on a narrow wooden bench between his guards. A cigarette dangled from his mouth and just as Dallin was about to crush it beneath his boot, the office door swung open and he was ushered inside. As he approached the desk, with the two guards in tow, Dallin noticed that Hata was eyeing him with fresh interest.

"I spoke with Tientsin," he said, "and had a very curious conversation with Kempetai commandant there. Very curious."

Spreading the fingers on both hands against the seams of his trousers, Dallin dug his heels into the floor and fought the queasy feeling that was rising from the pit of his stomach. Curious conversations, he thought, were hardly what he needed now.

"He said that before a Russian emigrant named Maximov Dallin left Tientsin there were certain conversations held with the Kempetai concerning a large sum of money stolen from an elderly Russian widow. The result was the—"

The telephone rang, interrupting Hata in mid-sentence. Grabbing the receiver, he unleashed a torrent of abuse, then, letting the instrument slide down into its cradle, he turned his attention back to Dallin.

"The Kempetai commandant insists that before Maximov Dallin left Tientsin he agreed to become an informer for the Kempetai."

While Dallin was still trying to come to grips with this revelation, Hata stunned him further by unraveling plans of his own—long-nourished plans of making a fortune from the flourishing black market trade going on between Shanghai and Chungking.

An hour later, as Dallin sat cross-legged on a tatami mat drinking hot saké from a tiny porcelain cup, the Kempetai commandant was intently outlining a proposition which included the White Russian. It was nearly midnight before Dallin finally reached the Cathay Hotel. As he had previously arranged with Gustav Torg, he went directly to the Tower Nightclub, had a double Scotch, then, eluding the Kempei agent tailing him, left the hotel through the service door.

Ten minutes later, Dallin stepped out of a dark blue Buick onto a street corner in the French Concession. Led by the same toothless Chinese man who had awaited his parachute drop earlier, Dallin entered a large apartment building and passed through a complicated maze of passages and stairways until he eventually arrived in the wine cellar of Gustav Torg's elegant mansion on Avenue du Roi Albert, one block away.

The butler, a tight-lipped northerner, nearly the same height as Dallin, escorted him into the Norwegian's presence in the rosewood-paneled library. Dallin accepted a shot glass of Scotch from Torg, then launched immediately into a detailed summary of his meeting at Bridge House and the startling plans Colonel Hata had in mind.

The long and short of it was that Dallin would be expected to continue serving the Kempetai as an informer, but his more important duty in Shanghai was to persuade Gustav Torg to give him a job with Torg & Company. Once employed, Dallin was to use the extensive network of representatives associated with Torg & Company to move large quantities of black-market merchandise, in equal partnership with Colonel Hata, whose Kempei troops would safeguard all their dealings.

But that was not all the ambitious Hata had in mind. The profits from these black-market operations would be converted into American currency, gold bars, and Chinese antiques of museum quality. Why antiques, Dallin had asked? Because, Colonel Hata had replied, in his opinion these ancient objects were certain to rise in value, keeping pace with the murderous rate of inflation that was sweeping China. To this end, the Kempetai commandant had already placed in custody the foremost scholar of Chinese art: Professor Koo, former curator of the Palace Museum at Peking, who would guide them in acquiring only the most valuable antiquities, steering them away from forgeries. Colonel Hata had been very concerned about that point, since, as commandant of the Shanghai Secret Military Police, his office had unearthed all sorts of fraudulent schemes, including counterfeit currency, stocks, and bonds, and especially bogus art. The Japanese officer did not intend to be similarly duped. Judging by the precautions he was taking, Dallin was sure that this master plan had been brewing in Hata's brain for some time.

As Dallin finished recounting the details of his interview with Colonel Hata, he took his first real look at Torg's library. It contained a staggering collection of books on a wide variety of subjects and was furnished with an actual ship's bar from an East India Clipper; over the bar hung an enormous portrait of one of the loveliest women Dallin had ever seen.

"Well," Torg said finally, "it's a very shrewd plan. Shrewd, but hardly unique. Many Japanese officers and officials, men far less influential than Hata, have been dealing in heroin, gold bullion, diamonds, even war materiél. Some even stashing their proceeds in Swiss banks against the day when it all comes to a halt. Colonel Hata is bound to end up enormously rich, and we will most likely end up very dead."

"How's that?"

"In your case, as a Caucasian informer serving the Kempetai in Shanghai," Gustav Torg elaborated, "it's just a question of time until your identity is known. Simply the fact that you're a White Russian will be a giveaway."

"Why?" Dallin asked.

"Because it's common knowledge in Shanghai that if you want someone to do a dirty job, the most likely candidate is a White Russian. You know, the Russians came by the thousands from Vladivostok, fleeing the Communists after the Revolution in battered ships, all that remained of the once-proud Czarist Navy; and they've been stranded on China's east coast ever since. Even back in those prosperous times when the white man reigned supreme, there were very few well-paying jobs. The better-looking women, and there were many, became taxi dancers in the nightclubs. The men, including aristocrats and high-ranking Czarist officers, took work wherever they could find it, as doormen, bodyguards, chauffeurs. Conditions were so harsh it wasn't very long before many of the women turned to prostitution and the men to racketeering.

"So, given that history, as a White Russian in with Hata, you'll be very visible. Once word gets out, Communist or Nationalist gunmen, or the Shanghai police acting in their behalf, will begin hunting you. From that moment on, your life is not worth the price of a rice bowl."

"It's a tight corner he's put me into," Dallin said.

"That's only half the problem," Gustav Torg said, refilling both their glasses. "You can hardly expect the people I've recruited to have much confidence in me if I permit a known collaborator to work on my premises."

"You could tell them upfront. Say you know all about me and that I've been planted by the Kempetai to keep an eye on you."

"Yes," the Norwegian replied thoughtfully, "that might protect me, but it only increases your danger. Some of the people I've recruited are hardly pacifists. One, for instance, made a habit during the Spanish Civil War of strangling traitors in retaliation for the atrocities committed by the Falangists. A man like that wouldn't think twice about acting on his own and getting rid of you. Assuming he could, of course."

Bowing his head to acknowledge the compliment, Dallin rose from his chair and went over to the bar to look at the portrait of the beautiful woman.

"Anything else troubling you, Mr. Torg?" he asked, keeping his eyes on the painting.

"There are still a couple of things. Yes."

"Such as?"

"Dealing in the black market. Selling merchandise, including vital medicines, at several thousand times their true value."

"What about it?"

"It doesn't bother you?"

"Everything about this war bothers me," Dallin said. "But if it has to be done, why worry about it?"

"If only life could be that simple," the Norwegian replied somberly. "But the deception involved! Pretending to be someone you're not. Taking people in and exploiting them for your own ends. This too is justified by war, I suppose?"

"Right again."

"I see." Torg frowned. "Maybe I'm old-fashioned—but living another person's life . . . No one you can trust. Always on your guard. I mean even men like Hata need friends."

"If you're asking me how I can do it," Dallin said, "I admit it's not easy. But I've blocked out the past."

"Meaning you've become Maximov Dallin. Thief, informant, and collaborator."

"And war profiteer."

"In that case, there is one final thing I must warn you about. My daughter. Dominique. She detests fascists and informers. I've had my own problems keeping her from acting against the Japanese."

"I don't see what this has to do with me."

"You will if you'll hear me out. When Dominique discovers you are a partner of Colonel Hata's and have come to Shanghai to exploit the reputation of Gustav Torg and Company, she won't like it."

"That's her problem."

"Wrong. You see, Dominique has a very close friend, a Corsican gambler by the name of Robert Salat."

"Yes, I've heard of him. He runs the Roulette Club." Dallin scowled. "This daughter of yours has strange friends."

"You better not tell her that."

"I don't intend telling her anything. But I won't dump a mission I've come halfway around the world to carry out because of her or Salat. Besides, from where I stand, my being on good terms with the commandant of the Kempetai couldn't be better. It's a real stroke of luck."

"You believe in luck then?"

"I've lived in China."

"I didn't know." The Norwegian's brow was creased with thought. "Still, all things considered, I'd prefer to dissolve my company if it's the same to you."

"It's not the same to me," Dallin objected firmly. "You're going to sell out lock, stock, and barrel to Colonel Hata and me."

Incensed, the Norwegian sprang up and stood over Dallin, who remained remarkably unruffled.

"I know what this means to you, ruining a name you've spent a lifetime building," Dallin said softly. "But it must be done. We've got a nasty job ahead. Yours is only the first sacrifice. Before we're done there'll be a lot more to regret. Innocent men and women tortured and dead. Property destroyed. An establishment that's worked in China for decades overturned. But whatever it takes to get this job done, I'll do."

"I'm beginning to understand why the OSS sent you," the Norwegian replied, studying Dallin's face.

"You do. Why?"

"Because, Mr. Dallin, or whatever your real name is," Torg went on with a hint of grudging admiration in his voice, "you have the makings of a real son of a bitch!"

Chapter Fourteen

———————◆———————

The northern section of the International Settlement beyond Soochow Creek is called Hongkew. Apart from the Central Post Office, the Ward Road Prison, Bridge House, and Broadway Mansions, a luxurious apartment building owned by Sir Victor Sassoon, Hongkew is an essentially treeless, squalid area historically inhabited by poor working-class Chinese and Japanese. It was here in May, 1943, that the Japanese decided to establish a ghetto for the fifteen thousand Jews, many of them refugees from Hitler's Germany and Nazi-occupied Europe, who had fled to Shanghai because China was the only nation that would have them.

At dusk, Rabbi Marcus Feinbaum, a powerfully built forty-year-old wearing a black skullcap and prayer shawl, stood at the open window of his shabbily furnished room in a dank bungalow near the Hongkew public market and beseeched God to save the Jewish people from extinction.

On a narrow bed several feet away, Sarah Brodsky sat, her three-year-old son Abraham clutched to her slender body. Sarah felt miserable. Every night since she had arrived in Shanghai two years earlier, she had witnessed her childhood friend and protector as he carried out this agonizing ritual.

For Sarah, disembarking into the crowded chaos of China without money or friends, encountering Marcus had been the greatest stroke of good fortune in her life. Since the age of twelve, the two had been close friends, and later sweethearts. Their families had been neighbors in Warsaw. If the Nazis had not invaded Poland in September of 1939, she and Marcus hight have been married and the child now resting against her breast would have been his. Instead, Marcus, recently ordained as a rabbi, had volunteered to serve with the Polish Army; at the time of the surrender, he had slipped away and joined a Jewish partisan band battling the Nazis in the forests outside Warsaw.

Now, in the stifling August heat of Shanghai, with only one small window looking out on a narrow airshaft, their room was suffocating in summer and piercingly cold and damp in winter, so cold it cut through piled-up blankets and clothing. Still, they were considered among the more fortunate Jews in the ghetto. Their landlord, a kindly Chinese merchant who lived in the rear of his shop just below them, could have demanded and gotten several times the rent they paid. Other Jews forced to live in Hongkew by Japanese ordinances had been compelled to pay huge sums for key money alone. From penniless Oriental to penniless Jew, decided Sarah, a natural succession of human suffering.

Hearing her son sigh, she gently patted his fine blond curls, then glanced over at Marcus. His prayers finished, he was folding his talis and taking it over to the other side of the battered wooden dresser between their beds.

"Marcus?"

Instantly she felt his presence beside her in the dark, searching her face for distress.

"I'm all right. I only wanted you near."

In all their time together in this tiny room, he never had come any closer than now, had never touched her except that one time.

"While I pray, I try not to think of you, but I always fail." Marcus said, as though reading her thoughts. He turned away as her hand caught his wrist and held tight. "We agreed," Marcus went on, his voice cracking.

"Please?"

"No."

"Just this once," Sarah wept. "Sometimes I feel so afraid ... so alone in this room I could scream."

"You're not alone. Don't ever think I don't want to hold you. That I don't think about you late at night and early every morning. But you are married to someone else and we are civilized human beings with laws. Regardless of what those vermin the Nazis may say."

"There is no law in Shanghai. Only gold and power."

"In our minds and hearts there is a law higher than everything else. This I truly believe."

"If you believe so strongly then why don't you worship in the temple with the others? Or better yet, why don't you lead the congregation as you should?"

"You know why."

"All right, but Marcus, I know he is dead. Everyone in that camp is dead, I tell you."

"You don't know that. I don't want to hear you say that again. Now I must go. Otherwise I'll be late for work."

"Marcus!" Sarah cried out, nearly awakening her baby.

"What?"

"When will you stop running from me and accept things as they are? When?" Sarah wept, as she held her sleeping son in her arms.

Marcus looked at the fragilely beautiful woman before him, but made no attempt to reply. Instead, upset, blaming himself for their cruel predicament, he slid open the top drawer of the dresser. He removed a red armband with the initial A, for Austrian and pulled the crudely sewn cloth up over his left wrist and along the upper part of his arm. Armbands were compulsory for all foreign nationals with the exception of the rich and influential. So were identity cards, indicating country of origin. In the case of Jewish refugees, the identification cards had a yellow stripe across the top, while all others had a green one.

Yet, as Marcus knew, except for the recent Allied bombings, the Jews of Shanghai would have been much worse off, had they been left to the mercy of the local Nazis. For years now, the official Nazi representative in China, Obersturmbannführer Becker, had tried to persuade the Japanese to organize concentration camps similar to those in eastern Europe. Fortunately, his efforts had met with failure. One reason was because of a quirk of history. Before the outbreak of the Russo-Japanese War of 1904, when Japan had found herself in desperate need of a huge international loan to purchase armaments, she had been denied this help in favor of her enemy, Russia. Quite unexpectedly, Jacob Schiff, a prominent Jewish investment banker from New York and an ardent critic of the

Czar's virulent anti-Semitic policies, came to the aid of Japan and arranged that she get the necessary funds. This gesture earned Jews great esteem among the Japanese. Later, when the Third Reich insisted Japan carry out the Final Solution in Asia, the Japanese were reluctant, chiefly because of Schiff's act, to do so.

Ultimately however, the Japanese decided it was politically expedient to pacify their Axis partner's demands by setting up a ghetto in Shanghai and introducing laws forbidding Jews to live or work outside its boundaries without special permission. While this measure fell far short of the Nazi ambitions, it did serve to create enormous problems for the Jews, who were locked behind guarded gates in the squalid dwellings of Hongkew.

Here, cut off from help abroad and from the rest of Shanghai, Jews awakened each day to begin anew a bitterly contested struggle for survival. The soaring rate of unemployment in Shanghai did not make their lives any easier. Some like Marcus Feinbaum were daring. By pretending to be Aryan he had secured a position as a wireless operator, a skill he acquired years before from his father, an electrical engineer with a fondness for building and operating radio equipment. While the job paid enough to feed and shelter Marcus, Sarah, and the baby, the possibility of the death penalty, strictly enforced by the Kempetai against any Jew caught defying ghetto restrictions, weighed heavily on him.

Nevertheless, by eight o'clock, one hour after passing through the ghetto barrier, Marcus was seated in the brightly lit offices of the Iberian Navigation Company on the Bund. His tattered cotton jacket with a red armband bearing the initial A on the left sleeve hung from a nearby coat rack. Ten feet away, Pak, an elderly Korean assigned to monitor all radio transmissions, snored loudly. Accustomed to the disturbance, Marcus swung around in the swivel chair facing his equipment. The transmitter, an outmoded British Hartley, with a triple row of dials and knobs, was encased in walnut and half the size of the table. Since its maximum range was two thousand miles, communications were severely limited, but repeated requests to the Kempetai for a more powerful transmitter had been ignored. The receiver, an amalgamation of German and American equipment, had been assembled by Marcus from salvaged prewar parts.

Marcus switched on the fifty kilowatt Hartley transmitter

capable of traversing over forty frequencies. Then he pulled open the table drawer for his logbook, which recorded the latest movements of the Iberian fleet of merchant ships, movements that corresponded to the red pins on the British Admiralty charts on the wall.

Several minutes later, Rossio, the director of the Iberian Navigation Company, entered the room. He was a heavyset Portuguese with dark circles under his eyes. He had grown rich using his neutral fleet to carry illegal cargo between the Axis-ruled nations, but he spent vast sums as well, reveling in the gaudy fleshpots of Shanghai and losing huge amounts at chemin de fer at the plush Roulette Club, pleasures Rossio could easily afford until, almost overnight, with Germany's capitulation and American subs controlling the China Sea, the demand for cargo vessels suddenly lessened. To compensate for this sudden drop in business, Rossio began offering safe passage to Portugal and Spain. More than a score of frightened Europeans with fascist leanings accepted his offer and had already reached a haven in southern Europe, but many clung to the desperate hope that Japan somehow would overwhelm the Allies at the last moment, or that a triumphant Chiang Kai-shek, in his quest to crush the Communists, once again might require their professional services as he did before Pearl Harbor.

"Where is the *Isabella* now?" Rossio asked.

"En route to Singapore," Marcus replied, reaching for his headset.

"Good. Advise her captain to stand by for an important message."

Marcus checked with the logbook, switched over to the proper frequency, then tapped out the order to the *Isabella*. He was getting his pencil and pad ready and Rossio had just started to speak when Pak raced across the room.

"Go back to sleep, Pak. This has nothing to do with the military," Rossio insisted patronizingly.

"So sorry, Senor!" Pak objected, flashing a gold tooth. "Kempetai says when you use wireless you must let Pak listen."

"Suit yourself." Rossio shrugged and, drawing a pale brown cigar from the pocket of his suit jacket, he began pacing between Marcus and the suspicious Korean.

"Order the *Isabella* to off-load all her cargo in Singapore," Rossio instructed. "Then tell her captain to proceed directly for Shanghai, advising us daily of his position over the same frequency."

"Usual code?" asked Marcus, jotting the message neatly into his logbook.

"Of course," responded Rossio, biting the end off his cigar.

Marcus telegraphed the order, and as they both waited in silence for the reply from the *Isabella,* a profusely sweating Becker entered the office complaining about the Japanese night patrols.

"Goddamn yellow dwarfs. Think they can shove me around. Three times they stopped me coming over here. Three times, even though the swastika still flies from my Mercedes."

Marcus had his back to the Nazi, but hearing the thick Berlin accent, he whirled around in the chair, getting his first glimpse of Ernst Becker. What he saw drained the color from his face and left his hands quivering.

"Something wrong with your operator?" Becker asked Rossio.

"Wrong?" questioned Rossio, puzzled.

Just then the signal from the *Isabella* came clicking back noisily on the receiver and Marcus quickly began recording the dots and dashes. After he had deciphered the code, he read the message aloud:

ISABELLA TO KINGPIN. AFTER SINGAPORE OFF-LOAD WILL PROCEED TO SHANGHAI AS OR-DERED. REPEAT. WILL PROCEED TO SHANGHAI AS ORDERED.

"That's your ship now," Rossio explained deferentially to Becker.

"You don't say!" The Nazi beamed. "How long before she gets here?"

"My operator is a better judge of that than I."

"Well?" Becker demanded, turning away from Rossio who was standing beneath a portrait of Salazar, the dictator of Portugal.

Absorbed in his nightmarish recollections of the German invasion of Poland in 1939, Marcus answered haltingly, "With port conditions so difficult in Singapore and the American fleet carrying out searches in the China Seas, you must allow a minimum of eight or nine days."

"Nine days," Becker repeated. "The fifteenth, *Ja?* Well, that's not bad. Not bad at all. In fact, that's about what I told my friends."

"In that case we should finally be able to settle our arrangements," Rossio interjected, anxiously seeking the promised initial payment from the German.

"Arrangement? *Ja!* Sure we can settle. Only in private, *ja?*"

"You heard Herr Becker," Rossio said forcefully, casting a withering glance at Marcus and Pak. "Go on now. We won't be long."

Marcus was barely able to rise from his chair. He heard Pak snort with disgust, then start for the door, leaving him alone with Rossio and Becker. "Don't you hear? What's wrong with you anyway?" the Nazi snapped angrily.

Although with every second he remained in the room the danger of his being discovered increased, Marcus was frozen to his seat. Finally, getting control of himself, he got up and was halfway across the room when Becker called out: "One moment."

Marcus wanted to run, but experience gained in the streets of occupied Warsaw had taught him the necessity of brazening it out. Slowly, he turned toward the Nazi.

"My friend, you are a Jew!" Becker announced, a smile on his freckled face. "We never met, but this nose of mine never fails me."

"Nein, mein herr. Osterreicher," Marcus protested, gesturing to the initial A for Austrian on the sleeve of his jacket, then reaching into his inside pocket for his carefully forged papers, he offered them to Becker.

Pushing them aside, the Nazi hissed, "Jew! I can always smell a Jew!"

"Be reasonable, Becker," Rossio interrupted. "The man's papers are in order. Look them over for yourself if you don't believe me."

"Papers! In times like these we all have papers saying we are who we wish to be." Becker jeered, suddenly shoving Marcus toward the door. "Oh, go on. I don't care if you're the chief rabbi of Warsaw, you hebe bastard . . . just see I get to Buenos Aires."

Marcus did not wait to be told twice. Bolting into the corridor he ran out of the building. He dodged past Pak, who was waiting on the front steps, then lurched around to the side of the building where, feeling sick to his stomach, he doubled over and vomited.

Chapter Fifteen

The Kempei guard slipped quietly into the small metal cage. He stood over the pitiful figure asleep on the stone floor, then kicked him hard in the ribs with the pointed toe of his hobnailed boot. The blow brought the Norwegian to his senses and sent him reeling up against the wall, clutching the few good ribs he had left. What had he done wrong now, he wondered, catching a blurry glimpse of a young guard coming at him.

Then Torg realized he must have dozed off. Must have fallen asleep and rolled onto the floor, violating the mandatory squatting position the Kempetai required all prisoners to maintain while locked inside their cages. Squatting was easy for the Japanese, Torg thought with a groan, but infinitely painful, hour after hour, for a Caucasian. Still, this guard seemed to have something else on his mind. Instead of giving him a tongue-lashing he was gesturing to the Norwegian to rise.

Torg tried but could not move his badly burned legs and swollen feet. Finally, losing patience, the guard reached over and, grabbing the Norwegian by the hair, dragged him out of the cage. Hoisting him to his feet with the help of another guard, the two men drove the Norwegian before them through the long corridor by pummeling him over the kidneys with the stocks of their rifles.

Staggering blindly ahead, the Norwegian entered the stairwell, misjudged the first step, and went tumbling down, ending up in a crumpled heap on the landing below. For a moment Torg thought he heard giggling; then darkness swept over him and he passed out.

He was revived by a bucket of cold water thrown by a loinclothed Kempei torturer. As consciousness returned with the sensation of being wet he pried open his puffy eyes and he found himself in the cellar corridor with Colonel Hata not three feet away.

"You look terrible," Hata murmured, "so be sensible and tell me where you hid the black book."

As the Norwegian opened his mouth to reply, blood burst from his throat and ran down over his cracked lower lip.

"You should be in the hospital getting medical care," Hata went on softly. "Help me and I'll see you get there."

The Norwegian did not even bother trying to reply. Instead he gazed stubbornly off at the cell door nearby.

"I can understand why you might prefer to die rather than tell me what I wish to know. In your place I too would feel the same way. But these are unusual times. A great deal has happened that you know nothing about. I need that book, Torg, and I need it now."

The Norwegian did not move so much as an eyelid.

"You'll soon change your mind," Hata threatened, motioning for the loinclothed torturer to open the cell door.

As his pale blue eyes followed the movement of the door opening, the Norwegian heard a familiar cry from inside the cell. Peering closer he saw Dominique dangling from a beam by her wrists, her feet barely touching the floor where her clothing was piled carelessly.

She was totally naked. Her full breasts accentuated her slender hips and rounded thighs where a patch of golden hair shimmered invitingly. Her distraught face signaled the shame and fear she was experiencing. Her captors, the same pair who had delighted so much in tormenting Gustav Torg, waited close by, anxious to have a chance at her.

Groaning, Torg turned away, unable to bear the sight any longer.

"Now do I get it?" Hata asked harshly.

The Norwegian was about to reply when Dominique cried

out. Tears streaming down his ruined face, he turned around to look at his daughter again, condemning herself for allowing this tragedy to befall her.

Dominique tried but could not keep from sobbing. She wept for both of them. She had expected to be treated cruelly when she surrendered, but the reality of it was far more terrifying than she had ever imagined, and seeing her father in this condition only deepened her despair.

Salat had warned her. He urged her to reject Hata's ultimatum. He insisted her surrender would not help her father and he pleaded that she wait until dark and then escape with him over the side of the building into the racetrack gardens. But Dominique never really had any choice. How could she abandon her father, even to save her own life?

Only now it was clear that Hata had always intended to deceive her, to use her as a pawn to extract a confession from her father. Her presence here in Bridge House had robbed her father of his last vestige of dignity. She knew now that things would never again be the same, because less than ten feet away, sprawled on his hands and knees before the commandant of the Kempetai, was Gustav Torg, a man who had kowtowed to no one.

At the same time the Norwegian's delay in yielding was incomprehensible to Hata. True, an Oriental might be expected to sacrifice a child, especially a female, to improve his position, to save face and particularly his fortune. But a Caucasian? A prominent Occidental? Their kind supposedly placed enormous value on family ties, most of all those between parent and child.

Finally, dragging himself painfully across the floor until his back was to the wall, the Norwegian said, "I agree provided you accept two conditions of mine."

"You dare set terms?"

"Either we do things my way," Torg warned, "or not at all!"

"And your daughter? You'd let her suffer with these two, become a barracks girl? A whore for our troops in the field?"

"If I must, yes."

"You're mad! Insane!"

"Two conditions."

"All right," Hata relented, unnerved by this defiance and anxious to put an end to a situation he found disturbing. "All right, but what is it you want?"

"First, you deliver my daughter into the custody of the Swiss consul with a promise that she will not be arrested again."

"And?"

"Then we meet in total privacy. No guards. No aides. No one but you and I. Then I shall tell you what you wish to know."

"Never!"

"When you hear what I have to say you will be grateful, believe me," the Norwegian insisted, spitting out a mouthful of blood.

Hata was about to repeat his refusal when a sudden burst of curiosity overcame his pride and he acquiesced.

"Very well. You wish privacy? I wish to hold your daughter until I can be certain what you say is the truth."

His pale blue eyes sparkled for a brief moment, revealing the Gustav Torg of old. Then he replied in a firm voice. "Agreed. But cut my daughter down first."

Nodding, Hata gave instructions for Dominique to be returned to her cell. Then he ordered the two guards escorting the Norwegian to accompany him upstairs to his office. Disappointment filled their coarse faces as the two severed the ropes securing the naked girl's wrists. Then, ogling her openly, they watched as Dominique struggled into her clothes and dashed out, overtaking her father, who was being dragged through the corridor by the two guards.

She leaned down, kissing him gently on the forehead, and murmured, "I love you. I always will."

The Norwegian hardly had time to whisper, "Forgive me," before his guards shoved Dominique aside and flung him into the elevator.

A few minutes afterward, Hata rested both elbows upon his desk and, puffing on a cigarette, waited for Gustav Torg to keep his part of the bargain. Instead the Norwegian rubbed his grizzled chin with the mutilated fingers of his right hand and asked softly, "Do you have any children, Colonel?"

"No! No children."

"I didn't think you had," Torg went on calmly, "otherwise you never could have done what you have."

"My country is at peace with Norway. It was you who violated the terms of your neutrality."

"That's true," Torg confirmed sadly, "but you Japanese destroyed not only my world but yours as well. And a samurai who disregards the Bushido code of honor is worse than a coward who dies in shame."

"What do you know of our Bushido code?"

"Enough to know it doesn't call for torturing women and children."

"No more, I say," Hata insisted sharply. "All I want from you is the location of the black book."

"You still have no idea what you've done. How far from common humanity this authority of yours has taken you."

"'I said no more, Torg," Hata screamed, pounding the table with his fist. "I will not be lectured like a schoolchild."

"I intended no lecture, Colonel. Merely a hope that you still had enough self-respect left to keep you from this final act of shame. I see now I was wrong to hope . . . wrong even to plead. Your kind only understands one thing."

The Norwegian took a deep breath and straightened up to his full height, well over six feet, dwarfing Hata.

At that moment, it dawned on Hata that he was alone with the Norwegian, not that he was frightened, but Gustav Torg did have a steely glint in his eyes, an expression that troubled Hata. He had encountered fanatics before in China, frequently enough so that he wasted no time in sliding open the desk drawer and snatching the German Luger he kept there.

As it was, he barely made it. Coming for him, his jaw set, the Norwegian was only half a step away when Hata leveled the four-inch barrel at his chest.

"Damn you, Torg!" Hata screamed, "don't make me kill you."

"You give me no other choice."

As the Norwegian threw himself across the desk, Hata swung the barrel. The blow caught Torg on the forehead, blunting his attack and turning him around.

"Tell me where the black book is?"

"Never, damn you!" Gustav Torg whispered hoarsely as he whirled and, summoning all his remaining strength, flung himself at Hata's throat.

This time Hata took no chances. He squeezed the trigger. The first bullet caught Torg high up in the chest, yet hardly checked his advance. Two more shots saw him come even closer. Then, determined to stop him, Hata emptied the

Luger. Torg came to a halt, his hands near Hata's throat, and collapsed on the desk.

"Fool! You fool!" Hata raged, as he dabbed at the splotches of blood covering his uniform and desk. "Now we both lose."

Chapter Sixteen

Shanghai sweltered under the searing August sun. At four o'clock as the chimes of Big Ching rang out, a sudden downpour made hardly a dent in the temperature, which had been ninety-six degrees while the humidity still remained unchanged at ninety-nine.

Halfway across the Whampoo River, three heavily ladden black Shanghai junks with their main sails furled were gliding toward Woosung carried by the slow-moving current. Off the Bund, a few sampans, their crews hawking fresh eel and octopus, drifted lazily among the anchored Japanese gunboats whose blistering hot steel decks were devoid of life.

Nearby on the wharves, not far from the pillboxes and anti-aircraft batteries, a horde of emaciated coolies, teaboys, and beggars rested on their haunches besieged by the shrill cries of traveling kitchen vendors offering choice bits of salted fish heads and duck eggs. In the center lane of the Bund, lines of people waited under the broiling sun at tram and bus stops. As each electric car and motorbus screeched to a halt, passengers eagerly swarmed aboard, jostling for a place inside the packed vehicles moving south into the French Concession and Nantao, or north over the Garden Bridge onto Broadway and the Yangtzepoo industrial district, where the great cotton mills of Shanghai were located.

Six stories above all this, inside a luxurious penthouse suite in the Palace Hotel, a modern air-conditioning system installed in the late thirties kept Salat, elegantly dressed in a silk smoking jacket, from feeling the tropical heat. The windows of the suite faced east, overlooking the Whampoo River. Its plush furnishings were a rich mix of genuine Louis XVI antiques and excellent copies made by Chinese artisans. On the walls were several fine oil paintings, including one especially favored by Salat: a Paris street scene in late autumn with crowded cafés and poster-cluttered kiosks. It stirred memories of a city that Salat had all but forgotten. Gazing at the painting now made him wistful for those uncomplicated days and nights so long ago.

Across the room, behind him, two Corsicans in dark suits were quietly playing cards. Within easy reach lay a pair of American-made Thompson submachine guns and a stack of ammunition clips. Salat, on the run, had deliberately chosen the Palace as his hiding place. It was a bold decision considering that the lobby and roof restaurant were popular haunts for Japanese officials and well-known collaborators, but to the Corsican, with his long experience as a fugitive from justice, it was for these very reasons the last place the Kempetai would ever think to look.

In case he was proved wrong, however, the suite was equipped with an escape hatch—a secret passageway off the master bedroom that led to a private elevator that opened onto the back alley below. Although the elevator had been frequently used by the original owner of the hotel, a passionate Frenchman, it was known to only a few, including the current hotel manager, a Romanian whose credit at the Shanghai Roulette Club would have been exhausted long ago if it were not for the generosity and foresight of Robert Salat.

A light tap on the door diverted Salat from his contemplation of the oil painting. By that time the two Corsicans were on their feet, cradling the submachine guns in their arms. One covered the other as he stared through the peephole and then opened the door, saying, "It's Caro."

A toothpick of a man with an olive complexion greeted the pair at the door with a very wry smile and then made his way across the room to Salat.

"Sorry I'm late, *mon ami*," he murmured apologetically, "but they've got an army of Kempetai agents watching the club and at least half of them were assigned to tail me."

"That's only natural, Caro," Salat grinned. "So is the fact you got here safely."

It was meant to be a compliment, and was taken as one. Salat and Caro had been through a great deal together over the past decade. What the slender Caro, also a Corsican, lacked in raw strength he made up for in wits and loyalty, qualities highly prized by Salat and the principal reason Caro, his most trusted aide, had been placed in charge of the Roulette Club during his absence.

"Drink?"

"Whiskey, thanks."

Salat turned to his bodyguards and asked for two Scotches on ice. He motioned Caro to the couch, then occupied the chair opposite him.

"How goes it? You've heard from Macao?"

"It's what we expected. They want you out of here."

"How soon?"

"Two or three days at the latest."

"Can you arrange it?"

"If I move quickly. The safest way would be overland to Canton. Then by sea to Macao."

Salat was about to reply when one of his bodyguards interrupted with their drinks. Clinking glasses, the two friends sipped their whiskey, then got back to business.

"I could get you aboard the flight to Hong Kong," Caro went on, "but there'd be too many people involved. Consular officials, Kempei guards, other passengers. Someone might recognize you. Then what?"

"I think you're right. By car to Canton is the safest way out."

"Then I better get busy," Caro replied, emptying his glass in one long gulp.

"Not just yet," Salat said, gesturing for Caro to stay seated. "Any news of Dominique?"

Frowning, Caro replied, "The Norwegian's dead."

"And Dominique?"

"Alive but for how long no one knows. It's not easy getting information out of Bridge House, especially for us. Not after what's happened."

"You can use Pockmark Shen's people."

"I have. They're not as good as dealing direct. Best I can make out is she's being held in solitary."

"How did the Norwegian die?"

"Hata handled him personally. Word is it took half a dozen Kempei to scrub the blood off his office floor."

"Then it doesn't look as if Hata got what he wanted after all."

Caro shook his head.

Salat rose from the chair and began pacing the room. "If that's so, then Hata won't release Dominique."

"No. He won't."

"Of course we could try Dallin."

"No good. Rumor is he's missing on the Yangtze. Up past Nanking."

"That should make Hata happy."

Caro's hollow cheeks and small mouth curled into a sardonic smile. "There's another rumor that Becker and Hata were planning to flee to South America but the Jap backed out."

"Is this true?"

"The Hungarian woman who runs the brothel over on Rue du Consulat swears it is! Claims Becker tried to borrow money from her. He promised to send the money back to her from Buenos Aires."

Salat nodded. Then he moved over to the draped window and peered through at the canopied entrance of the Cathay Hotel. Joining him, Caro stopped to gaze at the Paris street scene on the wall.

"*La belle France,*" he murmured, strongly affected by the painting. "What I would give to be back there."

"Caro?"

"*Oui?*"

"I want Dominique Torg freed," Salat said forcefully. "Do you understand? Freed."

"It won't be easy."

"But it can be done. What's the name of Hata's friend . . . that White Russian girl?"

"Niki Orlov. Why?"

"I might want to snatch her, then arrange a trade."

"*Mon Dieu!*"

"But maybe to be on the safe side," Salat went on, "it's better to knock off his warehouse."

"Fantastic!" Caro murmured, shaken by the thought. "But fortunately impossible. The place is guarded day and night by a full platoon of Kempetai. Even if we did fight our way in—

side we'd never have enough time to get away with all that loot."

"Suppose I said there is another way inside that warehouse. One that requires no gun battle."

"I'd still be against it."

"But it can be done."

"*Oui.* But at what cost. You already have every Kempei agent looking for you. If we go near that warehouse, you'll never get out of Shanghai alive."

"But Dominique will be free."

"Perhaps. One can't be sure." Caro hedged.

"You mean, Macao won't like it?"

"They're angry, Salat. And if you looked at things from their side you'd see they're right. It's taken us years to get into the good graces of the Japanese after that trouble with Bastia. Now we're back where we started and who knows how much squeeze it's going to take to sort out things."

"The Japanese are finished in East Asia. They know it and Macao knows it," Salat replied resentfully. "A few more months . . . a year at most . . . and we needn't put up with them anymore."

"In the meantime we do. Unless you want them to shut us down from Shanghai to Singapore."

"I know what Macao thinks. But Dominique Torg isn't just any woman. She is extraordinary and I love her."

"Keep in mind that to the bosses in Macao business comes first."

"But not to me. Not anymore," Salat insisted. "I gave her up once. Never again."

All this could have been avoided if Dominique had listened, Salat thought. If only she had stayed, escaped from the Kempetai with him. Still, deep in his heart, he could not blame her. If their positions had been reversed, he would have done what she did. In fact, according to Caro, he was about to do it now.

The upper echelon of the Corsican syndicate based in Macao would never understand his motives. In their hard-edged world there was little place for personal sentiment. Because of them, Salat had long ago broken with his past—his family, the island where he was born—and had gone to China with another man's name and a new identity.

There had been many women in his life, but finding one he could genuinely love was not easy. There had never really been anyone until he met Dominique. Despite the fact that she was from such a different background, they were drawn together naturally.

The syndicate had done nothing to save Bastia. Now they were prepared to force Salat to watch Dominique die. However, Salat had no intention of allowing this to happen. If he survived, from now on he would be his own man. He would take Dominique far away from China to a place where they might start a new life. Even Caro, could no longer be trusted. Just by looking at his face, thought Salat, it was clear that pressure had already been brought to bear to oppose the director of the Shanghai Roulette Club.

"Caro?"

"*Oui?*".

"Make your arrangements. I'll leave for Macao tomorrow night."

"A wise decision, *mon ami*." Caro smiled. "And Dominique?"

"I'll miss her," Salat replied, "but the syndicate comes first."

Nodding, Caro thought, if only what you are saying is the truth. If not, then a man who excels at obtaining information can also pass it on, especially to a certain individual at the Cathay Hotel.

Chapter Seventeen

The calendar beside the Hacker and Torg files on Hata's desk read August 6, 1945. Hata noted that his office no longer bore the signs of the bloody confrontation with Gustav Torg. He was in no mood to find it otherwise. After stalking angrily out of Bridge House, he had spent what was left of the night with Niki. They had planned to stop at the Pleasure Palace for a drink before going to Broadway Mansions where Hata had confiscated the sumptuously appointed duplex apartment of a wealthy cotton exporter. The lower floor of the apartment had a large swimming pool and steam bath where he could escape from the responsibilities of his command and be alone with Niki.

The recollection of Niki, resting damp and naked on the cool ceramic tiles framing the pool, stirred Hata. Her bare thighs spread apart, she had commanded him to come closer—crawl closer and bury his face between her legs. This ritual of theirs had revealed to Hata what an erotic woman could do to a man. It was not her looks which mattered to him. It was something in her attitude which tapped into some basic desire of his.

However, one drink at the Pleasure Palace had led to another. The piano player, a young Neapolitan with long black eyelashes, was singing romantic songs from the twenties. Niki

doted on the nostalgic melodies, and much as Hata wanted to
be alone with her, they had stayed on to drink.

The brothel was filled that night with Kamikaze, young
men recently trained as pilots, en route to a secret base outside Osaka. Some of them had served with the army on Okinawa, and their descriptions of the bitter fighting there were
very graphic: Japanese infantrymen hounded from cave to
cave, blown up by satchel charges, burned by flamethrowers,
driven by starvation to cannibalism, and beyond, to insanity
and suicide. Their tales did more than just repel Hata; it reminded him of how westernized his relationship with Niki
and Dallin had made him, for listening to these harrowing
accounts of battle left Hata with only one overriding feeling:
life not glory; life not honor; life not Emperor or country,
was all he really wanted.

Yet the Japanese military code that governed him forbade
surrender. In part, this explained the harsh treatment the
Japanese accorded Allied prisoners of war. For them, surrender was a sign of total disgrace, so, consequently, defeated
soldiers were undeserving of respect and decent treatment.
The Japanese soldier was expected to die fighting on the battlefield, and in the event he survived, tradition then required
that he commit hara-kiri to remove the stain of dishonor.
Should he refuse, his countrymen would ostracize him, leaving him no other choice but exile.

Hata studied his ornate samurai sword lying on the edge of
the desk, painfully aware of its symbolic meaning. He
frowned and turned his attention to the recently arrived pile
of communiqués and reports.

JAPANESE HIGH COMMAND
FIRST GENERAL ARMY HQ
TOKYO

RECENT REPORTS OF EXTENSIVE AMERICAN
TROOP TRANSFER AND SUPPLY BUILDUP FROM
EUROPEAN THEATER OF OPERATIONS FOR USE
AGAINST THE HOME ISLANDS CONFIRMED.

KEMPETAI HQ
TOKYO

RUMORS OF PEACE NEGOTIATIONS IN SWITZER-
LAND BETWEEN MEMBERS OF JAPANESE PEACE

FACTION AND OSS REPRESENTATIVES VERIFIED. TO DATE SUCH MEETINGS APPARENTLY HAVE PROVEN FRUITLESS.

JAPANESE ARMY HQ
CHINA EXPEDITIONARY FORCES
SHANGHAI

NATIONALIST CHINESE PLAN TO LAUNCH INVASION UPON CANTON FROM THE SEA HAS BEEN ACTIVATED. ATTACK EXPECTED NO LATER THAN MID-SEPTEMBER.

KEMPETAI HQ
PEKING

URGENT

DESPITE AMERICAN-SPONSORED COALITION BETWEEN KUOMINTANG AND COMMUNISTS, NOTED GUERRILLA LEADER COMMISSAR HSU UNDERSTOOD TO BE EN ROUTE TO SHANGHAI WITH ORDERS TO IMPLEMENT COMMUNIST TAKEOVER THERE IN ORDER TO DENY CITY TO NATIONALISTS.

IN A RELATED DEVELOPMENT OUR RELATIONSHIP WITH THE SOVIETS IS DETERIORATING RAPIDLY. WAR APPEARS TO BE IMMINENT.

Staggered by the enormity of the collapse these communiqués outlined, Hata studied the weekly evaluation made by his own command of the situation in Shanghai.

IN PAST WEEK STATISTICS OBTAINED FROM AIRPORT, PORT, AND RAILWAY STATIONS INDICATE NUMEROUS FOREIGN NATIONALS, PARTICULARLY OF FORMER AXIS PARTNERS, DEPARTING SHANGHAI. OTHERS ARE ASSUMED TO HAVE LEFT BY AUTOMOBILE. SIGNS OF IMPENDING DEPARTURE BY SEGMENTS OF JAPANESE CIVILIAN POPULATION HAVE BEEN NOTED.

UNREST AMONG CHINESE WORKING CLASS CONTINUES DUE TO MAJOR UNEMPLOYMENT IN MILLS, SHIPPING, AND FACTORIES.

PRICE OF GOLD AND U.S. CURRENCY RISING
SHARPLY. LOCAL CHINESE AND JAPANESE CUR-
RENCIES DEVALUATING TEN PERCENT DAILY.
HOARDING OF FOODSTUFFS GREATLY INCREASED.
LOCAL STORES REPORT LOW INVENTORIES OF
RICE, GRAIN, AND OTHER STAPLE ITEMS. SITUA-
TION IS PARTICULARLY DESPERATE INSIDE HONG-
KEW JEWISH GHETTO.

SHANGHAI POWER COMPANY EXPECTS SHORT-
AGE OF FUEL WILL COMPEL FURTHER SHUT-
DOWNS BEYOND PRESENT FOUR-HOUR-A-DAY
USE. MUNICIPAL TRANSPORTATION MAY BE DIS-
RUPTED.

MORALE OF NANKING GOVERNMENT OFFICIALS
VERY LOW. SOME HIGHER RANKING INDIVIDUALS
HAVE ALREADY FLED TO INTERIOR. SIGNS OF
INCREASING DISOBEDIENCE TOWARD COLLABO-
RATION GOVERNMENT IN SHANGHAI BECOMING
MORE FREQUENT. IT MAY BE NECESSARY FOR
ELEMENTS OF JAPANESE OCCUPATION FORCES TO
TAKE OVER THEIR FUNCTION SHOULD SITUATION
DETERIORATE ANY FURTHER.

As Hata put this last report back on his desk, there was a
knock on the door and two Kempei guards escorted Dominique Torg into his office.

She shuffled wearily into the office. She was dressed in gray
cotton pajamas and cloth sandals, standard prison garb, and
her blonde hair fell in tangled strands. Her face, paler than
usual, made her hazel eyes seem more pronounced.

In the last twenty-four hours her faith in humanity had
been sorely tested. She had seen men and women cry out for
mercy while their Japanese tormentors watched dispas-
sionately. She had been stripped and physically abused, and
then, most devastating of all, she had witnessed the effects of
the barbaric treatment her father had suffered, all in the
name of Japanese nationalism.

Through it all, her one wish had been to be able to close
her eyes and make the nightmare disappear, to restore her
life to the way it had once been. But rationally she knew that
for her to emerge intact from this experience she had to face

reality, to accept things as they were. But she realized that it was too soon for a rational look at what had happened. Fate had thrown her life off course and only when the evil cycle of events was completed would she be righted again. Although passivity had never been part of her makeup, what could she or anyone do, confronted by the raw power of the Kempetai?

"I regret to inform you," Hata said stiffly, "that your father Gustav Torg has died of natural causes."

"Natural causes?"

"Exactly," Hata said forcefully, prepared for an argument. "Now I want to honor the agreement I had with him, but how can I without the black book, the record of the occupation kept by Felix Hacker. "Do you understand my problem?"

"I think so," Dominique answered vaguely.

"Good. Then where is it?"

"Where is what?" Dominique asked, her face vacant.

"The black book! Tell me where your father and Felix Hacker hid it and you can go free."

"Free?" she repeated dully.

"That's what I said!" Hata turned to the guards in a rage. "What's wrong with her?"

Before either of them could answer, Dominique's face went slack and she fell to her knees. Grabbing for her, the guards managed to break her fall and hold her up between them.

Hata pounded his fist against the desk in exasperation, then after one more attempt to get the information from her, he ordered the guards to take Dominique to the prison hospital with instructions that the doctors notify him the moment her condition improved.

The door had hardly shut behind them when the telephone rang. Hata lifted the receiver from its cradle and sat back. Five minutes later he replaced the receiver, amazed by what the Kempetai commandant of the Nanking Section had just told him. A patrol boat had found the *Ikado Maru* adrift on the Yantze, forty miles north of Nanking. Dallin was not aboard, but the body of Colonel Juzo, a recent deserter from the Kwantung Army, was discovered in the wheelhouse with his throat slit. Locked inside the forward hold were the detachment of Japanese guards from the Shanghai garrison and the crew of the *Ikado Maru*, who insisted they had last seen Dallin with Juzo holding a gun to his head.

So the worst had happened. Most likely Dallin was dead. The thought left Hata disconsolate. Aside from Niki, their friendship was the only close personal contact he had allowed himself in Shanghai.

He could still recall their first meeting in January of 1943. He remembered how his sharp questioning had never shaken Dallin, not even when Hata uncovered the fact that the White Russian was a common thief and had agreed to become a Kempetai informer in Tientsin. Despite Dallin's initial attempt to conceal his past, Hata had responded to him instantly, and to the possibilities that his arrival in Shanghai had brought about. The pair had struck a bargain right away, and in the years that followed, the two men shared many interests, not to mention enormous wealth. With Shanghai as their base, they had achieved a mutual dream: together they operated the most successful black-market syndicate on the China coast.

It was Maximov Dallin who had introduced Hata to Niki, and to countless other western pleasures, including jazz, French cuisine, all-night partying, and gambling, all things for which the White Russian had a keen appreciation. Even the idea for the Pleasure Palace, the most luxurious brothel in Shanghai, had been his.

The only area that held no interest for the White Russian was politics. Outside of his abiding hatred for the Americans and British, he did not think it really mattered who dominated Asia. Often, after many drinks, he would confide in Hata, telling the Kempetai commandant how a close study of world history revealed that in time every government became corrupt. The basic nature of man, Dallin frequently insisted, was rooted in hypocrisy and personal gain. He claimed his only loyalty was to their partnership. In supporting Hata, he was ultimately bolstering his own self-interest. The candor of the statement startled Hata at first, but later, after listening to Niki's description of how the Bolsheviks overwhelmed Czarist Russia, the Kempetai commandant decided the White Russian's cynicism was well justified.

And now Dallin was gone! It was more than Hata could take in. Suddenly the door to his office was thrown open and Lieutenant Sumato, his haggard face more agitated than usual, burst in.

"There's been a bombing," he said, handing a communiqué to Hata. "Better read it for yourself."

"Why the excitement about a bombing? The Americans have already leveled most of our cities———"

"This one is different," Sumato interrupted, his voice tinged with doom. "See for yourself."

Annoyed by his subordinate's manner, Hata made a mental note to have him disciplined, but first he decided to read the communiqué.

> KEMPETAI HQ
> TOKYO
>
> HIROSHIMA TOTALLY DEVASTATED BY TREMEN-
> DOUS EXPLOSION CAUSED BY ONE BOMB OF
> MYSTERIOUS AND REVOLUTIONARY QUALITY.
> MORE THAN ONE HUNDRED THOUSAND CASUAL-
> TIES REPORTED SO FAR. FIRES STILL RAGING
> OUT OF CONTROL. ALL VITAL SERVICES HAVE
> CEASED TO FUNCTION.

"One bomb? One hundred thousand casualties?

"According to an official broadcast," Sumato said tremulously, "just after eight o'clock this morning, two B-29's passed over Hiroshima. There was a bright flash, then an incredible concussion, and the city was destroyed."

"How is this possible?"

"Our radio room picked up a broadcast from San Francisco. Truman refers to the weapon as an atomic bomb, the equivalent of twenty thousand tons of TNT."

For a few moments Hata could not trust himself to speak. Then in a dull monotone, he said, "This means the Home Islands . . . Shanghai . . . the Americans can blow up any place they wish. Madness!"

"It was madness to fight the Americans in the first place," Sumato said, staring down glumly at his mustard-colored leather boots and thinking of his beloved family in Nagasaki.

"Keep your defeatist thoughts to yourself," Hata exploded, "unless you want to share a cell with some of our prisoners."

"Yes, sir," Sumato bowed before turning toward the door.

"Sumato!" Hata called out. "Find Obersturmbannführer Becker and bring him here."

"Shall I place him under arrest?"

"Did I mention arrest?"

"No, sir."

Hata reddened. "Then do exactly what I ordered. And bring me the file on Becker."

"Immediately."

"And Sumato?"

"Sir?"

"A few days ago I asked you to prepare a plan for destroying all our files. Is it completed?"

"No . . . I——"

"Never mind the excuses," Hata interrupted brusquely. "Just have it finished and turned into me by morning. Is that understood?" And without waiting for a response, Hata dismissed him with a wave of his hand.

Every sofa and chair, every foot of space in the lobby of the Cathay Hotel was occupied, as Occidentals, Japanese businessmen, Chinese collaborators, and regular patrons clustered together in stunned groups. The broadcast from the Domei Agency, the official news service of Japan, had come over the wireless only an hour earlier.

Hiroshima, the eighth largest city in Japan, had been blasted apart by a single bomb! Leaflets dropped by American planes elsewhere in the Home Islands had warned that more bombs would soon follow unless the Japanese accepted the Potsdam Declaration and capitulated.

The end was not far off for collaborators and officials of the Nanking puppet government. If Nippon did not surrender, then she would be bombed into extinction. The only choice now left to those who had sided with the Japanese was to flee, or wiser still, go into hiding until a new regime was installed whose favor could be curried.

But to the canny war profiteers, the speculators and black-market operators, defeat meant something totally different. An era of vast opportunity was ending, to be sure, but another, with infinitely greater possibilities, lay ahead. Japanese propaganda to the contrary, America was wealthier and more powerful than ever before. Her factories churned out goods at rates incalculable to minds still frozen in terms of the world depression. What the ambitious of Shanghai needed now was to take lessons from the Chungking crowd on how to fleece "Uncle Chump from over the Hump." Soon thousands of American officials and soldiers with U.S. dollars would be stationed in Shanghai. A whole different market could be tapped. New merchandise, western-style restaurants and nightclubs, and women would be in demand. The profits envisioned in U.S. dollars, aside from gold the best hedge against inflation in China, was tantalizing.

Not so for Plitov, the bearded night manager, poised at the edge of the marble reception desk. Personally he relished the day that exploiters and thieves, made respectable by the Japanese Occupation, would stop patronizing the Cathay. His views had been seconded only a few moments earlier by Zabar, the maître d' of the Tower Nightclub upstairs. But Zabar, more cynical in his outlook, cautioned Plitov against expecting too much change. Only the Communists could cause a total upheaval, he said, and then where would Zabar or Plitov be?

In the next five minutes the noise and confusion in the lobby mounted as waves of Europeans and Orientals swarmed down from their rooms and in from Nanking Road to join the crowd already milling about there.

"Extraordinary, isn't it?" Ferrara observed, joining Plitov at the reception desk.

"Started just after that radio broadcast. I'll bet the night flights to Hong Kong will be fully booked from now on."

"They have been for weeks," Ferrara replied. "But, unless I'm wrong—which I doubt, most of the cleverer ones won't be going anywhere. There just aren't that many places to run."

It was true. To the west were the Allies and the Nationalists. To the east the Pacific was filled with American land, sea, and air forces. Up north were the Russians. Only south, through Hong Kong into Southeast Asia, was there any hope of escape—and that was limited.

"Odd, isn't it?" Plitov remarked suddenly, catching a glimpse of an Argentine munitions dealer encircled by a horde of Japanese collaborators.

"What is?" Ferrara asked.

"We are. Throughout all the turbulence of the warlords, the Communists, the Nationalists, the puppet government, the Japanese, and now this—we have always remained."

"It's not so remarkable, Plitov. After all, we are the Swiss of the Orient. We manage a grand hotel in the finest international tradition. We take no sides, offer equal services to all, whether they be fascist, capitalist, or communist, and have made it clear that regardless of regime we shall always remain impartial and unbiased."

"The Swiss of the Orient," murmured Plitov, with new-found admiration.

"Exactly," Ferrara replied, extracting an American cigarette from a slender gold case. "But instead of providing a safe haven for gold and foreign currencies we pamper the body and spirit. And judging from the wellbeing of our guests, I would say that under the most difficult circumstances we've done quite nicely by them."

"It hasn't been easy. Truly I don't know how you've managed to keep us open."

"Nonsense, Plitov." Ferrara smiled modestly. "Any Venetian trained as I have been would have done the same. You see, centuries of experience have prepared us for coping with intrigue and betrayal. You forget, *amico mio*, I personally am a seasoned veteran of world instability. I was at the Adlon in Berlin during the days of the Weimar Republic. The streets were filled with the unemployed, with rabble-rousers. And while I served at the Ritz in Madrid the Spanish Republic fell. Why, socialists and Falangists were battling in the tea room. Believe me, *amico mio*, when you've been through what I have, even Shanghai has its good points."

Nodding, Plitov recalled other tales with which Ferrara had regaled him in the past. He recalled the occasional travelers, normally the very wealthy or influential, who knew the managing director from his days at the Danieli in Venice, the Adlon in Berlin, and the Ritz in Madrid. It was ironic, Plitov thought, that a man who epitomized culture and civilization invariably turned up in the midst of a battlefield.

Chapter Eighteen

———••◆•◆••———

Dallin decided to avoid Nanking altogether. Although the city was nearby, the approaches to it were simply too dangerous. So instead he trekked due east, then swung south in a loop, planning to link up with the Shanghai Railway Line well below Nanking and away from the bandits and guerrillas roaming the area.

Traveling on foot was grueling. The sun was blistering. There was no breeze, and the cloying humidity quickly forced him to strip off his jacket and shirt, wrapping them into a bundle. Before he had traveled much farther, he added his shoes and socks as well.

By then he was in rice country, flat, treeless, and marked by lush green patches of rice submerged in water and hemmed in by natural dikes of tightly packed mud which served as paths. Around him the heat shimmered above the water, making his vision seem fuzzy and out of focus. Reluctantly, Dallin dragged to a halt. He untangled the soiled handkerchief from his forehead and wiped the sweat from his eyes and face. Then, with a groan, he gave up and sank down on the damp earth.

Dallin was not sure how far he was from the Yangtze. He only knew that with each step, his misgivings increased. Something kept telling him to change directions, to turn his back on Shanghai and move directly west to Chungking and safety. Christ, the idea was appealing! But how could he ever justify abandoning the ring? Still, the notion kept nagging at him, as if his instinct for playing hunches was struggling to prevail. According to an ex-soldier, a nineteen-year-old double amputee, the town of Wuteh, once a prosperous railhead on the Shanghai-Nanking line, lay an hour ahead on the path he was following, which meant the worst part of his journey was nearly over.

Dallin crawled over to the edge of the paddy and scooped up a handful of water, letting it drip slowly onto his grimy face, making sure the water never entered his mouth. Then he applied the same technique, only not as cautiously, to his bare chest and feet. It brought instant relief. He was almost tempted to quench his thirst, but reason won out, and instead he rolled over on his back, resting his head on his bundled-up clothes. Overhead the sun had slipped behind a dense blanket of low-lying clouds. It looked as though it might rain. If so, it would not last, sighed Dallin knowingly.

Off to his right in the paddy a bunch of naked children giggled and pointed their fingers at him. Farther away, a line of peasants in broad bamboo hats and black cotton pajamas, cut above the knee, were working their way across the field, planting rice sprouts and filling straw baskets with fish plucked live from the water, where they had purposely been left to fatten.

Dallin waited till the line weaved closer to him. Then, heaving himself onto his haunches, he shouted, attracting their attention. Eventually one of the peasants approached. A woman's face, as wrinkled as a dried prune, peeped out beneath her bamboo hat. Her few remaining teeth were blackened stumps.

Smiling, Dallin politely asked how far Wuteh was. After long contemplation the woman shook her head. In Li, the equivalent of a third of a mile, she had no idea. By foot, along the path Dallin was on, it was usually a journey of two full hours. That meant either she or the amputee was wrong. But only by half, which for China was not bad. Relieved, Dallin went on to his next question, asking details about the town. Were there soldiers? What time did the train pass through on its way to Shanghai?

Again the woman contemplated. Then she wheeled and shouted to one of the children playing at the edge of the paddy. An incredibly scrawny boy, whom Dallin guessed to be ten or twelve, came over and stood nervously beside the woman. Dallin repeated his questions. At first the boy shrugged; then, encouraged by the woman, he started to talk.

Wuteh had been badly shelled several years earlier and abandoned by most of its population. The main street was boarded up. Only a few merchants, mostly the poorer ones, remained. There were others, however—beggars, thieves, and squatters—living in the deserted and wrecked buildings, while a company of puppet troops guarded the railway station in the center of town. But the boy, who visited there during daylight to sell fish and rice, had neither seen nor heard a train, which was possible since trains in occupied China ran only at night to avoid strafing from American planes.

Dallin thanked the two for their help; then, on second thought, he dug into the bundle and removed his keys, giving them the silver chain. By his standards, the gift was hardly very munificent, but for the peasants it meant the difference between life and death in the winter months that lay ahead.

Then, certain of his safety, Dallin gave in to his fatigue and rolled over on the ground to sleep. He awoke at dusk to find a thick mist drifting over the paddies, and the peasants gone. He hurriedly flung more water on his face, stuck the bundle under one arm, and started along the mud path toward Wuteh. His plan was to arrive there after dark, so that his presence might go undetected until the final moment when he boarded the Shanghai-bound train. Puppet troops were usually undisciplined and as prone to molesting unprotected travelers as any other lawless band in China, so he decided to keep away from them.

Dallin made his way at a steady trot across the flat rice paddies. Gradually the terrain ahead sloped upward and, leaving the paddies behind, he came to a ridge overlooking an irregular formation of low-lying structures outlined against the darkening sky. Quickening his pace, Dallin began narrowing the gap between himself and the first row of buildings, which from their size he judged to be factories and warehouses.

On open ground now, Dallin skirted several deep trenches that had been dug during the bitter fighting earlier in the war. The desolation was complete here. It brought Dallin to a halt. He put on his shoes, shirt, and jacket, and, taking no chances, started ahead slowly, glancing warily from left to right as he drew near the outlying buildings. Up close he saw they were really little more than facades, barren walls shot full of holes and left standing like silent sentinels guarding mounds of debris from their caved-in roofs.

It was darker now, the moon full but pale and not yet luminous. Beyond the ruins a winding road led into the town. It was pitted with shell holes and craters and lined on both sides by houses boarded up to keep out prowlers. Even the lamp posts were casualties of the battle, twisted and bent out of shape as though they were made of wood rather than cast iron. The bulbs had been destroyed by gunfire, and Dallin guessed the electric current had been disrupted as well.

He slowed to a crawl, groping past burned-out hulks of trucks and automobiles, some overturned, others parked wherever they had been hit. So far there was no sign of life, but Dallin knew his luck could not hold forever. As he rounded a curve at the far end of the road, he saw a crowd of beggars and refugees hunched over a roaring bonfire. Nearby a dead horse lay on the ground, its ribcage showing and flesh gouged crudely from its haunches. One man in rags held a hunk of meat skewered on a wooden stick over the fire. Suddenly a loud argument broke out among the crowd and another man snatched the meat from the pole and dashed off down the road.

Dallin dove sideways into the doorway of a ruined building just as the thief approached. He watched as the mob, howling for blood, rushed past in pursuit. Then the street fell silent again. Dallin checked carefully to make sure he was alone before he pushed on down the road. He slipped past alleys and narrow lanes where men gambled and drank before fires. A girl, no more than thirteen, sat in a broken chair with her black trousers pulled down around her thighs. In the shadows, a group of figures, ignoring the shrieks of a trapped dog, tore at the pitiful animal with their bare hands.

The inferno neither sickened nor surprised Dallin. Experience had taught him what to expect in lawless areas. This was the debris of the long war in China, the natural heritage of a vast mass of people who had been marked expendable by various power blocs and discarded. Left to die, with no authority or community force to guide them, these outcasts had slid back centuries, far beyond the first gleam of civilization. Wuteh was horrible, but Dallin kept telling himself that the Honan famine only a few years before had been far worse. There Kuomintang officials had sold off grain at enormous profit to the Japanese and then had done nothing as millions of people ate bark from trees, grass, even one another in a futile effort to avoid starving to death.

Suddenly the road wound sharply to the right, bringing Dallin to a major intersection. Here the cross street was much wider and lined by more imposing shops and homes, which led Dallin to believe he was on the main street of Wuteh. These buildings too were shuttered and dark. The moon was bright yellow now, a perfect sphere. Even so there was no way of telling where the railway station was.

Following his hunch, Dallin turned left and almost immediately stumbled over a jagged pile of household goods. Alarmed at his miscalculation, he quickly retraced his steps and headed in the opposite direction. The wide avenue eventually ended in what seemed to be a patch of open ground. Sure it had once been a park, Dallin made his way between two uprooted concrete blocks long ago stripped of their valuable wooden benches. Catching the erratic hum of an electric generator off to his right, Dallin followed the sound till he came to the edge of a clump of thorny bushes.

On the other side of the thicket, a half dozen badly battered trucks and jeeps were parked in front of a two-story building, its windows lit by low-wattage bulbs. Just off the entrance, below the flags of Japan and the Nanking government, a portable generator was rumbling away. On both sides of the doorway, concealed by sandbags, were heavy machine guns manned by Chinese soldiers in the tan uniform of the puppet government. Bareheaded and puffing on cigarettes, the gunners sat behind their weapons exchanging comments.

Edging closer, Dallin studied the windows. In the corner room at the left four soldiers were playing Mah-Jongg and drinking hot tea; in the middle one, several soldiers dozed as a wireless blared, while in the room to his extreme right, two trouserless soldiers pinned a teenage girl to the wall as a third one slapped her across the face, then pawed brutally at her naked breasts. The girl squirmed and pleaded, which only aroused the soldier further. She was still struggling when Dallin averted his eyes. If he made an attempt to enter puppet headquarters he might never leave alive, and if he backtracked into Wuteh and encountered that hungry mob things could go even harder for him. Yet somewhere between lay the railway station. If he only knew exactly where.

He never got the chance to find out. A hobnailed boot struck the pavement, then the glare of a flashlight blinded him.

"Who are you?" a voice demanded in a guttural tone. Before Dallin could reply, a baby-faced Cantonese in a puppet uniform swept forward, prodding his chest with the snub-nosed barrel of a revolver.

"Who are you?" the soldier repeated.

"My name wouldn't mean anything to you. I'm up from Shanghai."

"What you want in Wuteh?"

"I was separated from my party. Figured I'd get back home by catching the train here."

"Papers?" the soldier demanded, prodding him with the revolver again.

"Got none," Dallin replied wearily. "Lost them on the Yangtze."

"The Yangtze's a long way from here."

"Look, maybe you better take me to headquarters. I'll tell my story to your superior officer."

Dallin meant this to be a bluff. It failed dismally. The Chinese slammed him on the side of the face with his revolver, then swung Dallin around expertly and began frisking him.

"I tell you I've got nothing on me. The steamer I was on was raided by pirates."

"Turn around!" the soldier ordered.

Dallin did as he was told. He planned to do a little more than was asked, but as Dallin spun, the soldier retreated, his youthful face creased with suspicion.

"All right, I'll level with you." Dallin shrugged. "In the heel of my right boot is a platinum bar."

"Show me!"

Smiling, Dallin bent over, then, giving no warning, straightened up. The top of his head caught the puppet soldier on the jaw. There was a sickening crunch and the soldier staggered backward. Dallin went after him. He swooped in, hitting him low with a jarring left to the gut, which sent the soldier sprawling to the ground. His revolver bounced against a concrete slab and exploded with a deafening blast, nearly hitting Dallin and bringing the sentries running.

His ears still ringing from the gunshot, Dallin took off the way he had come. He wove across the derelict park, then ducked into a squalid alley bordering the wide avenue, the tramping of hobnailed boots and shouts to stop piercing the darkness behind him.

Onward he raced, heaving himself over a low fence and getting a whiff of unwashed body as he did so. He had dropped down beside an elderly Chinese beggar, huddled on the ground, feeding off a garbage pile. Terror-stricken, the beggar started to scream. Dallin wrapped a hand over his gaping mouth and said, "Just tell me how to get to the railway station."

"Shanghai railway?"

"Which way?"

"That way," the beggar replied, motioning in the direction Dallin was heading. It was not a moment too soon. The puppet soldiers were in the alley, their flashlights sweeping the low fence, their voices getting louder. Dallin shoved off at a full run. Thirty feet away, he tripped and, skidding on his belly, went hurtling to a stop against the wall.

At the same time the puppet soldiers were already bounding over the fence in pairs. Long-barreled rifles at the ready, they pushed the elderly beggar aside, then swept the alley with their flashlights. When the entire squad was over the fence, their officer, a middle-aged captain, led them deeper into the alley. At a cry from one of the squad, every flashlight came to rest on a man lying face down on the ground. Pleased with himself, the front-rank soldier flipped the man over on his back, only to let out a shriek as he did so. A family of rats melted into the darkness, revealing a face eaten to the bone.

Moaning, the soldier swung around and vomited. The captain cursed, then taking one look at the defiled corpse, ordered his men back to headquarters.

"Let him go," he explained. "Only fools roam these streets at night."

"So Dallin finally caught it!" Igor, the chief barman of the Tower Nightclub, said as he set a chilled martini on the bar in front of Giacomo Ferrara. "Murdered on the Yangtze no less."

"From your amazed tone you'd think Dallin wasn't mortal."

"Oh, he was mortal, all right," Igor said. "But what a conniver! What a manipulator! Sure, people die every day in Shanghai, die in droves. But Maximov Dallin? That White Russian scoundrel being killed . . . that's something! And if you ask me, I bet Colonel Hata isn't half as surprised about what happened as I am."

Reflecting, Ferrara sipped his drink, then asked softly, "So you think Hata's responsible?"

"Who else? They made millions, those two. If only half of what people around here say is true, they amassed one of the great Shanghai fortunes. Dallin left no wife or kids. So I ask you? Who gets his share?"

"Igor, my dear friend," Ferrara smiled, shaking his head, "for an excellent barman you have a most imaginative mind."

"It's not imagination!" Igor protested. "Look at the facts. In Shanghai, anything can happen. Take this club, for instance. Just look around. After the terrible news about Hiroshima, a whole city wiped out, wouldn't you think this place would be empty, out of respect for the dead, for the tragedy! Instead Zabar tells me we have more reservations than on a Saturday evening! So go figure out China!"

It was true, realized Ferrara. The dance floor packed. Every table was full. There was even a crowd fifty deep at the door, waiting to get in. Zabar was having a difficult time keeping them calm. People seemed to be bubbling over with excitement, hatching plans, scheming new ways for making money; the intoxicating aroma of gold bars and U.S. currency was in the air.

"I mean go figure China!" Igor complained. "If I was one of those people, I'd be home packing. Trying to find some way out of here. Instead they sit there like they just inherited billions. And you know why? It's simple. The Americans are coming to Shanghai. That's why!"

"Some of our former patrons will come as well," Ferrara said half-heartedly. "The great steamers will be running . . . Pan Am Clippers . . . ocean-going yachts . . . perhaps even the Trans-Siberian."

"I hope so!" Igor replied gloomily.

A bone-thin Corsican emerged from the crowd and slipped past the maître d'; he headed to the bar where Ferrara was standing.

"Your man at reception said I'd find you here," Caro said quietly.

"Well?" Ferrara replied, his tone far from gracious.

"I'd like a word with you in private."

"You've caught me at a bad time. If you phone tomorrow, perhaps we can . . ."

"By then it will be too late. We must talk now."

"Have we met before?"

"No."

"Then why are you so sure I'd be interested in what you have to say."

"Because I just am, Monsieur Munk," Caro said with a knowing smile, resting his hand confidently upon the managing director's elbow, "or do you still call yourself Senor Pacheco?"

Chapter Nineteen

———◆——————◆——————◆———

Fourteen hundred miles west of Shanghai lies Chungking. The city is situated on a rocky peninsula that juts out between the confluences of the Yangtze and Kialing rivers. In 1938, following the Nationalists' retreat from the coast, this minor treaty port in the backwater province of Szechuan became the wartime capital of Free China.

It was generally an awful place. In winter a constant dense fog lay over Chungking, bringing with it a damp cold that chilled even the sturdiest souls. Spring brought heavy rains and flooding, while in summer, the most unpleasant season of all, a torrid sun turned the city's mud and bamboo buildings into ovens and made the inhabitants slow-moving drudges at the mercy of foul odors, thick gray dust, and swarms of annoying flies.

Several hundred thousand people, including foreign diplomats, newspaper correspondents, and European businessmen, had accompanied Chiang Kai-shek here from the cosmopolitan cities of eastern and northern China, swelling the local population to almost a million.

The wealthier and more influential ones lived in hastily built houses with primitive plumbing. The majority survived as best they could behind fences in caves burrowed deep into the reddish cliffs of the peninsula, which, as it turned out, were the safest places to live in Chungking until the Japanese bombers stopped their daily raids on the city, at the end of 1942.

There was little food to eat in Chungking and most of it was spoiled. People suffered from the intense heat and penetrating cold. They were cut off from newspapers, mail, films, family, and friends, with only the wireless radio to sustain them, and the knowledge that, given time, the United States would enter the war and then Japan would be doomed.

By 1945 these predictions had come true, but by then the defiant spirit of the capital of Free China, which had for a brief time won the respect of the beleaguered democracies of the world, had been corroded by corruption, war profiteering, and the chronic turmoil of runaway inflation.

Thousands of residents, who had formerly gone on foot about the steep streets or moved in rickshas and foul-smelling alcohol-driven motorbuses bearing huge posters of Chiang Kai-shek and his New Life Movement, now whizzed through Chungking in U.S. Army-issue jeeps stolen from American bases or sold illicitly by the Nationalists.

Shop windows overflowed with luxury items and food brought in from Tokyo and Occupied China, or obtained illegally from American sources. The postal service, never dependable in peacetime, now functioned efficiently between the interior and the coast, as did the flow of coded messages on a radio frequency linking banks in Chungking with their affiliates in Shanghai and Nanking.

But to Major Christopher Blake, the OSS officer charged with organizing clandestine operations in Shanghai, one of the strangest anomalies in this most unconventional of wars could be found in the row of small buildings that stood side by side on a crooked Chungking street. They housed, in order of appearance, the offices of the unofficial Japanese peace representative, the Communist delegation, a branch office of the Nationalist Secret Police led by General Tai-Li, and Blake's own undermanned, overworked covert operation, crammed inside a suffocating and poorly lit cubbyhole.

A lanky six-footer with light brown hair, Blake's crinkly gray eyes reflected his irrepressibly positive nature. A graduate of Columbia University and a budding Sinologist, his sharp insight into Chinese life had earned him the respect of the "old China hands," that tiny group of scholars and diplomats who devoted themselves to bettering the legitimate interests of the Chinese people, even at the expense of her self-serving leadership.

The China theater was a complex arena in which to fight a war, and no one was more ready than Christopher Blake to acknowledge his own confusion and inadequacy in unsnarling its mysteries. Yet, for nearly three years now, hour after hour, late into the night, Blake had sat at his desk, between two overloaded bookshelves, sifting through the enormous flow of information from his agents on the China coast. It was a curious existence for a scholar, but Christopher Blake was no stranger to war. His beliefs had taken him years before to Spain to fight against Franco, and they had kept him in Chungking despite threats on his life; relentless interference by the intelligence branch of the Nationalist Army, who were his supposed allies—even despite his vehement opposition to the conduct of the clique that now ruled Nationalist China.

A piece of disturbing news had just reached his desk, a response to an inquiry he had sent earlier. The communiqué had come from a source seldom tapped before, a high-ranking inspector at the Shanghai police station.

NO SIGN OF SHANGHAI BLACK BOOK. TORG, HACKER, AND OTHERS EXECUTED BY KEMPETAI. WHEREABOUTS OF WHITE RUSSIAN MAXIMOV DALLIN UNCERTAIN.

Blake crumpled the paper into an ashtray and set fire to it. He had grasped the implications at once, but his authority was severely limited. His official orders prohibited him from carrying out any further operations in the Shanghai Zone. This included rescuing Maximov Dallin and obtaining the black book.

The atomic bomb had changed the course of the war. The carefully planned and long-awaited invasion of Canton and the southern coast of China was cancelled. Official peace was expected at any moment. If not, scuttlebutt had it that the President would loose another atomic raid over the Japanese Home Islands. The streets of Chungking were overflowing with celebrating GIs. No one wanted to bother with the Japs anymore. It was a job for the big-shots and the State Department boys in Washington. Unfortunately, Blake thought ruefully, neither they nor the atomic bomb could do much good for those members of the Shanghai Ring who were already dead; or for Dallin, whose life might be on the line at this very moment. Nor could they recover Felix Hacker's black book.

Years of risk and hard work with no payoff! The idea rankled. Even Blake, a quiet, very controlled individual, had his breaking point. And this was it!

He had expected trouble for almost three months now, ever since he had sent an urgent request to the Shanghai Ring, asking them to pinpoint newly constructed Japanese defense positions on the coast. It was only logical the Kempetai would use every resource at their disposal to break the ring after its conspicuous success in uncovering the Japanese Navy's movements on the China Seas. After all, it was well known that the High Command was infuriated with Colonel Hata for his failure to plug these leaks of military information. Nevertheless, Chungking needed more information for their impending invasion, and the ring was the only group for the job. Never, however, did Blake think that it would cost all their lives.

Now the Norwegian, Hacker, Chung Lee, Hansen, and Knoll were all dead. While he had never met any of them, or even seen their photographs, Blake felt he knew them as well as his own family, or as well as his best friend Dallin. Dallin, of course, was not his real name. He had been born Stephen Tarabrin. His father, Nikolai, had been a brilliant Russian emigré, a financier with a flair for languages, exotic women, and complex business dealings. Following the Russian Revolution, the widowed Nikolai Tarabrin and his young son had settled in New York City. Several years later, just prior to Black Tuesday, Nicolai had made a substantial fortune selling short in the stock market. Shortly thereafter he died mysteriously, leaving sixteen-year-old Stephen an independently wealthy orphan.

A natural linguist like his father, Stephen subsequently graduated with honors from Columbia University in the class of 1935 and went abroad. He arrived in Canton, found employment for two years as a roving representative for an American oil company, and, during this time, acquired a working knowledge of both the Cantonese and Mandarin dialects. In 1937, deciding to move on, Stephen Tarabrin traveled by Trans-Siberian Express to Moscow. He arrived there at the height of Stalin's purges, finding thousands executed and more condemned to long sentences in remote camps. It was a harrowing experience, all the more disillusioning to someone like himself with a growing commitment to social justice. Disenchanted with the Soviets he went to Germany, where the sight of Nazi storm troopers beating up several elderly Jews got him into a nasty street brawl; he was subtly advised by the American consul to beat a hasty retreat for France. Once there, Stephen began running guns to the beleaguered Republican forces battling Franco in Spain. During one such smuggling venture he learned that his old college roommate Christopher Blake was being held in a fascist prison. With false papers he traveled into enemy territory in a battered Citroën roadster and bribed a prison guard into leaving a door open long enough so that Blake could walk out; then, with his grateful friend, Stephen made a wild, all-night drive back over the border into France.

So, for Blake, the thought of Dallin on the run from the Kempetai, or even worse returning unknowingly to Shanghai, was terrible, but what was he to do? All operations in the Shanghai Zone were henceforth terminated. The precise language of his orders made any evasion on his part subject to a court-martial. Of course, there was always the possibility of requesting help from the espionage network run by General Tai-Li or from the underworld minions ruled by the gangster chieftain Du Yueh Sen, but every time Blake had depended on their resources, the results had been at best odd, at worst chilling.

If only China were different, Blake thought wishfully. If only the in-fighting that characterized the relations between the Kuomintang government and the U.S. Army were not so cruel. But Free China oozed with deceits, half-truths, and exaggerations, even about several hard-won battles against the Japanese, which some said had never taken place at all, except in the imaginations of those high up in the Chungking government.

There was only one solution possible, Blake decided. It was contained in a neatly typed in-house memo on his desk, informing him that Major-General William B. Donovan, chief of the Office of Strategic Services, was making an around-the-world tour of OSS operations and was scheduled to arrive within the next seventy-two hours.

Chapter Twenty

———••◆••———

Dallin had survived. In running away, he had tripped over the legs of the dead man, on whom the rats had been feeding, and had fallen down a stairwell, escaping detection as the flashlights of the puppet soldiers passed by overhead. Once again, his *joss* had held. He succeeded in boarding the night train for Shanghai and left the blasted ruins of Wuteh far behind.

The train was a rattling conglomerate of rolling stock that had been manufactured by British, French, and German companies, some of it thirty and forty years old and collected from all over Occupied China. It stretched for half a mile and was made up of broken-down boxcars and gondolas with a moth-eaten coach next to the caboose. Dallin deliberately stayed away from that, slipping instead aboard a drafty boxcar in the middle of the train just as it was leaving the Wuteh station. He found he was not alone. At least fifty others, including grandmothers and young children, had made the same desperate run, joining another hundred or so passengers already inside the car for the miserable journey to Shanghai.

By rail the distance between Nanking and Shanghai is one hundred and ninety-five miles. In peacetime the Shanghai-Nanking Express normally made the journey in eight hours, but the passengers sharing the boxcar with Dallin would be

lucky to reach Shanghai in twice that time. At top speed the
train never exceeded thirty miles per hour, and stops at every
local station, time spent on sidings while military trains sped
past, and the frequent delays at bridge crossings while guards
searched for mines reduced this substantially.

Six hours into the trip, they were not even halfway to
Shanghai. Through it all, Dallin stayed tucked into a corner
of the boxcar. Jammed around him, both squatting and
standing, were entire families, complete with crying infants
and weary grandparents, as well as minor puppet government
officials with bulging briefcases, Buddhist monks, merchants,
including some carrying songbirds in wooden cages (particularly prized by the Chinese), a sprinkling of impoverished
Japanese factory workers, bearded Sikhs in turbans, and the
usual complement of noisy tea-boys who, despite the constant
swaying and bumping of the train, managed to keep their
hot-water jugs boiling over small fires, delivering their
sought-after tea in even the most out-of-the-way reaches of
the densely packed boxcar.

Almost everyone seemed to be resigned to the prolonged
journey; many slept or dozed fitfully, but not Dallin and the
spartan-like Chinese who shared his corner. Neither of them
shut their eyes for even a second. The Chinese was of
medium height but gaunt to the point of emaciation. A hairy
mole protruded from the lower left side of his leathery face,
and his clothing, a Western jacket and trousers, were oddly
matched. His eyes burned with intensity and, if he was weary
of the long journey, his stolid expression never betrayed it.
He neither smoked nor fidgeted, only kept watching the
crowd and Dallin. The curious part was he looked familiar.
Dallin, trying to place him, decided finally that perhaps he
had seen a photograph of him at Bridge House.

Finally the man spoke. His voice was low and hard, and
strangely commanding, as if he were accustomed to being
heard and obeyed. "You think you know me?" he asked.

"How can you tell?" replied Dallin warily.

"Habit."

"I know the feeling."

"I'm sure you do, Maximov Dallin, White Russian."

"And you?" Dallin asked, more puzzled than ever.

"Hsu."

"From Yenan?"

The Chinese nodded. So Dallin was right after all. It had been a photograph, a photograph Hata had shown him, of Commissar Hsu, the right-hand man of the astute Communist leader, Chou En-lai, and one of the Eighth Route Army's most skillful guerrillas and saboteurs, which meant Hsu would not be traveling alone. Dallin shifted his eyes slowly around in an arc. Less than six feet away, to the left, buried behind several rows of people was another gaunt face. Off in the opposite direction a third. They all looked the same; wary and restless, with the eyes of the hunted, the eyes of Communists.

"You needn't fear," Hsu said, confirming his thoughts. "We are not aboard because of you. Much as your actions in the past would justify it." His words were blunt, yet fell short of being a threat. "In fact," Hsu went on, "you might be of service to us."

Dallin kept silent, waiting before he reverted to his role of opportunist and war profiteer. Outside the wind howled through the splintered wood sidings of the boxcar. Then the floor of the car shifted and swayed as the train swerved around a steep bend of track.

"Before we get to that," Hsu continued, squatting down, "you might oblige me with an explanation of why you are aboard this wretched conveyance the puppet government chooses to call a train."

Complying, Dallin briefly related the history of the *Ikado Maru*, of Juzo and his own cross-country trek to the railway line. When he finished, Hsu replied, "You did well to bypass Nanking. The puppet troops have been unsettled ever since they got word of Hiroshima."

"Hiroshima?"'

"Ah!" Hsu exclaimed softly, "that's right. You could not possibly have heard."

As Hsu spoke, the horror and meaning of Hiroshima became apparent to Dallin at once.

"The end of the war," he murmured. "Some time ago a group of Japanese physicists wanted to duplicate a similar Nazi project, but they never got the support of the War Cabinet."

"Fortunately for all of us." Hsu smiled. "But tell me, until now how would you describe the morale of the Japanese soldier in Shanghai?"

"Reasonably good. Considering most haven't seen their

families or been in the Home Islands since they left there years ago.'"

"They are well disciplined?"

"Depends on the command. Five divisions are based around Shanghai. They vary greatly in quality, but are generally obedient. Should Japan surrender, though, you never know. If their officers run, there might just be another sacking of Nanking."

"I see." Hsu frowned. "So you feel that as long as the high-ranking officers remain, the rank-and-file will follow orders?"

"Yes."

"Even if it means joining the Americans and Nationalists to fight against us?" Hsu asked, raising his voice to offset the screeching of the wheels as the train rattled downhill.

The question jolted Dallin. "A second front against the Communists?" he asked, recovering slowly.

"Exactly."

"Well, I don't know," Dallin answered thoughtfully. "On the whole, I'd say they'd probably welcome it. Be a remarkable face-saving device for them. Sure, the average Japanese soldier is willing to die for the Emperor. Their military code really doesn't give them much choice. If they surrender, they can't go home. So that leaves them hara-kiri or exile."

"Still, the political implications stun you?"

"To say the least, Commissar.'"

"Thank you, Mr. Dallin," Hsu replied. "It's always refreshing to speak with someone who is direct and forthright. But then, Felix Hacker told me what to expect."

"Felix Hacker?"

"Yes. The Swiss librarian from the Municipal Council. When I was a student years ago at St. John's University in Shanghai he was kind enough to help me obtain certain books I needed. He also spent many hours teaching me English."

"I'm afraid I don't know Hacker. We never met," Dallin said guardedly.

"Then you will be a little more than surprised to learn he saved your life not very long ago. As you know," Hsu explained, "we marked you for liquidation several times. On the last occasion, just a day before our plan was to be executed, I encountered Felix Hacker en route to his cottage in the Munkanshan Mountains. At that time he overheard your name mentioned and, taking me aside, without revealing too much, insisted that liquidating you would be a serious error. Life is curious, is it not?"

"It is indeed," Dallin agreed. It was no news to him that he had been earmarked for death, not only by the Communists but by rival black-market operators and even eager college students idealistically embracing the Nationalist cause. Most of these attempts had been stymied by the Kempetai; some by Hata and Dallin personally; and now one, it appeared, by the kindly but highly proficient Swiss librarian, a man Dallin often wanted to get to know, but could not, for security reasons.

"What do you wish of me?" Dallin asked, aware of the silence that had fallen.

"I want you to arrange a meeting for me with Colonel Hata."

"He'd never risk it," Dallin said flatly.

"He can choose his own spot. I assure you, assassination is not what I have in mind. All I wish is a private conversation. No more."

"I'll see what I can do."

"One other thing," Hsu went on. "In your opinion, can Hata be trusted? For instance, if he was offered certain guarantees is it reasonable to expect he would live up to his part of the bargain?"

"Depends on what guarantees we're talking about. Reputation aside, Hata has never been a sadist. From what I can see, the war made a moral degenerate of him. As it did with so many officers, on both sides. Basically, he's a loyal Japanese officer who tortured and murdered in the belief it was his duty. He goes on doing so now because to stop would mean his own life."

"You seem to like him?"

"Hata? I don't like or dislike him. We're business partners. We've gotten rich together. He's got his work, I have mine. It's that simple."

"Then you don't judge him?"

"If I do, only to myself."

"Most interesting," Hsu murmured. "I can see why Felix Hacker felt the way he did. You seem an unusual man, Dallin. Although I base that more on what you leave unsaid than on what you say. My only regret is that you chose to make money from this war rather than take sides. If, in fact, that is what you have done."

Dallin decided to let it drop right there, although he was tempted to do otherwise. Commissar Hsu was not the only one who had been refreshed by their conversation. But Dallin had to be careful; far more than his own life was at stake. There was the safety of the ring and the work they were doing.

Still, some response was called for. Before Dallin could make any, the locomotive gave a shrill whistle and the train jolted past a Japanese bunker guarding a stone bridge.

"You may sleep now, Mr. Dallin," Hsu murmured. "And be assured you will reach Shanghai unharmed."

"How do I contact you?"

"You live at the Cathay. Suite 1500, I believe. We'll reach you there."

Hsu gave one of his rare smiles. It was the last thing Dallin remembered as his eyelids drooped shut and he slipped into a deep sleep against the wall of the swaying boxcar.

Chapter Twenty-One

The Deutscher Garten Klub on Avenue Haig in the International Settlement was the Shanghai version of a traditional Bavarian beerhall. Heavy timber beams crisscrossed the ceiling. A line of mooseheads studded the whitewashed stucco walls beside colored photographs of the Black Forest, the medieval university city of Heidelberg, and the lavish Schloss Herrenchiemsee built by mad King Ludwig II. There were also marks left by the oversized portraits of Hitler and Goering, which had been replaced by those of two famed heroes of the First World War, Baron Manfred Von Richthofen, the Red Baron, and Field Marshal Von Hindenburg.

It was almost curfew. Rudolph, the brawny proprietor, stood behind the bar, washing and drying glasses. Nearby, his remaining patron, Ernst Becker, sat at a long wooden table, clutching a stein half full of beer to his moist lips. His usually spotless starched collar was stained and his narrow black tie askew.

Becker was desperate. He had only managed to put off Rossio, the director of the Iberian Navigation Company for a few days. But that was it. Beyond that time, no money; no freighter. It was that simple. The Portuguese made no attempt to be polite or understanding. The fortune he had earned from the Axis meant nothing. That was the past, perhaps still a glorious time to the Nazis, but of no significance to Rossio's present.

Becker gazed enviously at Rudolph tending bar. How much simpler and more comfortable life would be if he too had been born in the German settlement of Tingstao up north. At one time it had been regarded as a little Berlin, and its pleasant beaches and the lovely Prinz Heinrich Hotel had made Tingstao a popular summer resort.

"Another glass," Becker called out, draining the one he held.

"Sorry, sir," Rudolph shouted back, pointing at the clock on the wall. It was nearly eleven.

"Curfew be damned. Give me another beer."

"But, Herr Becker, you know how difficult the Japanese have been with me lately. I cannot afford to take the risk."

"To hell with the little yellow dwarfs," Becker ranted. "Are you a true German or some half-Asiatic worm."

"A German," Rudolph replied, his face reddening at the slur. Then he reluctantly filled the stein and brought it over to the table.

"That's better!" Becker belched, hoisting the glass into the air. "To the good old days, *ja?*"

"*Ja,* Herr Becker," sighed the proprietor, returning to the bar with growing disgust and impatience.

It was not only the avarice of the Portuguese that left Becker in despair. The news about Hiroshima, and the fact that it was the goddamn Yid scientists who were responsible for it, ate at his guts and stripped away his last bit of courage. Until earlier this morning, Becker had figured there was at least a year of fight left in the Japanese. Six months for the Americans to conquer the Home Islands, then that much more time to extend their victory onto the Chinese mainland. But now the Bomb changed everything. The timetable was ludicrous and as absurd as the Third Reich's hope that the Ardenne offensive in Christmas of 1944 would alter the course of the war in Europe.

To make matters worse, his car, his precious Mercedes-Benz, a gift from Himmler no less, had been stolen out of the garage of the Kaiser Wilhem Institute. At this rate, Becker moaned, the Americans would have him before very long. His Berlin friends might reach safety in Buenos Aires but he never would.

"A cooked goose, that's what I am," Becker murmured, draining the stein, then slamming the empty glass onto the wooden table and laughing as it skidded over the edge and onto the floor.

From the bar, Rudolph studied the mess on the floor with dismay as he heard Becker shout for another beer.

"Please, Herr Becker. I told you it's almost curfew and the Japanese will not permit . . ."

"What did you call me?" Becker screamed, rising shakily to his feet. "It's Obersturmbannführer Becker. Or are you another one of those ungrateful swine who forget it was the Nazis that made it possible for sheep like you to hold your heads up high."

"We were sheep," Rudolph admitted nervously, unable to contain his temper as he leaned over the bar, his florid face turning red. "But the good old days that you refer to are over, Herr Becker. And I, for one, am glad."

"Glad are you, you swine!"

"*Ja*, glad! Glad you and the other bully boys are finished. *Kaput!* Gangsters, pimps, and dope addicts, that's what you were. And we should never have allowed you to get in power. We were duped. I only wish we had kicked you out on your lousy no-good asses years ago. Instead you brought ruin and shame on us all. Even here in Shanghai, with that mad 'final solution' of yours, Herr Becker, official Gestapo representative."

"You dare . . . you dare say this to me!" Becker hissed. "Why, I'll break your neck . . . I'll take your eyes and gouge them from your head . . . I'll hang your damned carcass . . ."

The heavy oak front door swung open, striking the stucco wall with a bang. A full squad of Kempei, followed by Lieutenant Sumato, his shoulders drooping, swept inside, forming a semicircle around Becker and Rudolph.

"I was just closing," the proprietor of the Deutscher Garten Klub insisted anxiously, eyeing the fixed bayonets on the rifles of the Japanese, "only this customer wouldn't go. I'm sorry. Truly. I know I should be shut because of the curfew."

"Stop begging, you swine," Becker ranted. "And get me another beer."

"Excuse me, Obersturmbannführer," Sumato said politely, "but Colonel Hata wishes to see you."

"He does, eh? Why?"

"Only the Colonel can answer that, Obersturmbannführer. Please. You will come with me now."

"At least you still use my correct title," grumbled Becker. "But how about one more before we go? One last beer?"

Turning toward the proprietor, Sumato said, "You will give Obersturmbannführer Becker whatever he wishes."

"If the Lieutenant says so," Rudolph said, his face tinged with embarrassment. He slid a fresh stein under the spigot and filled it with local beer. Then, carrying it over to the table, he placed the glass before Becker and started away.

"Just one moment," Becker insisted. "The table. You have not wiped it clean."

Rudolph muttered; then, removing a cloth stuck into his waistband, he bent over and began drying the table. A second later Becker brought the full stein of beer crashing down on his skull.

"More coffee, Obersturmbannführer?" Hata asked, signaling his orderly to pour another cup for the disheveled Nazi seated across the desk from him in his office at Bridge House. It was close to midnight but the humidity still hovered in the upper nineties and only a slight breeze was blowing in from nearby Soochow Creek. Overhead the wooden fan merely kept the hot stale air circulating. To make matters even worse, American bombers had struck Shanghai again; destroying three ships and causing further havoc at the airport by delaying the overbooked Tokyo flights. "So! Tell me," Becker said, sitting back, the cup and saucer in one hand, "why have you brought me here at this time of night?"

"Surely you know why."

"My dear Colonel, after what those Yid scientists did to Hiroshima my mind is on one subject only."

"Escape?"

"Precisely."

"Mine too!" Hata agreed. "Now, tell me, what news of your Portuguese freighter?"

"So! You know about the *Isabella*, ja?"

"You can charter her?"

"*Ja!* Of course!"

"Only you cannot afford to pay for her."

"So you know that too!"

"I tried reaching you by telephone. And I've heard about the electricity. You should have been honest with me, Obersturmbannführer. I would never have permitted this to happen, for things to go so far."

"A question of pride, Colonel."

"Of course. But now that fate has thrown us together, your concerns are also mine if we are to reach Argentina safely. So, tell me, what's required? Passport, visa, papers?"

"*Ja, ja!* You will need all those things," Becker agreed, beaming like a man who had been given a new lease on life. "But I have a list, and the man, the expert at forgery, who can do everything quickly and properly. You may depend upon it."

"Good. Before you go, leave me his name and where he can be reached."

"To be sure. But, tell me, how many will be going in your party?"

"Three of us. Two men and a woman."

"Very good. And a bodyguard, will you be taking any men along with you?"

"One squad of my best, most loyal Kempei. Any objection?"

"No, Colonel, no," Becker said, mopping his perspiring forehead. "I was only asking so as to be able to complete all the necessary arrangements."

"Your people in Buenos Aires can accommodate us?" Hata asked, suddenly concerned.

"Accommodate? Why, Colonel, please believe me when I say they will be most delighted that a man of your caliber has chosen to seek refuge in their country. You don't know how often I've said there is a natural and deep common bond that is shared by the Japanese and German people. It is not for nothing the world refers to us as master races."

"Thank you, Obersturmbannführer," Hata murmured. "This should make your task even easier."

He slid open the drawer at his knee, removed a thick envelope, and spread six bundles of crisp American one-hundred-dollar bills across the desk.

"*Gott in Himmel!*" The Nazi sighed. "My compliments, my dear Colonel Hata, my compliments!"

After Becker left, Hata opened the desk drawer again. Inside were three manila folders. The top one had ERNST BECKER printed across the top in bold lettering. The bottom two were marked GUSTAV TORG and FELIX HACKER, respectively. Hata

took only the Becker file, then closed the drawer. He emptied
its contents on the desk before him. There were reports from
the Gestapo and SS and the Japanese Secret Service as well as
the Kempetai. The ones written in German had Japanese
translations attached to the back.

Hata flipped through the various reports until he finally
came to one marked GESTAPO—SECRET AFFAIRS IN WARSAW,
meaning it held the most confidential material. His eyes
scanned the single-spaced typewritten page dated January 9,
1940. It was addressed to Reichsführer Himmler and signed
Governor-General Hans Frank.

> OBERSTURMBANNFUHRER ERNST BECKER IS TO
> BE COMMENDED AND CONGRATULATED FOR HIS
> EXCELLENT RESULTS WITH THE POLISH RABBI
> SITUATION. IN A FEW SHORT MONTHS HE HAS
> EXPEDITED THE ARREST AND LIQUIDATION OF
> TWO HUNDRED AND SIXTY-THREE ORDAINED
> RABBIS AND OVER FOUR HUNDRED TALMUDIC
> STUDENTS. ALSO HE HAS UNCOVERED A PLOT TO
> SAVE SOME OF THESE JEWS AND HAS PERSON-
> ALLY EXECUTED THE JEWISH PARTISANS
> INVOLVED.

What Hata read came as no great shock to him. In fact, he
had known about the Jew-hunter from the day he arrived in
Shanghai. But now this information had far more importance.
If Hata was going to place himself in the Nazi's care, then he
needed to protect himself. More desperate men than Ernst
Becker had been kept in line by the threat of exposure. And
from his recollection the dossier on Obersturmbannführer
Becker contained still blacker information.

Hata decided to have several copies made at once, one to
be left behind in Shanghai for safe-keeping, another to be
given to Niki, and a third to remain in his own possession at
all times. Suddenly he was reminded of the record of his own
deeds that was contained in that elusive black book compiled
by Felix Hacker.

It must be found. The question was how? His own Kempei
had gotten nowhere in their investigation. Even Hata was
stumped as to where to look. All the members of the
Shanghai Ring were dead and, according to the latest report,

Dominique Torg had stopped eating completely and appeared to be deranged.

Besides, there was so much else for Hata to do. The fifteenth of August was getting closer. Niki would need help in getting ready. Then there was the nagging problem of untangling the business affairs of his partner Dallin. And, most important of all, the valuable objects in the warehouse had to be checked and readied for embarkation aboard the freighter. The more Hata pondered, the more he realized how pressed for time he really was.

Then he got an inspiration. Of course, Hata decided, who else was better trained to find the black book than the man who had told Hata about its existence in the first place. Reaching into the desk drawer, Hata drew out the two remaining manila folders. He quickly wrote a note, put everything into a large envelope, sealed it, then rang for his orderly. A bowlegged Japanese in a sweaty khaki uniform rushed in. Hata finished jotting the post office box in the upper left-hand corner; then added *Monsieur Munk*, the *Cathay Hotel* and PLEASE HOLD FOR ARRIVAL in the center.

Some time later, the personal motorcar of the Kempetai commandant, an armor-plated Mercedes Benz, carried Obersturmbannführer Becker past the Palace Hotel. Six stories above, in the penthouse, the two Corsicans guarding Salat were sitting, tied hand and foot, on the bathroom floor, staring helplessly at one another.

Salat had completed this part of his plan easily enough. Deceiving Caro required more finesse. To lull Caro into believing he was willing to abandon Dominique, Salat had agreed to leave Shanghai as soon as his departure could be arranged. It did not take Caro long. The escape he devised was by motorcar to Canton, then by fishing junk on to Macao. In four or five days, depending on Japanese patrols, Salat would be safely installed in another syndicate gambling operation well away from the Kempetai. It was very neatly thought out, and Salat had few doubts about its success.

Even now, Caro was awaiting him at the Columbia Country Club on Great Western Road—only Salat never had any intention of joining him there. Instead, he had tricked his two bodyguards and gone directly to the home of a friendly moneylender, a Chinese with an ivorylike face, who owed Salat a favor worth thirty thousand in gold.

Then Salat crossed over to the east bank of the Whampoo into the industrial zone of Pootung, a flat stretch of marshland opposite the Bund, separating the river from the sea, where the sprawling warehouses of the British-American Tobacco Company were located alongside several large cotton and textile mills and a score of native godowns. Here, not far from the customs signal station, amid rows of sampans and junks, Salat found the floating headquarters of Wu-Ting, the hulking leader of the boat people, whose intense hatred for the Japanese barely exceeded the respect in which he held the Corsican.

Salat gave Wu-Ting six thousand in gold. That, plus a sizable share of the anticipated booty, bought Salat the immediate services of two dozen sampans and their expert crews. A further thousand bought protection in the form of a small band of gunmen armed with Mauser pistols. This left Salat with twenty-three thousand in gold, enough to take Dominique and himself far away from war-torn Shanghai, provided the rest of his plan went as smoothly.

By then it was well after midnight. Ideal weather, a pale sliver of moon peeped through the dark sky. Salat was crouched on his knees between two wiry polemen in the middle of a sampan. Strung out behind him, concealed by the tall reeds of the marsh jutting from the Pootung side of the Whampoo, were the rest of the sampans manned by their crews.

From mid-river the steady hum of an engine signaled that a Japanese patrol boat was approaching. Suddenly her powerful searchlight fell over the marsh, licking futilely at the tall weeds sheltering Salat and the sampans, making him grateful for placing himself in the experienced hands of the master smuggler Wu-Ting. Then the patrol boat swept on southward, her searchlight completing a one-hundred-and-eighty-degree arc and landing finally on a pair of rusting freighters lying half-sunk off the French Bund.

In the same instant, Salat tapped the shoulder of the bowman. The wiry Chinese swung his bamboo pole over the side, then thrust downward and, giving a violent heave, sent the sampan hurtling into open water. One by one, the other sampans followed in a single line, their crews agilely switching poles for broad-bladed oars and never breaking formation, keeping their sampans on a diagonal course across the

Whampoo toward the west bank. To the south the engines of the Japanese patrol boat could scarcely be heard, its searchlight leaving only a faint ribbon in the distant sky. In the opposite direction, up north, the towering buildings of the Bund remained shrouded in darkness.

Her hull skimming the water, the sampan carrying Salat sped west, leaving the marsh behind. The waves grew higher and the current choppier. Water sprayed his face as Salat held tightly to her gunwales. Then a hard-hitting wave struck the stern of the sampan, sending her hurtling upward where she hung in mid-air before crashing down under a solid sheet of water, drenching Salat, who was glad he had traded his linen suit for a padded jacket and trousers. The crew, cursing loudly, paddled furiously against the choppy water.

Each minute felt like an hour now. In the darkness, Salat could not tell how much farther they had to go. All he could make out were brief glimpses of the bowman's bony shoulder as he kept up the relentless rhythm of his paddling.

Finally the sampan broke free of the strong cross-current and sped smoothly toward shore. A few more minutes passed and then the bowman cried out a warning. Salat threw himself flat against the deck of the sampan, as the crew veered her around at a ninety-degree angle and brought the sampan gliding beneath the pier of a warehouse.

Her gunwales scraped between the concrete posts that supported the warehouse overhead. Then her crew shipped oars and rammed their bamboo poles down deep into the thick mud, bringing the sampan to an abrupt stop.

Salat unbuttoned his padded jacket swiftly. He bypassed the Browning automatic fitted snugly into the waistband of his trousers and took out a flashlight. Flicking the beam aft, he saw the glistening faces of the perspiring crews aboard the other sampans. Then he shone some light on his wristwatch. Quarter past the hour. It had taken them six minutes to get across the Whampoo. The patrol boat ran past this point precisely on the hour. This meant they had another forty-eight minutes to break inside, take what they needed, and get back to the Pootung side. It would not be easy.

Salat shifted the beam upward, fixing on a section of the heavy timber floor of the warehouse. He motioned to the crew, now holding steel saws, and they began cutting their way through the floor.

Ten minutes later, Salat wriggled into the warehouse carrying a Thompson submachine gun. He threw himself down on the floor immediately, listening for any noises. Hearing none, he edged the flashlight slowly around in a circle. On every side were crates of all sizes, marked in English and Chinese. Peering closely at a few, Salat saw the labels: BRONZE LION, MING DYNASTY PORCELAIN PLATE; T'ANG DYNASTY HORSE. Beside each one was a different number.

Salat shifted the beam, uncovering an aisle that ran through the crates. He followed it, eventually coming to the entrance of the warehouse. Switching off the flashlight he put his left eye up against a crack in the thick steel doors.

In front, guarding the only entry to the warehouse, were twin machine gun nests manned by Kempei soldiers. At the edge of the curb not far away a light tank was parked, its cannon covering the dark street. A grizzled sergeant with torn leggings squatted before a fire between the tank and the doorway. He was pouring boiling water from a kettle into a tin cup.

Salat turned away. So far things looked good. He switched the flashlight back on and made his way quietly to the hole in the floor. Two short blinks followed by a longer one brought a Chinese gunman up into the warehouse. Within moments, five more Chinese waving Mauser pistols stood beside him. They kept watch as members of the crew fanned out across the warehouse, lifting only the smallest crates and bringing them back to the hole where two of their number passed them gingerly below into the waiting sampans.

The system worked well; Salat was thinking about the good-sized dent he would make in the loot Hata and Dallin had amassed, when the lights overhead went on and there was a guttural scream in Japanese ordering the raiders to surrender.

Salat ended the speaker's demand in midsentence, as a pair of Nambu machine guns barked, setting up a deadly crossfire and turning the warehouse into a shooting gallery, with Salat and the Chinese for pigeons. Two of his gunmen went down in the first salvo. Salat dropped beside them, using one still warm corpse for cover. Then he shifted the barrel of his Thompson from left to right, squeezing off short bursts of gunfire at three Japanese charging at him from different angles. One flopped sideways, giving out an anguished cry. Another dragged to a halt, clapped his hands over his blood-soaked face, and collapsed. The third, Ganghi, the most highly rated executioner in the Kempetai, dove lightly onto the floor with a Nambu submachine gun cradled in his arms, then rolled behind a five-foot-high stack of crates.

"Close shave, eh?" a bearded Kempei said, huddled upon his knees. "It's that damn Corsican again. The one who gave us so much trouble over at the Dome Café."

"Don't worry about him," Ganghi grinned, jamming a fresh magazine onto his gun, "He's all mine."

"You can have him. Six of us he took out that day on Bubbling Well Road before he got away in the dark. And now he's already finished off Tanaki and Kurota."

It was true. Nearby, two of their fallen comrades, blood still dripping from their wounds, were curled up dead, while the jarring blasts of gunfire grew scarcer as both sides jockeyed for position.

"Least this way they get into Yasukuni!" Ganghi laughed, starting off on his belly between two crates in a flanking movement behind Salat.

Beneath the warehouse the patrol boat was churning up the water. Her bow was lined with Imperial Marines firing short-barreled rifles. Her searchlight, blinding at close range, swept over the sampans shining on the Chinese still aboard. Some leaped into the shallow water, hoping to escape. Others tried to get away in their sampans. All were cut down by the twin machine guns mounted on the stern of the patrol boat, as fifty-caliber slugs tore into the sampans, splintering their wood hulls.

Above, Salat kept up a deadly fire pattern. The barrel of his gun was burning hot. The floor around him was strewn with the bodies of dead Chinese and Japanese. More lay near the hole, a few feet away. Salat ordered the last surviving Chinese to try for it. Flat on the floor, with his arms outstretched and forging a path through the dead, the Chinese edged his way bravely toward the hole, when a Kempei charged from the flank, swinging his rifle with fixed bayonet. Hearing the shrill cry from the Japanese, Salat whirled and drilled him with a burst across the groin. Just then, another Kempei poured gunfire down on the Chinese. Salat wheeled, nailing him too, but a shade late to help the Chinese.

Salat was down to his last ammo clip. His daring plan had turned into a well-oiled trap. Someone betrayed him to the Kempetai, and he knew just who that person was. The problem was, first, how to get through that hole in the floor and into the river. He nursed his ammunition carefully, inching his way backward. Then picking off the last two members of the original squad, who lay in ambush, Salat swung around to make his escape.

Ganghi, the bandy-legged Kempei gunner, his weapon gleaming in the crook of his elbow, got there first.

"Colonel Hata say, can do Corsican!" He snickered.

Not bothering to reply, Salat opened fire. Only there was a dull clunk as his Thompson submachine gun jammed, followed by the snarling rat-ta-ta-tat, as Ganghi's did not.

The force of the bullets knocked Salat over on his back, a wound the size of a grapefruit gouged in his upper chest and a look of genuine surprise etched on his handsome face.

Swaggering closer, Ganghi chortled smugly. "Thompson no damn good. Any Yank Marine on Iwo or Okinawa tell you same!" Then his Nambu barked again, tossing Salat, bloody and helpless, all over the floor.

Later Colonel Hata stood inside the circle of crates, surveying the carnage, while Ganghi, his favorite gunner, looted the dead Corsican's pockets, then trotted over to report.

"Five enemy wounded. Twelve dead, including Salat."

"Good," Hata replied with a faint smile. "You can keep what you found in his pockets."

"Thank you, sir."

"Ganghi?"

"Sir?"

"Was the Corsican tough?"

"See for yourself, sir."

Hata could easily see. The number of Japanese wounded and dead far exceeded the Chinese. All around him medics and stretcher parties were moving out the wounded.

Scowling, Hata turned back to the gunner. "Escort the Chinese survivors back to Bridge House. Make certain none get away."

"Sir!" Ganghi snapped and trotted off.

Hata lit a cigarette and leaned thoughtfully against a stack of crates. Some of his men had been stationed in the warehouse since he was warned of the raid. Originally he had planned to move the treasure trove of antiquities. Then he realized it would be too dangerous. Instead, he assigned a full company of Kempei to a nearby factory, within easy distance of the warehouse, expecting the raiders to mount a frontal attack on the entrance. But the Corsican had been more imaginative.

Hata suspected the damage to the crates around the hole was extensive. Its equivalent in hard currency would be considerable. It irritated Hata. He bent over the closest crate, probing inside the splintered boards with his fingers, and felt cool, smooth stone. Surprised, he studied the outer markings of the crate again: SHENSI BRONZE RHINOCEROS. Puzzled now, Hata pried apart the boards, pulling out straw stuffing and exposing several flat white stones. How could a crate marked Shensi bronze be stones? Unless. . .? Hata did not like it. He ordered the Kempei around him to break open every crate within reach.

In a few moments his order was carried out. The results confirmed his worst fears. Incredible as it seemed, every crate they opened contained only flat white stones. An hour later, with still more crates to open, the situation remained unchanged.

His hawklike face a mask of fury, Hata walked slowly across the warehouse past a long line of Kempei standing at attention beside the unsealed crates. The noncoms and enlisted men alike kept their eyes pinned to the floor, none of them wanting to catch their commandant's wrath.

Although only Hata and Dallin knew the true value of the objects stored in the warehouse, for years it had been common knowledge at Bridge House that the amount was stupendous by anyone's standards. Now everything was gone: the ninth-century Shangbronzes in the shapes of elephants and tigers, Ming porcelains, the huge palace vases and bowls, the T'ang horses, the bells from the Warring States period, the Yuan Dynasty temple vases, the solid gold flasks, the scrolls from the fourth century B.C., and even the stone reliefs and Buddhas from the caves of Yun Kang.

It was all missing. Stolen! What other possibility was there? Hata decided. Seething at the thought, he barked out orders. He waited as the guard detail stationed outside was disarmed, then led them into the warehouse. They bowed low before him. Hata fired a series of questions at each man, inquiring who else beside his partner Dallin had accompanied the shipments to the warehouse. The replies were identical. No one ever accompanied them but Dallin.

"Only Dallin!" Hata snorted bitterly. The infamy was almost too enormous to believe. Years of implicit trust and loyalty wiped away in a matter of seconds. There had to be some mistake. Dallin would not do this, Hata kept repeating to himself.

Finally Professor Chu, the Mandarin scholar and former curator of the Palace Museum of Peking, was brought in under guard. He was very old and tiny and moved with Buddha-like serenity. He wore a silk robe of traditional dark blue and a cap over his balding head. His narrow face bore the marks of his advanced years, but his brown eyes sparkled with youthful curiosity and defiance.

"Professor." Hata greeted him with obvious respect for his age and status.

"Commandant."

"Tell me, Professor, what do you see about you?"

"Stones."

"Are they precious . . . valuable ones?"

Professor Chu peered at one crate and ran his long fingernails lightly over several flat white stones, then looked up at Hata with a quizzical expression.

"These are from the Yangtze Valley. There must be millions of them."

"Billions," Hata confirmed. "Tell me, are these crates familiar to you?"

"The markings are mine. They are from my studio in Chapei where you keep me prisoner against my will."

"And when they left there they contained antiques? Objets d'art?"

"Of course. What else?"

"What else indeed," Hata cried, unable to control himself. "And yet you can see that the treasure, my treasure, is missing. And these worthless stupid stones are all that's left of years of work."

"You mean this isn't meant to deceive thieves? Professor Chu asked, amazement filling his voice. "This wasn't your idea?"

"No, Professor. Not my idea," Hata replied softly. "Tell me, after you inspect an object for authenticity and dating, what happens to it then?"

"Why, it's crated and labeled. As you see."

"And then?"

"Shipped here by trucks belonging to the Kempetai."

"Here?" hissed Hata vehemently, "not somewhere else. Not

to a place chosen by you or one of your patriotic liberal friends?"

"You think I stole those priceless objects?" Professor Chu asked, his eyes filled with wonder. "A cultural treasure of China?"

"No. Unfortunately I do not," Hata replied sadly. "And the man who I'm certain did is either dead or missing. And in either case, I'm afraid I'll never see him again."

Afterward Hata sat alone in his office at Bridge House and stared solemnly at the ornate samurai sword on his desk. His thoughts were violent. He should have known this would happen! Amassing such enormous wealth had required a shrewd, manipulative mind, someone capable of weaving through a complicated maze of intangibles, including shifting power blocs, ruthless greed, and changing markets.

Early on in the war, even before he met Dallin, Hata knew he was not cut out for such work. It was true he could organize. His success as Kempetai commandant of Shanghai had proven that. But with his dignity and rigid pride, he had been unable to deal with the sort of people that Dallin was routinely in contact with. Until now, the White Russian had been an ideal partner. His ability to act deceptively and move with ease among all sorts of people had been the perfect compliment to the naked power that Hata wielded on the China coast. Yet it was exactly this ability to deceive that had doubtlessly led Dallin to do what he had done. Hata should have realized this and been prepared for it.

An Oriental never should trust a Caucasian. That's what it came down to, Hata thought bitterly. The world belonged to the Caucasian. What he did not own outright, he controlled. What he did not control, he influenced. Nothing moving on the face of the earth escaped his widespread domination.

The Korean who had been assigned to accompany Dallin was not protection enough. Dallin had warranted more watchdogs, to guard against the day he made his run. In retrospect, Hata realized it was as instinctive an act for the stateless White Russian as was his own desire now for vengeance. His wrath unabated, he slid the ceremonial sword from its jeweled scabbard and ran his finger cautiously over the razor-sharp edge.

The idea of hara-kiri, or seppuku, as Hata preferred to call it, for the ancient ceremony meant far more than ordinary belly-cutting, was an inviting prospect. It offered a swift end to all his problems. Buenos Aires never seemed so far away as it did now, nor were his thoughts ever so bleak and without hope. Dallin had betrayed him, had caused him to lose face.

Long before he had ever joined the army, somewhere back in his early childhood, Hata had envisioned committing suicide. The ritual was a natural part of his upbringing. Only the weak and the servile endured personal shame and the scorn of their peers and their community. A man, a samurai, had to act and do so boldly and without fear. How else could he hope to regain his name and honor. By now word of his humiliation would surely have spread throughout Shanghai. In another day or two it would reach Tokyo.

The telephone rang and Hata let it ring several times before answering. He murmured a response, then slipped the sword into its sheath.

A moment later, Niki entered, wearing a sleeveless blue checked cotton dress with a revealing neckline. On her right hand was a huge pear-shaped diamond ring and a matching bracelet circled her wrist, both gifts from Hata.

"It's so goddamn hot I couldn't sleep," she complained, "so I had my chauffeur bring me over here."

Hata remained silent. Somewhat miffed, Niki rounded the desk and kissed him tenderly on the lips. She sat on the edge of the desk and let one bare leg dangle invitingly before him.

"You look tired. It's Hiroshima, isn't it?"

"It's Dallin."

"What's our enterprising friend done now?" Niki asked, toying with his long black hair. "Trade Bridge House to the Nationalists for a Chungking bank?"

"I only wish!" Hata answered sharply, moving his head away with a frown.

"My! You *are* in a bad mood. What's wrong? Maybe I can help."

Hata shook his head, then realizing she wanted to help, he relented. The account of the stolen antiquities left Niki almost breathless.

"Good Christ!" she moaned. "Just like that? I don't believe it."

"Everything is gone, I tell you!"

"But what's going to happen to us?"

"That depends on your courage," Hata replied somberly, lifting his samurai sword from the desk.

"You can't be serious?" Niki suppressed her impulse to laugh.

His dark eyes flashing with indignation, Hata insisted, "I have always been serious about seppuku!"

"Suppose Dallin isn't to blame?" Niki asked haltingly.

"Who else could be? Only a handful of people know where the crates are stored. And we were the only two who had permission to get past the guards."

"All right," Niki agreed reluctantly, "maybe Dallin did it. But why can't you find him and get back what he stole?"

"I'm trying," Hata explained, "but it may not be easy. It may not even be possible if Dallin's dead."

"But the treasure may still be in Shanghai?"

"Who knows? By now it could even be aboard a ship bound for Europe or Latin America."

Niki nodded, impressed with this explanation. "Pretending all these years to be our friend and now to do this to us. Especially now when——"

"When the Americans have won the war," interrupted Hata gravely.

"Then it *is* true about Hiroshima?"

"Many wish to go on fighting, but one way or another the end is near. A month perhaps . . . but no more than that. So now you see that for me there is no other choice."

"You can't mean it."

"I do!"

For Niki it was like a nightmare unfolding before her eyes. First her father, then Dallin, and now Hata. All the men she cared for, the ones she had relied on to protect her and care for her, were already gone or soon would be. And then what would happen to her?

In a low haunting voice, she pleaded with Hata. "All my life, all I ever really wanted was to be happy. I never meant to hurt anyone. I never wanted enemies, people who hated me enough to wish me harm. I only wanted to be happy. Even when I disappointed you at the Pleasure Palace it was not something I did deliberately. I just couldn't help myself."

"It's not you. It's Dallin. It's me!"

"Darling, please."

His face a mask, Hata held his tongue.

"Please?"

"I must do as custom demands. There is more than just

happiness in life. For a Japanese, a samurai, there is tradition and, above all, honor."

"Where will your honor get you? If you use that family relic lying there to rip open your belly and bleed to death, how will that improve things? So Dallin betrayed you. He also betrayed me and many others. Why must you take your life because of what he did?"

"You care . . . you really care about me?" Hata asked, disbelief marking his voice. "This is not some trick? You really want me to live?"

"Yes, I do!" Niki murmured. "More than anything I've ever wanted in my whole life, I want you to stay alive." Her cameo-like face was tense and her eyes pleading. She ran her hand caressingly along his muscular thigh. "You do this for me," she murmured huskily, her eyes glazed, "you stay alive, and I promise, I swear, you'll never have cause to be sorry."

Chapter Twenty-Two

———◆———

At five-thirty in the morning the sky was still gray with just a tinge of orange at the horizon as a taxi pulled to a stop beneath the canopied entrance of the Cathay Hotel. Dallin got out, told the uniformed doorman to pay the driver, and entered the nearly deserted lobby.

At the reception desk, Old Lu, the aging Chinese desk clerk stood motionless in his navy blue jacket with its brass buttons. On a bench nearby three bellboys in white gowns and caps dozed. Across the opulently decorated lobby, on the far side of the lush Persian carpet and the row of Victorian palms, a perspiring Korean was mopping a narrow length of marble floor.

Dallin greeted Old Lu politely, picked up his key and a thick bundle of messages, and took the elevator to his suite on the fifteenth floor. He stopped in the bedroom with the mirrored ceiling only long enough to phone room service, then went into the bathroom, an immense marble-lined chamber. He ran a bath, then he flung off his soiled clothes and slid with a groan of pleasure into the warm water. After a brief soak, he began flipping through the bundle of messages. One from Giacomo Ferrara immediately caught his attention—an urgent matter concerning Gustav Torg, which the managing director wished to see him about. The combination of the two men's names in the same note struck Dallin. Ferrara was an old bird, a trifle too slick for his taste. Still, he had proven useful in the past. Dallin shut his eyes, letting the steaming water soak away the grime of the past several days.

In the lobby, the Korean stuffed the wet mop into a bucket, then used the service staircase to reach the lower level. He looked around carefully, making sure he was not being observed, then used the pay telephone on the wall between the restrooms to contact Colonel Hata at Bridge House. Yawning, the operator advised him that both the Kempetai commandant and his aide, Lieutenant Sumato, would not be available before ten o'clock. The Korean hung up abruptly and ran back to his duties in the lobby.

Dallin got out of the tub, rubbed himself dry, and put on a maroon dressing gown. He examined his face in the sink mirror, took a closer look at the dark pockets beneath his eyes, then, shaking his head, went to the dining alcove off the living room. A pot of Turkish coffee, sweet rolls and butter, and a long Havana cigar from his own silver humidor rested on the oval white marble table beside the picture window overlooking the Whampoo River. Dallin drank the strong coffee black.

Below, outside the hotel, traffic on Garden Bridge was at a trickle. The construction crews, who had been frantically building gun emplacements before Hiroshima, had abandoned their work. Dallin had noticed other signs of defeat during the taxi ride from North Railway Station. Pondering on the consequences of recent events, he shifted his gaze slowly over at the river. It was then he caught sight of a long line of sampans, crewless and badly demolished by gunfire, being towed north past the Cathay Hotel by a Japanese tug.

A knock on the door brought him back to his present predicament. It was Giacomo Ferrara, wearing a brown velvet smoking jacket, light gray trousers, and suede slippers.

"Forgive me for disturbing you so early,"' the managing director apologized, "but Old Lu notified me you had arrived. We heard you'd disappeared on the Yangtze. Were presumed dead. I'm elated to find it wasn't so."

"So am I!" Dallin smiled. "Will you take a coffee?"

"Please."

Dallin poured another cup of dark Turkish coffee from the sterling pot and handed it to Ferrara.

After pausing for a sip, Ferrara said, "Since you've been

gone, your friend Colonel Hata has been very active. And, how shall I say it, from his point of view very successful."

"What's he done? Arrested your pastry chef? Or has your barman's son-in-law gotten himself in trouble again?"

"The fact is he's broken up the Shanghai Ring," Ferrara said bluntly, watching Dallin's reaction closely. "He's arrested and executed five men, including Felix Hacker and Gustav Torg."

Expressionlessly, Dallin reached for a cigar, peeled away the wrapping and, using a special tool, nipped off the tip. Then, looking directly at Ferrara, he lit the cigar and said, "That's too bad for them but I don't see what any of this has to do with me. After all, Hata gets paid to uncover and execute spies, and a man like the Norwegian surely knew the risks."

Despite his bland response, Dallin was shaken. Chung Lee, Hansen, Knoll, the outwardly benign but lethal Felix Hacker, and most shocking of all, the Norwegian Torg. All dead?

Yet somehow Dallin's facade held. The question now was how much did Hata know? And what sort of game was Giacomo Ferrara playing?

"I thought Torg's death might affect you more. Obviously I overestimated his importance to you," Ferrara said finally.

"All I did was buy his company. Oh, don't get me wrong. I didn't mean the man harm, but he's been around Shanghai and China long enough to know you can't cross the Kempetai and get away with it. At least not forever."

"Interesting that you, of all people, say that."

"Really. Why?"

"Forgive me," Ferrara apologized hastily. "I've already put you out enough.'"

"You're not putting me out," Dallin said, indicating that the managing director should remain. "But I don't see what your involvement in all this is."

"Gustav Torg was a good friend. I feel I owe his daughter Dominique something."

"What's his daughter got to do with this? Is she a spy too?"

"Not even Hata thinks that," Ferrara replied coldly.

"So what's her problem?"

"She's at Bridge House. Hata insists she knows about a black book that her father and Felix Hacker put together. Apparently the book was hidden, and Hata wants it.

"A black book?"

"You never heard of it?"

"Should I have?"

"No. I suppose not. It's a list of war criminals and collaborators active here in Shanghai, with enough evidence to convict them."

"Whose idea was that?"

"The Americans. They did the same thing in Europe with great success, I'm told."

"You seem to know an awful lot about it," Dallin observed. "I can see why Hata would like to know where it is. I wouldn't mind knowing myself."

"I thought you might." Ferrara smiled. "The problem is, I doubt very much if Dominique Torg knows anything about it. Besides, in her condition, dazed, confused, frightened, she no longer cares if she lives or dies. And the terrible news about Robert Salat just makes matters worse for her."

"You've lost me."

"Ah, you haven't heard. Last night the Corsican raided a warehouse south of here with a fleet of sampans. It seems the Kempetai were alerted and he was killed trying to escape."

"So that's what all that traffic on the river was about," Dallin murmured, drawing on his cigar. "You aren't wrong when you say my friend Hata's been busy. Maybe a little too busy."

"Pardon?"

"Salat's Roulette Club paid us ten thousand U.S. a month to stay open. Even more than you do for the Cathay."

"I see." Ferrara blushed.

"Well! So much for that." Dallin sighed, getting up from the chair. "In the meantime I'll see what can be done for Torg's daughter."

"I assume your price will be high?"

"You assume right. Unless you can get her to say where this book is hidden."

"That wouldn't be possible. Besides, take my word for it, even if she knows, she'll never tell. Not after what's happened to her father. She loved him very much, you know."

"Torg never should've spied against the Japanese."

"There's a rumor he may have been coerced."

"Blackmailed?"

"Something like that. Of course, it's only a rumor."

As Dallin started across the room, Ferrara fell into step beside him, pausing for a moment to examine an Albers on the wall. His lack of appreciation for modern art reinforced, he joined Dallin at the doorway.

"Tell me," he said, "how do you think Hiroshima will affect things?"

"Just means the Japs are finished that much sooner."

"You're not worried? Concerned for your own welfare, I mean?"

"Sure, I am. But there's more sides than just one in any conflict."

"So when Japan does fall you don't expect to fall with her?"

"Is that what I meant?" Dallin smiled, clenching the cigar between his teeth.

"You're an interesting man, Dallin," Ferrara said sincerely. "Unfortunately, you have more enemies than friends. So I trust when the Americans place the rope around Hata's throat, they won't leave enough room for yours as well."

After Dallin closed the door behind Ferrara, he sank down on the cushioned leather couch. Chung Lee, Hansen, Knoll, Hacker, and the Norwegian—all dead! How was it possible? Who slipped up? Or had they been shopped? Betrayed by an informant or discovered by a Kempei agent? Was it a stranger or someone who had been watching them a long time? And did he or she have an inkling of Dallin's involvement? This was one godawful mess, for certain, and here he had battled to get back to Shanghai! For what? A Kempetai firing squad?

Giacomo Ferrara bothered Dallin too. In the past, they had maintained distant but cordial relations. They had made every effort to show respect for one another but had never permitted their relationship to grow into a friendship. Dallin preferred it this way and so apparently had the managing director. Now, despite his usual urbane manner, there was something odd about Ferrara's behavior. He was pressing, trying to dig information out of Dallin. On the surface it seemed quite harmless but in actuality it could only benefit the Japanese. Why? What was his game? And was there actually a game at all, or was it merely Dallin's paranoia?

As if in answer to the question, there was a clatter of hobnailed boots in the corridor, and the door swung open, revealing four Kempei with fixed bayonets led by Ganghi.

"Hello, Dallin," the bandylegged gunner snickered and barged in, toting his gleaming Nambu submachine gun.

"What the hell do you want, Ganghi?"

"You, my old friend."

"How come?" Dallin asked nonchalantly, rekindling his cigar with a wooden match.

"Haven't you heard? Colonel Hata found his Whampoo River warehouse sacked, and guess who he thinks did it?"

Half an hour later, Hata asked sardonically, "So you're alive after all?" He was poised beside the open window of his eighth-floor office. The flowerlike star insignias of the Kempetai stood out boldly on the collar tabs of his freshly laundered tan shirt. Dallin sat by the desk. He seemed rested and relaxed, but in actuality he was neither. He had hoped to learn something about the Norwegian from Ganghi during the ride from the Cathay Hotel, but the gunner apparently knew nothing about the annihilation of the Shanghai Ring.

Bridge House appeared to Dallin like a fortress under siege. Two heavy tanks, the most powerful in the Japanese arsenal, guarded the gates facing Szechwan Road. Within the courtyard a pair of machine-gun nests flanked the broad concrete stairs leading to the main entrance.

For Dallin, falling from grace was a chilling experience. He was no longer treated as a privileged friend of the commandant but merely as another prisoner of the dreaded Kempetai.

"By this time I was sure you'd be en route to Europe," Hata went on in the same biting tone, barely managing to contain his rage.

"Europe?" Dallin asked, genuinely surprised.

"Isn't that where Occidentals go after making a fortune in the Orient?"

"Look, Hata . . ."

"*Colonel* Hata!"

"All right. Colonel Hata. What's going on? Why am I being treated as if I did something wrong . . . like I was the enemy?"

"Aren't you?"

For a moment Dallin thought that perhaps the Norwegian had talked. Then he rejected the idea entirely and fell back to another line of reasoning he had devised.

"All right, so you found the crates full of stones instead of antiques. That doesn't mean I meant to steal them."

"What does it mean then?" Hata asked sharply, moving away from the window.

"Must I tell you about Shanghai? Everyone in this town is touched by greed. Show me an honest person and I'll show you a fool or a fake. And that includes your men as well."

"So now the Kempetai cannot be trusted," Hata said, slipping into the chair across from Dallin. "I suppose that includes me as well."

"Goddamnit!" Dallin exploded, "if you want to be serious let's be serious! But don't play your clever little games with me, because for nearly a week now I've been shot at and chased and I'm damn well not in the mood to be accused of treachery by my friends."

"Friends?" snorted Hata. "And the one thousand four hundred and thirty-four objects missing from the warehouse? I suppose that's a sign of friendship? Of trust? Loyalty?"

"I don't know about you, but I need a drink," Dallin replied, rubbing his smoothly shaven chin.

"Drink it all!" Hata offered, yanking a bottle of Scotch from his desk drawer and placing it in front of Dallin with a shot glass. "Only tell me where they are."

Dallin needed more than just a belt or two. He needed time to find a way out of the corner Hata had so cleverly backed him into. His mind racing, Dallin poured himself a shot and knocked it back neatly.

"I'm waiting," Hata warned, lighting a cigarette and staring coldly at Dallin.

"You're holding Dominique Torg?"

"So?"

"Has she told you anything about the black book?"

"No."

"She can't, you know. Ferrara swears she knew nothing about her father's activities."

"What has this got to do with you?"

"I need her . . . to trade for something I want."

"Never!" Hata replied forcefully, stubbing out his cigarette in the large brass ashtray.

"What good is she to you?"

"I might ask the same question."

"If I give her over to the Nationalists . . . if I save her life . . . I'm off the hook."

"You're lying!"

"Why should I lie? You think I asked Juzo to attack the

Ikado Maru? That I swam ashore, then walked fifty miles around Nanking to the railway and nearly got killed by puppet soldiers in Wuteh from choice? I'd hardly call any of that the act of someone trying to steal a warehouse full of priceless antiquities."

"Why did you take them?"

"I told you."

"And I don't believe you, Dallin. Not anymore. Not after last night."

So it was a stalemate after all. But Dallin did not delude himself. It would not be a stalemate for long. No White Russian, regardless of his influence, could defy the Kempetai commandant of Shanghai and not eventually suffer the consequences.

"If I don't get the exact location, I'll turn you over to my people downstairs."

So he was right, Dallin thought, keeping silent.

"I mean it, Dallin."

"I know you do. But that won't help either of us."

"It'll help me in some ways."

The way Hata said it, Dallin knew he was telling the truth. He had known Hata long enough to realize how easy it was to offend his enormous sense of pride. Dallin had shamed him, and Hata clearly meant to make him pay for it.

Still, Dallin knew better than to plead for mercy. That was the last way to reach Hata. There was no mercy in his own world so why should he extend any to his enemy?

"I'll say it just one more time," Dallin said stubbornly. "I need the Norwegian's daughter so I can save myself."

"And me? What of me?" Hata spat back.

"I tried including you on the deal. Ask Fat Ling if you don't believe me. The word from Chungking is you're high on their blacklist and they won't make any concessions. But that doesn't mean I'm through trying. It just means I can't do a damn thing for either of us without Dominique Torg alive and free."

Hata said nothing, studying this explanation, while Dallin congratulated himself on devising a story that even he could buy if the positions were reversed.

"What you say is true," Hata admitted finally. "Chungking's representative here in Shanghai has given me the same story."

"So what do you want me to do?" Dallin replied angrily,

keeping up the pressure. "Die with you? Is that what you want? Will that make you feel any better about Japan's losing the war?"

"Dallin . . ." Hata said haltingly, "just give me the address where you stashed everything and you can walk out of here. Don't, and I promise the only way you'll ever leave is on a stretcher."

Hata was a master all right, Dallin conceded silently. He had played every card he knew and still the Japanese wasn't buying. Shrugging, Dallin fished in his jacket pockets for a cigarette. He found a crumpled one and lit it. Inhaling deeply, he sorted quickly through his alternatives. In the end, he decided that if he gave Hata the treasure, there would be nothing to stop him from fleeing, and all the ring's efforts to bring Shanghai's number-one war criminal to justice would have been for naught. Nor would there be any guarantee of Dominique Torg's survival.

He studied the Japanese for a moment and then said coolly, "Let's get on with it, shall we?"

"Fool!" Hata ranted in frustration, as he jammed one knee against the button on his side of the desk.

Two minutes later, Dallin found himself in one of the tiled cubicles in the cellar, stripped to the waist and chained by his wrists to the wall. On the other side of the narrow wooden table bisecting the cubicle was a metal sink with several shelves that held gruesome-looking tools, some of them medieval in design and horrendous in impact.

Working intently by the sink, Yoshijiro, the huge torturer with the shaven head, and his pop-eyed assistant Koki, prepared for Dallin. Yoshijiro, dressed in only a loincloth, sliced off slivers from a long stalk of bamboo while Koki, in white baggy pants ending at the knees, heated iron pincers over a small charcoal stove on the floor. They worked solemnly, as if carrying out a ritual, paying no attention to their prisoner.

The irony of his situation did not escape Dallin. Ever since he had arrived in Shanghai, he had visualized himself here and at their mercy—but for being a spy, not because he had defied Hata over a warehouse of treasure.

Seeing these two subhumans up close reminded Dallin of what the others had suffered, especially Hacker and the Norwegian, both of whom had had information that could have saved their lives. That was the real test, and Dallin wondered how he would fare under the same circumstances. Not now, he thought, but later, in the long hours to come, when there was nothing to protect him from his torturers.

In a sense, everything up till now was only rhetoric. True, he had not known the ring was broken and its members executed, but even if he had, Dallin would still have returned to Shanghai. His purpose in being here had not changed with his arrest. Somehow the commandant of the Kempetai had to be kept in the city until the Allies arrived. And the only way Dallin knew to bring this about was to withhold the whereabouts of the antiquities.

But Dallin did not delude himself. No one, man or woman, regardless of physical strength or personal conviction, could say with any positive assurance how they would react under torture. Dallin had seen too many victims of the Kempetai in the past. Priest or whore, general or gangster, Caucasian or Oriental, Dallin had witnessed them all begging for the chance to reveal anything they knew to save themselves from the sadistic skills of Yoshijiro and Koki.

And the rigors that lay ahead for Dallin were no different, particularly since the words that might save him were his to tell. Only his *joss* could save him.

"Okay, Dallin!" Yoshijiro smirked, waving a lead pipe, "time for you to say hello good-bye!"

Upstairs Hata paced his office. Torturing Dallin gave him no pleasure. At first he thought it might, but the more he reflected on it, the more apparent it became that it was Hata who stood to lose face, not the White Russian.

By sending Dallin to the cellars, the Kempetai commandant was admitting publicly that his partner had deceived him. He too was under no delusion: the White Russian was sturdy and tough. Breaking him would not be an easy or quick process, even for his experienced henchmen. And Hata had no patience for delays. No! Not with Hiroshima! The peace faction in Tokyo must be girding for a last assault, Hata thought, and it was a moot point how long the War Cabinet could ignore them. It was not something Hata wished to risk his life on.

The idea of releasing Dominique, as Dallin demanded, crossed his mind. Hata considered it for a while. According to Sumato, she was still in a daze, incapable or unwilling to help him. If the truth be known, Hata respected the Norwegian for the way he had chosen to die. Why not yield and give the girl over to Dallin? On the surface, it made sense. Was it to save face that he hesitated? Was it mere stubbornness? Or was it something intangible, a feeling he had about the White Russian's story which kept him from accepting it, despite all logic?

Still, there was time left, Hata realized. At best, the Portuguese freighter was five days away from Shanghai. "Five days," he murmured aloud. Certainly enough time to get information from a prisoner, even from someone as determined as Dallin. Provided, of course, he did not die during the ordeal.

Hata returned to his desk. Determined to clear his mind of the whole matter, he set himself to his paperwork when suddenly there was an abrupt rap on the door and Sumato, his face awash with tears, staggered inside.

"What is it?" Hata asked, taken by surprise.

Sumato tried to reply, but was unable to do so. Instead he began weeping as he moved across the room, holding out a sheet of wrinkled rice paper.

Hata was disgusted. He was about to denounce Sumato for his cowardly behavior when some inner sense told him to read the communiqué first.

KEMPETAI HQ
TOKYO

MOST URGENT

SECOND MYSTERY BOMB HAS FALLEN UPON NAGASAKI. EXPLOSION DESTROYED CENTER OF CITY AND LEFT MANY THOUSANDS KILLED. MANY MORE WOUNDED AND HOMELESS.

Shaken, Hata slowly reread the communiqué. From across the room he could hear Sumato weeping. It was incredible. Two bombs! Two major Japanese cities left in rubble, a vast portion of their citizenry killed.

"Nagasaki too," he eventually murmured.

Sumato broke down, sobbing violently, his entire body quivering. His brown eyes, normally haunted by his internal conflict, were wild-looking, and his gaunt face reflected the despair of an unhinged mind.

"What is it, Sumato?"

The still sobbing Sumato made a valiant attempt to reply but gave up, too overcome with grief.

"What is it?"

"Nagasaki!" Sumato finally managed to whisper.

"What about it?"

His hands clenched at his sides, the haggard Japanese peered at Hata, an odd expression on his face. "Nagasaki is my home. Three generations of the Sumato family live there. My entire family."

Then, shoulders drooping more than ever, Sumato walked abruptly from the room, moving blindly past a young lieutenant in a visor cap and battledress.

"Yes, Tokura?" Hata asked, relieved at the sight of his most outstanding junior officer.

"Sir. We've searched over one hundred godowns and foreign warehouses on both sides of the Whangpoo, from Nantao to the Yangtzepoo district. There's still no sign of them."

"You've done what?" Hata asked, still distracted by the communiqué from Tokyo.

"The search for the missing antiquities, sir. You instructed me to report three times daily."

"Very good then, Tokura."

"Sir. Shall I recall the men?"

"No!" Hata snapped. "Keep looking until I say otherwise. Is that understood?"

"Yes, sir." Tokura bowed low, then hurried into the corridor past Sumato who was slumped over on the wooden bench between the office and records room.

Hata gazed back down at the communiqué resting on his desk.

"First Hiroshima, then Nagasaki, and now the Emperor," he murmured, swiveling to study the portrait of Hirohito on the wall. "The next logical step must be surrender. What else can he do?"

And what else is there for me to do, Hata asked himself, but escape. Get as far away from East Asia as possible before the trap closed around him.

But to do this, Hata had to have one man's help—the prisoner in the cellar—Maximov Dallin!

Sumato stumbled into his room at the far end of the barracks on the sixth floor. He sank to his knees on the tatami mat. His head throbbed, blurring his vision and making his thoughts muddled. His quarters were modest in size and decor. Other than the traditional tatami mat there was just a pinewood chest and neat row of books in several languages. Perched among them was a family photograph. The sight of his precious family underscored the shocking phrase . . . Nagasaki struck by bomb . . . Nagasaki struck by bomb.

It would be days, perhaps even weeks, before the names of the dead and wounded would be listed. Attempting to reach Nagasaki by telephone or wireless was impossible. Not even the Kempetai could cut through the wall of death and chaos that surrounded the city now.

Until today Nagasaki had been a lovely city, a prosperous cosmopolitan port, that, for some unaccountable reason, had been one of the few major Japanese cities spared by the American Air Force.

Nagasaki was an intellectual oasis, a harmonious environment in an otherwise repressive land, especially for a curious scholar like Sumato. For three generations his family had been renowned for the bookshop they owned in the center of the city. Since the turn of the century when his great-grandfather established Sumato and Company: Fine Books and Maps had become a landmark. Foreign sea captains and university professors from as far away as Edinburgh, Scotland, and Princeton, New Jersey, were regular patrons. The shop had even supplied rare books of poetry to Felix Hacker at the Municipal Council Library in Shanghai. It was this connection that had formed the basis for Sumato's friendship with the Swiss librarian.

Sumato was proud of his heritage. And his family had taken great pride in the honors he had received at the university and later at the good job he had done managing the family bookshop—until he had been drafted into the Kempetai.

Sumato moaned as he studied the photograph on the chest: his grandparents; his father and mother; his wife and their four children. Only a miracle could have saved them from the horrible fate that had befallen Nagasaki.

Shuddering, Sumato groaned and threw himself on the tatami mat. Beating both fists on the floor, he writhed from side to side; until, finally exhausted, he lay curled in the fetal position. He had feared for a long time that the Pacific War would lead to this. His last letter from home, written by his wife, had told of the fire-bombings that had changed Tokyo from a thriving metropolis into a great wasteland of rubble.

And why? For what reason was nearly two thirds of his nation destroyed, millions killed or left maimed and without homes? So the industrialists and bankers could have larger markets and greater profits? So militarists like Tojo, Kenji, and Araki, even men like Colonel Hata, could gain glory and public esteem? What folly it was, reflected Sumato, permitting this greedy and ambitious minority to enforce their will on the entire population.

Of all the officers at Bridge House, Sumato was the most knowledgeable in analyzing foreign affairs. A year and a half ago he had begun to suspect that his nation faced a crushing defeat. How could a nation of seventy million people, taught to believe they were the divine race, accept humiliation and humble themselves before their conquerors? And how would their conquerors behave, considering that very few understood the language and customs of the Japanese people. So many changes lay ahead, and Sumato could not help wondering if the Allies, in wiping out the establishment, which seemed a logical step, would not alter Nippon beyond recognition. It seemed unthinkable that the Allies would permit the Zaibatsu families, those few clans controlling most of the wealth of Japan, to remain in power. Then, Sumato thought bitterly how often he had been wrong in the past.

He still flushed with shame every time he thought about how proudly he had sailed from Osaka aboard the crowded troopship bound for China, taking with him the noble expectations of the true believer, even if he was among that tiny minority who never totally accepted what they had been told.

Asia for the Asiatics! A new order in the world! Eight painful and disillusioning years had passed since that gray, rainy day when his ship departed the Home Islands. But instead of convincing the Chinese people to join Japan in her drive to rid Asia of the hated Caucasians, Sumato had witnessed her troops, led by the Kempetai, ruthlessly brutalize and corrupt the native populace until the Chinese came to despise their "brothers" from Nippon far more than they had ever hated their white oppressors.

It was a bitter pill for Sumato to think that he, an educated man, a devoted scholar, and heir to a family tradition that valued the life of every single human being, would stand in the docket beside barbarians like Colonel Hata to be tried and judged as a war criminal.

How had he reached this point? How had all his countrymen? It was a question he knew fascinated the Allied nations about the citizens of the Third Reich. How had the same cultural heritage that had produced Luther, Beethoven, and Thomas Mann also given birth to monsters like Hitler, Goebbels, and Himmler.

Somewhere Sumato knew there must be a reason for the Nazi death camps and gas chambers. Infamies like these did not spring up overnight and without roots any more than the Japanese atrocities at Bataan, Nanking, and Singapore had lacked underlying causes. After some reflection, Sumato decided that their blind respect for authority had brought the Japanese and German people to their present plight, for obedience to one's superior was instilled in every Japanese and German from birth.

In the Germans, Sumato had observed that this respect was originally based on fear, then brought to maturity by force, whereas for the Japanese the concept of blind obedience had different origins.

Until the second half of the nineteenth century, Japan had been largely shut off from the world. Before then she had been an insular nation, held together by the worship of the Mikado, the theory of divine descent. Every Japanese was taught to believe that their heritage was the most ancient in the world, that it went as far back as a deity who created Nippon and established the Imperial Dynasty. Total devotion to the Emperor was considered by his loyal subjects to be their sole reason for existence. All men, women, and children were expected to fulfill their responsibilities to the Emperor as outlined in a fixed social and cultural code that covered every situation. Independent thinking was taboo. The rights of the individual were always regarded as secondary to those of the group. Hard work, respect for one's elders, obedience to one's superiors, keeping emotions under control, plus, most important of all, the commitment to live and die for the Emperor were the guiding tenets for every Japanese.

Sumato concluded ruefully that, in adhering to the standards set by their traditions, both the Japanese and Germans had ultimately made themselves vulnerable to exploitation by unscrupulous and power-hungry leaders. And, given the turbulent world economic conditions, it had not been long before such ruthless individuals assumed control.

And, in the end, who was sacrificed for this madness, moaned Sumato, but innocent people such as his own family in Nagasaki!

The noon rain was falling in dense gray sheets. Drops bounced from the wet windowsill of the open window, forming shallow puddles on the highly polished wood floor. Hata sat at his desk. He had instructed his subordinates that he wanted no telephone calls, no disturbances for any reason whatsoever. He sat erect, waiting; his desk was cleared of everything but the ornate samurai sword, a neat pile of official reports, and a calendar marked July 9th, 1945.

A light tap on the door was followed by the entrance of two Kempei in sodden khaki. They helped Dallin, his nose bloodied, inside the office and to the chair across from Hata. Then they bowed low and left.

Hata handed Dallin a clean handkerchief for his nose, then he removed a bottle of Scotch from the drawer and filled two shot glasses.

"Whiskey?"

Dallin wiped the last bit of dried blood from his battered nostrils, then downed his Scotch in one fast gulp. His hand trembled and he spilled some whiskey on his shirt; Hata noticed it.

"Another."

Complying, Hata refilled the shot glass. Then he emptied his own as Dallin finished the second one at almost the same time.

"How do you feel?"

"Like you'd expect," Dallin replied, cracking a small smile. "Only worse.'"

"The whiskey will help dull the pain."

"But not the memory."

Nodding, Hata swung both his legs onto the edge of the desk. He did not seem eager to say whatever was on his mind, and Dallin welcomed the postponement.

Yoshijiro and his pop-eyed assistant, Koki, had proved more proficient than even Dallin had imagined. His OSS training, brief though it was, had taught him roughly what to expect, and what gaps it left had been filled in by his glimpses of Kempetai victims in the past. Yet he was not prepared for what they had done, and he doubted that anyone could ever be.

"Hello good-bye!" meant knocking him unconscious. He awoke to find himself naked and strapped on his back to the wooden table. Koki beat his legs and buttocks with a rough board, making his skin raw and sensitive to the slightest touch, and Yoshijiro then added to the pain by rubbing coarse sea salt over his flesh.

After that, they turned him over on his stomach, and Koki held a glowing iron pincers between his thighs, scorching a tiny patch of skin until the cell stank of burned flesh. Koki shifted the red-hot pincers up his leg when the order came, terminating the session. Displeased, Yoshijiro sought instant gratification by slamming Dallin in the face with his clenched fist. Actually, he was their human toy for only a few minutes, but it was enough time to leave Dallin more convinced than ever that when one was helpless and in the hands of amoral brutes, bent on inflicting pain, no one could say with any assurance what he would do.

"Perhaps we can come to an agreement after all," Hata said, finally breaking the silence.

"On what terms?"

"Dominique Torg for our goods."

"Half of them."

"All!"

"Half."

"Have another drink?"

"Thanks but I'd rather not," Dallin replied with a smile. His body had taken a terrible pounding and he had no intention of letting Hata see him tremble again, not if he expected to get out of Bridge House intact and alive.

"If the girl is so important to you then she is worth everything."

"Not everything. I'll need a stake to get started when all this is over."

"You have cash . . . gems . . . some gold."

"I'll need more. The Chungking crowd are well heeled. It'll be difficult enough competing with them."

"Still . . . a White Russian like yourself," Hata said bitingly, "without ideals and loyalties, shouldn't have any problem."

"I emptied those crates to protect us."

"You told me that once before."

"You didn't believe me."

"I don't now."

Again a tense silence engulfed the office. This time Dallin sat back, trying to conceal the pain as he crossed one leg over the other. But the pause was quickly shattered by a rap on the door, and a bushy-haired corporal with a handful of messages entered.

"I said no disturbances," Hata screamed.

"I'm sorry sir," the corporal whined, "but Lieutenant Sumato is not available and these communiqués are marked urgent."

"Give them here and get out."

"Sir." The corporal did as he was told, then bowed low and retreated back through the door, closing it behind him.

Hata pushed the messages to one side, then had second thoughts and reluctantly reviewed them.

> KWANTUNG ARMY HQ
> HSINKING, MANCHURIA
>
> THREE RUSSIAN ARMIES INVADING IN FORCE. HAVE OVERRUN OUR POSITIONS. SITUATION GRAVE. EXPECT TO FALL BACK IN DIRECTION OF HARBIN, TAONAN, AND TSIHAR.

Scowling, Hata went onto the other communiqué:

> KEMPETAI HQ
> TOKYO
>
> IN LATEST BROADCAST BY CABINET DIRECTED AT ALLIES THE TERMS OF THE POTSDAM DEC-LARATION ARE DEEMED ACCEPTABLE PROVIDED THE SOVEREIGNTY OF EMPEROR IS RESPECTED.

"You've heard about Hiroshima?" asked Hata, glancing up from the rice paper. "Now they've hit Nagasaki."

"Same type of bomb?"

"The same type."

"So the end's finally come."

"Yes, but hardly the one I had in mind." Hata answered, crossing to the window. The rain had stopped and the sun, a flaming orange fireball, was set against a turquoise sky. To the southeast a faint rainbow hung over Garden Bridge and the shuttered British Consulate. It was a propitious omen, Hata felt.

Turning away, he said, "I'll give you Dominique Torg provided you turn over my share of what was in the warehouse today."

"I can't do that," Dallin replied reluctantly.

"Why can't you? You forget who is in power here. One word from me and you go back downstairs. Perhaps forever."

"Do that and neither of us gains."

"I don't understand you," Hata seethed. "Have you gone mad?"

"I can't do it."

"You realize, punishing you would give me enormous pleasure . . . would please my dignity."

"Dignity won't help you escape the Allies. It won't take you to Buenos Aires."

"I am no longer interested in going to South America."

"Then Europe, or wherever it is you're going."

"You really think a Japanese like myself could be safe in Europe?" Hata asked with intense interest.

"Don't see why not. Assuming you've got the means."

"Naturally," Hata replied uneasily. "It so happens I have been considering Spain."

"Wise choice. Franco has a long tradition of being hospitable to fascists and Axis supporters."

"So I understand," Hata agreed, "so I understand."

Nodding, Dallin thought, the hell you do. Hata was running, that was obvious, but his destination was something Dallin would never learn from his lips. Not anymore. Nearly overnight their three-year-old friendship had ended, leaving only the bitter dregs of suspicion and distrust.

Hata too was reflecting on the sudden change. He could not get over how much had altered between Dallin and himself. The White Russian was the only Caucasian, other than Niki, he had ever regarded as loyal and faithful, the only one in whose presence he ever felt comfortable and secure. Now that was destroyed.

"Here's my counter offer," Dallin said, measuring his words carefully.

"Your counter offer!" Hata scoffed. "Truly, you amuse me. Were you always so bold? So daring? I mean when we first met?"

"Bolder, probably. I was hungrier then. Had nothing much to lose."

"And now you feel you do?"

"As much as you."

"Yes," Hata agreed thoughtfully. "What's your proposition?"

"When you're ready to leave, I'll turn over half the goods . . ."

"Dallin!"

"Hear me out, damnit!" Dallin shouted back. "Until you do leave, you can keep Dominique Torg under house arrest and me under guard if it makes you feel any safer. Now, I think that's goddamn fair unless you're planning to murder me?"

Hata smiled. "How do I know you won't try to make off with the girl and the cargo?"

"It's *your* military police. Make sure I don't."

"Strange," Hata said calmly, "I never noticed till today how tough you really are."

"No tougher than you. Otherwise we never would've made it as partners. Now, is it a deal?"

Hata was unsure. He would have given anything to take the White Russian into his confidence. If ever he needed the services of a charlatan like Maximov Dallin it was now. No one else knew better than Hata how ill-equipped he was to face the uncertainties that lay ahead. Becker; the voyage aboard the freighter; his reception by the Nazis living in Argentina; all these were exactly the sort of problems that the White Russian was adept at handling.

But Dallin had lied and deceived him, and before Hata left Shanghai he would make the White Russian pay for it.

"Very well," Hata replied finally, "if you keep your end of the bargain, I'll keep mine."

Dominique was kept in a cage on the third floor, not far from the room where her father had spent his last hours. She did not know this, which was just as well. In the past three days she had cried enough. Still, she was not nearly as distraught as she had made the Kempetai believe. What other defense had she but deception? Being a woman added fuel to the ferocity of her tormentors. When she first arrived at Bridge House and was taken into the cellar, the Japanese had fought among themselves over who would take charge of her.

Finally the strongest, Yoshijiro, had won Dominique for himself. Afterward, alone with her in the tiled cell, he strapped her wrists to the beam overhead and, with saliva dripping from his mouth, slowly stripped off her clothing, one piece at a time, until Dominique was completely naked and at his mercy.

His meaty fingers pawing at her undraped breasts, Yoshijiro anxiously edged nearer, poking his huge shaven head between her bare thighs. If Hata had not made an appearance just then, Dominique had no doubt what would have happened next.

Later, spared, and alone in a cell, she had time to think over her situation. Just how the idea of deliberately acting odd, off-balance really, in the presence of Hata had occurred to her she was not certain. Nevertheless that is precisely what she had done and it had succeeded. Somehow her pose triggered the paradoxical behavior that was so typical of the Japanese. It deflected Hata's compelling urge for brutality. Dominique remained a prisoner, but as yet she was still unmolested physically, beyond what had happened that first day.

Niki had told her about Salat. Coming so close upon her father's death, she took the news without a tremor, for it seemed unreal, impossible. Salat had been her first love, in fact, her only true love. There had been many flirtations, although not as many as some would expect, for Dominique actually preferred to be alone, quiet and reflective. Just talking with Salat, being with him was enough; and during the brief time they were together, sleeping with him was the most tender and loving experience Dominique had ever known.

The Corsican was understanding and adoring. His affection was constant and boundless. Awakened sexually by him, Dominique yielded willingly. Their lovemaking was marvelously natural, a truly shared experience, something they both wanted and needed. And because of that it was extraordinarily good. They surrendered to one another in body and spirit. Dominique knew then that what they had was very rare, and now, even with Salat gone, it was very precious to her. She had been fortunate in finding a man who was not just a lover but a brother, a friend, and a father all in one.

Now that both Salat and Gustav Torg were dead, her own world seemed diminished. Their deaths had robbed her of a safe harbor, a loving refuge, and she was left to face life alone. Although she might comfort herself with memories, in time she knew this would be destructive; she must use the cherished past to somehow help her go on.

Dominique was stunned when Maximov Dallin, someone totally unexpected, unlocked her cage door. At his insistence, Dominique was given back her clothing, and then, too shaken too walk, was carried downstairs to a waiting Bentley roadster.

Dallin had forgotten how appealing Dominique was. Even when he saw her in soiled cotton pajamas, squatting inside that foul cage, she exuded a loveliness and purity that kindled long-forgotten memories.

A year or more had passed since they had last met and spoken. Dominique had never concealed her antipathy toward him for forcing Gustav Torg to sell his company, and she had never forgiven him for ruining its fine image in China by his black market activities and war profiteering.

The Norwegian had never felt he could reveal the real purpose behind these manipulations to his daughter. In fact the more bitter Dominique became, the better Dallin's position was with Hata. Still, the cost was high, and never was Dallin more aware of it than now, as he slid next to Dominique in the back of his elegant Bentley.

A Ronin with a smashed face, one of the plainclothes members of the Kempetai, who wore their dreaded insignia on the reverse side of their lapels, was seated on the other side of Dominique. Two equally repellent Ronin were seated in front.

Dallin's Chinese chauffeur glowered at these two, then wheeled the Bentley away from Bridge House. They sped past the two tanks at the massive gates, then headed over Soochow Creek, mingling with the flow of army trucks, rickshaws, and bicyclists on Szechwan Road.

The European-style buildings of the International Settlement had never looked so inviting to Dominique. The familiar granite architecture, crowded streets, and busy shops were a reassuring sight. Just as she was beginning to relax, a lumbering army truck swung abruptly into their lane, forcing their driver to veer sharply to the right and onto the curb to avoid a collision. Dominique was flung up against the Ronin beside her, and by the time the Bentley had come to a full stop, his beefy hands were halfway up under her skirt, and he was leering at her.

She was on the verge of screaming when Dallin reached

over and, seizing the Kempei agents wrists, tore his hands away from her body. The Ronin cursed and struggled to break free, but Dallin increased his pressure until the Japanese fell back against the seat a beaten man.

"You ever touch her again and I'll maim you for life, understand?"

The Kempei agent nodded, then let out a loud sigh as Dallin drew away. Up front the other two Ronin had swiveled around and were watching the White Russian. Seeing his grim expression, however, neither felt any impulse to come to the aid of their comrade.

Dominique kept telling herself to remain firm. She had refused to give in to Niki and she had no regrets. Now it seemed as if the Kempetai were using Dallin to influence her, although, so far, his actions were hardly those of someone in league with them. There was a curious aura of security about being with Dallin, Dominique found, a kind of comfort in having this confident White Russian with his rugged shoulders and strong face at her side. It was much too early to make any sense of the way she felt.

So much had changed in such a short time. A few minutes earlier she had been locked in a Bridge House cage. Now she was riding in the chauffeured car of the most notorious black marketeer in Shanghai. It was all very mysterious, and judging from his somber look, Maximov Dallin hardly seemed on the verge of explaining anything.

He gestured down at her lap, and Dominique saw that her skirt was still pulled halfway up her bare thighs.

"Thank you," she said, embarrassed, as she yanked the hem down over her knees.

"When we get you home, stay there," Dallin said brusquely.

"Is that where you're taking me?"

"Where'd you think?"

"I had stopped hoping for the best back there."

"I'm not surprised," Dallin said, not unpleasantly. "Bridge House can do that to people."

"But not to you," Dominique retorted sharply, giving way to spite. "Only the people *around* Maximov Dallin end up at Bridge House. You never have."

"I wouldn't be too sure of yourself on that point," Dallin answered, still aware of the effects of the beating he had taken. Stung by her words, he fell into silence, as the Bentley proceeded south on Szechwan Road toward the French Concession.

But Dominique was not through. Not just yet. The one person she could repay for all the anguish she had experienced was Maximov Dallin.

"It's not fair," she went on. "So many good men, like Felix Hacker and my father, have died and you are still alive. And they're not the only ones who have suffered because of you. Believe me, I don't know how, but one day I hope you get what you deserve.'"

"Have you had your say?"

"No!" Dominique said, flashing her first smile in days, "but I'm too tired to pursue it right now."

With a frown, Dallin lit a cigarette and peered out the side window at a mob surrounding the ticket booth of a theater advertising German and French films. The shops grew more luxurious as the Bentley neared Avenue Edward VII, the dividing line between the International Settlement and the French Concession.

For the first time, Dominique believed that Dallin was telling her the truth: she was being driven home. Before she could stop herself, she blurted out, "Why did Hata free me."

"He didn't!"

"I don't understand."

"No one says you have to!"

"You're rude and disgusting."

"So what else is new?" Dallin asked with a faint smile.

"If it's the black book . . ."

"Relax. I know you don't have it. And if it's all the same to you, you've recovered pretty quickly for someone who just a short while ago was said to be suffering from a bad case of shock."

"What do you want from me?"

"Not what you think. We made a bargain, Hata and I. He wants something I have. I need you. It's that simple."

"But why do you need me?"

"You don't let up," Dallin said, annoyed. "But if you really want to know, I intend to use you to save my life with the Allies."

"Then the war is nearly over?"

Dallin filled her in on the most recent developments, and by the time he finished telling her of the Japanese War Cabinet offering to accept the Potsdam Declaration provided the sovereignty of the Emperor was respected, the Bentley had turned right on Avenue du Roi Albert, passed through the tall steel gates into a walled courtyard, and drawn to a stop on the circular driveway before the entrance of the Norwegian's white Georgian-style mansion, where a detachment of Kempei were already stationed.

"So what it all means is the rats are finally deserting the ship," Dominique said, noticing her guards.

"Rats have to live too," Dallin replied with a half-smile. "So just be sure you're around when I need you. After all, Gustav Torg was a hero, and saving his daughter should be worth at least my own freedom."

"You're very shrewd, Mr. Dallin," Dominique said, following him out of the Bentley. "And also quite contemptible." She stalked off, blond and leggy, and, entering the mansion through the heavy wooden doors, disappeared from view.

Dallin was relieved. Dominique Torg had been a little bit more than he had bargained for. The description Gustav Torg had given of her years earlier had been very accurate. She was clearly quite a woman. Salat had been a fortunate man, in another time and place, perhaps Dallin would be as well. But for the present, Dominique represented as much of a danger as the Kempetai.

Chapter Twenty-Three

————◆————

At sixty-two, Major General William B. Donovan, the leader of the OSS since its inception, was hearty, silver-haired, and impetuous. A winner of the Medal of Honor during the First World War and a noted patriot, he was personally charged by President Roosevelt with forming an intelligence unit capable of operating on a worldwide scale.

A prominent and highly successful Wall Street attorney with connections in the Vatican, and a member of the most elite social circles, Donovan amazed lethargic Washington with his energy and organizational ability. Just weeks after receiving the OSS assignment he managed to recruit a colorful cross-section of highly perceptive and skilled men and women from half a dozen countries, among them college professors, famed athletes, international businessmen, celebrities, explorers, and Hollywood stars.

The task of developing an intelligence-gathering and counter-intelligence service overnight to match the highly seasoned German and Japanese agents was not easy, even for a well-qualified group of American bluebloods. For a while members of the OSS were regarded as errant playboys bent on mischief and a good time, but eventually, with the aid of the British SIS and some serious knuckling down to hard work, they began operating effectively in every theater of the war.

They served in neutral Switzerland, Turkey, and on the Iberian peninsula, as well as behind the lines in Occupied France, Italy, and other countries dominated by the Axis powers, and in South America, the Mideast, and North Africa. Wherever the enemy was to be found, agents of the OSS were on the spot. For the most part they were a pampered, eccentric bunch, proud of their independence and even prouder of their unorthodox leader, who at present was receiving Christopher Blake's salute inside the American Embassy in Chungking.

"At ease, Major."

"Thank you, sir."

"What's on your mind, son? My people say you've been badgering them for this appointment ever since my plane touched down in India."

"Well, sir . . ."

"Don't sir me, son. Just tell me what's on your mind." They were standing in a large conference room beside a couple of battered easy chairs and a table strewn with reports. Blake felt uncomfortable and looked it.

"Sorry, General. The short of it is I want permission to go into Shanghai, and my C.O.'s against it."

"And you don't mind going over his head?"

"There was no alternative," Blake said soberly.

"Must be pretty important then." Donovan motioned Blake into a chair and took the opposite one for himself.

In the old days, bold propositions used to reach his ears every hour. Some were real beauts and left the late President Roosevelt in stitches.

"General," Blake went on forcefully, "my outfit, the Shanghai Ring, was the finest intelligence unit in China."

"You did say was?"

"The ring's been shopped. Five men are already dead and a sixth one, our man, has his life on the line this very minute."

"And you want to save him?"

"We must save him. And recover the black book they put together. It will expose all the important war criminals and collaborators in the Shanghai Zone. Which, I respectfully remind you, sir, was the basis of a directive from your own office several months ago."

"You take this job of yours seriously, don't you, son?"

"A lot of good people sacrificed themselves for that book, including Jews from the Shanghai ghetto, working class Chinese, as well as students and even some decent-minded Japanese."

"You also build a pretty convincing mousetrap," Donovan concluded with a wry grin.

"It was my trade, sir. I was intercollegiate chess champion for New England three years running."

Donovan nodded. Then he went over the situation in his mind and, after tossing it around for a while, said, "Your C.O. isn't exactly crazy, you know. This mission you have planned could rub a lot of important people the wrong way and that can be dangerous."

"Truc," Blake admitted, hunching his narrow shoulders over the table. "Fact is, Tai-Li's already has wind of my plan. Last night someone emptied a double-barreled shotgun in my bunk. Blew a damn good mattress and pillow all to hell!"

"Where were you at the time?"

"In the bathtub, where I've been sleeping ever since I sent off that first radio message to you."

Donovan laughed exuberantly, then turned somber and said, "Son, with your idealistic views, it's a wonder you're still alive."

"General, don't think I don't appreciate your concern. There's little doubt that what those pages contain will injure a great many reputations, even topple some very important people. But we came to fight a war and keep the largest nation on earth free, not to coddle and enrich crooks who wouldn't last in power ten seconds in even the most corrupt city in the States.

Donovan sighed, "If you're referring to who made us Uncle Chump from over the Hump, I can't fault you there. I just saw those multimillion-dollar airfields we've been paying for at the official rate of twenty Chinese dollars for every one of ours, when the black-market rate is more like three thousand Chinese to our one."

"Sir, I'll get into Shanghai fast and be gone as soon as I can. That's a promise."

"I believe you, Major. Problem is, we've got to look at the overview. Right now the wires between Tokyo and Washington are burning with talk of peace. Ambassador Hurley's just persuaded Chiang to sit down with Mao, and now he's in the other room trying to close the arrangement with the representatives from Yenan, the whole point being, what use is peace if this country's just going to break out in a civil war. Not that the Kuomintang don't deserve to get their noses rubbed a bit. However, if Tai-Li doesn't want this black book of yours found, that means the Generalissimo and his cronies don't either. And if the establishment is dead set against prosecuting the enemy, not to mention their own, seems to me your mission's an exercise in futility. Least in this respect."

"Then the answer's negative?" Blake asked, his voice reflecting disappointment.

Donovan's steely gaze hooked into Blake, judging him. "No, only things would've been simpler if you had never brought up this whole thing."

"General, with respect, if we forget the black book now we might as well forget it forever, because if the Japs don't destroy it, then Tai-Li or Du's gangsters will."

"Your work attracts some nice people."

"Blame Chiang. They're his cronies, not mine," Blake said heatedly.

"Pretty saucy, aren't you, son?"

"Lot of good men invested their lives in China."

"So they have," Donovan agreed. "And according to what you say, there's one more at stake."

"General, after what that man has been through for us, he deserves better than he's getting. He deserves a break."

"I think he does too!" Donovan replied, brightening suddenly. "So why don't you go on back to that bathtub of yours and give me the rest of the night to think things over. That fair?"

"Eminently, sir." Blake smiled, relieved he was still in the ball game.

Chapter Twenty-Four

By noon of the following day, the tenth of August, word of a Tokyo peace overture had reached Shanghai. Rumors that the Pacific War was over and the Allies victorious spread quickly, setting off a reaction that had never been anticipated by Colonel Hata or the general staff of the Japanese Expeditionary Force or the Governor-General.

The citizens of Shanghai believed that peace had finally come. Within minutes of hearing the rumor, excited crowds sprang up in every quarter of the city. American, Nationalist, and British flags were hung from windows, and huge photographs of Chiang, FDR, and Churchill were draped across building entrances. Mobs of marchers gathered and began storming through the crooked streets and bylanes of Hongkew, Chapei, and Nantao, spilling over onto the major avenues of the International Settlement and French Concession, shouting Peace! Peace! while others stood on the sidewalks, hugging, cheering, and crying. In the plush places like the Cathay and the Palace and Park hotels, residents and visitors alike milled about noisily in the corridors and lobbies, celebrating with expensive imported champagne and Havana cigars.

At first no one in the occupational government sought to dispel the rumor or declare it false or premature. Even the

Japanese sentries, normally swift to quell the slightest disturbance, ignored the spontaneous din going on around them. Stranger still, the soldiers on guard at Garden Bridge, on the wharves, and at all official buildings refused to be goaded into violence, as crowds of Chinese swirled past, cursing the Japanese and stoning their detested Korean underlings.

Finally news of the demonstrations reached Colonel Hata in the dining room of the Cercle Sportif Club on Route Cardinal Mercier near Siccawei Creek. Leaving Niki, Hata climbed into his armor-plated Mercedes Benz and, flanked by four Kempei motorcyclists, raced toward Bridge House. Once inside his office, he took personal charge of the situation, putting every army, air force, and naval command within fifty miles of Shanghai on alert.

By this time it was two o'clock, the sun a blistering lump of torrid orange in the azure sky. The humidity stood at an even one hundred, and Hata saw that his own uniform and that of every other officer in his steamy office was soggy with sweat. Some of his officers were dizzy and turning ill from the soggy air. Around them phones kept ringing and harried messengers arrived with reports that the rioters were taking over the city and had immobilized vital services.

The demonstration had assumed catastrophic proportions. Communiqués from the Governor-General and the High Command conveyed their fear that, if the demonstration were sustained long enough, the Communists or gangsters under Du might exploit the situation to overthrow the occupation forces. They demanded that Hata act immediately to restore order in Shanghai.

On Rue du Consulat, the clamor of marching people echoed through the walls of Madam Tabor's brothel, disturbing Ernst Becker, who was half-drunk and in bed with a pair of heavy-breasted naked women. Alarmed by the outcries, Becker shoved the two attentive women aside, climbed hurriedly into his rumpled white linen suit, and raced downstairs. He pushed past several half-nude prostitutes, gathered in the foyer, as he darted through the front door.

Outside, the white glare from the summer sun blinded him. Shielding his bloodshot eyes with both hands, he stumbled around the corner onto Avenue Joffre and came to an abrupt halt. The mass of demonstrators gathered there left Ober-

sturmbannführer Becker astonished. Only once before, at
Nuremberg in 1939, had he ever seen anything like it. And
those crowds of Germans were cheering for war, not peace!

Marcus Feinbaum and Sarah were at the public market
shopping for fresh milk when news of peace reached the
Hongkew ghetto. For Jews, peace represented dreams of
Palestine and America, the safety and comfort of the family
and loved ones, the end of their nightmare. Once again, they
could hope and dream and live.

Within moments, hard-bargaining stall vendors abandoned
their meager merchandise and ran about, clutching customers
and one another with soaring relief. Hasidic Jews in black felt
hats and long coats came swirling madly by from all directions. Other Jews, less religious, their faces flushed with excitement, threw their starved bodies into a circle and began
dancing the hora, while from the rooftops and windows of
the tenements ringing the market, people celebrated and hung
out photographs of famed Zionists Theodore Herzl and Chaim
Weizmann.

As the emotions of the Jews heightened, some stripped off
their hated armbands and ground them into the pavement.
Only one Jew, Marcus Feinbaum, knew better and resisted
the temptation. Instead he quietly drew Sarah aside, leading
her between two abandoned footstalls. There he told her in a
calm, matter-of-fact tone that, according to his radio at the
Iberian Navigation Company; as recently as one hour before,
negotiations had broken down between Washington and
Tokyo, and official peace was not expected for days.

His words left Sarah dazed. How could the news be a lie?
And if so, then why hadn't the Japanese reacted with force?

Commissar Hsu also was convinced the news was false, for
his radio operator manning a wireless at the ancient city
temple in Nantao had already told him so. Although he knew
how widespread the demonstrations were, Hsu was not deceived into believing they could be utilized to seize control of
the city. That would require more than just manpower; he
would need armaments, which his cadre lacked, to combat
the well-entrenched Japanese. Even at this late stage in the
occupation, a premature attack could only end in total disaster.

Instead, in the midst of all the confusion, Hsu followed a

young boy in ragged short pants off the Broadway tram and into the heart of the Yangtzepoo industrial district. They were nearing the sprawling complex of the Shanghai Power Company buildings when they heard the frantic cries of a mob. A solid wave of humanity poured around the corner, sweeping them against the side of the building. Taking refuge in a doorway, Hsu heard the low rumble of approaching tanks, and the pavement nearby began to crack. Hsu and the boy retreated in the same direction, swept by the mob. When they reached Broadway, Hsu signaled the boy to follow him across to the north side, ignoring the panicked demonstrators who were heading for Garden Bridge. They bowed low before two sullen Japanese soldiers guarding the tram stop and entered a gray concrete building. With the boy in the lead, Hsu climbed five stories to the roof. Hugging the low wall at the southeast corner, he watched as a column of tanks flying the flag of the Rising Sun from their steel turrets lumbered toward Garden Bridge and the Bund.

From the windows of his suite in the Cathay Hotel Dallin stood observing the action below on the Bund. He was dressed in a beige silk dressing gown and a long Havana cigar jutted from his mouth. Behind him, across the black and white living room, the pair of coarse Ronin assigned to watch him were sharing a plateful of fried squid and fresh abalone at his expense. Outside, thousands of Chinese and Occidental demonstrators were waving Allied flags and photographs of the Free World's leaders.

Dallin gazed down at the crowd and took in the line of Japanese gunboats in the Whampoo. Finally, his eyes caught the dull glint of the steel-turreted tanks followed by several regiments of infantry with fixed bayonets, converging on the Bund from opposite directions in a classic pincer movement. The tanks rolled south over Garden Bridge and north from the Quai de France, squeezing the mass of unarmed and helpless civilians between them, until those milling at the eastern tip were forced into the murky brown waters of the Whampoo. The rest surged west into Nanking Road, pursued by the tanks mowing down the stragglers with long bursts of gunfire from their heavy machine guns.

Those demonstrators who sought refuge in the Palace and Cathay hotels, rimming Nanking Road, met the steel-tipped bayonets of the waiting Kempi barring the entranceways.

Waves of confused and frightened demonstrators reeled away, plunging down the avenue, seeking whatever escape they could find. The column of Kempei, rifles at the ready, stretched from one side of the fashionable shopping street to the other, intent on crushing all resistance to their rule.

As the anguished cries of the maimed and dying drifted upward to his fifteenth-floor suite, Dallin turned away, unable to watch the tragedy any longer. He walked past the two Ronin who seemed totally absorbed in their food.

Five floors below, on the tenth floor of the Cathay Hotel, Giacomo Ferrara viewed the scene outside his windows with clinical interest. Nothing short of enormous profit could have dragged him away from the spectacle of thousands of stupid Chinese and Caucasians trapped in a bloodbath of their own making. Sights such as these only reinforced the cynical Venetian's low opinion of his fellow man. He would never have allowed himself to fall victim to rumor or be caught in a violent maelstrom as they had been.

Ferrara smiled as he sipped a glass of dry English sherry. The Bund ran with the blood of the sheep; the naive; in many ways what was occurring before his eyes was similar to the carnage in the Colosseum in Rome nearly two thousand years ago, a show doubtless observed by his own ancestors.

The barracks and interrogation chambers at Bridge House were deserted. Every officer and enlisted man, regardless of rank, was at his assigned post. Only Lieutenant Sumato remained in his quarters. He had ignored the order directing him to lead a hastily formed unit of Kempei to crush the demonstrators. Instead he knelt quietly before the photograph of his family and the replica of the ancient Shinto shrine in Nagasaki where his family had always worshipped. On the tatami mat near him lay a recently arrived communiqué from a personal friend at Kempetai headquarters in Tokyo. The message was brief but devastating: the entire Sumato family had perished in the bombing of Nagasaki.

Of the thousands congregating on the Bund, only a few found refuge in the buildings lining Nanking Road and the streets nearby. Most, hemmed in by tank columns advancing from three directions, streamed west into the French Concession and Chapei. Prodded by machine-gun fire and drawn bayonets, people clawed and shoved to get out of the path of the oncoming Japanese. Some managed to hide in cellars and the stairwells of buildings, others crawled under parked vehicles while the dead and wounded lay nearby unattended in the streets.

A greater number, too terrified or exhausted to run any further, simply gave up. These people were herded into groups and forced to squat on the burning asphalt of the main thoroughfares or public parks. Anyone unwise enough to resist was swiftly clubbed and kicked to the ground. Some women, encircled, with no way to escape, were singled out and dragged into alleys where they were raped. Others, including a number who were pregnant, found themselves escorted into the shade or comfort of nearby homes, and many helmeted Japanese in puttees and hobnailed boots were observed comforting lost and weeping children. The sharp disparity in mood among the Japanese troops defied explanation, but, faced with it, those civilians still free tended to get off the streets as quickly as possible to avoid the soldiers who were roaming Shanghai.

By sunset the crisis was over. The major threat to the Japanese occupation had been thwarted and order had been restored. Mopping-up operations continued in some parts of the city, but in most areas the Japanese troops had already been withdrawn.

At Bridge House, Hata sat with both legs propped up on his desk. His tan shirt and dark brown breeches were soaked through with sweat, his face etched by fatigue. In general he was pleased by the success of his strategy. At the same time he was acutely aware now that a single rumor of peace could bring forth thousands into the streets intent on overthrowing their Japanese rulers.

Unable to rid his weary mind of this thought, he stared at the date on the calendar—August tenth—and began to worry even more. He had managed to restore order in Shanghai today, but could he do so when a flotilla of American warships were anchored in the Whampoo or when a sky full of paratroopers were descending on the city. Then, Hata fretted, not even the sight of cold Japanese steel could stem the natural tide of the subjugated Shanghai residents. Which meant that if Hata did not escape soon, he never would.

At twilight Commissar Hsu boarded the Broadway tram. He took a seat beside the rear door, five rows behind the young boy. Then, scratching the hairy mole on his cheek, Hsu rested his head against one wiry arm and reviewed the situation.

Few of the spectators who had watched the ruthless methods of the Kempetai were as appreciative as Commissar Hsu. In the course of a single afternoon, Colonel Hata had managed to plan and execute a complex operation to regain control of a city of nearly four million people. It had taught the Communist from Yenan a hard lesson. Even now, with only hours or at most days remaining in the war, the population of Shanghai still lived in fear of the Japanese. After today, judged Hsu realistically, their reluctance to resist would be even greater.

The tram struggled uphill toward Garden Bridge, then, passing a row of machine-gun emplacements manned by Japanese, rattled across Soochow Creek into the Bund. The wide avenue with its promenade, swath of lawn, and quays running alongside the muddy Whampoo was strewn with badly wounded Chinese. Heavily armed Kempei were looting the bodies of the dead. Commissar Hsu was seeing without seeing, lost in speculation as to how the Kempetai commandant could be maneuvered into effecting a peaceful transfer of the city to the Communists, without another bloodbath and the pointless waste of more innocent lives.

Meanwhile Suite 1500 at the Cathay Hotel was jammed with Oriental and Caucasian collaborators, businessmen, and war profiteers. Billie Holiday sang wistfully on the phonograph while Chinese waiters in white robes moved quietly about serving vodka, champagne, and hors d'oeuvres.

The two Ronin stood awkwardly at the door checking the people moving in and out of the suite. Hardly any of those arriving seemed to see anything out of the ordinary in their presence. In fact, most envied Dallin the protection of the Kempetai.

In the bedroom, Tung, the rotund gold specialist employed by Dallin, had just concluded a transaction with a Vichy art dealer. He peeled away his jacket, revealing a vest weighed down with gold bars in the shape of tiny cigars, and began counting them out.

Over in one corner of the living room Dallin pretended to

listen as a smug Argentine armaments merchant related a recent request by the Communists for munitions. In actuality, Dallin was mulling over his own situation. His last contact with Christopher Blake in Chungking had been weeks ago. If the Allies had a plan for taking control of Shanghai, Dallin needed to know what it was. The black book also concerned him. Incredible as it seemed, he had no idea where Felix Hacker had hidden it. The project had been directed by Torg. Now with both Hacker and Torg dead, Dallin was left to find it on his own. But where, he wondered?

During all the unrest that gripped the city, Niki stayed by herself in the deserted bar of the Cercle Sportif Club. Originally founded decades before by the French residents of Shanghai, the Cercle Sportif was one of the most fashionable social clubs in prewar China. Its vast lawn was the scene of bowling and tennis matches. The enormous swimming pool was a welcome relief during the sultry summer months, while the canopied verandah, oak-paneled bar, ball room, and roof garden provided the finest European food and drink in Shanghai.

Niki was on her fifth vodka gimlet. Taking in the empty stools and tables, she complained to Old Koo, the Cantonese barman who had been with the Cercle Sportif long as she could remember, "What's keeping everyone? The damn riots must be over."

"Riots over but not for long!" Old Koo replied from a high stool on the other side of the bar. His dark brown eyes were sunk into his withered flesh. He wore a starched white robe and was seated near a shiny brass cash register in front of murals of Deauville, Biarritz, and the Côte Azure interspersed by shelves of whiskey.

"Good Old Koo." Niki smiled. "You and I are the only ones left from the old crowd. Do you know that? Everyone else is long gone."

"Gone now but be back soon maybe."

"I doubt it." Niki frowned, crossing her right knee gracefully over her left. "So what do you say we have another drink for old times?"

"Much too much Missy drink. Better go home."

"First Missy needs just one more vodka," Niki insisted, draining the glass in her hand, then holding it out to the barman. "Because Shanghai's all finished and so am I! All finished! All over!"

"Big city never finished. Big city people come. People go. New ones. Old ones. Come and go all time."

"Not anymore. Colonial China's had it. And we have too. Now give me that drink."

"Missy very very sad today. Better go home now come back tomorrow. Old Koo make her very good drink."

"I want another one now," Niki pouted. Then, noticing the hurt look on the elderly Chinese barman's face, she softened her tone, adding, "Please, Koo. For old times and because the General is terribly ill and it makes me even sadder to go home."

Niki had yet another reason for wanting to remain at the Cercle Sportif. Dallin. The idea he could have deceived Hata the way he did had stunned her. Niki thought she had witnessed every conceivable treachery. She had certainly executed many of her own. But somehow she always felt that the interests of the White Russian lay with those of Hata and herself. Of course, she knew there was always a first time for everything. No one—child, brother, sister, friend—was above deceit when money was involved.

But her resentment toward her fellow White Russian went even deeper. Not only did Dallin turn his larcenous ways against Hata, and ultimately herself, but he had freed Dominique from Bridge House and had somehow been able to bring off an arrangement with the Nationalists and the Americans. Whereas Niki, far less detrimental to the Allied war effort, was being forced out of Shanghai, he would remain. Niki was bitter and envious of his good fortune.

Yet she had to laugh. The General had been right. He had advised her to find a shrewd Caucasian and use him to provide her with security. He had even mentioned Dallin by name. The only trouble was, the grim-faced Maximov Dallin had been at least one step ahead of her.

It was a pity, Niki thought, toying with her empty glass. She had often been tempted to sleep with Dallin. In fact, she had almost succeeded on several occasions, despite his reluctance, but then Hata had arrived, and instead, Dallin had ended up with her own pet, the luscious redhead from the Pleasure Palace.

Niki was pleased to see that Old Koo had finally relented. With a few deft movements he placed another vodka gimlet in a tall glass before her. As he watched her sip the cocktail, he nagged gently. "Maybe Old Koo see too much. Maybe see nice girl grow up and do bad things. Stay with bad people."

"How did it happen, Old Koo? Everyone I went to school with, except for those who've been interned—or Dominique, seem happy enough. They're either married and have children or they went to America."

"Missy stay too long. Not get out when she could."

"I suppose you're right," Niki hesitantly agreed, downing half her drink in one gulp.

"Sure Old Koo right. Old Koo know Missy since she little girl. Old Koo make Missy first cherry punch."

"Do you really remember?" Niki asked, misty-eyed. "All those birthday and swimming parties. The Sunday dances. Tennis matches. God, it was so much fun! Maybe it will all be the same again."

The barman hesitated, then leaning nearer Niki, said, "Missy make bad bad mistake. Stay with wrong people. Missy smart she leave Shanghai before more trouble come her way."

"But I don't want to!" Niki cried. "I don't want to!" Tears ran down her face, leaving streaks on her pale cheeks. She swiveled around on the stool, turning her back to Old Koo. The telephone beside the cash register rang. She heard Old Koo answer, then heard his shout: "General no good. Say Missy better come home quick!"

The moment Niki entered the dimly lit bedroom on the second floor of the red brick mansion, she could tell by her father's face that there was little time left him. The glum expression on the faces of the doctors in attendance confirmed her suspicions.

She steeled herself and approached the bed. His breath was labored and coming in long, slow gasps. His sunken cheeks were a dingy gray, and his old-fashioned sleeping cap had been removed, exposing the few remaining strands of white hair.

Niki sat down near her father on the edge of the bed and gently stroked his heavily veined right hand. His eyes opened wide at her touch and he gazed up at her groggily.

"Where have you been?" he asked in a hoarse whisper.

"I came as soon as I heard."

"Tell them to get out."

"Papa?"

"Out, I said!"

Niki did as she was told. Seconds later the two doctors followed a pair of servants through the door. Then she turned back, still stroking her father's clammy hand.

"Niki?"

"Yes?"

"Niki, you must—"

He broke off suddenly as a stabbing pain sent his whole body lurching upward against the pillows; then he fell back, his face slack, his mouth open at a crooked angle. The purplish veins on his forehead pulsed wildly.

"Papa, please let me call the doctors back," Niki insisted, starting to rise.

"No! No more doctors!" her father whispered, gripping her elbow with his withered fingers. "There's no time. No more time left for me to . . ."

Once again he stopped in midsentence as another wave of pain surged through his emaciated body, jerking him up against the pillows; he writhed for a moment, teeth clenched and his fists futilely pounding the mattress.

"Papa! You must rest now. We can talk later."

"No! There won't be any later for me."

Frustrated but knowing how stubborn her father could be, Niki watched him struggle to rally what little strength he had left.

Finally, he whispered, "The gold is deposited in a numbered account . . . a numbered account in Switzerland . . . the number is . . ."

He battled to get the information out against the rattle of breath in his throat. Then his head sagged to one side and, emitting a deep sigh, he closed his gray eyes forever.

It was a full minute before Niki realized the end had come, that her father, Count Aleksandr Orlov of St. Petersburg, was dead, and it was only much later that she realized her father had gone to his grave without telling her the name of his bank in Switzerland or the number of the secret account.

Chapter Twenty-Five

———————◆◆◆———————

For the next three days, rain fell in heavy sheets. A typhoon far to the south was registered on the delicate equipment at the Meteorological Station in Siccawei, the most important observatory in the Orient, built in 1900 and operated by Jesuit priests. Storm warnings were flashed from the signal tower on the Bund, keeping the vast flotilla of fishing sampans and coastal vessels in port. The sky turned darker, almost black at times, as winds of more than a hundred miles an hour blew in from the South China Sea, threatening Taiwan and as far north as Shanghai.

But more than just the fear of a major storm hung over the city. A thick pall of terror had been produced by the brutal reaction of the Japanese occupiers. The people of Shanghai had been taught a painful lesson. Peace might be at hand but they still remained under the guns of the Japanese. They were disappointed and frustrated but, wise to the ways of China, they decided to do nothing more for the present and let all the Asian power brokers sort out their future.

In the International Settlement and the French Concession pedestrian traffic slowed to a trickle. The normally crowded luxury shops on Nanking Road were deserted. Even the dance halls, cabarets, bars, and restaurants, where Europeans and affluent Orientals had habitually gathered, felt the pinch.

The citizens of Shanghai were scared; those who could afford to, stayed indoors, while those who could not, moved warily and respectfully past the heavily armed Japanese soldiers patrolling the quiet streets.

Even so, the Japanese High Command was not content. To remind Shanghai of their lingering presence a squadron of tanks was stationed on the Bund. Two hundred Occidentals were rounded up at random and kept at the Murray Road prison, and a thousand Chinese, mostly beggars and coolies, were pressed into cleaning the streets of the International Settlement and the French Concession.

Colonel Hata attended the funeral services of Count Aleksandr Orlov at the Russian Orthodox Mission Church on rue Paul Henry. Fewer than two dozen mourners, mainly elderly Russian women, came to pay their respects. The service, rich in pomp, was remarkably impersonal in its remarks about the deceased. After all, what was there to say about a general who had stolen millions for his own comfort, leaving an entire command to starve and make their own way into exile? Some of his former officers, shabbily dressed and clearly accustomed to the lowest depths of life in Shanghai, waited outside the church, hoping vainly for justice even at this late date.

Gustav Torg was also put to rest, or rather, services in his name were held; the Kempetai had refused to release his body. Dominique was given permission to leave her house and, along with nearly five-hundred mourners, she witnessed the final rites at the Church of St. Andrews, a long-time favorite of many seamen. The Protestant minister, a fellow Norwegian, extolled Gustav Torg as a loving father and as a man noted for his fair dealings, his philanthropy, his dedication to Shanghai, and, this despite the presence of several Kempetai agents, his noble sacrifice in the cause of freedom. When he had finished, hundreds of Caucasians and Orientals filed past Dominique to shake her hand and offer their condolences. Letters and telegrams also arrived from all over China, expressing sympathy at the death of Torg.

Haunted by memories of her father and Robert Salat, Dominique prowled restlessly about the three-story Georgian mansion, reading, sorting through letters and mementos, doing whatever she possibly could to avoid reality. Finally, recognizing the futility of her attempts, she agreed to meet with her father's attorneys for the disposal of the estate. Gustav Torg had made Dominique his sole heir. Aside from several generous bequests to loyal servants and friends, among them the late Felix Hacker, the amount earmarked for her was a sum of astounding proportions.

Dominique was shocked to find herself enormously wealthy. She had believed that the war had ruined her father. Instead, she discovered, that despite several years of relative inactivity in China trade, her father had bequeathed her several large parcels of real estate in San Francisco and New York City, as well as a home in Bergen, Norway, her father's native city, and a palatial villa in the south of France, near the village where her mother had been born.

Nonetheless, within minutes of the attorneys' departure, Dominique was overwhelmed by sadness and a sense of isolation. Nor was she free from concern at the sudden intrusion of the White Russian Maximov Dallin into her life. Try as she might, she could not avoid the idea she had gone full circle, from daughter of a patriot, to lover of a hero, to unwilling yet not totally disinterested pawn of a wily collaborator.

Meanwhile Dallin reverted to his old habits, behaving precisely as he had since he first arrived in Shanghai. He was seen frequenting the Tower Nightclub, the Cercle Sportif, and the Pleasure Palace, where, between necessary but not unenjoyable bouts of leisurely lovemaking with the willful redhead whose perfect breasts and exquisite derriere never failed to arouse him, Dallin managed to elude the two Ronin long enough to use the transmitter concealed behind the mirrored wall in his private office.

The news from Chungking was disquieting. A lieutenant, fresh from officer training school and new to China, had taken over Christopher Blake's duties. To make matters more upsetting, this replacement, a ninety-day wonder, was not only unseasoned but curiously indifferent to the tense situation in Shanghai. His only advice to Dallin was to lie low until peace became official and the Allies could arrive in force. But just when this event might occur the lieutenant had no idea. Even the news he passed on regarding the status of the peace talks and the coalition between the Chinese Communists and the Nationalists shed no light on the numerous rumors circulating in Shanghai. Equally disturbing, in answer to Dallin's query as to the whereabouts of Major Christopher Blake, the new man claimed total ignorance. The sum total of this radio contact left Dallin wondering about the fate of his friend Blake and feeling more isolated than ever from the outside world.

Then, one day, outside the Cathay Hotel a Chinese boy in ragged clothes approached Dallin ostensibly for money but actually to convey an urgent message from Commissar Hsu. The man from Yenan wished to meet him at the Da Ching Temple in the native part of the city. Before Dallin could reply, the youth raced away, unaware that the two Ronin lurking nearby had recognized him from a recent Kempetai report on the presence of Commissar Hsu in Shanghai.

Giacomo Ferrara made the most of his time during the bleak lull that gripped the city. He wrote several letters, entrusting them to the care of the hotel concierge for future mailing. Then he deposited a legal document with the Swiss consulate providing for his personal possessions to be forwarded by ship to his family's palazzo in Venice in the unlikely event he should disappear or die.

Finally, he pored diligently over two manila folders lying on his desk, until he had finished circling certain items in both dossiers in red pencil.

FELIX HACKER SPENT HIS SUMMER VACATIONS AND WEEKENDS AT A COTTAGE IN THE MUKAN-SHAN MOUNTAINS NEAR HANGCHOW.

AT THE TIME OF HIS ARREST HE WAS ABOARD A TRAM EN ROUTE TO SOUTH RAILWAY STATION. FOUND UPON HIS PERSON WERE A TICKET FOR HANGCHOW AND SEVERAL INCRIMINATING PAGES DETAILING KEMPETAI INFORMANTS OPERATING IN SHANGHAI.

AMONG THE LENGTHY LIST OF PROPERTIES OWNED BY GUSTAV TORG IS A SUMMER COTTAGE IN THE MUKANSHAN MOUNTAIN RESORT NEAR HANGCHOW.

Satisfied that he had done his best with the meager materials at hand, Ferrara slipped both folders into their original envelope, wrote *No longer at this address* on the cover below the name *Monsieur Munk*, and then had a hotel messenger drop it off at the Central Post Office on Peking Road, never suspecting the envelope would get lost in the huge pile-up of mail caused by the disruption of services in Shanghai.

At Bridge House, Lieutenant Sumato was taken under guard before Hata and given a severe reprimand. Only the extraordinary circumstances in Nagasaki and the death of his entire family saved him from a summary court-martial and firing squad for his failure to obey orders during the crisis. In truth, Hata cared little if the quarrelsome and rebellious scholar was executed, but out of respect for the tragedy that had swept over Japan and the tradition of honoring one's ancestors, he decided to spare him. Instead, Hata confined Sumato to Bridge House and stripped him of all privileges and duties save one: the complete and total destruction of the official Kempetai files stored in the records room on the eighth floor.

Disappointment at the false news of peace was especially high in the Jewish ghetto in Hongkew. For years now the Jews living there had been trapped between the Nazi-influenced Japanese authorities and the advancing Allied war machine. It was only recently that many of these refugees had begun to believe they might actually survive. In their minds each day was a race against starvation and the Final Solution. So when the news of peace finally reached the ghetto it was considered God-given, and when it was discovered to be untrue, not only did it undo the good that had been done but it plunged the spirits of people even lower than before.

For Marcus Feinbaum, however, it gave more time to reach a decision about Ernst Becker. Obviously the Gestapo officer deserved to be killed, but Marcus was a rabbi, not a murderer. True, he had defied the Nazis in Poland. He even helped organize a group of Polish rabbis who rescued yeshiva students from the SS death squads. In fact, Marcus was the only rabbi from that group to survive an SS Einsatzgruppen operation in September of 1940 in a forest outside Warsaw.

This SS group had been led by Obersturmbannführer Becker.

Ever since Adolf Hitler rose to power, Marcus had asked himself one question: If God existed, where was he during this ordeal for the Jewish people? When a disillusioned Marcus reached Shanghai, after a flight across Russia to Japan, he hid the fact that he was a rabbi. Only Sarah knew his secret and she swore never to reveal it.

As the months of exile turned into years and further horrors were perpetrated on the Jewish people, Marcus began asking himself another question. Why had he not acted more boldly against the Nazis? Why had he not taken up arms and slain them as they had slain his own people? This time he had an answer: because he believed in the Ten Commandments. He regarded the life of every human being as precious. But was the life of a Nazi to be cherished, Marcus wondered in despair. Did God intend the Torah to include the Obersturmbannführer Beckers of this world? Or was this not the time for a devout Jew like Rabbi Marcus Feinbaum to put down his Bible, remember the haunted faces of his people being led into the death camps, and personally see that Ernst Becker, and other Nazis like him, paid with their lives for their crimes against humanity. Not so much out of vengeance but to serve as a warning to others that Jews would no longer tolerate annihilation.

In the end neither Colonel Hata nor Obersturmbannführer Becker could forget the spontaneous response by the people of Shanghai to the news of Japan's defeat. The New Order in Asia had failed. Asia for the Asiatics ultimately bore little more meaning than had the Thousand Years of the Third Reich. Both plans for economic domination and the subjugation of people's minds had only ended in misery and ruin for Japan and Germany, leaving only one avenue for Hata and Becker. Escape! Through Rossio at the Iberian Navigation Company, they had anxiously followed the progress of the *Isabella* as she off-loaded her cargo at Singapore, then steamed across the South China Sea, which was heavily infested with units of the Allied Fleet, on her way toward Shanghai.

Ten sets of forged papers had been ordered from a German refugee recommended by Becker; eight for a group of Tibetan monks en route to a remote monastery in the Andes, one for Niki, describing her as the daughter of an Argentine missionary who was returning to her native country, and the last set for a male Caucasian of Latin origin whose false Uruguayan citizenship papers showed he was affiliated with the International Red Cross.

Hata continued to maintain his tight surveillance on Dallin. Nothing the White Russian did evaded his notice, including the fact that he had been approached by the young companion of Commissar Hsu outside the Cathay Hotel. Hata had long held a grudge against Hsu for his successful actions in and around Shanghai. It therefore came as no surprise to his staff at Bridge House when he assigned his favorite gunner, Ganghi, to personally dispose of the man from Yenan.

Chapter Twenty-Six

———◦❯═❮◦———

The pilot leaned hard on the stick, cutting his ground speed, and brought the lumbering twin-engined Dakota to a bumpy stop between the two bonfires. A minute after getting the all-clear from his navigator, he swung the nose of the aircraft around and, gunning his engines, sent the Dakota hurtling skyward, bound for a base in Southern China. Behind, on the ground, Major Christopher Blake was rocked by the gust of wind caused by the departing aircraft. Then, getting his bearings, he ran over to a Chinese in black pajamas who was dousing one of the bonfires with a bucket of water.

"How do?" Blake grinned.

"Do lot better we get away from here fast," the Chinese answered, stomping out the last remaining flames in the dirt. Then, taking Blake by the elbow, he steered him across the dark field, away from where another Chinese in black was putting out the flames of the second bonfire.

Three hours later, undetected by the Japanese guardpost on Penang Road, near Jessup Park, Blake hopped off a broken-down truck outside North Railway Station in Shanghai.

He waved good-bye to the elderly Chinese couple in the cab of the truck, then made his way into the crowded station where he joined a large group standing around a newspaper stand. Not until he was certain he had not been observed did he slip into an empty telephone booth and dial the Cathay Hotel.

Dallin was just getting out of the shower when he heard the telephone. He answered on the first ring.

A familiar voice filtered through the wire. "Your Spanish friend said to say hello and give his best regards."

"Tell my Spanish friend his regards are always welcome," Dallin replied, replacing the receiver just as the suspicious face of the smaller, slow-witted Ronin appeared in the bathroom doorway.

Downstairs at the hotel switchboard, the Kempei agent monitoring Dallin's telephone gave a puzzled look, then wearily jotted down what he had just heard on the sheet with forty other calls the White Russian had received during the night.

At exactly noon, with the temperature hovering at ninety-six degrees and the humidity about the same, the maroon Bentley roadster deposited Dallin and the two Ronin in the heart of the Hongkew Jewish ghetto not far from the sprawling complex of Ward Road Prison.

Telling his chauffeur to wait, Dallin went into the Danube Kosher Restaurant, the two Ronin in tow.

The restaurant consisted of a narrow whitewashed room with a dozen small tables covered by white tablecloths. On the walls hung faded photographs of Theodore Herzl and Chaim Weizmann. The gray-haired Viennese proprietor rushed across the crowded restaurant and greeted Dallin warmly. He gazed doubtfully at the two bewildered Ronin, then led all three men over to the only available table, where two Jews with beards and skullcaps and a younger woman wearing a scarf on her head were already seated, eating borscht. Ignoring the menu brought by a gaunt waiter, Dallin asked for a plate of boiled beef and cold Kirin beer. Then he insisted on ordering gefilte fish and tea for the two Ronin, advising the pair of impassioned fish-eaters they would especially enjoy this traditional Jewish dish.

When the waiter reappeared with their food, Dallin took a few bites, then excused himself to go to the bathroom. He passed through the cluttered kitchen to reach the outhouse in the rear. Not long after, the two Ronin, belching with obvious satisfaction, pushed aside their empty plates. Five minutes later, nervous over his absence, they went after Dallin. They found a note from him in the outhouse, promising to return to the restaurant in less than half an hour.

Angered, the smaller, more volatile of the pair was all for rushing to telephone Bridge House. The larger, more intelligent Ronin, desirous of keeping in the good graces of Colonel Hata, opposed the move. He pointed out the practical advantage of waiting to see if the White Russian kept his word, since thirty minutes hardly mattered either way if Dallin was not coming back, and if he was, there was no point in letting Hata know of their blunder.

It was precisely this sort of logic that Dallin had counted on, he observed, as he dropped into a seat opposite his old friend Christopher Blake at the Roy Roofgarten Restaurant, an open, European-style café on top of a large factory building around the corner. The Roofgarten, a popular meeting place for the affluent Jews of the ghetto, also attracted many Europeans from the International Settlement and French Concession. An orchestra played Strauss and Mozart while patrons sat beneath umbrellas, dining, reading newspapers, and exchanging gossip as they once had in the cafés of the Old World.

For the first minutes of their meeting neither Dallin nor Christopher Blake spoke. It had been a long time since they had seen one another. A lot had happened in the interim, and dozens of patriotic men and women had suffered and died in order to achieve their aims.

The effect of the war on both men had been considerable. Blake looked a good ten years older than his age and the smile that had once lightened his lean face did not come easily or often now. Dallin seemed grimmer than ever, as if the sights his eyes had witnessed had left permanent scars on his mind.

Over an espresso, Dallin gave Blake a quick update on the Shanghai situation.

"So the Kempetai haven't got the black book," Blake concluded with obvious relief.

"Well, neither do we!"

"But we can find it?"

"Maybe. Like I said, I never even met Felix Hacker. The Norwegian controlled him and the dossier."

"What about Dominique Torg?"

"She doesn't know. And if she does, the last person she'd help is me."

"That leaves the library. A perfect spot to conceal his work."

"There must be three or four thousand books there."

"Still, I'll have a go there first."

"Uh . . . uh!" Dallin shook his head. "Best thing for you to do is get out of Shanghai today. Right now, in fact."

"Now look here, I came to see this through. I want to see it through!"

"This isn't Chungking! The Kempetai may pick you up at any moment."

"My I.D.'s good as yours. Maybe even better!"

"What about Tai-Li or Du's people? Think they'll stop to look at the false papers you're carrying?"

"I can handle them *and* the Japanese."

"I don't get it! I really don't!"

"Don't you?" Chris Blake smiled warmly. "Nearly three years I've been sitting in Chungking watching you people risk your lives while I've played politics with those jokers in the Nationalist Government. I'm tired of it, I tell you. Now I want to stay and find the black book because it's the only way I know to clean up this stinking mess in China."

Dallin grinned. "You haven't changed. Not after Spain or four years in Chungking. You're still the same optimist."

"Oh, I've changed all right. And so have you. But we aren't licked yet. Not by a long shot."

"The General's right, you know, about the chances of the black book even being used."

"I still want to take the odds."

"All right, but do me a favor," Dallin all but pleaded. "Let me get the dossier. This is my territory and I'm stuck here anyhow. I couldn't get out even if I wanted to."

"That's not so and you know it!" You're only sticking because otherwise the Norwegian's daughter buys it and Hata gets away to Argentina or wherever he's going."

"Always the same analytical Chris Blake." Dallin was upset and his face showed it. The last thing he wanted now was more lives on his conscience.

"Actually my chess game's a bit rusty." Blake shrugged, trying to relieve their gloom. "But one thing's certain, this war can't last more than another few days. By then I'll have found the black book and you will have kept Hata from leaving."

"Yeah, sure," Dallin agreed, unable to look his friend in the eye.

"Tell me?" Blake asked, deliberately changing the subject, "any idea exactly who shopped the ring?"

"Just that he isn't Japanese and rumor has it he lives at the Cathay."

"Same hotel as you. That's a bit chilling."

"This whole war is! But that's what the smart money in Shanghai says and they've never been wrong yet."

"Speaking of money, my rich friend," Blake laughed, "just how much have you and Hata stashed away over the years?"

"In antiquities, it runs into millions."

"That much!" Blake said, awe-struck. "No wonder Hata won't leave Shanghai without his share."

"No, he won't leave," Dallin agreed. Then, noticing a couple of stocky East Europeans in white suits and straw hats mounting the stairs at the other end of the terrace, he said, "Tai-Li's people. We'd best be moving."

Dallin and Blake rose calmly from their seats and casually made their way past the other tables. As they did, they picked up speed until they were racing down the stairs.

As Blake neared the sunlit street below, Dallin shouted, "You go on. I'll take care of these two."

"Not a chance!" Blake objected vehemently, glancing over his shoulder at the stocky pair poised behind them at the top of the stairs.

"I said I'd handle them!" Dallin insisted forcefully.

"Don't worry so much, old friend." Blake grinned. "Nothing's about to happen to me."

"That's what you think!" Dallin shot back grimly. "I've lost everyone else."

"Well, you won't lose me and that's a promise. But if it makes you happier, they're yours!" Blake relented, moving away from the doorway.

By the time the two Europeans were halfway down the staircase, Blake had disappeared in one direction and Dallin in the other. Calling for Blake to halt, they drew revolvers from their jackets and charged wildly out into the street.

It was a mistake. Dallin swooped in from their blind side, catching them off balance and ramming them to the pavement. Then, his elbows and knees flashing, he barreled in close, leaving the pair bloody and stunned. Making certain they were disarmed, he warned them to stay away from Blake or risk an unpleasant end. A few minutes later, Dallin had made his way back to the Danube Kosher Restaurant where the two Ronin were leaning restlessly against the gleaming fender of his maroon Bentley.

Among the patrons of the Roy Roofgarten were Sarah Brodsky and Marcus Feinbaum. It was Sarah's birthday and Marcus had decided to splurge this one time. Ever since Sarah had discovered that Obersturmbannführer Becker had confronted Marcus at the Iberian Navigation Company, she had insisted that he stop working there, but Marcus refused. Even if peace did come quickly, their very existence depended on the small but steady salary he earned as a radio operator. If he quit, it would spell disaster for them. They had no savings, nothing of value to sell on the thriving black market; nor did either of them have family or friends they could turn to for aid. They were strictly on their own.

For all they knew, their families had perished in the death camps. The stories reaching the ghetto were too horrible to contemplate: Buchenwald, Auschwitz, Treblinka—each revelation more gruesome than the one before it, until the stories formed an unbearable nightmare that touched every Jew living in Shanghai. The fate of European Jewry had been sealed in blood, and with it the dreams of those fugitives of the Third Reich whose tragic exile had until now at least offered the possibility of reunion with their families and return home after Germany's defeat. Now this hope too was gone.

"Have you decided what you will do?" Marcus asked, haunted by these thoughts.

"Yes," Sarah hesitated. "I'm going back to Poland. Look for my parents and Peter."

"And if I asked you not to go? To stay with me."

"You wouldn't." Sarah smiled wanly, gazing longingly at the few crumbs of the almond cake still remaining on her plate. It had been her first taste of any sweet in months. "Your upbringing won't permit it."

"True," Marcus admitted, "but I've come to another decision."

Her curiosity piqued, Sarah looked closely at Marcus, realizing more than ever before how much she cared for this sensitive, honorable man who had accepted responsibility not only for herself but for her child by another man, without ever once asking anything in return.

"Yes," Marcus smiled warmly, "if you'll have me, I'll go back with you."

"To Poland?"

"And after we find out what's happened and you're settled with Abraham, then I'll go on to Palestine."

"But I don't understand. Why don't you go there directly? You said you'd never set foot in Poland again."

"I know! But I read the newspapers. Hear broadcasts on the wireless. It's a troubled, uncertain Europe you'll be going back to. I lost you once. I won't let it happen again."

"And if Peter is alive? If he wants me back?"

"Then I'll shake his hand, kiss you and Abraham good-bye, and wish you all well."

"Oh, Marcus! Marcus!" Sarah murmured, biting her lips as her eyes filled with tears. "What am I to do with you? When will you finally understand this world was not made for a moral man."

"If, as you say, Sarah, it wasn't made for a moral man, then how is it that all of us, and even Christians everywhere, are shocked by what the Nazis have done. I know it sounds strange after all I've said, but for the first time in years, for the first time since I fled Warsaw, I'm starting to believe again."

Nodding thoughtfully, Sarah leaned over the table and asked, "If this is true, then why do you wish to kill that Nazi Becker?"

"Who says I—"

"Marcus, please," Sarah interrupted. "I've seen the gun in your drawer. What else could it possibly be for?"

"Sarah, in my heart I know I'd be right to do it. But my mind, the mind of Rabbi Marcus Feinbaum, says how could I dare do such a thing."

"Then let others deal with him."

"Suppose they don't! You've seen how arrangements are made here in Shanghai. The Third Reich lies in ruins, yet every time I walk along the Bund all I see are Nazis in big cars with as much money and influence as ever. They act like they never lost the war."

"I don't care about the Nazis. I only care about you, Marcus, my friend . . . my love!" Sarah murmured haltingly, as she stroked his hand.

Chapter Twenty-Seven

———◦◦◦———

At Bridge House, Hata signed what he hoped was the last order of the day and leaned back in his chair. He felt caught in a whirlwind of events that swirled around him, completely out of control. Communiqués arrived almost hourly signaling that peace was at hand any moment. A confidential message sent under the highest priority reached Bridge House advising certain Kempetai officers, including himself, to consider the unpleasant realities of unconditional surrender. The alternatives left officers such as Hata were dire: seppuku or exile.

This however, was not his only problem. The black book was still missing and nothing new had turned up to indicate where it could be found. Dallin was still at large, although under the surveillance of Hata's two most reliable agents. Niki was reacting with unusual bitterness to the death of her father. Also Becker had informed him that the *Isabella* had encountered rough weather in the South China Sea but was now heading full steam toward Shanghai. Meanwhile the forged papers had been completed by the European expert and Hata had sent Ganghi to collect these vital documents. When he returned, he produced the most remarkable set of papers Hata had ever encountered as Kempetai commandant. Even under a powerful magnifying glass they were flawless and looked as authentic as possible. Hata was equally gratified by Ganghi's report that the forger had been left incapable of ever betraying his client. In the light of Hata's recent experience with Dallin, this was an important consideration, especially since the longer he dwelt on the White Russian's treachery, the more intense his resentment became.

As he now saw it, Dallin was shuffling all the pieces in his own favor: Hata, Commissar Hsu, Dominique Torg, with the ultimate result that whichever side took power when the war ended, the White Russian would continue as he had in the past. Hata envied Dallin for having this freedom. Frustrated over his own limitations, he left his desk, shut the sliding wood panels behind him, and, stretching out upon the tatami mat, reached for the silver cocaine box resting on the shelf beside the shrine to Yasukuni.

On Nanking Road, a recently conscripted Japanese private sprang to attention, then bowed low before a party of senior officers in dark green breeches and tan leather boots filing hurriedly from Town Hall. The sentry, his broad face impassive, remained at attention, his long-barreled rifle at his side, while most of the officers walked toward the Cathay Hotel half a block away; the others climbed into waiting putty-colored sedans and sped off into the sweltering summer night. Left by himself at last, the sentry wearily shouldered his rifle and resumed his lonely vigil in front of Town Hall.

Across the street, hidden inside the doorway of a camera shop, Christopher Blake breathed a bit easier. He studied the luminous dial of his stainless-steel wristwatch, noting it was eight forty-five. Precisely five minutes later, as the Japanese private was marching with his back to the Bund, three Chinese bicyclists whipped around the corner onto Nanking Road, racing flat out toward Town Hall. Legs pumping, all three veered their sleek machines over toward the curb and in one simultaneous motion swung their right arms, pelting the sentry with eggs just as he was whirling into his next turn.

One egg splashed his face, another hit his knee, and the third soaked the white puttees wrapped around his legs. At first shocked, then infuriated, the sentry wiped the dripping yolk from his eyes and tore down the street after the fleeing Chinese. Spewing curses, he flung his Nambu rifle up to his right shoulder and took aim. As he did, the bicyclists made a sharp left turn into Szechwan Road and disappeared from view.

At that moment, Blake strolled nonchalantly across Nanking Road into Town Hall. Once inside, he scanned the dimly lit gray marble foyer, steered clear of the elevator, and climbed the steps to his left. At the landing he turned into a short corridor, which brought him to a solid oak door marked MUNICIPAL COUNCIL LIBRARY.

He tried the knob and, discovering it locked, took out a specially made set of keys supplied by OSS headquarters in Washington. After a few hurried attempts, he found the right one and opened the door.

A blast of stale hot air greeted Blake as he stepped into the library. Several rows of tightly packed bookshelves lined the walls of the large room as far as the lofty French windows, which overlooked Nanking Road. Against his better judgment he opened two of the windows just a crack, but it still didn't help much. By the time he turned back to scan the bookshelves in front of him, his suit was already wilted by perspiration. He swiftly peeled off his jacket, shirt, shoes, and socks, and then with beads of sweat dripping from his bare chest, he started to work. He soon found himself ripping volumes from the crowded shelves almost hysterically, flipping through the pages, then shoving them back into place.

Meanwhile, Dallin stood anxiously at the window of his air-conditioned suite in the Cathay, the ever-present cigarette dangling from his mouth. Behind him, across the stark black and white room, the two Ronin were happily smoking his Havana cigars, drinking his most expensive imported Scotch, and playing a game of dominoes for high stakes with his money. It was the cost of his brief foray in the Jewish ghetto. Their initial reaction to his vanishing act was little short of violent. Only a stack of precious American currency plus the generous use of his apartment had blunted their desire for revenge. The larger of the pair, a husky six-footer with a round face, was still taking no chances. He had telephoned Bridge House, obtaining immediate approval for placing Maximov Dallin under house arrest. Dallin could no longer move about Shanghai at will, even accompanied by the two Ronin. From now on, he was confined to the Cathay Hotel and any attempt to leave would be dealt with accordingly.

This new development complicated his life enormously. He

had two urgent appointments: one with Commissar Hsu in the native quarter; the other with an employee of Torg's in the French Concession, but now, because of the Ronin, he could keep neither, a condition that added considerably to his tension.

Not half a block away, Christopher Blake was risking his life to find the black book. No matter how much Dallin tried, he could not stem his concern for his old friend's safety. More than once in the past two hours he had nearly bolted from the suite. Only the realization that his going would mean an open confrontation with the two Ronin and the possible exposure of his own identity had kept Dallin from leaving.

Inside the library, Blake mopped the sweat from his face, as he put the remaining volume back on the last shelf he searched. So far the venture had been in vain. If Felix Hacker had left the black book here, it was not on any of the shelves, nor in his office. Blake had flipped through every volume. Except for bookmarks and occasional personal notes left by library patrons, there was no hint of the valuable dossier on the Japanese occupation of Shanghai.

He switched off his small flashlight and moved over to the window. The Japanese sentry was still on patrol directly below. Blake got back into his clothes and shoes, then glanced at his wristwatch. It was almost midnight, time to be going, Blake realized. He looked again at the soldier marching below, then scanned the bookshelves once more. Shrugging in defeat, he moved swiftly for the door, not bothering to lock it behind him. He made his way rapidly along the corridor and down the stairs, edging carefully alongside the entranceway.

On the other side of the glass doors the sentry moved across the pavement. Watching him march past, Blake felt his throat constrict, his breath coming more slowly. Suddenly the Japanese jerked to attention, gave a piercing cry, and took off at a run for Szechwan Road. Blake reacted at once. He flung open the door, darted onto the sidewalk, and, glancing once to his right, saw the sentry frantically chasing the same three bicyclists west along Nanking Road.

Blake turned the other way, toward the Bund. A dozen yards from the Cathay Hotel, two Eurasian prostitutes in tight satin dresses hovered at the edge of the alleyway, giggling at an elderly Chinese in a flaring navy robe who was waving a business card in front of them. Swinging wide of the trio, Blake kept to the curb and hurried by, but the elderly Chinese, moving fast for someone his age, blocked his way.

"Please?" he asked in a whining tone, presenting the small business card to Blake, "you tell me where I can find?"

"Sorry!" Blake replied in Cantonese, sidestepping around him.

Again the elderly Chinese was too quick for him. Holding the printed card with both hands, he whined insistently, "You look, please! No want trouble with yellow dwarfs!"

Relenting, Blake bent over to peer at the inscription, trying to decipher the tiny printing. Nodding appreciatively, the old man let go of the card with one hand, scratched the back of his neck, then suddenly shoved six inches of British steel between Blake's ribs.

Blake groaned and attempted to scream, but nothing came out. The elderly Chinese clapped a large bony hand over his mouth, stifling him. Still Blake struggled, fighting to break away, but the old man shifted ground expertly and, pulling the blade from his ribs, transplanted it skillfully to his chest just below his heart. Blake shuddered as the blood came in thick spurts. Satisfied that his victim was a dead man, the elderly Chinese shoved Blake aside and followed the two Eurasian prostitutes into a black limousine that had come to a stop at the curb.

Abandoned to die, Blake stumbled forward, hugging the side of the building. His eyes glazed, mumbling for help, he somehow managed to walk past the uniformed doorman, who had his back to Blake, and to stagger through the revolving doors into the lobby of the hotel. The usual contingent of well-dressed European and Oriental black marketeers and war profiteers were gathered there, accompanied by a sprinkling of stunning women in lavish gowns. The sight of Blake, his face drawn and his jacket soaked with blood, falling heavily against a brocaded Louis XV chair, brought all conversation and laughter to a nervous halt.

Only Plitov, the bearded night manager, grasped the situation at once and, ordering the bell captain to get the hotel doctor, he ran to aid the dying stranger. "Try and hold on," he pleaded. "The doctor won't be long."

Hunched over, Blake whispered hoarsely through clenched teeth, "Thanks, but I don't think I can wait." Then coughing and spitting blood, he fell onto the Persian carpet and rolled over on his side.

Across the lobby, Dallin and the two Ronin emerged from the center elevator and joined the throng gathered around Blake. "What's wrong?" one of the Ronin asked loudly.

"Someone got stabbed," came the reply from a white-haired man in a tuxedo.

"Not just once either!" added a lovely blonde whose low-cut gown gave her pillowy breasts maximum exposure.

"Anyone we know?" Dallin asked casually.

The crowd suddenly parted and he saw Blake stretched out on the floor, his head resting in a pool of blood. Kneeling beside him, Dallin heard his old friend murmur, "Nothing there. Get out . . . save yourself while you can." A moment later, he was dead.

Chapter Twenty-Eight

Now that her father was gone, the big house seemed alien to Dominique. It was true the servants, especially her old amah, were overjoyed to see her. With the sudden loss of Gustav Torg, who had been a ballast in their lives, they clung to Dominique for their security. Only Big Han, her father's taciturn butler, made no fuss, although Dominique could tell from the way he always hovered near, that he too was gladdened by her presence.

She could not seem to come to terms with her father's death. Before this, the idea of dying had never preoccupied her at all. Her mother had died when Dominique was very young and she never really knew her, so she had not suffered the void she now felt.

Gustav Torg had been more than just a power in Shanghai and the China trade. He had been the central figure in her life; her world had revolved around him. He had been far more than just a parent; he had been a friend, an ally, someone she could go to with all her problems. Ever since the end of her affair with Salat, the Japanese occupation of Shanghai, and the sale of Gustav Torg & Company, Dominique had spent more time than ever with her father.

They often took long walks in the late afternoons when the

sun was milder and a fresh breeze offered respite from the oppressive heat. Their favorite spot was the French Park not far from their home. In its wide expanse of manicured lawn, lush lily ponds, and sweet-smelling flowers, Dominique and her father found refuge from the brutality around them.

Often, while they were seated on a stone bench amid the blossoming wine-red chrysanthemums, her father would speak of the past, of how he had landed in Shanghai at the turn of the century and decided that this was where he would make his mark. He had overcome many hardships to establish Gustav Torg & Company, and had endured years of loneliness after her mother's death from cholera. Often as she walked back to the large Georgian mansion his toil and energy had built, Dominique would take hold of his sinewy arm, grateful to have such a father.

Now, curled up on the massive leather sofa in the rosewood-paneled library, under the portrait of her mother and the etching of an early opium clipper, Dominique wondered about the fate of Shanghai. The Allies had already given in to the Nationalist demands and abolished their extraterritorial agreements. Without these covenants, Shanghai and the other Treaty Ports would never be the same again. The old days were gone for good and nothing could ever bring them back.

Thinking of what lay ahead, her thoughts strayed to Maximov Dallin. The White Russian was the moodiest, most unprincipled man on earth. Small wonder, Dominique thought, that the Russian emigré women who had taken refuge in Shanghai had sought to marry men of other nationalities.

As she huddled in the mansion her father had built to shelter and protect her, Dominique trembled. What if her father had not achieved the success he had? Would she too have been forced to share the sordid life of the White Russians and Oriental girls in the street outside, selling their bodies to any stranger, in return for enough to eat and a place to sleep.

If these last ten days had done anything, they had taught her how incredibly thin was the line between the haves and the have-nots. And woe betide the people who believed they were secure. Anything could happen at any time, anywhere. There were no guarantees.

Suddenly Dominique had an urge for a glass of wine. None of the bottles on the bar interested her, so she reached for the button on the nearby wall that connected her with the servants' quarters, then changed her mind. It was late, well past midnight, and she had troubled them enough in the past few days. Instead, she decided to go down to the wine cellar herself. Besides, she thought, getting up from the sofa, selecting a bottle would be a diversion.

In the hallway leading from the library was a narrow door which fitted so perfectly into the wall that it was almost undetectable. Dominique opened it and started down the wrought-iron spiral staircase. At the bottom she switched on a light, then went through another door on her right. Before her lay row upon row of wooden racks, each one taller than she and holding over a hundred bottles of wine.

As she moved purposefully toward the row set apart for Bordeaux, she thought she heard footsteps echoing from the other side of the wall. Realizing the garden was beyond the cellar and that there was nothing below that but earth, she dismissed the footsteps as a fantasy. Just then, a portion of the wall between the two racks where she stood swung open, and Big Han, the butler, stepped inside.

Dominique gasped, then watched in amazement as Han calmly closed the door behind him.

"I was looking for bottle of wine," she blurted, still amazed at what she had just seen.

"Big Han get one. Red or white? French or Italian?"

"Never mind that now, Big Han. First tell me where that door leads and how is it I never knew about it before?"

"Papa say no can do."

"That's all over now—my father's gone. So I'd be grateful if you'd tell me what I want to know."

The butler shook his massive head, then started past her.

"Please, Big Han? You know you can trust me."

"Big Han know you since baby. Never know day he could not trust daughter of Gustav Torg. But Papa say no can do!"

"You must do!" Dominique insisted, her hazel eyes fixed squarely on him. "If this involves my father, and I'm sure it does, then I want to know everything I can."

For several moments Dominique was not sure she was getting through to the taciturn Chinese. Centuries of cultivating the traditional mask of indifference had made it all but impossible to really tell what a Chinese was thinking by looking at his face.

"Door goes into passageway under garden," Big Han finally explained.

"It ends there?"

"End across street in cellar of apartment building."

Dominique leaned back and grabbed at the rack beside her for support. For a moment she was dumbfounded. Then something suddenly occurred to her.

"My father didn't need the passage. Who did? Felix Hacker?"

Big Han nodded.

"Anyone else?"

Again the stubborn Chinese nodded.

"Who else? Tell me please."

"Anton Knoll from airport. Hansen from docks. Chung Lee from railway station."

"Then everything Hata said is true. All those men were involved in the ring. All the men who died."

"Not all die."

"You mean one is still alive? Of course! That's why you're here now, isn't it? You're expecting someone to meet you? Who is it, Big Han?"

"Papa make Big Han swear he never say. Big Han already talk too much."

"You must tell me. Don't you see. If he worked with my father and he's still alive, then he must be in great danger. Unless, he has another reason for coming. Has he?"

The bulky Chinese squirmed but nodded.

"What reason?"

"Felix Hacker left book. Book tell all about Japanese and collaborators."

"I know all about the black book. The Kempetai wanted Father to give it to them. You mean all this time you've known where it is and you never said anything?"

"Big Han never say anything about Shanghai Ring. Big Han always loyal to Gustav Torg."

"And you were right. But now it's up to us. You and me. We must carry on. We must make the Japanese pay for what they've done."

This time her words hit home. Almost with relief, Big Han said, "Black book at Mukanshan cottage your papa give Felix Hacker."

"So that's where," Dominique murmured. "And the man you were expecting to meet? I must know his name?"

"No can do!"

"He's overdue, isn't he? Maybe something's happened to

him. Don't you see? Maybe the Kempetai have already arrested him and he won't ever be coming. If that's so, we must find out and get the black book before the Japanese do."

Big Han's immobile face creased with concern. "If you know man's name, maybe Kempetai kill you to get it," he said in a whisper.

"I want to know," Dominique said forcefully, sweeping her long blond hair away from her hazel eyes. "No matter what the Kempetai do to me!"

"Then man's name," Big Han whispered, "man's name . . . Maximov Dallin!"

The Tower Nightclub was nearly empty by two-thirty in the morning. Most of the night people went off to the Roulette Club or for a late supper at one of the flourishing Russian cabarets. Only a few of the stalwarts remained.

Mendl, a Vichy Frenchman, was at a table with two Chinese in double-breasted striped suits. Six tables away from them, directly opposite the podium, which was deserted, a Hungarian countess, a cocaine addict, was telling her Eurasian boyfriend, some twenty years younger than she, about her family's fabulous landholdings outside Budapest. From the rehearsed way she told the story and the bored manner of her listener the account was not new to either of them.

The only other patron left from the earlier crowd was Dallin, who was seated alone at his regular corner booth. The two Ronin were at a table across the aisle. Dallin was hunched over a half-empty shot glass. By his elbow was a totally drained bottle of Scotch. The grief he felt at the death of Christopher Blake was all-consuming. At the time he saw the body he had been heading for a restaurant off the lobby. Stricken by what he had seen, Dallin led his guards up to the Tower Nightclub where he had stayed, drinking steadily. During the whole time he had not uttered a single word except to order a second bottle and to tell the Ronin, who were agitating to go to sleep, that they could go without him if they were so damn tired. His reply upset the Japanese and they were tempted to use force, but the larger Ronin, seeing the grim expression on Dallin's face, realized that the only way they could drag him away was at gunpoint, and he decided not to make a scene.

So Dallin stayed on, morose and drunker than he had ever been in his entire life. Why not, he reasoned. Everyone he had worked with since the war began was dead. And now his old college roommate Christopher Blake. Thinking about it deepened his despondency. What had been the point of it all?

Suddenly Ferrara intruded upon him, following in the wake of the waiter who was carrying an unopened bottle of Scotch over to the corner booth.

"Quiet tonight, isn't it?" the managing director observed.

Looking away from his shot glass, Dallin studied the urbane Italian in thoughtful silence, then asked him to join him for a drink.

"Only for a moment. To thank you for getting the Torg girl out." Ferrara smiled, signaling the waiter to leave the bottle and go. "This time of night, whiskey ruins my sleep."

He lowered himself into the booth opposite the White Russian and lit a cigarette. "You heard about the dead man in our lobby, I suppose?"

"What about him?" Dallin asked, giving himself a shot from the new bottle.

"The Kempetai found papers showing he was a German from Alsace-Lorraine."

"Nothing strange about that. Shanghai's full of them."

"Yet Plitov swears he spoke English like an American. And our doorman claims the murderers left in a 1939 black Packard."

"So?"

"The car belongs to Tai-Li's people."

"Hell!" Dallin cocked one eye irritably, "you know well as I that in Shanghai the Communists hunt Nationalists, the Japanese hunt everyone, and there are hundreds—no, better make that thousands—of Occidentals caught in between."

"Quite true," the managing director conceded, "but the Nationalists seldom kill Americans. Particularly at this late stage. Which makes things all the more odd."

"My friend, all I can say is let dead men lie in peace."

"You're absolutely correct," Ferrara answered warily. "And now I must get some sleep. I have an early condolence call to pay at the Orlov home tomorrow. You're going, too, I assume?"

"Uh . . . uh. Not the way things are. The last person in the world Niki wants to see is me."

"Of course," Ferrara agreed, without inquiring as to why. "It's a pity about Niki. She's left herself in a rather awkward position with the Allies. Not that your own is any less precarious unfortunately."

"I'll get by." Dallin smiled faintly. "You forget, I was the one who got Dominique Torg released from Bridge House."

"I don't follow."

"Well, you didn't think I did it for love or friendship, did you? I'm here in China to stay. At least until I say different. Nobody is making Maximov Dallin run away. For that, I need influence. Rescuing the girl gave me just that, maybe even a little more. After all, Gustav Torg is a hero to the Allies. Get me?"

"I'm afraid I do." The managing director frowned. "Now I must get some rest. *Buona notte.*"

"*Buona notte* to you, pal!" Dallin muttered, raising the glass to his lips and watching the elegant managing director bid his barman good night before leaving the club.

"May we join you for a moment?" It was Mendl, the Vichy Frenchman, a short, dapper man with dyed black hair. He was accompanied by the two Chinese from his table.

"Suit yourselves."

"Thank you. You know my associates Charlie Sung and Victor Kuan," Mendl went on, following the two Chinese as they slid into the booth opposite the White Russian.

"Charlie Sung and Victor Kuan," Dallin repeated in singsong fashion. "Who can ever forget the pair responsible for turning over those Catholic nuns to the Kempetai. You boys should be real proud of yourselves. That was a swell piece of work."

"Wasn't it!" Mendl agreed dryly. "But we haven't come for compliments."

"No! Then what have you come for?"

"We heard of your falling out with Hata. It's clear times are changing very rapidly. Well, Charlie and Victor here, not to mention myself, would like to forget the past. We are looking for someone clever like yourself to work with in the future. The Yanks spend money as if it was water and, handled properly, we can make more off them in peacetime than we did off the Japs in war."

"Let me see if I follow all this. You three want to replace Colonel Hata. You want to handle all the assassinations, betrayals, extortions, and rough stuff. So to speak, move hand in hand with me on to the next wave of profit-making."

The two Chinese were eyeing Dallin with curiosity, as was Mendl, although he seemed more willing to be conciliatory.

"There's no need to crude about things, Dallin. We're all aware of what's at stake and what it takes to do the job. The basic question is whether you'd be inclined to merge your interests with ours."

"So what you're asking for is a partnership?"

"Exactly," Mendl replied, as the other two nodded their heads vigorously.

Dallin stared sourly at the men one by one. Then in a hard chilling voice, he replied, "Before I ever did what you propose I'd cut off my balls. Does this answer your question? Or must I make myself clearer?"

"No. I think you've said quite enough," Mendl responded icily. He gave the two Chinese a cautionary glance, checking their move for the guns stowed under their jackets, then added, "I only hope with time we can some day oblige you."

Dominique entered the club just as they were leaving. The Harlem Five had returned to the podium and were playing a Duke Ellington tune as she approached the corner booth. She wore a white linen safari jacket with a matching skirt. Her golden hair had just been washed and fell to her slim shoulders. Her high-cheek-boned aquiline face had taken on a new look of resolution and her walk had an energetic swing.

Dallin was very aware of her, which made his job just that much more difficult.

Dominique had spotted Dallin at the same time he saw her and she headed directly across the club to the corner booth. She had left home feeling guilty about the way she had treated the White Russian, but now, seeing him, she became indignant that Dallin and her father had treated her with so little respect. Why had they refused to take her into their confidence? Why had they insisted on treating her like an untrustworthy immature girl? The questions galled Dominique, particularly when she remembered how insistent Gustav Torg had been to make certain she did nothing to displease the Japanese.

"You too, huh!" Dallin grumbled at her approach, not giving Dominique a chance to explain the reason for her presence. "Must be my night. Don't tell me you have a proposition too?"

"You're drunk!" Dominique frowned.

"And getting drunker! But if you want booze, get your

own bottle. Around here my popularity is not exactly at its highest level."

"I came here to talk, not drink, and certainly not to argue, okay?" She sat down opposite him.

"Who says it's okay?" Dallin shot back nastily. "Did I invite you over? Did I ask you to sit? What the hell are you doing out of your house anyhow? You're breaking my deal with Hata, and I'm in trouble enough with that sonofabitch!"

Dominique ignored the tirade and sat down opposite him. "Something's gone terribly wrong, hasn't it?" she asked, making no attempt to conceal her concern.

"Wrong? In Shanghai?" Dallin replied, knocking back another shot of Scotch. "What could possibly be wrong? Unless, of course, you begin to rate knifing and shooting people as being out of the ordinary?"

"Did someone you care about just die?"

"Only a German from Alsace-Lorraine."

"I don't understand. I'm trying to but I don't. Won't you explain it?"

"Why should I? Look, why don't you just get lost, okay!"

Dominique was thrown by his hostility, but still she did not stir. She was staying no matter what he said. Dallin scowled, poured another shot, and knocked that one down as well.

"Will you please listen to me for a second?"

"Look! Let's face it. I don't like you and you don't like me. So why not leave things that way and go about our business."

"Because I don't want to go after Felix Hacker's black book myself."

Her remark took Dallin completely by surprise. Lowering his glass to the table, he leaned nearer and asked softly. "You mind repeating that once more?"

"Dance with me and I shall," Dominique offered, glancing quickly at the two Ronin across the aisle, who were showing signs of interest in her.

"Sure, but I can hardly stand."

"Lean on me, I don't mind."

Dallin did just that. They were alone on the dance floor, her body supporting his as the Harlem Five obliged with a slow, moody foxtrot. As they danced, Dominique told him where the black book was hidden and how she had evaded her Japanese guards by using the passage beneath the mansion. Dallin rested his cheek against her lovely face and, acutely aware of how appealing she was, whispered, "You realize you're confusing the hell out of me."

"Why?"

"Because for two and a half years I had you figured all wrong."

"That makes two of us. But tell me about it after. First we have to find a way out of here."

"I know one way but you're not going to like it!"

"How do you know until I've tried." Dominique smiled and tightened her grip on Dallin just in time to prevent him from toppling over backward.

Half a pot of coffee later, Dallin stood at the open closet of his bedroom, putting on a freshly laundered shirt. Dominique paced anxiously nearby, every now and then throwing a worried glance at the living room. Beyond the closed door the larger Ronin dozed in a chair while his companion was fast asleep on the leather couch.

Checking her wristwatch, Dominique asked, "How much longer?"

"Just about now," Dallin replied, stuffing his shirt-tails into his trousers.

"Were you really drunk!"

"I still am. First time in years, unless you count the occasions with Hata."

"How come?"

"How come what?"

"You drank so much tonight?"

Dallin paused to light a Camel before he told her about Christopher Blake. At the end of the story he turned away, his back to her. Dominique understood how he felt. She only wished she could somehow relieve his anguish. But she couldn't, anymore than he or anyone else could help her get over the loss of Gustav Torg. Some things had to be faced alone.

Dallin moved past her to the head of the bed and released the mirrored panel on the wall. The sight of his concealed arsenal amazed her. Dallin offered no explanation. Instead, he removed a snub-nosed .38 caliber Smith & Wesson from the peg, checked to make sure it was fully loaded, and handed it to her. Dominique slipped the gun into her pocketbook without a comment.

Dallin took the remaining Bolo Mauser from the shelf and,

putting on his jacket, filled the pockets with twenty-round clips. Gripping the Mauser in his right hand, he started toward the doorway.

"Dallin?"

"What?"

"Why can't we ask Ferrara for help. He's on our side."

"Maybe a little too much."

"Meaning?"

"I'm not sure," Dallin explained. "Call it a hunch. Anything you want. But that's one of the reasons I'm still around. So we'll play it my way."

Dominique accepted his judgment and sipped her coffee in silence.

"One more thing," Dallin went on. "I thought a great deal of your old man. I can't tell you how sorry I am he's dead."

Dominique looked up at him, her hazel eyes aglow with warmth and gratitude. Before she could reply, he told her to stay put, then disappeared into the living room.

At his entrance, the larger Ronin, unaware at first of the Mauser in Dallin's hand, straightened up slowly in the chair. Then seeing the gun trained on him, he mumbled a stream of angry curses, awakening his partner.

"Easy now!" Dallin cautioned. "One at a time. Drop your hardware on the floor and back over against the windows."

Dallin waited, glacier-eyed, as the Japanese carried out his instructions. By the time they stood with their backs to the windows overlooking the Bund, Dominique was standing between them and Dallin, collecting their pistols off the floor.

"Keep a good distance from them," Dallin said, never shifting his gaze from the Ronin. "If there's any trouble, aim low," he went on somberly. "That way, if you hit me instead, I'll still be alive."

"Funny man," Dominique replied wryly. Just the same, she was not entirely confident of what she was assigned to do, but gathering up both pistols, pointed them at the two Japanese.

Meanwhile Dallin was busy over at the bar in the corner of the room. He removed a harmless-looking decanter from behind several rows of bottles, poured off six drops apiece into a pair of crystal tumblers, then added more than a finger's worth of soda water to each.

Recrossing the room, he passed Dominique to where the oval marble table separated him from the Ronin and put the tumblers down.

"Drink up!"

The Ronin balked, shaking their heads vehemently.

"Sleeping drops." Dallin glared. "You may not feel so good when you wake up, but at least you'll be alive. Now drink it!"

Intimidated, the Japanese obeyed, reaching onto the table for the tumblers, and emptying them with a great show of reluctance.

"Very nice." Dallin smiled faintly. "Now go back to where you were sitting."

Fifteen minutes later, with both Ronin fast asleep, Dominique trailed Dallin out of the suite and into the elevator.

"You do good work," Dominique said as they emerged in the hotel garage, which was lined by costly American and European cars. "But then you've had a lot of practice."

"We have a long drive ahead." Dallin scanned the rows of automobiles. "And it's safer we do it in someone else's car."

"How about this one?" Dominique asked, pointing to the next row where an immense white Cadillac roadster was parked, the key dangling invitingly in the ignition.

A two-lane blacktop highway connected Shanghai with Hangchow, 131 miles to the southwest. A picturesque city situated at the southern outlet of the Grand Canal and overlooking the lovely and vast West Lake, it had been a flourishing metropolis well before the fourteenth century. A half-hour drive away was the Mukanshan Mountains, a densely wooded range with craggy ridges, some two thousand feet high, dotted by ancient monasteries, pagodas, and Buddhist shrines.

In the decades leading up to the war, the Mukanshan Mountains had become a popular summer resort for the foreign residents of eastern China, who sought relief from the steamy cities. Quaint hotels, rustic timber houses, and thatch-roofed cottages like those usually found throughout Europe, had been built among the towering green pines and silvery streams.

By sunset of the following day, August 14, Dallin and Dominique were deep in the mountain range. The white Cadillac, its fenders spattered by mud, bounced wildly over the unpaved, winding road, leaving a trail of thick dust. The journey from Shanghai had been long and tiring. They shared the wheel, taking time only to purchase the necessary gasoline and food. Even so, the drive, which normally took three hours, took nearly fifteen, and they were still some distance from the cottage.

The delays were caused by the heavy flow of Japanese military personnel and civilians moving frantically toward the coast, frequently hogging both lanes of the highway. It was eerie, seeing so many people in flight, and it left Dallin and Dominique feeling isolated and on their own.

Originally Dallin hoped to reach the cottage by early morning. Instead the sun was a blazing ribbon of yellow framed by a scarlet horizon, when the Cadillac skidded around a sharp bend, scattering pebbles all over the road, and Dominique announced the cottage was less than a mile ahead.

"Sure now?" Dallin asked, glancing sideways at a centuries old seven-story pagoda, its jade-green tiled roof glimmering in the distance.

"Positive." Dominique smiled. "I used to hike over to that pagoda before my father gave the cottage to Felix Hacker."

"I understood he rented it."

"That was father's way of doing things. He often made anonymous gifts. Helped those in trouble or, in this case made certain the underpaid and overworked librarian of the Municipal Council Library had a pleasant place to spend his summers."

"Sometimes even the best of wars seem stupid!" Dallin said.

"I agree. But why do you say that now?"

"Ask me another time."

Dominique let the question drop. In the last fifteen hours or so she had learned a great deal about Dallin. Aside from her father and Robert Salat, she had never met such a complex or fascinating man. Maximov Dallin had touched her heart. Beneath his calculatedly gruff exterior and hard-nosed way of viewing life, she detected a remarkably decent man, capable of love and tenderness. The fact that he openly deplored that he had lied, cheated, and killed—although he hoped he need no longer do so—only increased her respect and affection for this thorny American adventurer.

"Slow down," Dominique advised, as the white Cadillac swept around a wide curve lined by timber chalets with shingled roofs and balconies. "We're almost there."

"What were you thinking about?"

"A lot of things. I knew some people like you in Paris before the war. Mostly refugees from Hitler and Mussolini. Some had fought against Franco. They were sad, disillusioned, at their wits' end."

"This world can do that to you."

"Yes. But I'm glad I lived to see the day their cause won, because I know many of them never shall."

"I still would like to know what you were thinking?"

"And I'd like to tell you," Dominique smiled radiantly, "but here's the cottage now."

They descended into a crooked gulley, then shot around a bend into a wide expanse of high grass. Off to Dallin's left was a white picket fence. Beyond that, among a cluster of tall pines on the high ground, was a white stucco cottage with a red brick chimney.

Chapter Twenty-Nine

———◆———

Three pairs of Ronin working in teams took turns following the young Chinese boy across Shanghai. Wary and wise to the ways of the streets, the youth in short ragged pants moved cleverly by ricksha through congested Chapei, then boarded a tram along the Bund, until finally he slipped into Nantao on foot. Normally the boy would have eluded his pursuers, but the Ronin had been forewarned of his skills and had somehow managed to cling to his trail without alerting him.

Now, hours later, well after dark, Ganghi waited in the window of a silk shop near North Gate across the street from Da Ching Temple. The shop owner resented his intrusion and was alarmed at the possibility of damages, but he quickly relented when made aware of the fate that awaited him if he displeased the Kempetai. Ganghi rested on his belly with the trusted Nambu submachine gun and three magazines at his side. Two hundred cartridges in all to take out one commissar. The odds seemed in his favor, yet Ganghi, still not convinced, took a grenade from his trouser pocket and added it to the pile.

After all, this was no ordinary Communist. The man from Yenan had survived countless ambushes, betrayals, and assassination attempts. By now, Hsu, like other men on the run, had developed a keen instinct for danger. For this reason,

Ganghi deliberately chose the shop window. The street was well lit by lamps, but they fell short of illuminating his hiding place. So while the Communist would inspect the doorways and upper levels of the buildings near the temple, it was unlikely he would expect an assassin to open fire through the closed window of a harmless shop.

In the past, Ganghi had executed many followers of Mao. In fact, he had killed far more of them than he had Chinese patriots and Nationalist agents. Although he was never sure why, the Japanese High Command dreaded the Communists more than any other group.

For the first time, however, Ganghi had a personal stake in seeing his intended victim dead. Ganghi had been told about Hiroshima and Nagàsaki. He knew it signaled the end of Nippon. He had also been told about the Potsdam Declaration and he knew the fate that was in store for war criminals. But Colonel Hata had promised to provide a route to safety if Ganghi remained loyal and did as he was instructed.

There was a sudden burst of laughter and conversation as a group of Chinese students and scholars filed from the rock gardens surrounding the ancient temple. Ganghi hugged the floor of the shop window, watching them scatter in opposite directions on the street. He peered closely at each face, searching futilely for Commissar Hsu, but he was not among them.

Ganghi began wondering if the Communist was inside Da Ching. Then he saw the boy wandering slowly from the garden. He was alone. He sat down on the steps leading into the street, and his experienced eyes raked the buildings and doorways, probably for signs of the enemy.

Ganghi ducked low and curled his finger around the trigger of the Nambu. His first blast would shatter the shop window and with it, he hoped, take out Hsu as well. Beyond the rock gardens lay the Taoist temple. It closely resembled a stone castle. At the entrance stood a black-faced warrior statue, General Chow. On the second floor, where religious rites were observed, was the figure of Kwangti, God of War; to his right, Li Zung Yang, God of Medicine, and on the other side, Zung Wong, the Protector of Shanghai.

Commissar Hsu sat alone one floor above, among the gilt statues of the Taoist trinity. His situation made him anxious and tense. Only now did he realize his folly in trying to use Dallin to effect a meeting with the Kempetai commandant.

The boy had just brought news that the White Russian was in disfavor with Hata, which meant he was the last person the Japanese would trust. It also meant his own life was in jeopardy. Even now, he thought, Kempei agents might be surrounding the temple. The boy was worried too and determined to warn Hsu of the pointlessness of waiting for Dallin. Hsu, widowed now for years and childless, was grateful to the boy; he had come to mean a lot to him. He was diligent, uncorruptible, and idealistic. To Hsu, he represented the future of China and must be preserved at all costs.

Hsu studied his wristwatch. He would give the boy another five minutes. If he did not return by then, Hsu would follow. He had originally planned to use a rear way out of the temple, but the boy brought word that a crew of Chinese laborers, guarded by Japanese soldiers, was at work in the street. On the face of it, their presence seemed normal enough, but to Hsu, just the contrary was true. He was more troubled than ever.

He tried relaxing, stretching both legs and letting his arms dangle loosely at his sides. He tried forcing himself to stop worrying. After all, the war was nearly over. Any moment, word of peace might be announced and then his forces would take over the city. Then Chou en-Lai and Mao could march into the great port of Shanghai as liberators and heroes of the people, while that cowardly compromiser Chiang sat on his haunches in Chungking, having once again missed a wonderful opportunity.

Fortunately, Hsu had used his brief stay in Shanghai to good purpose. An Argentine armaments dealer had finally agreed to supply the necessary guns, and Hsu had drawn together an effective cadre to use them. All that remained now was for the commissar to show them how to carry out the uprising.

So why had he exceeded his orders and come to the temple for a meeting with Dallin? Hsu knew it was because of the past. The abortive revolt of 1927 and the subsequent rout of the Communists had impressed on him the value of having the support of the police and the local army. If he had managed to make an arrangement with Colonel Hata, then his mission in Shanghai might have been accomplished without bloodshed. Instead, he had failed and now he must get out of the Taoist temple alive so he could lead the fight for the city.

Meanwhile, Ganghi began to suspect the boy was a decoy,

sent only to mislead him while Hsu escaped by another route. He was tempted to sound the alarm, drawing other Kempei from the adjoining buildings. His free hand reached for the brass whistle in his shirt pocket when the boy shifted his gaze directly to the window of the silk shop. Ganghi muttered an oath, certain he had been spotted. Yet nothing happened. Nonetheless, Ganghi thought all was lost until he saw the boy rise to his feet and move slowly down the street.

Within moments Commissar Hsu, his dark cap drawn low over his gaunt face, appeared in the entranceway and began descending the stairs after the boy. Snickering, Ganghi fixed his sights on the lowest step and waited a split second before firing. The burst shattered the window, sending glass splintering outward in a thousand pieces. It caught Hsu in the chest, spinning him around and back up the stairs.

Crying out, the Communist crash-landed on his face. Blood seeped from the holes in his chest onto his hands. Another burst, this one even longer, struck his back, pinning him to the concrete staircase. Both eyes blurred, Hsu heard the boy running toward him long before he caught sight of his stunned face. His arm lay limp at his side and, much as Hsu tried, he could not wave the boy away. So, sucking in his final breath, he heaved himself down the steps, deliberately drawing all the gunfire.

Thwarted, Ganghi cursed bitterly as he instinctively followed Hsu down, mutilating the corpse until a dull clunk signaled that his gun was empty. Even angrier now, Ganghi swiftly replaced it with a fresh clip and leaped past the jagged pieces of glass protruding from the window frame into the street. The boy was already halfway to the corner by the time Ganghi began tracking him with short, near-lethal bursts. Agile and determined, the boy weaved expertly from one doorway to the next, narrowly avoiding the deadly hail of bullets. Finally, at the corner, he pulled to a sudden stop, lifted his clenched fist defiantly into the air, then vanished into the night.

At Bridge House, the two Ronin assigned to guard Dallin were themselves now prisoners, flanked by two Kempei with rifles, inside the eighth-floor office of the commandant.

"Dallin gone," Hata repeated dully. He was standing near his desk with both hands in his pockets. Overhead, two mosquitoes buzzed noisily about the revolving wooden fan.

The Ronin, frightened, their wrists manacled, nodded their heads sheepishly.

"I assigned you to guard him," Hata went on despondently. "To watch him day and night and to not let him out of your sight. Instead he gets away. For the final time, how could this happen?"

The larger Ronin, convinced they were doomed if they said nothing, tried to explain, unaware he was a clumsy liar.

"Colonel?"

"What? Tell me?"

"Dallin drugged us . . . there was something in our drink which put us to sleep."

Hata gave the Ronin an exasperated look, then turned toward the door where Sumato stood. Despite many reservations, Hata had been forced to reinstate the rebellious scholar because of the general incompetence of his own staff during Sumato's absence.

"What is it you found out?"

"There were knockout drops. But Dominique Torg also visited the Cathay Hotel," Sumato answered, reading from the sheet of paper in his hands. "She went into Suite 1500 with Dallin after spending some time at the Tower Nightclub."

"Dallin tricked us," whined the slower-witted Ronin suddenly. "We were sure he was in bed with the woman. We never thought he . . ."

"Fools!" Hata interrupted sharply. He ordered the Kempei to take the prisoners away. Then, overcome by weariness and disappointment, he lowered himself down behind his desk. It was a few minutes before he motioned Sumato closer and asked, "What else have you found out?"

"At five o'clock this morning Dallin and Dominique Torg drove past our Kiangnan Road outpost in a White Cadillac roadster stolen from the garage of the Cathay Hotel."

"Heading toward Canton?"

"Originally. According to a later report the Cadillac was seen turning southwest along the Hangchow highway."

"Are you sure?"

"It's all in this report," Sumato replied, putting the paper on the desk. "See for yourself."

"But why would Dallin head inland? It makes no sense. Does it?"

"Not to me, sir." Sumato answered indifferently.

Hata gave a scornful look. "Go back to destroying the records."

"Colonel?"

"What is it, Sumato?"

"Sergeant Yoshijiro and Private Koki wish to see you."

"Who?"

"Yoshijiro and Koki, the torturers from the cellar, sir. Apparently they read or heard of the communiqué you distributed regarding officers and enlisted men desiring to flee Shanghai to avoid prosecution as war criminals."

His face reddening, Hata seethed. "Persecution not prosecution! Honorable soldiers of Nippon, not torturers! You despise us all, don't you, Sumato? Everything we fought and died for?"

"Sir?"

"You heard me."

"Of course, sir," Sumato agreed, refusing to be goaded.

"Send them in and get back to your duties."

"At once," Sumato replied. Stifling thoughts which if said aloud would get him summarily executed. Soon after he left, the two torturers wearing poorly fitting western suits were ushered in. They bowed low before Hata.

"You want to flee?"

"Please, sir," Yoshijiro murmured.

"Where will you go?"

"We thought of Indochina, sir."

"There are jungles. Uncharted areas where a man could hide for years," Koki added in a high-pitched whine.

"And there are already many Orientals living among the natives. It won't be easy for anyone to trace us," Yoshijiro explained further.

"And how do expect to reach there?"

"Train to Canton. Then across the China Sea by junk."

"Very well," Hata sighed, "if you wish to go, then go. But you'll need money. See the paymaster and have him phone me for approval. And good luck. You'll need it."

"Thank you, sir." Yoshijiro bowed low. "Thank you very much."

"Thank you, Colonel," Koki replied. He bent over. "Also thank you very much!"

As soon as they were gone, Hata returned to his desk. Dallin had deceived him twice. It was more than the proud samurai could bear. He regretted not executing Dallin. Even the certain loss of the antiquities was better than accepting this latest humiliation. Before Hata could dwell further on his changing circumstances, he took one phone call, then quickly made another. The incoming one was from Ernst Becker informing him that the *Isabella* was leaving the South China Sea, nearing Hong Kong, and would anchor in Shanghai within two days. Bluffing, Hata assured the Nazi that all his preparations to get underway would be completed by the time of her arrival.

Then he hurriedly telephoned Suite 1010 at the Cathay Hotel.

"Ringing," the operator shouted in his ear. Eventually a cultured voice with an Italian accent came on the line with a cautious greeting.

"Forgive the intrusion," Hata began politely, "but something urgent has come up which needs your attention."

"Always pleased to be of service."

"Dallin's disappeared."

"Again?"

"Yes, and if I knew where, I wouldn't have called. He was seen driving toward Hangchow."

"You're certain?"

"Of course I'm certain."

"Didn't you get back the envelope you sent me?"

"No! Nothing."

"It must have been lost in the mail. In any case, the point is, at the time Felix Hacker was arrested he was en route to the South Railway Station. A ticket for Hangchow was inside his pockets along with incriminating pages from this black book I informed you about."

"Go on?"

"Well, according to the two dossiers you sent me, both Gustav Torg and Hacker have summer cottages in the Mukanshan Mountains near Hangchow. Recently I learned it's the same one."

"Then you believe the black book was hidden there all along?"

"Precisely."

"But why would Dallin . . . of course . . . with the black book and Dominique Torg, his own chances with the Allies would be more than excellent. You agree?"

"Absolutely."

"Thank you," Hata murmured. "Thank you very much."

"A pleasure."

After Hata replaced the receiver, he dispatched a detachment of Kempei led by Ganghi to the Mukanshan Mountains. Then, sinking back into the chair, his eyes strayed to the recently received communiqué atop the pile on his desk.

> KEMPETAI HQ
> TOKYO
>
> MOST IMPERATIVE
>
> HIS MAJESTY INTENDS TO PERSONALLY DELIVER
> RADIO BROADCAST TOMORROW, 15TH OF AUGUST,
> AT NOON.

Sumato leaned against the wall of the records room on the eighth floor. In one hand he held a cup of tepid green tea, in his other, two manila files. A steady stream of ragged privates carrying armfuls of documents moved past him out the door. Most of the loads were destined for the bonfire in the courtyard below. Considerably less were assigned to a putty-colored truck waiting at the gate.

The office itself was a colossal mess. Strewn about on cabinets, tables, and the floor were piles of manila files, envelopes, and loose sheets of paper. Some bore the official seal of the Third Reich, Mussolini's Italy, and Franco's Spain. Others had the mark of fascist secret services in Europe, Asia, and South America, while a surprising amount were from the OSS, Great Britain's SIS and the Russian NKVD.

To anyone passing, including Colonel Hata, the records room was in complete confusion. Sumato had deliberately created this chaos for one purpose only. Throughout the destruction of the official records of the Kempetai he was putting aside the most incriminating files to be placed aboard the truck at the gate for transfer to a safe location. Considering the peril he faced if caught, Sumato was remarkably calm and unafraid. It was because of Nagasaki. The blast had wiped away everything he cherished. Nothing was spared—not family, friends, or the bookshop.

At first he considered committing suicide. It seemed only logical in his situation. Then, recovering from his initial shock, he realized this would make a mockery of those who had suffered and died before him from this war. To Sumato, far from being noble, the ancient tradition of hara-kiri was a sign of cowardice. Human beings, in his opinion, were given a brain to reason, to come to terms with problems, not to shunt them aside when things went wrong and blindly take one's life. The longer and deeper Sumato reflected, the more apparent it became he must alter things. He must undertake some positive action to bring the truth of the Pacific war to the Japanese people. The most effective way, he decided, was by emulating his friend Felix Hacker and using the official files of the Kempetai.

If Sumato ever had doubts, they were swiftly dispelled the moment he began sorting through the documents in order to determine which he would retain and which he would destroy. The two he now held in his hand were perfect examples of the learning process in store for the people of Japan. One document contained a brief summary of a request made by Obersturmbannführer Becker, complied with by the Kempetai-Tokyo, to build gas chambers in Shanghai. At the bottom of the same document was a note certifying that the ovens had been constructed and were awaiting their first shipment of Jews. The other file, containing items yellow with age, portrayed a career of utmost perfidy and callous deception. It detailed the personal history of a genuine international spymaster, someone who was of enormous service to the Kempetai but whom Sumato, until now, had had no inkling of. His name was Giacomo Ferrara, alias Monsieur Munk from Paris, alias Senor Pacheco of Mexico City, and before that and in many other countries a long list of other false identities.

Giacomo Ferrara had been schooled as a young man by the Italian Secret Service during the Great War. Following the armistice he served as a double agent for both his own nation and Germany. At the personal request of Admiral Canaris, chief of the German Abwehr, Ferrara managed to get himself posted first to Spain as managing director of the Ritz Hotel in Madrid, then later to Shanghai at the Cathay in the same capacity.

Early on in the war, when Mussolini's regime showed signs of collapsing, the astute spymaster, ever an expert at personal survival, sold his valued services to a third client—the Kempetai. Thus, by maintaining his role as a staunch anti-fascist whose entire interest in life centered around the elegant Cathay, Ferrara was easily able to inform on many of Japan's enemies.

But his greatest coup, his greatest contribution to date, was the smashing of the Shanghai Ring. He received the assignment because intense pressure had been placed on Hata by the Japanese High Command to stop the leak of military information. Ferrara approached the intelligence problem in his usual meticulous manner. He began by studying the habits of every important official at the Shanghai railway station, airport, and port. By systematically checking and rechecking all the data provided by the Kempei agents watching the three sites, he eventually detected a curious pattern. Chung Lee, Karl Busch, and Peter Hansen all visited the Municipal Council Library routinely once a week. Twice during the same month each one of them met the librarian, Felix Hacker, in a different restaurant. On all three occasions there was ample time and opportunity for them to pass information.

Further investigation suggested that the four men were linked together in a common effort to spy against the Japanese. But the trail to the leader of the ring turned cold at a large apartment building in the French Concession. The Ronin assigned to follow Felix Hacker after each of his meetings with one of the other three lost the Swiss librarian there every time. A painstaking search of the apartments in the building in the hope of finding a secret passage or chamber proved futile. The hunt for the leader of the Shanghai Ring seemed to end with Felix Hacker, until Ferrara, poring over a street map of the French Concession, realized that the mansion of Gustav Torg was only one block away from the apartment building. This was of especial interest since until the outbreak of the war in the Pacific, the Norwegian had been the Municipal Council Library's most generous patron.

"Lieutenant?"

"Yes?" Sumato answered, turning to the buck-toothed private standing hesitantly beside him.

"Colonel Hata sent me. He wishes to have three copies of Giacomo Ferrara's file."

"Very good," Sumato replied, holding both files tighter. "Tell Colonel Hata, I shall do as he asks, assuming we still have that particular one."

"Sir!" The private bowed low and trotted from the records room.

Chapter Thirty

The mountain night air was sharp and invigorating compared to Shanghai. Dallin was against using the fireplace until it was dark, for he feared smoke from the chimney would attract bandits or guerrillas roaming the area, so Dominique went into the cellar and came back with two thick camel-hair sweaters from a trunk belonging to her father. From it also came tins of Danish cheese, Belgian sausage, English biscuits, and a ten-year-old bottle of French burgundy.

The Mukanshan cottage had six rooms—three small bedrooms upstairs, a good-sized living room, kitchen, and bath below. By midnight, they had searched each room, including all the closets and bureau drawers. There was no trace of the black book. Dallin had used the only available flashlight until its moldy batteries gave out. Then Dominique lit candles from the badly depleted stock in the kitchen. Finally, barely able to see what they were looking for, they decided to resume their search the following day.

After supper they rested before the fireplace. The pine logs burned crisply, giving off a fragrant aroma and soft glow which lit up the living room. The room, paneled in knotty pine, was furnished with a brown corduroy couch, four upholstered chairs, and a bridge table. Against one wall stood a bookcase laden with volumes in a half a dozen languages, mainly on the study of great civilizations. In another corner was a cumbersome American-made Victrola with an extensive collection of classical records. Between them were several faded photographs of Shanghai at the turn of the century, and one much more recent one showing the Municipal Council Library committee, including Gustav Torg and Felix Hacker posed proudly on the front steps of Town Hall.

Dominique had supposed they would sleep in the upstairs bedrooms, but Dallin was against it. He insisted they were much safer where they were in the living room. This way, if they did have callers, they could get away from the cottage through the windows or either the front or rear doors. Dominique brought bedding down to the living room and they made themselves comfortable before the fire.

Within moments, they were both asleep, fatigued by the long night and harrowing drive. At dawn, Dominique was awakened by what she thought was the cry of a wild animal, only to find Dallin thrashing about wildly under the blankets and mumbling a stream of curses. Dominique eluded his waving fists and held him tenderly in her arms. She caressed his perspiring face, murmuring soft words until he came awake in her embrace.

"Nightmare?"

"So you know about it."

"Get me a cigarette, will you?"

Dominique reached over onto the nearby table for a half-empty pack of cigarettes.

"Does this happen often?" she asked, lighting a cigarette for him.

Dallin nodded. "There were times I had to force myself to stay awake so I wouldn't give myself away."

His words left them both in a reflective silence. Dallin glanced over at her and smiled warmly. "I woke you, I'm sorry."

"That's all right," Dominique said, brushing a strand of blond hair back off her face. Crinkling her nose, she looked at him affectionately. "If you like, we can talk a while longer. I'm really not that tired anymore."

"I'd like. Thanks."

Dominique swung her legs around and sat up facing him. Dallin leaned back on one elbow, with the cigarette dangling from his lips, his eyes fixed on her.

"It must have been so frightening for you. The idea of

staying around Hata day after day, never sure when you might be found out, never sure when some freak accident might give away your true identity."

"It was that way at first," Dallin admitted, "but after a while I actually was Maximov Dallin. As though the real me, Stephen Tarabrin, stopped existing. Well, almost. There were moments when Stephen Tarabrin would rather have died than do the things I did."

"They made you play God. It's too much to ask of anyone."

"Someone had to do it. It was just a weird break, an odd stroke of luck that Hata decided to become my partner."

"Didn't you want to run? Disappear? Slip away from Shanghai?"

"Many times. Especially when I betrayed a patriot or got involved in a killing, in blackmail or extortion. Or, most horrible of all, the times I was forced to take measures to retain our monopoly in the rice and grain trade."

"And these nightmares," Dominique asked, haltingly, "they're because you question whether your efforts really were necessary to winning the war?"

"No. That much I'm sure of. But what I can't do is get those people I've hurt out of my mind. Especially the poor . . . the thousands . . . tens of thousands who went hungry . . . who starved."

Dominique straightened her slim shoulders. She sat up, gazing at Dallin, her hazel eyes sympathetic and misty.

"I can't tell you what is right. God knows I want to, but I can't!"

"I know!"

"But this much I can say," Dominique went on, "the war's nearly over. The Japanese are beaten, and beaten badly. Whatever you were forced to do, you won't ever have to do it again."

"But was it worth so many innocent lives?"

"Philosophically, maybe not. But to those people who felt the despair and agony of having wild beasts come to their door, who were dragged from their homes, torn from their loved ones, or who felt the fear and daily humiliation of living in a occupied city or country, those people, like myself, can only say it was worth it."

"Dominique," Dallin murmured, his haunted face softening.

"Don't say anything," she whispered, stretching out beside him on the blankets. "Only love me."

Dominique was awakened at dawn by the sound of a hammer tapping. She rolled over and found Dallin across the room on his knees in front of the paneled wall.

Noticing her incredulous stare, he explained. "Hacker was an accomplished Sinologist—he understood the Oriental mind. Which means he either left the black book out in the open, where it would be overlooked because it was in such an obvious place, or he hid it away where it couldn't be found unless you knew exactly where to search."

"Like behind a wall?"

"Precisely."

"Okay." Dominique sighed, and, yawning, dragged herself over to another section of the same wall. "I'm game."

As Dallin continued his search, he told her how Hacker had originally sought permission from her father for the black book project, and how the Norwegian had turned to Dallin for approval, which he gave. In the end they had all agreed that having a documentation of the brutality of the occupiers of Shanghai would be invaluable not only to future historians but to the world at large.

Then Dallin began describing the inner workings of the ring, how the information delivered to Hacker was passed on to Dominique's father, and then to Dallin for transmission by radio to Chungking. The Pleasure Palace had turned out to be the safest location for the wireless radio since Kempetai trucks monitoring illegal broadcasts stayed clear of the brothel owned by their commandant.

Later, as Dominique sipped a cup of tea and watched Dallin cover the last section of wall in the room with his hammer, she said, "There's a rumor in Shanghai that the Americans never would have used the bomb against Caucasians, not even against the Nazis."

"That occurred to me as well," Dallin admitted glumly, "the bomb's saved us a million lives by not having to invade the Home Islands. But it cost at least a few hundred thousand Japanese lives. So, either way, it seems a stupid waste of human life."

"You're pretty tired of it all, aren't you?"

"I have been for some time." Dallin smiled, his strong face marked by despair. "I fought fascism in Spain, then opposed it here, thinking maybe in China we would finally win. Well, it looks like we have and we haven't! And that's a hard fact to face. And it's hard to accept that my old friend Blake is gone too!"

"Then it's a good thing you're not going back to Shanghai," Dominique concluded, as she watched Dallin finish his search of the living room and shift his attention to the staircase in the foyer. "You're not, are you?"

Dallin kept silent, tapping the lower steps for signs of a hiding place.

"Dallin?"

"I have to go back."

"I don't understand. Hata will make you turn over the treasure. He'll try to have you killed. You've admitted as much yourself."

"Just the same I must go back."

"Why? You can't bear the burden for everyone who's died before you. You've done enough. Unless you feel so guilty at being alive, so alone, you want to die."

Dallin reached over and caressed her long blond hair and lovely face. "I don't feel alone, not anymore."

"Dallin, for God's sake. Hata has tortured and maimed and murdered. All right, perhaps much of what he did was done in the name of Japan, but he's also acted out of greed, something you may have exploited because it was your duty but you don't have to take the responsibility for creating it. Now let others be his judge and jury. You've done your share and more."

"Once Hata leaves Shanghai, he'll get away for good. I'm the only one who stands between him and freedom."

"Then let him go I say. Only don't you die too, please," Dominique implored. Just then the hammer struck hollowly against a stairboard. Looking at her in surprise, Dallin quickly repeated the blow, again getting the same hollow sound. Then, reversing the hammer and using the prongs, he pried the board loose from the step, exposing a bulky package wrapped in waterproof oilskin.

With Dominique urging him on, Dallin excitedly peeled away the oilskin, revealing a thick manuscript of almost five hundred typewritten pages. He turned to the first page on which was written SHANGHAI DOSSIER, with the dates, JANUARY 1942–JULY, 1945.

"Only a month before the Kempetai arrested him," Dominique murmured.

The next page listed the contents of the manuscript: an orderly breakdown of the entire Japanese occupation of Shanghai, listing alphabetically all the black marketeers, collaborators, informers, Kempetai agents, puppet government officials, and ending finally with the war criminals and profiteers.

His curiosity heightened, Dallin turned to the section marked Black Marketeers. There to his amazement in the margin of the page beside a highly detailed analysis of his activities was a penciled note: BEFORE ANYTHING IS DONE IN THE CASE OF MAXIMOV DALLIN, THE RESPONSIBLE PARTIES SHOULD CONTACT MAJOR CHRISTOPHER BLAKE, OSS, CHUNGKING.

"Oh, no!" Dominique gasped. "Felix knew all along about you but never used it to save his life."

Dallin nodded gravely. Then wrapping the manuscript in the oilskin, he said grimly, "Get your things. We're leaving."

"Where to?" Dominique asked, scrambling for her shoes and leather bag, but he was out the door.

She eventually caught up with Dallin halfway to the white Cadillac roadster parked in a clump of pine trees beside the road.

"Where to?"

"I'm dropping you in Hangchow," Dallin replied, swinging open the gate of the picket fence and waiting for her to pass through first.

"Which means you're going to Shanghai?"

"That's what it means."

"And if I won't go?"

"You'll go, believe me!"

They were beside the roadster now. Dallin opened the driver's door and Dominique moved around to the passenger's side.

"You sound just like the old Dallin again. Not the Stephen Tarabrin I care about, the man who loves life and freedom and me."

"I won't argue with you. Get in!"

Dallin slid behind the wheel, pulled out the choke, switched on the ignition, and the engine roared. Then glancing sideways, he realized Dominique was standing outside the roadster and leaning against the door.

"Get in, I said!"

"Go to hell!"

"Dominique!"

"I said go to hell, Maximov Dallin!" The tears rolled down her cheeks.

"I can't leave you here."

"Why not? Afraid I'll get raped or maybe stabbed or shot?"

"I said I won't argue with you."

"The Maximov Dallin I knew in Shanghai never would. But I've had enough of listening to you, to my father, to Robert Salat. They're both dead and you will be too. But at least I don't have to accept it in your case. I'll do anything I can to keep you alive. I'll never be treated like a little girl again. So if you're going, go!"

"I can't leave you here."

"Why? Because in your code it's all right for you to die but not me. It's all right for you to disappear from my life forever and for me to go on without you . . . without your . . ."

Dominique never got to finish her sentence. Her words were drowned out by a screech of tires as two massive black Packard sedans rounded the curve above the cottage, raced down into the gulley, and skidded to a halt on either side of them. The doors of both Packards burst open and out stepped eight Chinese in dark suits waving .45 automatics.

Dallin shoved the manuscript onto the floor beside his feet and reached for his Mauser, but he was a shade too late. The leader of the group, a young Chinese with the sleek, pampered look typical of those favored by the Kuomintang ruling clique, was already poised at the passenger side of the Cadillac, his pistol leveled at Dominique's head.

Dallin withdrew his hand from inside his jacket and rested it on the steering wheel.

"A wise move, Captain Tarabrin," the young Chinese said in flawless English. "Permit me to introduce myself. I am Major Ho, attached to the Central Bureau of Investigation and Statistics."

"Tai-Li's crowd. You're a little far from Chungking, aren't you, Major?"

"Our sentiments too," Major Ho replied, acknowledging the jittery state of his men, who were nervously watching the cottage and the road. "But then, we're no farther than you have strayed."

"Know all about me, do you?"

"We have been keeping a close watch on your friend Major Christopher Blake ever since he left Chungking. The two of you were photographed together at the Roy Roofgarten in Hongkew. And our records of OSS personnel stationed in China provided your true name, rank, and background."

"Too bad your people didn't spend as much time making sure Major Blake stayed alive," Dallin said bitingly. "But then, I gather your records don't contain the name of the Chinese assassin who butchered him."

"I assure you," Major Ho replied unruffled, "we all regret the untimely death of your friend. Now, if you don't mind, I would like you to turn over Felix Hacker's black book."

"So you know about that too?"

"The black book, please. If I'm not mistaken, it's beside your feet on the floor of the car."

"Sorry."

"I'm the one who should apologize. But, as you can see, my men are already quite anxious. There's a report that a Kempetai patrol is in the vicinity. Neither my men nor I wish a fight with the enemy so far from our own lines."

"This book is the property of the United States government. If you want it, write to Washington, D.C., care of General William B. Donovan, for permission. Until then, I'm obliged to see that these pages get into the right hands."

"They *are* in the right hands. The book concerns us, does it not? Now, please, no more delays."

Dallin stared out of the Cadillac window at the Chinese major, his face a taut mask. "If you walk away with this book now, it'll never be seen again."

"My orders are to confiscate the manuscript written by Felix Hacker. Nothing whatsoever was mentioned about destroying it."

"Like hell!" Dallin growled.

"Captain, if you don't mind my saying so, you are being unduly righteous, and you're interfering in a matter that only concerns China."

"Someone has to take a stand if this nation is ever to become a decent place to live."

"That is not up to me. Or up to you, for that matter. To be perfectly candid, it would not surprise me in the least if members of my own family, including my father, were mentioned by Felix Hacker. Now, would you have me betray my elders, whom I have been taught to cherish and respect, out of blind fanaticism."

"You mean patriotism, don't you?"

"I mean exactly what I said! Only a renegade would do as you ask. A bastard dog without a sense of honor or tradition. Come now, we have delayed long enough. The black book, please."

"Come and get it."

Pushing Dominique aside, Major Ho reached inside the car just as Dallin whipped out his Mauser; the sight of the gleaming barrel aimed at his head brought the confident Chinese to an abrupt halt.

"What's wrong, Major?" Dallin asked softly. "Lose your nerve?"

"If you fire, my men will kill the woman and then you."

"Meanwhile you'll be dead."

"Perhaps I am, as you say, wrong in my beliefs," the major murmured. "That is for others wiser than myself to say, but one thing I am not is a coward. I will die for my China."

Dallin was confused by the obvious sincerity and courage of the Chinese. He glanced over at Dominique, who looked at him imploringly, her only fear that he might be killed.

"Now, I must have the black book," Major Ho said forcefully, his fingers just inches from the bulky manuscript wrapped in oilskin. "Otherwise I can never return to Chungking again. And if I should not return, then my family would suffer disgrace and even worse at the hands of my superior."

"This is madness! All madness!" Dallin whispered hoarsely. "Will there ever be any end to it?"

"In China there never has been," the young Chinese replied, moved by Dallin's distress. "I can only say I'm sorry."

Nodding, Dallin lowered the Mauser and handed over the black book. A moment later, having issued orders in rapidly spoken Mandarin, Major Ho turned away as four of his men yanked Dallin from behind the wheel of the Cadillac and pummeled him about until he dropped senseless to the ground.

"Why did you do that?" Dominique moaned to the major as she cradled Dallin's limp body in her arms.

"Because among my men is one who reports directly to General Tai-Li. It would be politically unwise for me to be described as lacking determination or being overly friendly with the Americans."

"But they're your Allies."

"So it would seem," Major Ho answered sadly. Then he reached into the car and switched on the radio, adding as he did so, "I suggest you listen carefully. Unless I'm seriously mistaken, in one hour history will be made!"

Dallin felt as though his head was on fire. He tried sitting up, only to fall back against the seat of the Cadillac which was still parked in the trees near the cottage. Dominique was hunched over the radio beside him, fiddling with the dial but getting only static.

"I don't think we can get anything," she said, as she tried for clearer reception.

"Keep trying."

"Maybe he was lying."

"I don't think so."

Suddenly an authoritative voice, faint at first but gradually becoming louder, intoned solemnly: "All listeners will now rise for an rescription by the Emperor of Japan."

This was immediately followed by the strident cords of Kimigayo, the Japanese anthem. Then, at exactly noon on the 15th of August 1945, Emperor Hirohito began to speak, his high-pitched voice strained and painfully apologetic.

"To our good and loyal subjects. After pondering deeply—actual conditions in our empire today, we have decided to resort to an extraordinary measure. Our empire accepts the provisions of the joint declaration made by the government of the United States, Great Britain, China, and the Soviet Union. Should we continue to fight, it would not only result in the ultimate collapse and obliteration of the Japanese nation, but also lead to the total extinction of human civilization. The thought of those officers and men as well as others who have fallen in the field of battle, those who died at their posts of duty, or those who met with untimely deaths and all their bereaved families, pains our heart.

"The hardships and sufferings to which our nation is subjected hereafter will certainly be great. However, we have resolved to pave the way to peace for ten thousand generations by enduring the unendurable and suffering what is insufferable.

"Let the entire nation continue as one family from generation to generation, ever firm in its faith in the imperishableness of its divine land. Unite your total strength to be devoted to the construction of the future. And work with resolution so you may enhance the innate glory of the Imperial State and keep pace with the progress of the world."

When Hirohito finished speaking, Dallin leaned over and switched off the radio. He and Dominique remained silent, deep in their own thoughts, until she murmured in amazement, "It's really over . . . this time it's not a false rumor but the truth. The Japanese have truly given up!"

Dallin nodded, then clasping her hand in his, he leaned back against the seat, resting his throbbing head.

"Just think!" Dominique went on eagerly. "We can go anywhere, do anything. We don't ever have to worry about the Japanese again. It hardly seems possible. A minute ago we were in the midst of a war, and now it's over. *Fini.* Done with."

"It's not over yet."

"I don't understand. You heard the radio. You heard what Hirohito said."

"There's no one in Shanghai to assume control," Dallin explained, switching on the ignition and revving the engine. The nearest Nationalists are over a thousand miles away. The Communists are closer but without transportation. And the Americans couldn't reach there for weeks."

"Their air force can fly the Nationalist troops there."

"Move tens of thousands of men—enough to control a city of four million people? No. Not even the American Air Force can do that."

"You can't mean . . ."

"That's exactly what I mean. The Japanese will stay put until they can officially transfer power, leaving Hata free to make his escape."

Dallin shifted into reverse, backed the Cadillac out of the clump of pines, and then drove off in the same direction they had come the night before. Racing out of the gulley, he wheeled around the curve in the road, coming bumper to bumper against a dark blue Horch with Kempetai pennants.

Chapter Thirty-One

———◦—◦◆◦—◦———

News of the Emperor's broadcast, the first time his voice had ever been heard on radio, circulated rapidly around the globe, touching off a tumultuous reaction in every Allied capital but especially in those territories under Japanese domination. In Shanghai, hundreds of thousands of people mobbed the streets rejoicing that the war was finally over. At first many of them, still haunted by the memory of their premature celebrations only a week before, were wary of the announcement, but one glance at the doleful faces of the Japanese sentries standing guard told them that this time the news was really true. Japan had surrendered! The Allies had won! The eight years of brutal occupation were ended!

On the Whampoo River off the Bund dozens of tugs and steamers blew their whistles, while the Chinese aboard the flotillas of sampans and junks waved banners and cheered. On the Bund itself, tens of thousands marched about carrying huge posters of Chiang Kai-shek, Franklin Delano Roosevelt, and Winston Churchill and waving Allied flags.

Fire engine alarms sounded, church bells pealed, and temple gongs reverberated. In Chapei, impoverished Chinese celebrated in the ruins left by Japanese artillery more than a decade earlier. At Hongkew in the ghetto, Jews from every nation formed circles and danced in the streets. In the narrow bylanes of Nantao, shopkeepers and street vendors abandoned their businesses and joined the rejoicing crowds.

At the Quai de France, outside Town Hall on Nanking
Road, at the Shanghai Club on the Bund, wherever Japanese
sentries remained at their posts, crowds of Chinese and Europeans taunted their former rulers with words and gestures but
stopped short of outright violence since the soldiers still had
guns. Instead the crowds took their wrath out on hapless
Korean and Japanese civilians, beating some with sticks and
pelting others with stones.

At Japanese Army and Navy headquarters, at the airport,
the naval repair yards, the barracks and depots throughout
the city, stunned Japanese officers and enlisted men were
overcome by despair. Many got drunk; others, ignoring opinion, wept; a few actually felt relieved. Most, however, were
swept by intense melancholy.

The situation was far different at Bridge House; here there
was little time for regret or drinking. The Kempei had no illusions. In their case, peace could only mean two things: retribution and revenge. The persecution of the Chinese and
Occidentals of Shanghai had ended, and their own was about
to begin. Consequently, most of the officers and enlisted men,
except for a specially appointed detachment of guards manning the front gates, were busy stripping the Kempetai insignia from their uniforms or exchanging them for ordinary
street clothes and making ready to flee.

The front courtyard, which was normally reserved for incoming and departing traffic, was a pandemonium of overloaded automobiles, trucks, and motorcycles, piles of luggage
were strewn about carelessly, as their owners sought a way
out of Shanghai. From the window of his office Colonel Hata
viewed this chaos with disdain. Fortunately, the responsibility
for introducing order into this confusion was no longer his.
The speech by the Emperor released him from this burden.
From now on, Hata could lead his own life, and for the first
time in months, he felt convinced that everything was under
control. The *Isabella* was scheduled to anchor in the Whampoo the following day. Allowing a day to take on provisions
for the long voyage, the ship would be able to depart by August 17th at the latest.

The forged papers were in order and the European expert
who had done them had already been liquidated. Niki too
was packed and ready to leave. But most important of all

for Hata, a telephone call had just come in from Hangchow informing him that the White Russian Maximov Dallin was in the custody of his men and would arrive in Shanghai the next day.

So, while those around Hata were suffering from the dreadful impact of surrender, his own reaction was different. Admittedly the thought of Nippon surrendering was anathema to him, but his close association with Niki and Dallin had done much to mute his loyalty. His determination to be master of his own fate was so strong it had freed Hata of the rigid formal traditions that had intimidated him from birth. Well, not entirely freed, he corrected himself. The samurai sword that had been in his family for generations was among the objects being taken to Buenos Aires. Still, he was Westernized, at least in the sense that he was determined to emerge from the ashes of defeat intact and make a new life for himself in South America as a wealthy collector of Oriental antiquities.

Snorting scornfully at the sight of his men scrambling desperately to get away, Hata turned from the window and moved to his desk. A communiqué just delivered rested on the top of the pile of official papers and reports, and Hata picked it up and scanned it.

> JAPANESE HIGH COMMAND
> TOKYO
>
> MOST URGENT
>
> ALL MILITARY UNITS ARE ORDERED TO REMAIN AT THEIR POSTS UNTIL NATIONALIST FORCES ARRIVE IN SHANGHAI TO ACCEPT YOUR SURRENDER.
>
> UNDER NO CIRCUMSTANCES ARE ANY UNITS OF THE IMPERIAL ARMY OR NAVY TO TRANSFER POWER TO THE COMMUNISTS. REPEAT. UNDER NO CIRCUMSTANCES ARE ANY UNITS OF THE IMPERIAL ARMY OR NAVY TO TRANSFER POWER TO THE COMMUNISTS.
>
> ANY DEVIATION FROM THE ABOVE WILL BE SUBJECT TO PUNISHMENT UNDER THE OFFICIAL MILITARY CODES AND WILL BE DEALT WITH ACCORDINGLY.

Incredible as the directive seemed, Hata had expected one like it. Hatred for the Communists existed at the highest levels of the government and the military, and far exceeded their antipathy toward the Americans or Caucasians. Moreover, there was a definite logic behind this order. Ever since word of the impending Japanese surrender had reached China, Communist forces had been annexing territory formerly controlled by the Japanese. This communiqué, Hata realized, was the first conciliatory step the Japanese government had made toward the Allies, who wanted the Kuomintang and Chiang Kai-shek to rule the mainland.

In any event, Hata had absolutely no intention of carrying out this latest order. Other units of the Japanese Army might remain at their posts but for the Kempetai to do so was sheer folly. Any moment mobs of fanatical Chinese or Europeans seeking vengeance against their former oppressors could overpower the sentries and rush through the gates. Hata already had his armor-plated Mercedes-Benz parked and loaded in the rear courtyard out of sight. As soon as it was dark, he planned to make his way to a temporary refuge until the *Isabella* was ready to sail.

Several floors below, Lieutenant Sumato also waited for darkness. His belongings were already packed into two large canvas valises. He had left his uniform neatly folded in the wooden chest by his tatami mat. Sumato himself wore a white short-sleeved shirt, black trousers and shoes. To anyone who did not know him, he appeared to be a displaced civilian. No one would imagine that inside his two valises were the most important files from the official records of the Kempetai.

Obersturmbannführer Becker was waiting it out in the brothel on Rue du Consulat in the French Concession. He had been expecting Hirohito to announce the capitulation of Japan, and he had already burned all the incriminating documents left at the Kaiser Wilhem Institute and sold the few valuables he still owned for cash. Becker intended to remain where he was until Rossio of the Iberian Navigation Company telephoned, giving him the precise location of the *Isabella*. A whorehouse was a comfortable place to wait, Ernst Becker decided, as he caressed the pale dangling breasts of the naked blonde beside him.

A peace celebration had been underway for hours at the Cathay Hotel. The lobby, mezzanine restaurants and bar, even the Tower Nightclub were jammed. It was the second such celebration, but this time the news was true, and those well-heeled patrons with money to splurge were out to enjoy every moment of it.

Giacomo Ferrara spent most of his time wandering from floor to floor, making certain the festivities did not get out of control. He did not want any accidents or fires. He also wanted to be noticed in a state of optimism about his future by as many people as possible, for when the highly respected managing director was discovered missed and believed dead, he hoped there would be no shortage of witnesses to testify that he had been looking forward to continued employment at the Cathay Hotel.

Continued employment was not in the cards for Old Lu, the Chinese mail clerk, or for Plitov, the night manager, however. Both men had been a trifle too curious about the letters that arrived for Ferrara's personal friends, as well as various coincidences connected with the Italian aristocrat. Therefore, only hours before the speech by the Emperor, Ferrara had taken the precaution of giving both men dismissal notices. It was a pity, the managing director knew; after all, employment was very hard to find in these uncertain times. But, sighed the canny Venetian, survival, especially his own, was getting even harder.

At the Shanghai Roulette Club, Caro, the newly appointed director, lifted a glass of imported French champagne and toasted the memory of his illustrious predecessor, Robert Salat. As the sparkling wine passed his lips he wondered why those Corsicans seated around him on the balcony did not join him in drinking. Shortly thereafter he felt his throat constrict and a lump begin to form in his chest. His breath came in short gasps, causing his lean, swarthy cheeks to bulge with pain. Gradually the faces of those around him dimmed and Caro began to realize he had been poisoned.

At the headquarters of the Swedish Red Cross, Peterson, the official representative, wept with joy at the news of peace, while Father Joseph stood misty-eyed in the Union Church listening to the bells toll. And at the Roman Catholic Mission, the three Jesuit priests from the supply train made new plans to bring in rice and grain for the starving poor of Shanghai.

In the ruins of the working-class quarter of Chapei, among those spectators watching their fellow Chinese waving Communist banners and posters of Mao Tse-tung and Chou En-lai was a young boy in ragged short pants. Still haunted by the killing of his comrade, Commissar Hsu, the boy threw his bony shoulders back and stood erect as the flag-bearers, bloodied veterans of the revolts of the twenties and thirties, swept past.

In the ghetto, Marcus and Sarah, their faces flushed with excitement, hurried over to a nearby building and watched their neighbors dancing wildly about. They both felt happier than they had been in years. To think that they were free, that their ordeal was over. Free! Alive! Together! This last thought was not lost on Sarah or Marcus. It was natural for them to be together. From childhood on, they had always been so—until the war broke out, when Marcus had been reported dead. At least that was the news she had received from a fleeing partisan who told her that the SS had rounded up a group of rabbis, including Marcus, and shot them all.

The news left Sarah despondent, ill, and, even worse, terribly alone. The Gestapo had taken her parents and younger sisters. Despite repeated inquiries, no one in any official capacity could tell her their fate. Nevertheless, against the advice of her relatives, she went off into the countryside in search of them. It was there she met a Jewish engineer from Bialystok who was caught up in a similar nightmare. He proved generous and kind, qualities that seemed to have all but disappeared. When the Nazis began arresting every Jew in sight, he spirited her away to Russia. Only then, after they were safe and had purchased tickets aboard the Trans-Siberian Railroad to Harbin, did he ask her to marry him. Could she say no to this man, who, in the midst of all the violence and insanity, had been so good to her? Love, she prayed after accepting his offer, would come later. Only there was never time, because after fathering her child, he too disappeared in the snowy wastes of eastern Russia.

After a trek halfway around the world, Sarah miraculously encountered Marcus in, of all places, Shanghai. Now over three years later, they would return to Europe. To Poland!

And if her husband was alive, well, then Sarah would make her decision.

Marcus, too, was overwhelmed by his emotions. He was perspiring from the intense heat and dancing, but joy surged within him at the sight of his people clasping hands and swirling happily about in circles. Yes, Marcus thought joyously, his people. The tortured period of doubt that had afflicted him had finally ended. Whatever else, the love he now felt for his fellow Jews surmounted everything. It restored his faith in God and made him yearn to again serve them as a rabbi. His faith, buried under years of anguish, had reemerged, not from logic or meditation but out of a resurgence of love.

Of everyone it was Niki who was hardest hit by the news of the Allied victory. Despite her recent decision to regard her voyage into exile with Hata as positively as possible, she was still apprehensive over leaving the Orlov mansion. Niki had spent nearly all of her life there and certainly by far the happiest moments. Her memories of Russia were a lingering horror. Here in Shanghai she had found luxury and a wide circle of adoring friends. Whatever her father's stolen gold could not purchase, her willowy body and insatiable desire for sex had. Now, left nearly penniless, she was forced to abandon all these comforts and depend for her survival on the generosity of Hata, a war criminal.

The day before, forewarned by him, she had gone to the offices of a prominent German attorney and, in the presence of a notary, signed over the deeds to the Orlov mansion to a Swiss nominee as a preventive measure to keep the property from being confiscated by the Allies or the Nationalists. Then, unknown to Hata, she had taken the icon, the Fabergé miniatures, and the copper samovar—all objects cherished by Count Aleksandr Orlov—and sold them to a Chinese pawnbroker. Despite his reputation for giving good prices, the money she received was far below what she had anticipated, for his shop was already overloaded with items sold by people on the run. Still, Niki did manage to salvage something, and it gave her intense pleasure to be rid of her father's possessions. In fact, the mere thought of her father failing to reveal the hiding place for his gold left her in a cold rage. She had ransacked every room and closet in the mansion in search of some clue to its whereabouts, but her search had been in vain. She found nothing, not a scrap of paper, to indicate where the gold had been hidden.

Ironically, when her morale was at its very lowest, she received a telephone call from a former Czarist colonel, a friend of her father's. Bubbling with excitement, he told her of the recently announced guarantees of citizenship by the Soviet Union to White Russians in China and how many had already expressed their willingness to return. He wondered if Niki also wished to go back. The hell she did, Niki fumed, severing the telephone connection with the naive Czarist officer. Niki was desperate and broke, but she was not stupid. If she had learned one thing from her father it was that the Bolshies were never to be trusted. Return to Russia indeed! The notion was absurd. Besides, Niki was still young and beautiful and had the love of an immensely wealthy man. What if he was no longer in charge of a metropolis; what if he was a Japanese war criminal? She would go to Buenos Aires with him anyway. And once there, who knew what opportunities might present themselves.

By twilight things had settled down considerably in Shanghai. Apart from the vast piles of debris that filled the streets, most of the peace celebrants had already returned to their homes and businesses. Gradually, however, an uneasy calm fell over the city. People began to realize that nothing had actually changed. Japanese troops were still on guard at all the major intersections, official buildings, the port, airport, and railway stations, while other Japanese soldiers, many of them drunk and embittered, were prowling the International Settlement and French Concession, looting shops, attacking women and terrorizing families in their homes.

By the time the bewildered Chinese and Occidentals understood that the Japanese forces were not withdrawing, the overseas wireless had confirmed the strange situation. The Pacific War was indeed over, but there were no Allied units large enough or near enough to accept the Japanese surrender of Shanghai, which meant, the astonished citizens of Shanghai quickly learned, it might be days, weeks even, before Nationalist troops could be airlifted in by the Americans for the official transfer of power. In the meantime, hard-driving units of the Communist Eighth Route Army, nearing Shanghai, had been warned by the Allies to keep away, leaving the dejected Japanese standing between anarchy and a Communist takeover and still occupying the city.

In the midst of all this uncertainty, the freighter *Isabella* steamed into Shanghai, her hull painted white to signal she was neutral and ward off submarines. With the flag of Portugal waving from her masthead, the *Isabella* crawled by the mine-strewn mouth of the Yangtze, then steamed past Woosung, heading for the Whampoo River and the Bund.

Chapter Thirty-Two

———◆———

By nightfall the highway from Hangchow to Shanghai was clogged with fleeing Japanese. Convoys of trucks and motor-cars loaded down with war booty inched desperately along both lanes toward the coast. The 131-mile-long journey began to seem interminable as hope and patience quickly gave way to anxiety. Stalled vehicles that had run out of gas or needed repair were simply shoved aside and their passengers left stranded by the roadside begging for another ride.

Then abruptly, the mass exodus of Japanese seeking the safety of the coast became even worse. Communist guerrillas, hidden by darkness, began shelling the road. The deep blue sky glowed with red flashes from their American-made 105-mm guns, and the shelling ravaged long stretches of highway, leaving in its wake destruction and death. Some trucks and cars were blasted apart, others set afire, and countless more collided with vehicles nearby, sending their terrified passengers scurrying into ditches for cover or hugging the ground for their lives.

The cries of the wounded and frightened, especially the wails of infants, drifted pitifully back to the highway, and glimpses of these refugees standing at the edge of the road were picked up in the headlights of oncoming vehicles: Women in kimonos carrying dazed children in their arms;

gaunt men in western-style clothing, some still lugging briefcases; and khaki-clad soldiers, all stunned by the Emperor's broadcast and fearful of what would befall them next.

Yet despite every obstacle, the German-made Horch with the Kempetai pennants kept moving ahead. Inside it, Dominique sat stiffly between the driver and a stocky Kempei with bayonet scars on his face. Dallin was in the rear, his wrists and ankles manacled by thick links of iron chain, with Ganghi beside him, holding the lethal Nambu on his lap.

Thus far, the drive had taken several hours, yet they had hardly gone any distance at all. Most of the journey had been made in silence. The loss of the black book left Dallin depressed. The idea that he and Dominique were in the hands of the Kempei and en route to Bridge House was bad enough, but to make matters worse, the Emperor's speech had touched off a sadistic streak in Ganghi. Giggling, the Kempei gunner described killing Robert Salat at the warehouse, recounting every detail of the ambush with obvious relish, especially the surprise on the Corsican's face as his Thompson submachine gun jammed and Ganghi's weapon did not. Then the gunner mentioned Mimidzuka—the mound-of-ears shrine in Japan, commemorating a sixteenth-century Japanese victory when the heads of 39,000 Korean dead were cut off and their ears and noses sent back to Nippon for burial.

A withering glance from Dallin finally silenced the gloating gunner, but too late to spare Dominique from hearing about the horrible last moments of her father who had died in order to spare her from the cruelties of Bridge House.

As Dallin studied the realities of their situation, he realized that if he did not turn over the treasure, Hata would have them both executed. Even if he agreed, it was still likely that they would die, if not right away, then before the freighter departed or perhaps on the China Sea. Any way Dallin turned the possibilities around in his mind, the chances of escape for himself were slim. Ganghi was too skilled and experienced to be tricked into loosening his shackles or leaving his side. He was totally loyal to Hata, which placed him beyond bribery, the customary method in China, as elsewhere to get away from one's captors. The longer Dallin reflected, the more he realized that only Dominique might be saved, provided an opportunity arose to distract Ganghi.

His mind concentrated on just what that opportunity could

be, Dallin sank back against the seat and pretended to sleep. Next to him, he could hear Ganghi drumming his fingernails against the trigger of the Nambu, beating out a rhythm as the car glided past burned-out hulks of twisted steel, until, finally gaining the open road, it accelerated and sped off into the August night.

Twelve hours later, the Horch swept past Kashing, within twenty-five miles of the coast. The nightmarish shelling from Communist guns interspersed by raiding parties of guerrillas on horseback had continued almost till dawn. By the time they turned off the highway and began making their way along local roads to the French Concession, the sun was rising. It was getting hotter by the minute, and Ganghi ordered the other two Kempei to lower their windows to give them all some relief.

Japanese sentries stood quietly on guard along Avenue Pétain, watching Chinese laborers loading debris and enormous piles of colored paper strips onto wooden wheelbarrows. The Horch veered smoothly around the race course into Nanking Road, then on past the imposing Sincere Company and Wing On Department Stores. Suddenly the driver braked to a stop, jolting the car's occupants. Ahead, Nanking Road was blocked by Japanese soldiers on a rampage in the shops leading up to the Bund. Drunk and dejected by surrender, they had smashed shop windows, looted merchandise, and were now battling among themselves over the spoils

At Ganghi's command, the driver shifted into reverse and started edging the car backward, but the loud blare of a truck horn immediately to their rear scotched that idea. Then, at Ganghi's urging, he wheeled the Horch onto the sidewalk and, ignoring the mob of Japanese soldiers, plunged straight ahead for the Cathay Hotel.

Stubbornly the mass of soldiers remained in the path of the oncoming car. The driver, growing anxious, sounded his horn frantically, sending out a clarion warning as the motorcar doggedly nudged its way among the angry and dejected soldiers. Alert now, Dallin saw the soldiers close ranks behind them. A surge of resentment and frustration swept the mob and they released their fury as one upon the car. Screaming curses and hurling whatever they were carrying, the Japanese soldiers stormed forward, climbing over the fenders, ripping away the pennants, and trying to turn the car over.

In the midst of all this, as the Horch was being rocked

back and forth, Ganghi somehow forced his door open and, with one burst from his Nambu, cut down half a dozen attackers. A second blast proved lethal to a party of sailors, and a third stopped a pair of airmen as they were bashing in the rear window. Tasting blood now, Ganghi leaped onto the running board and, firing his submachine gun nonstop, he drove the rest of the mob back into the nearby buildings.

At that moment, Dallin swung both legs through the rear door and, kicking Ganghi with all his might, sent him toppling into the gutter. Then, yanking his manacled legs inside, Dallin smashed the Kempei seated beside Dominique in the back of the neck, sending him hurtling head-first into the windshield. The Kempei reeled from the unexpected blow, which cracked the glass and left his face bloodied, while his companion battled for his life with an infantryman who was leaning through the side window trying to slash his throat with a straight razor. Dallin shouted to Dominique to run, but she was too bewildered to move. Finally he reached over and opened her door, then again shouted for her to run, murmuring something about brass doors. Dominique crawled over the dazed Kempei, who was clutching his bloodied face, and got out of the car just as Ganghi lifted himself up from the gutter on the other side. Dominique took off at a run as she saw him raise the deadly Nambu.

She reached the sidewalk in a couple of strides, then stumbled over a fallen soldier. A burst of gunfire spewed over her head. She glanced back at Ganghi; he had paused to reload. Desperately, she pushed on, racing wildly along Nanking Road until, half a block from the Cathay Hotel with her escape blocked by a cluster of Japanese soldiers, she turned into a small office building.

The inside hallway was dim and long. A bulb dangled from the ceiling illuminating a stairway that led off to her right. As she neared it, she heard a clatter of hobnailed boots in the street. Then she saw a door at the far end of the hallway swing open and shut. Panicking, she ran toward it. She reached the door just as two Kempei came charging into the hallway entrance. She tried the doorknob, found it locked, and shouted for someone to open it. A French-speaking woman told her to go away. Dominique pleaded, but the woman did not relent. Trapped, she returned to face her two pursuers, who holstered their pistols and advanced toward her with more than merely capture on their minds.

An intense feeling of rage swept Dominique. She took off her shoes and, holding the high heels outward, went to meet her tormentors. The Kempei snickered at the sight of the enraged Caucasian woman, then exchanged a few lewd remarks before continuing forward. As they did, Dominique swung one shoe at the light overhead, shattering the bulb and pitching the hallway into darkness, and ducked up the steps.

The Kempei cursed and groped blindly for the stairs. Eventually they were successful and began to trudge up the steps after her. At the landing on the second floor they came to a halt. One Kempei reluctantly went on, while the other entered the hallway to search for Dominique. Meanwhile she hung by her hands from the railing several steps short of the second-floor landing. As the Kempei went in separate directions she gave a sigh of relief, then let herself drop down to the first floor below. She took her shoes from her jacket pockets, slipped them back on her feet, and raced from the building, veering east toward the Bund.

Ahead, outside the Cathay Hotel, a surly mob of Japanese soldiers were being denied entry by a cordon of heavily armed Imperial Marines. In the midst of this noisy commotion Ganghi was dragging Dallin, still in manacles, into the hotel. The lobby had a life of its own. It was filled with stunned Japanese, still reeling from the idea of Nippon's defeat. Around them guests and staff alike rushed about carrying luggage and spreading rumors. Over in one corner, a batch of jittery Occidentals, most of them notorious collaborators, were engrossed in a heated argument over the best means of escape.

Dominique entered the Cathay cheered by her successful escape. At first she expected to overtake Dallin in the lobby but after hunting for him in the crowd she abandoned all hope and admitted to herself that he was gone.

A tall European with plastered-down hair and a pencil mustache was manning the reception desk. Dominique had never seen him before and was put off by his oily looks, but since she seemed to have no choice she swept through the dense mob besieging his desk and asked for Giacomo Ferrara, saying it was urgent.

"The managing director cannot be disturbed under any circumstances."

"But I tell you this is urgent!" Dominique pleaded.

"Madam," he replied pompously, "is there anyone in this hotel whose problem is not?"

"Perhaps I better ask Monsieur Plitov or Old Lu."

"Perhaps you should; however, you'll find they are no longer with us." He smiled nastily and turned away.

Dominique slipped around a buxom German woman who was crowding in for information and darted over to a wizened Chinese in a black cap and robe who stood beside the bank of elevators. One quick study of his shriveled-up arrogant face and Dominique decided only money would win his cooperation.

"You know me?"

"Everyone in Shanghai know only daughter of Norwegian."

"Then tell me where have they taken Maximov Dallin?"

The man's narrow mouth closed like a trapdoor. "Maximov Dallin no longer guest," he said finally. "White Russian now prisoner of Kempetai. Big trouble Kempetai."

"The war is over."

"You tell that to Kempetai!" he said mockingly.

Exasperated, Dominique pushed her hair away from her eyes with a weary gesture. Then she remembered some of the tales Gustav Torg had told her of his early days in China. "How long have you been working?" she asked, her confidence regained.

"Sixty-two years. Since eight years old."

"That's a very long time. You must be entitled to a large pension."

His eyes flinty, the dispatcher answered coldly, "Shanghai company never give pension to Chinee. Never give anything!"

"But I'll give you plenty," Dominique countered. "Fifty U.S. dollars for every year, if you tell me what I wish to know."

"Kempetai plenty bad!" the dispatcher replied, mentally calculating the amount of the offer.

"One hundred U.S. dollars for every year."

"Daughter of taipan hard bargainer," the dispatcher negotiated, smelling the vast profit that could be made off the Torg family.

"Think so?" Dominique smiled. "Then you won't be upset when I tell you that by the time the elevator behind you opens if your answer isn't yes you lose sixty-two hundred U.S. dollars."

Whirling, with a startled look on his prunelike face, the dispatcher saw the arrow on the dial overhead dropping sharply below the third floor. In just a few seconds he would be much richer or, if he chose, still poor. His mind made up, he hissed, "Suite 1010," just as the doors of the elevator slid open.

Reaching the tenth floor, Dominique found herself alone in the deserted corridor. She followed the numbers of the doors, rounding two corners and moving into the southeastern section of the hotel before she finally saw the suite she wanted on her left.

Suddenly the service doors ahead on the right side of the corridor swung out and a food cart rolled through, pushed by a stooped waiter.

Dominique ducked into the service passage and watched as the cart stopped across the hall at Suite 1010. The waiter rang the doorbell. A bolt shot free and the door swung open, revealing Giacomo Ferrara in a velvet smoking jacket. He stood for a moment, then stepped aside to let the waiter enter, affording Dominique a glimpse of Niki and Colonel Hata, drinks in hand, toasting their about-to-be-embarked-on voyage.

Ten minutes later, still shaken by what she had seen, Dominique waited at the rear entrance of the hotel. A black Cadillac limousine turned into the alley and drew alongside her, Big Han in the front seat. Dominique got in quickly and the chauffeur wheeled the massive car off into the sweltering summer night.

Meanwhile, Dallin was being held in a tiny sitting room adjoining Suite 1010. He sat manacled opposite Ganghi, both of them occupying the only two chairs in the room.

Dallin had been blindfolded in the elevator so he still had no idea where they were. But he did know what to expect next, so it was no surprise when he heard a third person entering the room, then felt Ganghi tearing the blindfold from his eyes.

The Kempetai commandant wore a stylish white linen double-breasted suit cut by the same London-trained tailor that Dallin used. His beige silk shirt matched his woven leather shoes. He lit a cigarette with a gold lighter, then, addressing Dallin, said softly, "You have caused me far more difficulty

than I ever imagined possible. But now finally we have come
to the end of the road."

"You forget I still have the goods," Dallin replied, looking
directly at Hata.

"I've forgotten nothing. That is why I'll be blunt. If you
are not prepared to show me where the antiquities are hidden
by tomorrow morning when the *Isabella* is ready to depart,
then Ganghi here will empty an entire magazine from his gun
into your head."

"I expected as much."

"Good! Now, my men tell me a Nationalist action squad
was seen leaving the cottage. Since the black book wasn't
found on your possession, I assume they have it. Is this correct?"

"I'm afraid so," Dallin answered, playing out his role.

"Isn't there anything you regard as sacred? Anything you
prize dearly enough not to sell?"

"My friend, in a situation like this everything is up for
grabs."

"So it would seem," Hata frowned, maintaining his dignity
with difficulty. Then, turning away, he addressed Ganghi.

"You heard what I said about the boat leaving in the
morning!"

"Yes, sir."

"Then understand that this treacherous White Russian
would betray his own mother for a profit. Nothing he says is
to be believed. Whatever he offers you during the night as a
bribe I shall double from his share."

"Yes, sir!"

"One final order. If he should try to escape, fire at his
knees. Cripple him, but under no circumstances kill him."

Ganghi bowed low as his superior disappeared into the adjoining suite.

At that very moment, the *Isabella* lay moored at the White
Star Line docks north of Hongkew Creek in the Whampoo
River. Built in Hamburg in 1901 and christened *Siegfried*, the
vessel had been given to the British government for war rep-
arations in 1918, then sold to the Iberian Navigation Company in 1929 and renamed the *Isabella*. The boat was a
well-deck vessel, the deep open hold situated between her su-
perstructure aft and the forecastle.

The quay around the *Isabella* was alive with movement as

trucks carrying ship stores and provisions for her long journey, unloaded, and then drove off. Below deck, a crew of carpenters, specially hired for the occasion, were busy constructing a false bulkhead in the aft tool bin, leaving enough space behind a pile of spare parts and equipment for ten people to conceal themselves comfortably, provided they stood up.

On her bridge deck, inside the wheelhouse, Rossio, the director of the Iberian Navigation Company, was giving last-minute instructions to the captain of the *Isabella*, a gray-haired, ruggedly built fellow Portuguese of fifty in a white uniform. His orders to the captain were simple. At dawn the *Isabella* would take on her passengers, then her cargo, and set sail for South America. In the likely event that Allied warships detained her while en route, the captain was to stow his passengers in the false compartment.

Should an inspection of her cargo reveal the *Isabella* was carrying war contraband, which, considering the nature of her passengers, was entirely possible, then the captain was to immediately inform the detaining ship's officers that his passengers had come aboard and had coerced him at gunpoint into transporting them. Under no circumstances, Rossio emphasized, was he to admit that the *Isabella* had been chartered for illicit purposes. This, Rossio stressed, would be grounds for confiscation and would guarantee the captain's dismissal from employment by the Iberian Navigation Company.

That said, Rossio shook the captain's perspiring hand firmly and drove back to his offices, where, realizing he was already late for supper with the widow of a fabulously wealthy Swiss pharmaceutical manufacturer, he gave a message to his wireless operator to relay the whereabouts of the *Isabella* to Obersturmbannführer Becker in the brothel at 44 Rue du Consulat.

Several hours later, Marcus sat by his radio studying the note left for him by Rossio. He should have telephoned the information to Ernst Becker much earlier but something kept him from doing so. A thought kept recurring, giving Marcus no rest. He could not stop believing that if they were allowed to live, the Nazis would pass on their ideas of genocide to the next generation. Perhaps even Sarah's son Abraham would one day find himself sent fleeing into exile halfway around the world or swept away by stormtroopers and imprisoned in a concentration camp to be gassed.

At three o'clock in the morning, the air conditioner in the suite running at full blast to relieve the humidity and temperature which had not fallen below ninety-six degrees in the last twenty-four hours, Hata found himself too restless to sleep. He and Niki were sharing the bedroom while Ferrara slept in the living room. The managing director had offered to arrange for other accommodations, but they had felt it was safer to remain in his suite.

Hata glanced over at the other side of the bed where Niki slept with her back to him. They had been awake for hours talking about Dallin, Shanghai, and their hopes for a life in South America. The deep anxiety Hata detected in Niki he attributed to the recent death of her father. Still, her nervousness was surprising, Hata thought, considering how wealthy, and thus how independent, the General must have left his daughter.

Hata reached for his short black silk robe with the silver dragon embroidered on the back. His muscular arms filled the sleeves and he wrapped the sash tightly around his waist. Puffing on a cigarette, he slipped quietly out of the bedroom, past Ferrara asleep on the sofa, and into the adjoining chamber where Dallin was being held prisoner. The White Russian was standing before the window staring silently into the night, a cigarette in his mouth. Ganghi sat nearby, the submachine gun trained on his back.

"He's been this way for hours," Ganghi explained.

"No matter. Leave him be," Hata answered, moving beside Dallin.

Both men stood by the window for a long while without saying anything. The lights of Shanghai were lit for the first time in more than two years. Even the ships plying the Whampoo had their running lamps on.

Finally Hata murmured, "I once had great hopes for us. When I think what's happened in these past two weeks, I still cannot understand why. What possessed you to do the things you have? To empty the warehouse? To force me to release the Torg woman and then to slip away with her after the black book? I can only think these must be the blunders of a madman, someone I do not know. Not the Maximov Dallin I had come to trust and call my friend."

Dallin was at a loss for an answer. How could he tell the truth without giving away his identity? And what could he possibly say that would not smack of greater hypocrisy, more lies? By virtue of his actions Hata was a war criminal, but only by Anglo-Saxon standards, not in terms of his own traditions and culture.

"You don't answer," Hata went on, interrupting his thoughts. "I ask questions but you make no attempt to reply. Can it be you think so little of me?"

Dallin shook his head. "It makes no sense, yet I have had my reasons."

"What reasons?" Hata asked, genuinely perplexed. "What could be so important that you would disrupt an immensely profitable partnership and bring disgrace upon me? Have I not saved your life? Done everything in my power to insure not only that we were successful but that we survived to enjoy the spoils. What more could I have done? Where have I failed or given you cause to do what you have? A samurai, you know, must save face or die."

"I understand," Dallin replied, reaching over to crush out his cigarette. "I can only repeat what I already said. I had my reasons."

"No!" Hata objected strongly, "you have no reasons. You have lost your senses. This is not the Maximov Dallin I have known. True, you did hard things . . . we all have . . . circumstances have allowed us no other way . . . but for us . . . Niki, you, and I, we made our own world. Lived by our own code. So I say again, you are not well and I hope you come to your senses in time. Because I am weary of torture and killing and traditions. I want to stay alive. In return, I give you my promise I will take you with me."

That said, Hata turned away and returned to his suite, leaving Dallin profoundly troubled. For a Japanese, a samurai especially, to say what Hata had was remarkable. The man had bared his soul, pleaded to be spared having to do further violence to himself and others. Only Dallin stood in his way. Dallin. A spy and an imposter, a man shaken by the terrible toll the years of deception had taken not only on him personally but on others as well.

The 17th of August, a Wednesday, was overcast. By dawn the sun hung limp and pale to the east at the edge of an horizon covered by dense grayish clouds. The tramcars on the Bund and the other major avenues were already filled with industrial workers going to their factories. A regular detachment of Japanese troops stood sentry duty at the Municipal

Council Building, Town Hall, and Garden Bridge, while a
specially formed unit roamed the International Settlement
and French Concession rounding up those Japanese soldiers
who were still making a nuisance of themselves. The Japanese
High Command, acting on orders from Tokyo, had restored
order to Shanghai and was awaiting the arrival of the Nationalist Army to turn over the city. Ten floors above the Bund,
inside the suite of the managing director, Hata anxiously
studied the tightly packed wharves along the Whampoo with
high-powered binoculars. He was searching for the *Isabella*.
A phone call earlier to Ernst Becker at Madame Gabor's had
elicited no news whatsoever. Other calls to the Iberian Navigation Company and the Shanghai Port Authority had failed
to draw a response.

Less than two miles away, Marcus Feinbaum moved anxiously through the French Concession. Jammed into his waistband under his shirt was a rusted-out 9 mm Radom pistol.
Marcus had borrowed the pistol from a Jew who had served
in the Polish Army in 1940. It had never been fired since
then. All Marcus knew was that the detachable box magazine
held eight cartridges and was fully loaded. This was his first
visit to the French Concession. Marcus was amazed at the
size and splendor of the large homes along the broad, tree-
lined avenues. They were comparable to the finest homes in
Warsaw and surely were a world apart from his dank bungalow in the ghetto.

Number 44 rue du Consulat stood in a long row of red
brick buildings, each four stories high with tall French windows overlooking the street. Marcus peered at the numerals
on the heavy oak door, took a deep breath, checked to make
certain the Radom pistol was still under his shirt, then used
the brass knocker.

Minutes later, having explained the purpose of his visit to
an elderly Hungarian woman whose wrinkled cheeks were
thick with rouge, he stood hesitantly in the salon before
Obersturmbannführer Becker. The Nazi, awakened from a
deep sleep twice in the last hour, rubbed his bloodshot eyes.
He was in a horrible mood, and finding this Jew, of all
people, here to inform him of the location of the *Isabella*
hardly improved things. Still, he told himself, within a few
hours he would be away from this Asiatic paradise which had
turned out to be such a hell-hole.

"So?" Becker repeated, standing in his sweaty underwear a

few feet from a table covered with whiskey bottles, "where is this wonderful vessel of yours anchored?"

Numb, unable to speak, Marcus glanced around hesitantly at the oversized portraits of naked women that hung on the walls of the cluttered salon.

"Well, Hebe?" Becker demanded impatiently, "you say the *Isabella* is here. But where?"

"Off Yangtzepoo. At the old White Star quay," Marcus finally answered.

"White Star, *ja!*" Becker repeated, reaching for the telephone on the coffee table. He dialed the Cathay Hotel, asked for Suite 1010, and quickly relayed the information to Niki. Then, replacing the receiver, he turned back to Marcus and asked, "She has provisions, and her crew is ready to sail?"

"As soon as you're aboard."

"*Ja!*" Becker beamed happily. "So why didn't you say so, my friend. You looked so worried I said to myself, Ernst, prepare yourself for the worst. This Jew looks so sad he must be bringing bad news."

"I do."

"What did you say?"

"I do bring bad news. You're not going to South America."

"What do you mean I'm not going? I paid your boss, *ja?*"

"You killed Jews."

At first Becker was not sure he had heard right. But then studying the determined look on the face of his accuser, he jeered sarcastically, "More Jewish lies! Rumors! Slander and gossip! You Hebes get together and what's the first thing you do? Blame us Nazis for all the crimes committed in this world. You say we killed millions of you Jews! Thousands of Poles and Czechs and gypsies! Well, I say prove it, Hebe! Because I never killed anyone in my life."

"Strange," Marcus murmured, a haunted look kindled in his light gray eyes, "how in every newspaper report I read from Europe it says Germans everywhere, even Nazis, keep insisting they never killed anyone. So what, I wonder, happened in Warsaw? My aunts and uncles, my cousins and friends, and the rabbis I went to yeshivah with. Did they all die naturally? Or am I only dreaming they were murdered the same way I saw you gas and burn my fellow rabbis and students."

"You saw me do what?" Becker asked, shaken.

"*Ja*, Obersturmbannführer Becker. I, Marcus Feinbaum, saw you murder Jews with my own eyes."

"Where?" Becker asked, his face purple with indignation.

"In Poland. Near Warsaw."

Cursing, Becker rushed for the door, but Marcus was there first and, ripping open his shirt, he yanked the rusted pistol from his belt.

"What's this?" Becker demanded, regaining his composure. "A Yid with a gun. Now you're really getting me angry, you lousy Hebe punk!"

"Believe me, Herr Becker, your anger is mild compared to the rage that has gone on inside every Jew and decent-minded person since your leader Adolf Hitler assumed power."

As Becker stared at Marcus he noticed the hand holding the gun was trembling so much that it was no longer pointed toward him.

"Look at you shake, Hebe!" Becker gloated. "Why you're more scared of me than I am of you, even with that gun. Now why don't you just put it down and leave me in peace."

"Because Nazis don't deserve peace or liberty."

"*Ja?* Well, we'll see about that!" Becker jeered. Turning away, he reached for a bottle of cognac and a glass. He tossed down two shots in quick succession, then, grasping the bottle in his right hand as though to pour off a third one, he spun around, swinging the bottle at where Marcus's head should have been.

Eight bullets later, with every cartridge from the magazine of the rusty Radom still in his blood-soaked body, the cosmopolitan Nazi from Berlin realized that the disillusioned rabbi from Warsaw had made an irrevocable decision for both of them.

At seven o'clock, a black Pierce-Arrow limousine glided to a stop at the rear entrance of the Cathay Hotel, followed by a truck carrying six Kempei in Tibetan monks robes. Hata immediately led Niki, Dallin, and Ganghi into the Pierce-Arrow and the both vehicles sped off, turning right onto Peking Road, then left along the Bund. On the other side of Garden Bridge where the flag of the Rising Sun was still waving, they veered onto Broadway. Then beyond Hongkew Creek, the limousine trailed by the truck swung onto Yangtzepoo Road and turned off at the quay marked White Star Lines where the *Isabella* was moored.

Dark gray smoke poured from the funnel of the steamer. In the sunlight, large patches of her original red lead primer were evident beneath her fading coat of white paint. A work party of coolies were transferring the last few trunks belonging to Niki from a moving van onto the *Isabella*, while in the near distance a tender headed back across the Whampoo toward Pootung.

Hata ordered Ganghi to remove the manacles from Dallin; then they followed him aboard the *Isabella*. The captain awaited them at the top of the gangplank. He greeted Hata and Niki cordially, then had his first mate, a dour Swede, show them to their quarters on the bridge deck.

Afterward, Hata left Niki to unpack and joined Ganghi and Dallin in the wheelhouse. The preparations to get underway had been completed, but Ernst Becker was still not aboard. Hata, reluctant to delay his departure any longer, had someone ashore telephone the brothel on rue du Consulat. The reply was startling. A Jew employed by the Iberian Navigation Company had shot the Nazi and killed him.

Finally Hata gave his consent for the *Isabella* to cast off her lines and get underway. Any moment now, Dallin knew Hata would be after the whereabouts of the antiquities. If he refused, then Ganghi would take him ashore and open fire. If he agreed, then after the goods were located the same likelihood of death existed, unless Dallin made certain Hata kept his promise and took him to South America. But even that, Dallin concluded, only meant more deception and danger.

Nearby, the captain was starboard using a megaphone to issue instructions to release the lines securing his vessel to the quay. Hata conferred briefly with the pilot, a leathery-skinned Chinese, then turned to Dallin for the location of the treasure.

"Tell me?"

"Nantao," Dallin answered without hesitation. "Place called the Brass Doors."

"The guildhouse?" interrupted the pilot with strong doubts.

"Is there a problem?" Hata interjected.

"I have never known the guildhouse to hold cargo."

"It does now."

"This guildhouse is on the quay?" Hata asked.

"South of the Signal Tower."

"Then get underway and let's see for ourselves."

All the ship's lines were freed and the gangplank withdrawn; the tug standing by nudged the *Isabella* away from the wharf and she began steaming south along the Whampoo, still trailed by the tug. Under the expert guidance of the pilot, the *Isabella* moved by the rusted hulk of an American gunboat sunk following the attack on Pearl Harbor. At roughly half-speed, five knots, she sailed past a flotilla of junks and sampans, then slowed beneath Garden Bridge at the mouth of Soochow Creek. As the white buildings of the Bund loomed large off her starboard, Hata turned to Dallin.

"If you've told me the truth, then I will keep my promise."

"Why should I lie? With Becker dead you'll need me more than ever in Argentina."

Hata nodded, then glanced toward starboard. The *Isabella* was parallel to the Cathay. The hotel glistened in the brightening sunlight, while beneath her canopied entrance a long line of limousines were discharging passengers.

"Reminds me of old times," Dallin murmured, lighting a Camel with a wooden match.

"Doesn't it!" Hata replied. "And of a friendship that once meant something."

"I did what I had to!" Dallin answered, feeling the barrel of Ganghi's submachine gun against his ribs. The Kempei gunner was alert and wary of the White Russian. His colonel might exchange bantering words with the man, even hold out a promise of the future, but for Ganghi Dallin was strictly an adversary.

The *Isabella* was now steaming past the sprawling Customs House and Big Ching, then by the renaissance-style Shanghai Club and Signal Station with its one-hundred-and-fifty-foot tower for relaying weather conditions along the China coast, then past the mansion at the foot of the Quai de France and rue du Consulat that housed the French Consulate. Now the great godowns of Butterfield & Swire and Jardine Matheson & Company hove into view, then the brick warehouse of Gustav Torg & Company, and finally an imposing building constructed of Ningpo granite with a gabled redwood roof and immense front doors of solid brass at least ten feet wide.

"Guildhouse," the pilot announced. He telegraphed the engine room, bringing the *Isabella* to a dead stop. Then, with the tug nudging the steamer gently off the port side, he guided his ship expertly against the quay, while her captain saw to the lines.

Ashore a mob of idle coolies moved across the quay, eager to be of some service to the arriving freighter.

"Excellent," murmured Hata at the sight of the unemployed horde of coolies. "We'll use them to load the cargo."

Turning to Dallin, he asked, "How many guards?"

"Only a watchman and his family."

Hata scanned the guildhouse. Dallin's information sounded on the level. There hardly seemed any need for guards since the building was windowless, the granite walls several feet thick, and the brass doors capable of withstanding anything but heavy artillery.

"Ganghi?"

"Sir?"

"Take your men and form a working party from those coolies."

"What about him?" Ganghi asked, prodding Dallin in the back with his submachine gun.

"I'll watch Dallin," Hata replied, slipping the Luger free of his shoulder holster.

Ganghi trotted out of the wheelhouse and scrambled down the companionway ladder onto the catwalk overlooking the well of the steamer. There he waited for the gangway to be put into place, then led his squad of Kempei onto the quay. Once ashore, Ganghi barked orders at the coolies, and, turning away the elderly and sick, he marched the others off toward the brass merchants guildhouse. With Ganghi in the lead and the rest of the squad strung out in a triangle around the Chinese workers, they neared the granite building.

The brass doors, gleaming brightly in the sun, overlapped at the center and, apart from a tiny peephole cut at about shoulder level, no hinge or knob protruded. The doors were flat, glossy, and impregnable to everything but explosives.

Ganghi struck the door with the stock of his submachine gun. A full minute ticked past without a response. Then he tried again. This time an eye appeared in the peephole and an authoritative voice in pidgin English boomed: "What you want?"

"Dallin sent us. He's aboard that ship and wants his cargo."

"Where Dallin now?"

"Aboard the *Isabella,* I told you!"

"Bring Dallin."

"Don't be stupid, man."

"Only stupid is you, stupid Japanese. Dallin give orders only give cargo to Dallin!"

Ganghi slid the safety off his Nambu and brought the dull gunmetal-gray barrel alongside the peephole.

"You want to die?"

"Only Japanese like die. Not Chinese. Bring Dallin."

Then the peephole shut tight, leaving Ganghi no choice but to send a messenger back to the *Isabella.* A few minutes later Hata escorted Dallin down the gangway and across the quay. He stood a good five inches shorter than Dallin but his athletic body enabled him to easily keep pace with the White Russian.

Nearing the guildhouse, Hata looked sideways at Dallin, his thick black hair framing his tawny hawklike face.

"If something does go wrong, you have my word you won't live to profit by it," he warned.

Dallin nodded and pulled away without a word. He swept past Ganghi, cradling his precious Nambu, and tapped lightly on the brass doors. The peephole slid open and Dallin gave orders to release his cargo. The Chinese agreed, but it took nearly three minutes before he managed to loosen the massive bolts and steel pegs so that the solid brass doors could be opened. A blast of cool air shot from the arched dark tunnel beyond, and Ganghi, flanked by his squad of Kempei holding revolvers, swept inside.

Hata and Dallin followed, moving past Big Han, who was standing with his arms folded across his chest. A beam of sunlight penetrated the entranceway, lighting his chunky face and casting his giant shadow on the curved wall behind. Ganghi halted at the end of the tunnel. Ahead was a central courtyard piled high with wooden crates identical to the ones from the warehouse. They stretched in long rows all the way across the courtyard to the main building of the guildhouse, a five-story pagoda with green glazed-tile balconies, intricate teak carvings, and dangling brass lanterns.

Hata and Dallin stopped alongside Ganghi. The Kempetai commandant gazed approvingly over the long rows of wooden crates, then ordered his men to inspect the pagoda before transferring the cargo aboard the *Isabella.* The bandy-legged gunner shouted for his squad to follow him. Spread out in a single line behind their leader they advanced into the sunlight.

And then it began. In long, withering bursts, shifting from left to right, 50-caliber machine-gun fire raked the courtyard. The lethal bursts poured down on the Kempei from the upper windows of the inner side of the building above the tunnel. Taken by surprise and caught out in the open, the Kempei went down in the deadly hail of bullets.

Ganghi, alone, his throat torn open by a stray slug, took cover between the rows of crates. At the edge of the tunnel, Hata viewed the slaughter, then brought his Luger up to shoot Dallin. He was a second too late. Dallin slapped the gun aside, then drove his clenched fist against Hata's jaw. As he did, Ganghi loosed a burst of gunfire at him, driving Dallin into the courtyard behind a pile of crates.

Above, the ambushers, recruited from among the boat people, held their fire for fear of hitting Dallin as he weaved through the maze of crates, with Ganghi close behind. Meanwhile, Hata had recovered his Luger and, abandoning Ganghi to his fate, retreated toward the quay, barreling through a dense crowd of coolies, who were milling in front of the guildhouse, attracted by the gunfire.

Dallin went after him. Against his better judgment and impressed by the danger he risked, Dallin zigzagged across the courtyard. Just short of the tunnel, bullets tore up the flagstones at his feet, bringing him to a reluctant halt. Ganghi, his Nambu aimed at Dallin, was bent over a crate, blood dripping from his lips.

"You one dead White Russian," sneered the Kempei gunner as he curled his finger around the trigger of his submachine gun.

A woman's cry came from the pagoda. Big Han sprang up, toppling the crates surrounding Ganghi, and sent him hurtling backward. The Nambu dropped onto the ground, rolling several feet away from the Japanese. Infuriated, the blood spurting from the wound in his neck, Ganghi yanked two daggers out of his tightly wrapped puttees and advanced on the giant Chinese.

Big Han waited, his long arms folded across his massive chest. A plea from Dominique in the doorway of the pagoda went unheeded, as did one from Dallin as well. Slashing the air ahead with both daggers, Ganghi swept in for the kill, but his wily feint and fatal lunge fell short. Big Han pinned his arms to his sides and, lifting him off the ground, hugged Ganghi tightly, squeezing the last bit of life from him.

As Dallin grabbed up the Nambu submachine gun, a shout from Dominique brought him to a stop. She was standing in the doorway of the pagoda. He waved affectionately, disregarding her concerned look, and took off at a run through the tunnel. He emerged from the guildhouse onto the crowded quay, just as the *Isabella*'s foghorn piped a warning all-clear blast. The five-inch mooring lines securing her bow and stern were severed at the swivel and slid down over her starboard side into the water. Black smoke poured from her funnel drifting down onto the quay. With the tug at her stern, the freighter began edging her way slowly into the river. Dallin veered sharply, avoiding a pile-up of coolies. Running wildly, shielded from view by the side of the ship, he dove at the gangway just as the heaving motion of the *Isabella* ripped it from the quay.

High above, unaware of Dallin's whereabouts, Hata stood beside the captain on the bridge. The tug was now off the starboard, and the *Isabella* was nosing carefully around in a circle, heading in a northerly course toward the Yangtze and the East China Sea. The gangway hung at a twenty-degree angle. Dallin worked his way up the steps with one hand gripping the rail until he finally reached the main deck. He crouched on the catwalk, surveying the ship.

Three seamen were at the bow, another was halfway along the catwalk opposite him. On the bridge the Chinese pilot was arguing bitterly with the Portuguese captain. Hata stood beside the wheelhouse, listening to them, then suddenly broke away, moving toward the stern.

Dallin was after him in a flash. He rushed down the catwalk, climbed the companionway ladder, then threw himself up against the bulkhead. He caught his breath, then raced up the next companionway ladder and, gaining the bridge deck, came face to face with the captain.

"Anchor your ship in the Bund," Dallin demanded.

"Sorry, Senhor. My orders are to depart at once for South America."

"You'll be halted at sea, searched, and end up in prison for hiding war criminals."

"That is a risk I must take," the captain replied reluctantly. "But I will contact my superiors for further instructions."

Dallin could have used his gun as a bargaining point, but

the idea of one man against an entire ship hardly appealed to him. Instead, he circled the captain and came on a hatch leading into the interior compartments. Inching nearer, he glanced into the passageway. It was deserted and seemed safe enough, but Dallin was hardly about to bet his life on it. Grimacing, he cradled the Nambu tighter under his elbow and started in.

Dallin came to a stop at the point where the passage widened to form a T, leading off in opposite directions. His face dripped with perspiration and his suit was soaked through and hung limply against his legs. He felt unsure, wondering why Hata had abruptly departed from the bridge.

His hunch was go left, but he changed his mind and decided the safer way was right. Then it occurred to him that either way was just as dangerous because Hata had spotted him.

Believing that, Dallin held the Nambu with one hand and wriggled out of his jacket. He tossed the tangled bundle into the heart of the T. A deafening explosion of gunfire rocked the passage, reverberating off the bulkheads. The jacket, riddled with holes, settled in a heap on the deck.

So his hunch had been correct, his *joss* had held. Hata and Niki were covering both ends of the passageway. Just as Dallin had decided to give the whole mess up for a bad job, the cultured voice of Giacomo Ferrara broke the tense silence.

"Be sensible, Dallin. From what Hata tells me your ambush succeeded brilliantly. The antiquities are yours. So why not get off this vessel and leave us alone?"

"What's your angle in this, Ferrara?" Dallin asked, not completely taken by surprise.

"Forgive me. How could you possibly know. Permit me to introduce myself. I am Colonel Giacomo Ferrara, formerly of the Italian Secret Service, also affiliated with the Abwehr and more recently, because of circumstances, at the service of the Kempetai–Shanghai Section."

"So it was you who broke the ring?"

"Yes. Credit for that is due me. But what interest is that of yours? Why don't you come to your senses and leave us? You have my assurance you may disembark without the slightest danger to yourself. On this you have my word."

"I don't want it!"

"Then what exactly *do* you want? What pleases you? What

is it that brings you back aboard this vessel when I should think you'd be thankful to be off it."

Dallin had trouble answering. The moment had finally come for him to reveal his true identity yet somehow he could not get the words out.

"I warned you, he wouldn't listen to reason," Hata shouted, from off to the right of the T.

"Patience, my friend," the Venetian counseled from the opposite end. "Remember the advantage lies with us."

That's no lie, thought Dallin. The *Isabella* was steaming at full speed, her bow cutting through the murky waters of the Whampoo. In a few minutes the Bund would be left behind; then she would sail past Woosung and into the East China Sea. Once that happened, Dallin would be trapped alone on a hostile ship. It would be just a matter of time before Hata and Ferrara could deal with him any way they wished.

Dallin glanced over his shoulder through the hatch. The Japanese-owned cotton mills and factories of the British–American Tobacco Company on Pootung were off the starboard side. He had to force the issue or lose. He moved ahead, reaching the end of the bulkhead. It was a perfect spot for a grenade but he carried no explosives. Surprise too might have worked but that element was out of the question. His only chance now was to spring around the corner, hug the deck, and roll about, firing in both directions in hopes of getting Hata and Ferrara before they got him.

Ferrara and Hata also understood the situation. They braced themselves, their pistols aimed at the opening of the passage. If Dallin delayed until they reached the sea, then they had won. But even if he did not, which was how they now read things, they could still win.

Dallin wiped the sweat from his forehead and started forward. Suddenly there was a deafening groan from the bowels of the ship and the *Isabella* heaved sideways, her decks tilted at a sharp angle. Dallin lost his balance, nearly landing where the passageways converged. Hata and Ferrara fell hard against the cabin doors as Niki went sprawling backward on the bunk.

By the time they had recovered their balance it was clear that the captain had brought his vessel to a dead stop in the Whampoo. No one knew the implications of that decision better than Ferrara, who shouted, "Dallin?"

"What?"

"Speak plainly. What is it you want from us?"

"I'll tell you what he wants," Hata interrupted. "He wants to deliver me to the Allies in exchange for his own freedom."

"No!" Dallin replied finally, "not for my own freedom but because I'm with the OSS."

The frozen silence that ensued was shattered by the sound of a fist crashing against the cabin door.

"You are not White Russian?" Hata screamed resentfully.

"No."

"American?"

"Yes."

"OSS?"

"All along."

Ferrara inserted a fresh clip into his Beretta automatic, then glanced down the passageway at the opposite cabin. Hata was standing there, distraught and melancholy, his shoulders bent. Niki stood forlornly behind him.

"Come now, my friends," Ferrara said coolly. "We've all hidden things from each other in the past. So why argue over what's done when it's only the future that counts."

"No accommodation. No arrangement," Dallin insisted hoarsely. "You both surrender. Period."

"Never! Not to you! Not to anyone!" Hata screamed defiantly.

Dallin overheard Niki, her voice quivering, trying to reason with Hata. Whatever fight she once had was now clearly gone.

"You must give up," she pleaded finally, "otherwise we're doomed, don't you see."

"Go if you wish. But *not* me!"

Weeping, Niki screamed, "Dallin?"

"What?"

"You are a lying sonofabitch! You hear me. A cruel, lying sonofabitch!"

"I know," Dallin admitted grimly, hearing Niki sob. "Now tell Hata to come out before I come in."

"Enough of this madness," Ferrara interrupted. "Why be at each other's throats? Do any of our nations really care what happens to us? Of course not! What is one more Italian, Japanese, Russian, even American, more or less. Listen to me, my dear friend Dallin, or whatever your real name is; you are overrating our own importance in the general scheme of things. So let us benefit by our acquaintance and return

for the antiquities; then sail together for Buenos Aires, where
we shall not only pool our resources but our expertise as well,
and in no time at all have riches beyond our imagination.
Why, working together, I daresay we could dominate all of
South America."

"I don't want to control South America. I don't want to
dominate anyone. I just want to see a job done right and go
home. Now are you coming out or do I come in?"

"Come in!" Hata screamed, firing a shot in anger that
missed Dallin by a foot.

"Wait!" demanded Ferrara. "If you insist on murdering
each other, I cannot stop you. But personally I have never
yet seen a cause worth dying for. So I'm coming out. You
hear me, Dallin, I am coming out."

"Stay where you are," Hata threatened, swinging the dark
barrel of his Luger toward the Venetian.

"Don't be absurd! The Allies don't want me. I am a professional, above all nationalistic ties and prejudices. What's
more, I urge you to accept the terms of our OSS friend over
here. Face this so-called war criminal trial. Why, citizens from
every nation that ever fought a war will come to your defense.
Men of distinction, high birth, rank, and intellect will flock to
squash this nationalistic witch-hunt the Allies have unleashed
around the world."

"No trial! No surrender!"

"You are speaking nonsense!" Ferrara snapped, giving up
all pretense of equality. "Why, this outdated samurai code
and your rules of Bushido don't apply to me, a Venetian. We
Venetians have betrayed people since time immemorial and
no one has ever had the audacity to hold it against us personally. I am leaving now, unarmed and fully prepared to submit
to whatever is asked of me, is that understood?"

Dallin heard the Beretta thud against the deck. A blast
from the Luger overlapped it, reverberating down the passageway. With a scream Ferrara slumped over, clutching his
chest.

"I don't understand," he gasped. "I explained my views
. . . how could you ignore the realities . . ."

Dallin heard a moan as Ferrara collapsed. Then Hata was
shouting: "Dallin?"

"What?"

"If you want me, you must come and get me. You must,
you hear! No surrender. No trial. You or me. Understand?"

"I understand."

"Good. Then at least you treat me with final respect. At least you give me this much dignity."

Dallin was overwhelmed with remorse. Yet, as he inched forward along the bulkhead, the submachine gun ready, his regrets were dissipated by memories of Gustav Torg, of Felix Hacker, and finally of his old college roommate Christopher Blake.

As he drew near, he heard Niki cry out. "No! Oh, no! Please don't leave me alone!"

Dallin dove around the corner onto the deck. Before him, at the far end of the passage, Hata was on his knees in the cabin doorway, the jeweled samurai sheath in one hand and the naked blade in the other. A fatalistic smile creased his hawklike face as he gripped the sword with both hands and plunged the tip deep into his abdomen, then ripped upward.

Epilogue

———◆◆◆———

On August 22nd, advance units of the American Armed Forces arrived in Shanghai. Four days later, the sky was blanketed by silver C-47 planes bringing Nationalist troops into the city to accept the formal surrender of the Japanese Expeditionary Army.

About the Author

Barth Jules Sussman has lived and worked as a professional writer in London, Paris, Rome, Los Angeles, and Ibiza for the last decade. He is the author of over a dozen original screenplays, a large number of which have either been purchased or produced by Columbia Pictures, Dino De Laurentiis, Carlo Ponti and Shaw Bros. of Hong Kong.

When he is not writing, his time is usually spent roaming the world; visiting grand hotels, gambling casinos and cafés in an attempt to recapture a feeling for the not-so-distant past.

SIGNET Books You'll Enjoy

☐ **TRIPLE by Ken Follett.** (#E9447—$3.50)

☐ **EYE OF THE NEEDLE by Ken Follett.** (#E9550—$3.50)

☐ **THE REVENANT by Brana Lobel.** (#E9451—$2.25)*

☐ **THE BLACK HORDE by Richard Lewis.** (#E9454—$1.75)

☐ **COLD HANDS by Joseph Pintauro.** (#E9482—$2.50)*

☐ **A FEAST FOR SPIDERS by Kenneth L. Evans.** (#J9484—$1.95)*

☐ **THE DARK by James Herbert.** (#E9403—$2.95)

☐ **THE DEATH MECHANIC by A. D. Hutter.** (#J9410—$1.95)*

☐ **THE MAGNATE by Jack Mayfield.** (#E9411—$2.25)*

☐ **THE SURROGATE by Nick Sharman.** (#E9293—$2.50)*

☐ **THE SCOURGE by Nick Sharman.** (#E9114—$2.25)*

☐ **INTENSIVE FEAR by Nick Christian.** (#E9341—$2.25)*

☐ **SPHINX by Robin Cook.** (#E9194—$2.95)

☐ **COMA by Robin Cook.** (#E9756—$2.75)

☐ **AUCTION! by Tom Murphy.** (#E9478—$2.95)

☐ **ELISE by Sara Reavin.** (#E9483—$2.95)

* Price slightly higher in Canada